The Re

All of the characters in this book are fictitious, and any resemblance to actual persons, living or dead, is purely coincidental.

All rights reserved. No part of this book may be reproduced or transmitted in any form or by any means, electronic or mechanical, including photocopying, recording, or be any information storage and retrieval system, without the written permission of the publisher, except where permitted by law.

Warning: This book contains some adult language and may offend some readers. The intent of using such language was strictly utilized to maintain the integrity of natural dialog, and to make as real as possible a fictitious situation.

The Reunion Reaper

All Rights Reserved

Copyright © 2009 Scott A. Reighard

Scott A. Reighard

Acknowledgements

I would like to thank the following people whose patience, assistance, and advice have been invaluable to me. First and foremost, to my Lord and Savior, of whom I seek on a daily basis for inspiration, strength and forgiveness, I cannot express how blessed I am.

Next, my wife and children who are always patient as I hibernate for hours on end plinking away on my laptop. Daddy's done kids, for now.

I would also like to thank my papap, Dan Marketti. Pap has been hanging with the Big Guy since January 31, 1986, but he left an indelible impression on me when I was a young teenager. He encouraged me to write down my thoughts in a notebook; perhaps knowing I was either disturbed, or had a sense of saying or thinking imaginary things. Regardless, I did as he suggested, and those random thoughts turned into short stories, poems, and eventually what you see before you, a completed novel. I still miss you pap.

To my parents, who never stepped in the way, or tried to discourage me from what I enjoy doing. Thanks for buying me my first IBM typewriter at age 14. Somehow I think my pap influenced them to make this Christmas purchase for me.

To my former classmates at Palm Beach Academy who served as the inspiration for this book, in a good way that is. I think you all would agree we have some great stories of the old place. One person in particular I would like to recognize is Adam Dread, a fellow graduate. Thanks Adam for all of your great insight and input. Just in case you were wondering, Adam is a lawyer in Nashville, TN. He told me to say that. Just kidding!

I would be remiss if I didn't mention a few other very important people. First is my good friend and confidant

The Reunion Reaper

Page Fairchilds, of whom I go to for just about anything and everything when it comes to floating ideas. He's a natural devil's advocate, and I appreciate his candor. Also, there is Sonny Bishop. Sonny said it was okay to use his name, so I did. Don't sue me! You're a great father and husband, a great teacher, and a great human being.

Lastly, I would like to thank Ricky Lonker for the fantastic cover idea. Well done! And to those who posed for the photos, enjoy your fame. I hope my book is not an embarrassment to you.

I apologize if I left anyone out, I'll catch you next time.

Scott A. Reighard

Chapter 1

"911, what's your emer---"

"Please, you gotta help me, my mother's not breathing."

It was the desperate cry of a young female voice seeking help from the Palm Beach County, Florida Sheriff's 911 dispatcher.

"Okay, honey I need you to relax okay? Are you calling from 142 Hibiscus Drive?" The experienced dispatcher asked as she typed out the information to transmit.

"Yes, please hurry my sister is giving her mouth to mouth, but she's not moving. Oh my God please hurry."

The young caller paced hurriedly around her mother's bedroom.

"Someone is on the way okay? But I need you to relax, I'm right here." The dispatcher could sense the young girl's anguish.

"Okay," the young caller's voice continued with a quiver.

"What is your name?"

"Jennifer."

The dispatcher continued typing out the information.

"Jennifer my name is Linda. I'm going to stay with you all the way until the EMTs arrive okay?"

"Okay Linda."

"You said your younger sister is trying to administer CPR is that right?"

"Yes."

"What is her name?"

"Crystal."

"Has Crystal given CPR before?"

"She's a lifeguard so they have to know that don't they?"

Her voice was beginning to calm.

The Reunion Reaper

"Yes Jennifer that's part of the training. Good. The EMT's should be arriving very soon okay? Tell her to continue with the CPR."

"Okay. Crystal, the lady said don't stop giving mom CPR."

It was yet another sticky day in South Florida, and this was only May, when the emergency medical team arrived at the home of Judith Barnett.

Inside this modest sea foamed colored concrete home in a quaint neighborhood lie the fully clothed body of a woman who once flaunted good looks and a gleaming smile. Her body was sprawled on a queen size bed. Next to her bed on the nightstand were cocaine residue and an empty wine glass. Her daughters discovered her after they arrived home from school.

The EMT's intervened for the struggling Crystal, who was growing weary from the process. They did all they could to revive the girls mother, but the forty two year old divorcee was dead. The young and balling Crystal had performed so valiantly, but there was nothing she or the EMT's could do to save Judith Barnett.

Scott A. Reighard

Chapter 2

Earlier that day – West Palm Beach, Florida

There was a heavy knock that echoed through the stucco ranch home of Judith Barnett. As she pushed open the door she was completely shocked to see who it was standing in her doorway. Her eyes lit up and a smile adorned her face as she looked at one of her old classmates.
"Oh my God, look who it is."
"Hey, Judith!"
A broad smile creased the face of this old friend, as his pearly white chops joined perfectly. He could have been a candidate for one of those Crest commercials.
"How are you?" She asked as she stepped toward him for a hug.
"I'm doing great, and you?"
"Good, good. Wow, I haven't seen you in years. Come on in."
The still slender classmate stepped across the door threshold.
"Gosh, you look great!" She said.
Viewing the contents of her home, he saw that it lacked the flair of the once young girl who flaunted good looks and a smile that sent boys into a tizzy. There was perhaps no other girl in the graduating class of 1983 who made more boys look foolish than Judith Barnett. She was a streaky blond haired green eyed Florida native who was also an accomplished athlete. She played volleyball and soccer. She was a girl with that can't take your eyes off of her kind of look. She had the looks and charm that turned away more approaches from men than a bouncer turns away teens at a trendy club.

The Reunion Reaper

Her guest stood back and looked her over; "still killing the boys I see."

"Well, it ain't like the ole days, a few wrinkles here, some sagging there, you know, that middle aged look."

"I don't know about that with you, but I know what you mean." He took both of his hands and grasped at the negligible love handles in his midsection area.

As she turned he noticed her still slender legs and shapely rear that was covered by a pair of white cotton shorts. She wore a lavender tank t-shirt that complemented her tanned skin. Her blond hair was still streaky but in recent years cut to shoulder length.

She directed him over to a tan colored leather couch that matched the cream colored tile floor. "So, what are you doing here?" as she motioned for him to sit.

"Well, I was here on business, and I was looking up some old classmates and I found that you still lived here."

"So, what kind of business are you in?"

"It's a home based business, it deals mostly with sales on the internet, and managing accounts for partners who don't want to be directly involved."

"Oh, so you're like a broker?"

"You could say that. I got tired of making money for other people."

"There you go! Well, sounds like you've got a good thing going. You always were an ambitious guy. I am just about to make some lunch, would you like something to eat?"

"No thanks, maybe a glass of wine though," he said with a smile.

"Well, I see you haven't changed. You still like your wine."

"Yes ma'am, got off the hard stuff years ago, not that wine doesn't have its little kick though."

"Oh you'll like what I've got. I keep some special bottles for such special occasions, I'll be right back."

Scott A. Reighard

As Judith went to retrieve the wine for the two of them, he gazed about the living area, noticing a few pictures hanging on a wall that faced the outside pool area. There were large photos hanging on a lime washed painted wall that presented two young girls in studio like poses, both looked to be teenagers. Both of them were blonds, and the striking features left no doubt as to whom the mother was.

He could hear some faint noises emerging from the kitchen as he continued his visual inventory and judgment of the place. The furniture was modest and the various accessories strewn about the coffee table were of a tropical nature. He noticed a Cosmopolitan magazine on the glass coffee table. Although it was an older home it had apparently gone through some renovating and now displayed a more contemporary Florida home appearance, open floor plan with ceramic flooring throughout with plenty of windows, and white walls, that besides the pictures of her girls, were decorated with a variety of floral paintings which contained light tropical colors of blush pink, sea foam green and tangerine orange.

Through the opened blinds of the sliding glass doors he could see a small pool. It appeared empty because the water showed no movement, the wind was down, which meant the humidity was up. The room was bright and cheery, and a slight breeze filtered the room due to a vanilla colored Antigua style ceiling fan that was whirling away overhead. It appeared to be more for style than function. This was a modest place by most standards, but for a single mom with two teenage girls it worked. He stood and slid over toward the hanging photos of the young girls. He rarely missed a detail.

"Beautiful girls, they look like their mother," loud enough for her to hear in the next room.

"Thanks, they're all I've got."

"I don't see any pictures of Harry?" He was asking a question where he already knew the answer.

The Reunion Reaper

Judith walked back into the room with the wine. She handed him his glass.

"Nope, been divorced for almost six years now."

She married her high school sweetheart Harry Jordan, who was two years older than her. Although this old classmate gave chase when they were seniors, there wasn't much he could do to woo her, she was Harry's girl and that was that. So, no regrets, well, maybe a little.

After a whirlwind Bohemian lifestyle came kids. The marriage was never the same. Judith gave up the hard partying that consisted of straight vodka and cocaine. It was a risky combination, but pre-kids she welcomed risk. Harry became the guy who never wanted to grow up, and so the marriage was officially on the rocks, with no twist.

"I'm sorry to hear that. It's tragic that marriages end in divorce, mine did too."

"Well, here's to birds of a feather," as she slowly sat down on the couch.

The two of them clicked their wine glasses and took a sip. There was a moment of silence as both seemed to reflect on separate thoughts. Judith took a sip of her wine.

"Mmm, good flavor, has a silky feeling, Chenin Blanc?"

"Very good, it's Barton and Guestier, Loire Valley."

"Well, it's perfect like you," as he sat on the edge of a soft leather cream colored recliner

She blushed, "So, how long you in town?"

"A few days."

"Do you travel a lot?" Her eyes did a quick once over of her guest.

"You could say that, about once or twice a month."

"I used to travel all the time with Harry and the girls when they were little, but I haven't gone anywhere in years."

"Sounds like you deserve a vacation?"

"It hasn't been easy, I should have gotten more in the divorce, but Harry threatened to get dirty and mention my addiction, which was years ago by the way. I didn't want to lose my girls, so I caved and lost out on a decent alimony. Harry financially takes care of the girls so I do what I can." He could see her tense up at her remarks.

"I'm sorry to hear that." As she looked down in reflection he looked her up and down.

In front of him sat a woman who spurned his advances in high school and was part of a moment in his high school life of which he would never let go.

"I'm sorry...what did you say?" as her head bounced back up to look at him.

"I said I'm sorry to hear about that."

"Hey whatever, I get by. Listen, you didn't come all this way to hear me bitch about my life."

"No, it's okay. I hear more than you think about people's lives. You should hear my clients, bitch, bitch, bitch, you know what I mean?" He forced out a laugh, "I get so sick and tired of people who bitch about their lives."

"Exactly." She crossed her legs and the light glistened off her shaved and tanned legs.

"So, seeing anyone?"

"Nope, too busy trying to raise two teenage girls who mean everything to me."

"Well, for someone as beautiful as you I find that hard to believe." Commenting to a woman in need of a real compliment it seemed.

"Thank you, but I'm good you know?" She shifted her position more in his direction.

There was a moment that the two of them seemed uncomfortable with the direction of the conversation.

"Listen, I gotta throw my work clothes in the dryer, I'll be right back okay."

"Take your time I'll just be sipping my wine," as he flashed a wink.

"Okay, be right back."

The Reunion Reaper

Judith went into a small room just off the kitchen. A few minutes had passed by, and with that little bit of time, he removed a vial of powder from his pocket and proceeded to pour it into her glass of wine. *A little booger sugar for the old candy queen.* He then quickly stirred it around with his finger to ensure that it would mix in and not show any discoloration. He wiped his finger on the back side of his dark blue slacks as Judith returned.

"So, two divorcees. Got any kids?"
A slight pause and pall fell over his face, "Had."
"Had, as in the wife got them?"
"No, as in dead," Judith's jaw dropped "He was killed by a drunk driver. My wife suffered multiple injuries, but the lowlife drunk hit the back passenger door and my son died instantly."
Judith clutched at her breast feeling a mother's loss. "Oh my God, I am so sorry. How old was he?"
"Five, five years old, and not a bad bone in his whole body. He had his whole life ahead of him, and then suddenly, someone who lacked any social responsibility took away everything."
Both of them were silent as a tear rolled down the cheek of Judith.
"I wanted to kill him you know. They gave him a five year sentence, and now the son of a bitch is a free man, and my boy is still dead."
"I am so sorry." Another tear trickled down her sleek cheek and fell off onto her lap. She reached over and grasped his hand.
"It's okay I've gotten over most of it. It happened about ten years ago. Of course the wife and I were never the same; it was just a matter of time before the divorce. I forgave her a thousand times, but she couldn't forgive herself." A reflective look appeared on his face as the two of them sat quietly for a moment. He raised his glass to her,
"Here's to life, how precious it is."

They clicked glasses, "Amen."

"Anyhow, let's talk about something different."

The conversation of the old days continued until Judith began to feel sickly. She was swaying in her chair nearly falling to the floor. He caught her and escorted her to her bedroom; her body stiffening with each step. She plopped down on the bed and fell back. Her body was lying across the bed. She was having difficulty breathing and was trying to say something, but it was incoherent as the back arched and the neck jerked about. The guest just looked at her as she laid there, her eyes practically bulging from her head. Like a skilled surgeon he coyly pulled from his slacks a set of latex gloves and placed them on his hands. He then proceeded to go into the kitchen to grab a hand towel. He also carried with him both their glasses of wine. He cleaned his glass and put it back in the cabinet then he cleaned hers and put a little more wine in it. He wanted to remove any and all residue that might be on the glass. Then he went over to where they were sitting and proceeded to wipe down everything that he had touched.

He went back into the bedroom placed the wine glass up to her lips to get an impression, as well as using her hand to grasp it leaving fingerprints. She was still breathing, but it was quick and short. He knew what he was doing, and he was performing like a seasoned pro. After he completed pressing her lips to the wine glass, he wiped her hands and wrists. From his pocket he removed another vial of powder. This time it was the real stuff with just a hint of strychnine, and he placed it in her hand and then manipulated her arm as if to pour a little on the table next to the wine. He also manipulated some of the powder into her nose.

As he looked down her breathing was now becoming more erratic, it was only a matter of time before she would pass into an unconscious state and eventually her heart would nearly explode creating a massive cardiac arrest. He had done this before so he knew what the effects would be, but he was going to wait. He could not risk any one finding her alive. He waited for nearly thirty minutes to make sure she was dead. He glanced at his watch knowing soon that her daughters would be coming home from school. Sitting there watching his victim, gazing at her from head to toe he thought for a moment of freely taking advantage of her, but he was too smart for that, besides only perverts sex the dead he thought.

He sat there watching as her heart nearly exploded with the amount of strychnine that was in the cocaine. If everything went accordingly, her death would be ruled an accidental overdose by someone who bought bad blow. When he examined her pulse he felt none. He headed for the door and left the home as if he were never there.

The street was typical of a Florida neighborhood, the homes where so many of the models looked similar, was eerily quiet. Oftentimes the heat of the day keeps people in doors. There was no one wandering outdoors to see him leave.

As he made his way to the rental car, he began to quietly sing, "And I've been takin' care of business, every day; takin' care of business every way. I've been takin' care of business, it's all mine; takin' care of business and working overtime, workout, lookout, watch out, yeah, yeah, yeah." He embellished the last part, always thinking himself clever and quick with his honey tongue. Yes sir, nothing like a good ole Bachman Turner Overdrive song to a mission complete.

Looking at every conceivable angle looking for that nosey Mrs. Kravitz like neighbor from the television show *Bewitched,* he hopped into the champagne colored Taurus. No need to rent something that looked out of place or noticeable, he thought. In this case that would have been a great thing, but there was no such nosey neighbor lurking about, or a flashy car to catch someone's eye, and so Judith Barnett's surprise guest continued to sing his quiet little song and was able to slip away unnoticed.

The Reunion Reaper

Chapter 3

Journal entry: First order of business is to recognize a great entertainer Frank Gorshin. It was exactly two years ago that you passed on my friend. You will be sorely missed, for there was no greater impressionist than you. You were one of my favorites. You inspire me.

Okay, the next order is to express how I relieved someone from their PATHETIC existence.

Damn, I have to admit this one was tough! Judith looked glowingly for an ex- cocaine addict; although she did look a bit thin and older than she was. Who was it that said you have the face you deserve when you turn 50? Ah, whatever, she wasn't 50, but sure as hell looked it. Maybe a little too much Florida sun as well. Who cares right? By the way, this had nothing to do with her turning me down for the senior prom, but more so for being the bitch who screwed me over at my party. Payback's a bitch ain't it? But I was right about her boyfriend slash future husband in that, he was all wrong for her. He was the bastard who got her hooked on the junk. Maybe I should have killed him???

Oh Judith, the lies you tell. You weren't a very good mom. How many times I watched you, drinking alone, or sucking in on a cigarette thin spliff. You embarrassed your daughters, and your family practically wanted to disown you, not to mention the problem with keeping steady employment. Too bad! The once beauty queen fell off her throne, and all for the white powder. Well, it's been a few weeks since then and I see that her death has been ruled an accidental death. Then again, I knew that.. Man I am good.

I did her and the family a favor, now nobody has to worry about her. I loved the dead son hit by the drunk driver story, not bad for spontaneous, although for a minute there I got a little more emotional than I wanted.

Scott A. Reighard

Boy did she bite on that one; then again she always was a bit gullible. Also, I thought it was ironic that neither of us mentioned the fact that the day I visited was the same day as our graduation date 24 years ago. Well, I have now cast the net. Let's hope the rest goes according to the master plan; time to plan my next fishing expedition.

Judith Barnett: July 13, 1965-May 17, 2007. Rest in peace my little snow queen.

The Reunion Reaper

Chapter 4

May 17, 1983- Palm Beach, Florida

The 55th graduating class of Palm Beach Preparatory School was sitting anxiously in the front row of the school's meeting house, a detached building which resembled more of a chapel than a meeting house. Headmaster Colquitt was making what would be his final commencement speech. A career dedicated to education was now coming to a close as the 64 year old tried his best to amuse the class and those in attendance with a few jokes, or anecdotes. He had been the headmaster at this prestigious prep school for 12 years, but according to him it was time to move on to another chapter and make a little more out of his remaining life; there was a book to write he once told a colleague. Despite Headmaster Colquitt's attempts to connect to the young people this class of twenty four was typical of seventeen and eighteen year olds. *Get to the good stuff old man, like our diplomas!*

The 1982-1983 school year was a memorable year for this graduating class; most notably there was the huge 2-1 upset in soccer of the mighty Miami Pine High School, a school with nearly fifteen hundred students, and here was Palm Beach Preparatory School busting its admission doors with one hundred twenty five. And then there was the state lacrosse championship. For the second year in a row they had mowed down the competition, this year capping it off by going undefeated. Of course, it didn't hurt to have a few guys from Maryland and Massachusetts who basically grew up with lacrosse sticks in their hands, or a soccer ball on their foot. Academically it was yet another strong class, a virtual who's who of high school students. There was no lack for higher education schools like M.I.T., Dartmouth,

Vanderbilt, Mount Vernon, Columbia and many more that were all well represented from this class as well as previous classes.

It was one of those schools that was starkly divided between the have's and have not's. For the most part the only way the have not's were accepted by these social elites was if they were outstanding athletes or mean party animals that could rival the rich in their tastes for experiencing just about anything and everything.

Other than sports the only thing the whole school shared was a unique event called beach day. It was one of those school sponsored bonding days where faculty, staff and students would gather at the beach across from their school property and partake in a variety of events from Frisbee football to beach volleyball. Of course there were those who would sneak off to a designated "smoke" area for a little toke of the wacky weed; unbeknownst to the older members of the staff, but most likely having participation from a few of the younger faculty members.

It was a good day for the school; however, the most awkward part of these beach days was seeing the white haired Mr. Colquitt flexing his sixty plus frame in a pair of Ocean Pacific shorts from where his two very white, heavily oiled legs protruded. This of course contrasted with his tan arms. The students were so used to seeing him in khaki slacks, and a short sleeved button down shirt with a tie.

Yet another weird scene was seeing the same people who were trying to teach the importance of Aristotle's philosophy, or the genius of Shakespeare's sonnets milling about in bikinis or bathing shorts. A positive was that most of the faculty was young, most of them between their mid-twenties to mid-thirties. In fact, it was not beyond the norm to see faculty and students party together, and it would not be far fetched to say that perhaps there were a few dalliances between some of the faculty and students. No,

The Reunion Reaper

this was not your typical school atmosphere, but it worked and the success of hundreds of previous graduates gave credibility and prestige to the school.

And so here it was May 17, 1983 and the 55th graduating class was about to have their names announced, receive a final handshake and get handed their diploma. What the future held was as open as their parent's bank account or as vast as the Atlantic Ocean less than a few hundred yards from the historic school meeting house.

As the ceiling fans whirled overhead in the modest sized meeting hall, parents, family and friends fanned themselves amid the early evening humidity that had drifted in through the jalousie windows. Headmaster Colquitt began to call out the names and Clarence Darby the assistant headmaster greeted the new graduates with a firm handshake and a diploma folder. As they called the names alphabetically, the smiles of everyone grew larger, and the anticipation for the graduates of what was about to be would be a new adventure that each of them would embrace with arms wide open, and accompanied by a voracious appetite for life, or at the very least, financial or career assistance from influential family or friends. The names were called out:

Carrie Adams	Rodney Adams
Elizabeth Anderson	Sonja Apandopoulis
Judith Barnett	Dominic Bevacqua
Sharon Bloom	Riley Bradshaw
Gary Deitrich	Tucker Harrison
Brandon Henniker	Andrew Keane
Mark Lambert	Adam Levitz
Jeffrey Lewis	Greg Madison
Amy McMahon	Brian Morris
Patti Schwartz	Jacob Silverman
Jonathan Snyder	Paul Thurman
Kathleen Walker	Hank Wyatt

Scott A. Reighard

When Hank Wyatt's name was called Mr. Colquitt donned a broad smile then coined the usual phrase of all commencement closings, "Parents, friends, family, faculty, I give you the 55th graduating class of Palm Beach Preparatory School." A chorus of hand clapping echoed throughout as the new graduates went to meet their parents and whoever else had showed up for them on this most special day. Yes indeed, this class was a special class, a mix of gotta-be's, wannabe's and soon-to-be's.

Chapter 5

Zipping around an internet search of Sedona, Arizona, he finally came across what he was looking for, an article posted from The *Sedona Observer*. In the article, a Steve Roberts reported that hikers discovered the pretzel shaped and rain soaked body of Brandon Henniker just off a trail near the Sycamore Canyon area. The victim was a freelance photographer who worked for several outdoor magazine affiliates. Still clutched in Mr. Henniker's hand was a Nikon 430 35mm camera with a 24x zoom lens. National Park Service personnel were first to appear on the scene and from initial observations it appeared as though Mr. Henniker fell from an overhanging observation area while taking pictures. The Yavapai County Sheriff's Department arrived and conducted a thorough investigation, concluding there was no evidence of foul play. Mr. Henniker is survived by his wife Ruella and son Jauquin. *He sure as hell is.*

He clicked the little X box at the top right of his screen to reveal a Three Stooges background on his computer. He smiled, knowing another on the list had been taken care of.

Brandon was a freelance photographer who enjoyed taking nature pictures. His idol in the photo world was Ansel Adams. In fact, that's what brought him west to Arizona, the influence of Adams. Somehow Brandon felt that he could pull out of Arizona what Adams pulled from the Yosemite Valley of California. He kept a huge portrait of his idol on the wall of his study, along with some of his own work. Brandon decided to take his talents west after graduating from the University of Florida. He told a roommate of his that he was tired of taking pictures of palm trees, alligators and sunsets.

Scott A. Reighard

Brandon was a wiry, sandy blonde haired kid who looked at his prep school years with some indignation, and did his level best to get those shots of people in compromised positions. He called it the natural look; or at least that was his impression of it. Of course several of those photographed would rather have broken his camera over his head.

During his high school years Brandon took most of the photographs for the yearbook. He decided to major in photography at the University of Florida. After moving to Arizona, he got married, and had one child, a boy who recently turned fifteen. But after this apparent accident Jauquin would no longer be able to hike with dad, or learn photography the old fashioned way in a dark room. The fifteen year old was now fatherless, and the thirty-eight year old wife was now a widow, a widow because her husband had ventured too close to the edge of an overhang, probably trying to get that one special photo that required some obscure angle, or so it appeared that way.

Chapter 6

A few days before

The sun intermittingly beamed in the Arizona sky as the weather for early September in Arizona was mild and nearly perfect for picture taking. Brandon didn't necessarily enjoy cloudless days; they sometimes take away the character, or depth of the photos. Clouds appear to have their own personality as they float or stream across the sky, and he was in search of such dramatic imagery. The weather had called for thunderstorms later in the day, and Brandon Henniker felt that storm clouds moving in would make for some dramatic shots. He had been working as a freelance photographer for various outdoor magazines, but he was really building quite a portfolio to hopefully one day put together that coffee table book.

On this particular day Brandon was wandering the Sycamore Canyon Wilderness near Sedona, a place known for weird happenings. He was perched on a ridge of weathered and jagged rocks that displayed character. From the ridge there was a precipitous drop to hiking trails below that zigzagged through this majestic setting. He was preparing his equipment. The only way up to that point was a long meandering walk, but one well worth it. He gazed out at his paradise, his peace, his spirituality, and he proceeded to take some pictures using his preferred choice of equipment, a Nikon. It was an older model, but he preferred the traditional to the new fangled digitals that were drowning the market. As he was lying there snapping away at a certain rock formation he heard a noise behind him. After taking his final clicks he turned. Shocked and surprised he saw someone he had not seen in nearly twenty years who also was brandishing a camera.

"Holy shit! Man, I haven't seen you in ages, what the hell brings you here?"

"Well, like you I enjoy photography."

"Is this like an accident, or what?"

The old classmate just smiled as the two of them got close enough to shake each other's hands. As they did the old classmate looked out toward the edge.

"Well, not exactly, I called your house because I was in the area and your wife, lovely wife by the way, told me basically where you were."

After the handshake the two of them separated and Brandon quickly grabbed his camera from the strap that held it around his neck.

"Yeah, she's like that, says she's gotta know exactly where I am just in case of, you know."

"Right, an accident."

"Exactly, plus I love coming here there are some sweet shots to be had." Brandon claimed, "So, man what the hell tell me what's going on?"

"Well, as I said I was in town for a few days and I thought I'd look up an old classmate for a bit of a reunion I guess. I didn't know how long you were going to be out here, so I thought, what the heck, go for it, get your camera and head outdoors."

"Man you got that right, this is great isn't it?" Brandon turned and shifted his direction back toward the canyon area.

"Absolutely!"

"So what kind of equipment you got there?"

"Oh this," lifting up his camera, "it's just a Canon EOS. It's sort of a dinosaur really."

"Like this isn't?" said Brandon as he motioned to his.

"This is the way pictures were intended to be taken, people get too caught up in the new stuff."

The Reunion Reaper

"I hear ya."

"Well hell, if you're here you might as well take some pictures with me, come on over here this is a great spot."

"Wow, that's really close to the edge."

"Yeah I know, but the wind is down and the only way I can get some depth shots of the canyon below is to crawl near the edge. It's not too bad once you get over the initial vertigo shit."

"Really?"

Brandon chortled at his response.

"Come on you'll be fine. You were a live wire in high school; tell me you haven't changed that?"

"Well, things change you know, people, habits, lives."

"Come on don't go getting Dalai Llama on me alright?"

"You're right, but I get no closer than about five feet."

"Hey whatever man!"

For this surprise he knew this spot well. It was one of Brandon's favorites. Six months of surveillance led him to this very moment. To his benefit it was a weekday, and he knew people milling about would be negligible at best. From on this rocky point he carefully traipsed over to where Brandon stood and surveyed the area.

"Come here you gotta see this," Brandon barked out. "Tell me what manufactured theme park could recreate a picture spot like this?"

His high school classmate edged closer.

"Look down there."

He slid closer and attempted to peak, but it was obvious that this seemed to be an uncomfortable situation for him.

"No, that's okay," he said nervously.

"Come on, I told you the winds are quiet today, look, down there."

"I don't see anything."

"Right there!" as he guided his arm to point at the location of two promontory rock formations.

"Oh, you mean those?"

"Beautiful aren't they?"

"Absolutely!"

"I could come here a thousand times and find something new every time. It's almost like the canyon moves man."

Actually, you've been here ten times in four months. Brandon brushed by him to get to his bag where several cameras with differing lenses were packed. He quickly pulled out another camera with the zoom lens and headed back to near the edge. He fired off a few quick shots. He jumped around that ridge like a mountain goat.

"Man, this is why I come here, nature is so frickin' unpredictable, you know."

"Part and parcel with the land I believe Thoreau once said."

"Emerson!" Brandon shot back.

"Oh sorry."

"That's okay, they were like father and son anyway; maybe one said it and the other wrote it who knows."

Brandon bounced back over to his bag to place the zoom camera back and he retrieved the one he held earlier. He moved back over to the edge and began to take more pictures. After a few shots he hesitated.

"Well, you hear to take shots or what?"

"Hell yeah, move aside," he shot back.

He slid a little closer to the edge near Brandon as the both of them clicked away. As they clicked the conversation continued. Brandon and his old classmate made small talk about each other's lives, about old classmates, and old girlfriends. Brandon invited his old friend to stay with him and his family, but his friend had business to tend to and would be gone by morning. It wasn't long before the tone of the conversation shifted to a darker topic.

"So Brandon... how's your marriage?"

"What kind of question is that man; it's like most I guess, why?"

The Reunion Reaper

"Well, I talked to your wife a while and I sensed that she was troubled."

"Hell no man, we're fine, sometimes she just opens her mouth to say certain things and it comes out all wrong."

"Kind of like a misunderstanding!" he shot him a glaring glance but Brandon failed to see it as he was too glued to the view finder of his camera.

"Exactly, she doesn't always express her feelings the right way you know? She's got some of that Native American blood that makes it difficult for her to sometimes express certain kinds of feelings." He continued clicking away.

"Oh yes, women can be very difficult to read sometimes, but so can we, especially if we've had an affair."

Totally surprised by the blind side Brandon whipped around and pulled his camera away from his face.

"What the hell are you gettin' at man?"

"I'm just saying that men, like women have skeletons in the closet."

"Yeah, well there are no more skeletons in the closet, my wife and I got all that straightened out, it was a one night stand and that was it. How the hell did you know that?"

"I see, and you've not seen this woman anymore?"

"No! What the hell is your deal man you some sort of private investigator?"

"Maybe, maybe not."

"So what, did my wife hire you or something?"

"She didn't need to, I took the job willingly. You see, it's measly little pricks like you who screw around on their wives and think it's okay, when in fact, it destroys the most precious aspect of a relationship, trust."

"What are you fuckin' Dr. Phil now? We haven't seen each other in over twenty years, and you come all the way out here to razz my shit? I told you, my wife and I have patched things up."

"You know something you've got a dirty mouth."

"Yeah, well fuck you, how about that? You know something I never really liked your ass anyway."
Ignoring Brandon's retort then smiling, "You know she doesn't even know about your affairs."

"What the hell are you talking about; of course she does… we talked about it."

"Oh Brandon, Brandon, those little white lies need to come to an end."

"Look, don't lecture me about marriage all right."

"Well, I just wanted to set the record straight."

"The record? What record?"

"The fact that you are engaged in an extramarital affair, got the tramp pregnant, and now she's carrying your baby, but here you are, oops, you're married to another woman, hmm, what shall we do?"

"I asked you before, how do you know all this?" Brandon's voice was more hesitant now.

"You love to take pictures, well so do I."

"And?"

"I've got pictures of you and this woman; she is looking very pregnant by the way." Brandon's mouth could catch flies as his old classmate continued. "I find that ironic, given the fact that you were always the one taking pictures of people in awkward or uncompromising positions."

"So what do you want money?"

"I don't want money." He laughed at the gesture of bribery, "I'm an honest man, as opposed to you, who is a lying, cheating no good dirt bag who feels women are simply property to be borrowed and used like some library book—"

"Hey screw you man, who are you to lecture me on morals?"

"Oh, this is not a lecture, this is a lesson." He inched closer to Brandon.

"So, what kind of lesson is this, you tell me I'm all fucked up and I go home and tell the truth, and all that?"

The Reunion Reaper

"The whole truth, that there's been more than one woman and that she is not the only one you got pregnant." He smiled, "Oh my, forgot about that little bambino in Albuquerque?"

Brandon surveyed his old classmate.

"Man, what the hell have you become, what happened to the cat who called himself cooler than iced tea?" as he raised both hands to simulate the quote sign.

"Actually it was the master of disaster you idiot. I guess you could call me the redeemer now. You're a married man you don't go around screwin' anybody just to get your rocks off, especially if there are kids involved, you know, like your legitimate fifteen year old son.

His temples began to bulge like a heartbeat, visible to the surprised Brandon as he continued.

"You know why, because you said I do. You should be real careful of who or what you take pictures of. So much for creativity I guess."

"Oh, I see, this is all about that," again, using his hands to make the quotes, "little embarrassing moment of yours isn't it?"

"That was years ago."

"Yeah, but a little prick is always just that isn't it?"

"You're pretty funny for a screw up. You always enjoyed taking," he put up his hands in mock to Brandon's quote gestures, "pot shots didn't you."

"Yeah, that was a lot of fun; anything to make someone look ridiculous." He followed it with a laugh.

Stepping closer to Brandon he lowered his voice, "Well, here's a final lesson for you."

The smaller, five foot nine vengeful classmate lunged at Brandon, who was standing just a few feet from the edge. Brandon stumbled with the look of shock in his eyes. He was unable to keep his balance and fell over the edge. With camera in hand he plunged some one hundred or so feet to a crushing death. As he looked down over the edge, the fear of the edge an apparent ruse, he looked down upon his second victim.

There's nothing like eradicating two birds with one stone, a dirt bag and ridding oneself of an old memory.

And with that he picked up his bag, looked around the area for anything that may tie a second individual to the area and then smiled at the ominous clouds on the horizon. This gave him little worry of any evidence being discovered, for later that day it rained to beat hell there.

Chapter 7

Journal date: September 9: Saving a woman and son from a dirt-bag pecker-head.

Simply put, I am good! Have I said that before, probably not? Thank you, thank you so much. No really, please! I must admit that this one actually felt good. I sort of felt bad for Judith, but it was something that had to be done, but this is not about her, her case is closed, and so the master plan moves on.

Brandon Henniker was a player who got his. What a prick! He had very little reason to exist other than screwing up the lives of many people, especially a fifteen year old boy and a loyal and loving wife. What a bird-brain. If parents were just more aware of how impressionable they really are to their kid's maybe they would be a little more responsible with their actions. Unlike this prick who couldn't keep his pecker in his pocket. Maybe I should have whacked it off. This is almost too easy. This calls for a little ditty. Do do doomp doomp doomp... another one bites the dust... hey, I'm gonna getcha too another bites the dust.

I need to give myself some memorable name for all of this, how about, The Desert Vigilante, or the Reunion Reaper? Yeah, perhaps the book should be titled, Reunion Reaper: Fear what you do not know, or Desert Vigilante: Justice served with a side of flair, or something like that. Work on this you brilliant bastard.

What the hell ever happened to keeping your commitments and not betraying those who rely on you? Come Judas your silver awaits you in hell. You know what, he's taken up too much of my paper, and to be honest, his photos weren't all that impressive; damn self serving prick that he was. Who's compromised now dirt dweller?

Scott A. Reighard

Brandon Henniker: January 26, 1964-September 8, 2007. Rest in guilt you bastard. I wonder what level Dante would have you placed. May you forever toss in your death sleep, and you can take that camera and shove it up your view finder, cause that's about how you looked at the world.

Chapter 8

Andrew Keane, a detective with the Roanoke County Police Department of Roanoke, Virginia pulled into the driveway where sat his four bed room split level home. It was a home that exuded a warm and happy atmosphere. It was divided with two bedrooms, a master bath and a study on the bottom floor while the upper level boasted two bedrooms, a full bath, the kitchen and living area. It was a modest home given the incomes of Andrew and Stephanie, his wife of nearly fifteen years.

He sauntered through the door as another workday had come to a close. Life as a detective in rural southwest Virginia wasn't exactly a hotbed for Hollywood style detective dramas, but it was a life Andrew had adopted and with which he had no regrets.

"Hoyt!" Was the familiar call of Andrew's as he walked through the front door.

As the door closed behind him his nine year old son Michael tested his catching ability by tossing himself from the steps to his father.

"Daddy!"

"Hey there bud, how was your day at school?" He groaned as he gave his son a bear hug.

"Good!"

"Ugh, you're getting too heavy for dad anymore. So, where are your brother and sister?"

"Ryan is playing downstairs and Mary's in her room, duh!"

"Hey, what I say about that duh stuff?" Andrew put Michael down and placed his keys on a hook just inside the door.

"Sorry."

He and Michael walked up the remaining steps to the kitchen area.

"Ryan, daddy's home," Andrew shouted out down the stairs.

He skated over to his wife Stephanie and kissed her neck as a faint voice echoed up the stairs.

"Okay."

Andrew tilted his head to the side as he looked at his wife, "Okay he says, I can see he's excited that his hard working father, who could have been shot today by the way, is home."

"Shot?" His wife fired back.

"Just trying to make a point dear."

"That's not a very nice point."

"Okay, let me rephrase that. I can see that he's excited that his hard working father, who could have been slapped by some old lady today, is home."

"Much better."

"Thank you."

"Mail's on the counter," she said gathering plates from the cupboard.

"Thanks."

With the whole family together this was the usual scene, but by all accounts the Keane's were a pretty busy family. The kids were involved with sports, and both Stephanie and Andrew stayed active with triathlons and the church. They would often split the typical parental duties, although Stephanie would often comment otherwise.

"Dad, can we play a game?" asked Michael.

"Not now son, daddy just got home. Let's wait until after dinner, okay?"

"Okay!" responded Michael in a dejected tone.

"Hey, I promise, after dinner we'll play a game. You choose okay?" said Andrew as he flipped through the mail.

Michael was working on his homework as Andrew slid into the bench style corner table next to him. Andrew was a man whose frame was slender yet muscular. He stood a solid six foot, his short cropped sandy blond hair, blue-gray eyes and twin vertical age like lines that creased his cheeks on either side suggested a man with rugged looks. The demeanor of his walk and posture were strong despite a man who had experienced a lot of athletic wear and tear so far. Many of his friends commented that he looked a lot like Kevin Costner. He joked that he wished he had Costner's money. He recently turned forty two, but took great care of his body, mind and soul.

Stephanie removed the chicken from the oven, "So how was your day sweetie?"

"Good! It was basically quiet except for an accident involving a student from the high school." He ripped up the junk mail.

"Really, what happened?"

"Well, I didn't want to get involved, but I went by there just a few minutes after it happened, so I figured what the heck it's been a while. So the kid says, get this, that his cell phone went off and when he went to answer it, some old lady pulled out in front of him, so he had to slam on his brakes, but there wasn't enough space between them so he plowed into her from behind. My guess was that he was probably more focused on the phone than he was on driving. I tell ya, these kids and their damn cell phones." Michael didn't bother calling out dad for swearing like he did his mom when she cursed.

A voice shouted and questioned from down the hall, "When am I getting a cell phone?"

Mary, their fourteen year old daughter, subtly reminded her parents that she was the only student in the entire school not to have a cell phone.

"When you become a doctor or a lawyer, someone who really needs one," dad shouted back.

Mom carried on without missing a beat, "Well I hope no one was hurt."

"Ah, the kid was fine, but he took a pretty bad rap to his head because he didn't have his seat belt on, so you know he got pretty upset when he was ticketed for reckless driving and not wearing his seatbelt. As for the old lady, she suffered a slight whiplash, but I'll guarantee it turns out to be more serious when she talks to a lawyer."

"Probably!"

"So, how was your day?"

"Fine, but the contracts are piling up as we near the end of the month."

"Typical end of the month BS huh," He was sympathetic to end of the month deadlines. He recalled those days when he and his fellow officers were constantly reminded about quotas for the month.

"It just gets old sometimes," as she pulled the bag of steamed vegetables from the microwave.

Andrew looked over at Michael and smiled as he was doing math homework. Rummaging through the last pieces of mail, he came across an envelope written with calligraphy style writing addressed to him. He looked at the return address and saw that it was from the Palm Beach County Historical Society. He opened it up only to discover an invitation to a high school class reunion. It had been nearly twenty five years since Andrew graduated in 1983.

"Well, I'll be."

"What is it?"

"Huh, it's an invitation to my twenty fifth year high school class reunion."

"Really, I thought you said the school wasn't around anymore."

"It's not this is from the Palm Beach Historical Society. Maybe they're handling all the archives and what not for the school."

"It's hard to believe twenty five years is right around the corner isn't it?"

"Thanks for the reminder."

After Andrew graduated from high school he attended Roanoke College in Salem, Virginia. He played lacrosse,

The Reunion Reaper

hustled girls, and studied criminal justice. These were merely appetizers to his burning ambitions, and when he decided on the exciting life of international security escort and enforcement protection over sitting behind a mahogany desk in a suit sucking up to just about whomever would give him business, it was obvious the competitive juices still churned, and so he decided that the field of law enforcement held the challenges he needed. He was a man bent on doing the best with which the tools God blessed him. Oh how the years had passed it seemed.

At work Andrew received news that he was most likely going to get promoted to lieutenant of detectives within the police department, despite his college degree and initial goal, something that indicated that he was a man destined to become a lawyer, but destiny turned the pages on what could have been. Now the chapters were being written on this profession. His distaste for the legal field, and all the politics that went along with it seemed to tire quickly as he gave that ambition its due process, but his decision to forego the lawyer track steered him into the man he had now become.

"What does it say?"

"It says *The Palm Beach Historical Society on behalf of Palm Beach Preparatory School would like to cordially invite you to a reunion to celebrate the graduating classes of 1983 through 1988 on May 19, 2008...*blah, blah, blah."

"Wow, that's just a week before our anniversary."

"Anyhow, it's at the Breakers Hotel in Palm Beach, Florida and more blah, blah, blah. Wait, here's a name at the bottom for the RSVP. It's a Gloria Steinbach."

"Hey, wouldn't that be a great anniversary gift, you and me back to Florida on our fifteenth wedding anniversary?"

From down the hall Mary shouted, "We're going to Florida?"

"No honey, your dad and I are just talking."

"Well, it sounds good, but who says we're going?" dad retorted.

"Oh come on, it's your twenty fifth high school reunion, who wouldn't want to go to that?"

"Me!"

"You old fart you can't tell me that you wouldn't want to see your old high school chums."

Michael, never looking up but keeping his attention on his homework, "Mommy, you said a bad word."

"That's really not a bad word honey it's just rude like shut up."

"Now let's not get too far ahead of ourselves, we need to look at our finances."

"We are solid financially, besides, when is the last time you and I went on a vacation alone."

"Alone... what about us?" Mary shouted from her room.

"God she's like radar in there. Mary nobody's going anywhere right now. We're just talking."

"Well I want to go to Florida."

"Yeah me too," echoed Michael.

"Everybody just zip it. Gees, thank God Ryan isn't within ear shot, it would be a virtual coup." Andrew looked at Stephanie and just shook his head.

Stephanie just smiled and whispered to him, "We'll talk privately later."

"Come on dad, Florida would be so much fun."

"What, is this my estranged daughter emerged from her lair?"

"Funny. No seriously, can we go?"

"First of all it's in May, you guys are still in school, and do you know how much a trip like that would cost for the five of us? Besides, I think you all are going to grandma and pap's this summer."

"Fine, but I still think we all should go."

"Dad will consider that, thank you for your input."

Mary plopped down on one of the kitchen table chairs.

The Reunion Reaper

"So, how was your day?"
"Great, yours?"
"Good." She said as she picked at a fingernail.
"Good, is that it?" he asked.
"Yeah, good."
"Good." He raised his eyebrows in a sarcastic manner. "You hear that honey, she's good."
"Okay I get it, uh, let's see, I have a stupid social studies paper due tomorrow in Mr. Penn's class, and let's see, I have a Geometry test on Thursday, and—"
"Okay, I get the point you don't want to talk with your old man."
"No, that's not it; I just needed a minute to think."
"Well, I appreciate you going out on a limb to think for me."
"Ha, ha, funny!"
"What, no kiss and hug for the man who helps to feed, cloth and—."
"Andrew, be nice to her, you know how teens can be," as she winked at her husband.
"All too well my dear, all too well."
Mary walked over and gave him a hug and a kiss on the cheek.
"You know, despite the fact your ole dad is ignored quite a bit, I still love you Mary."
"I don't ignore you…all the time…I love you too dad."
That's all he needed to hear, *I love you.* Daddy's little girl wasn't so little anymore, she was becoming a woman, and quicker than he and Stephanie had hoped.
Everyone gathered as dinner was placed on the table. Michael asked if he could say the blessing. They then proceeded to dig in to mom's chicken in gravy. During this time together conversations of school, sports and Ryan's new fort downstairs were tossed about the table. Overall, it had the impression of a house that was content with its residents, and resident's content with one another.

Scott A. Reighard

Chapter 9

Spring 1983- Palm Beach, Florida

"Hey, idiot, stop messin' with the record player. Keep playin' *Stairway to Heaven*, and I'm gonna help you get there sooner than you think."

Tucker Harrison, the bruising defensive leader of the school's lacrosse team and team mouth who often made his thoughts instant words was commenting on the repeated playing of Led Zeppelin's famous song. One thing was a common denominator for Tucker, he liked to hit, not just on the lacrosse field but on the young ladies. Despite being a senior he was in the arms of one of the school freshman Andrea Pruitt. Tucker liked the younger girls, his last girlfriend was a sophomore, but of course that was in the fall during soccer season. This was lacrosse season, time for new territory and a new squeeze.

The night was a special night; Palm Beach Preparatory School had just defeated the previous three time state champ, St. Francis Prep out of Ft. Lauderdale earlier that day fourteen to ten. It kept their undefeated hopes alive and the path to the state championship one step closer. This undefeated, experienced Palm Beach team was confident and coached by a man who was used to winning, Todd Hill, former Division I All-American goalie out of Johns Hopkins.

The party was at the home of Jeffery Lewis. By all accounts, Jeffrey lived a silver spooned life. He was a single child and much attention was given to him. At his Bar Mitzvah there were three hundred guests, and yes, three hundred gifts; mostly by way of cash. He drove a new Saab 900, canary yellow, and he wasn't afraid to throw huge parties while his parents went back to their old haunts

The Reunion Reaper

in New Jersey. This particular party was for his fellow lacrosse players, and he was a pretty good host. There was alcohol, weed, and for the hardliners, cocaine. Jeffrey dabbled in a little trafficking of high demand goods for his friends, and basically socked away every dollar he earned from his side business. On this night, Jeffrey once again had his eye on Judy Barnett. Although she was practically betrothed to Harry Jordan, a graduate of 1981, he still had visions of stealing her away from someone he considered a jerk. One thing for sure, Judy liked to experiment with various substances, and Jeffrey was sure to offer her cocaine. Jeffrey made up his own jingle when it came to drugs. He used to say, "Weed makes 'em easy, but the 'caine drives 'em insane."

Ever since they were freshman Jeffrey was hot after Judy, but he couldn't overcome the charm and jois de vive of Harry Jordan. But like an opportunistic cat, he was always lying in wait for a chance to pounce. Plus, he was hoping that since the two of them were seniors and Harry was away at college perhaps she would be into one last high school affair. It was hard to tell whether Jeffrey was now looking for something meaningful, or to just say he laid Judy Barnett. That night he gave her his best "Hebrewski," as he used to call it. The good news for him was that Judy appeared pretty well coked out. He managed to slip in a few clever lines that persuaded her to venture upstairs to his bedroom. He offered her some goodies that only he would share with her.

As the rest of the party continued downstairs the music and noise slowly faded as Jeffrey guided her into his bedroom. He clicked on his liquid lava lamp then he slid from an album sleeve his favorite Journey album. He twirled the album in his hands then carefully placed it on the record player. It didn't take long for Steve Perry to start belting out *Don't Stop Believin'* and for Jeffrey to begin putting the moves on a spoken for girl. At first she was receptive, and Jeffrey's confidence was gaining strength with every advance, and then, to his total shock, she said, "Look, I know what it is we want…the two of us both."

"What?" Jeffrey responded, not understanding her.

"I mean, I know what the two of us want. You wait here, I need to get my purse, there's something in there we'll both need."

Jeffrey smiled as wide as his lips would stretch, "Okay."

"Now, you go and get ready for me okay," if a slight wink and a gentle sway of the golden blond hair didn't get his juices flowing then he was clinically dead, "light some incense, or whatever. I'll be right back."

"You got it!" he answered with enthusiasm as she snuck out the door. He danced around the room quietly exuding joy like a kid at Christmas. Then he dashed into the bathroom to check all the goods and such he hoped to lay on her.

Judy went downstairs to get her purse and began to head back up stairs. Meanwhile, Jeffrey was preparing his bed as well as himself for the arrival of his affection. There was a light knock at the door.

"Open for business."

Jeffrey was lying on the bed as the door knob slowly turned. Suddenly a throng of people bust through the door. He was sitting on his bed, and all those in attendance could see his proud tower of manhood smiling for the camera. Brandon Henniker was quick to strike with his camera.
Rodney Adams pointed out, "It looks like the leaning tower of Pisa. Mmm, a leaning tower indeed."

"Yeah, but a tiny tower at that," laughed Tucker Harrison.

Jeffrey leaped from the bed and darted into the adjacent bathroom as everyone began laughing hysterically. Although many of them tried to convince him it was just a joke, Jeffrey was in no mood for humor, especially at his expense. He was usually the one pulling the practical jokes, or finding someone to embarrass, but this time he was the victim of the turnabout is fair play game.

Judy yelled for everyone to get out, but a few verbal jabs were thrown at him as they were hustled out the door.

"Hey I got some pills that may help that whole leaning thing Jeffrey," shouted a boisterous Tucker.

When the last person was shoved out of the room she tried to console him from outside the bathroom door by apologizing, but he just quietly told her to tell everyone to go home, the party was over.

"Listen, I'm really sorry, you know they don't mean it, everyone loves you."

She placed her face close to the door and explained,

"Jeffrey, why did you have to go and do something like that? You know I'm with Harry, what were you thinking?"

"What were you thinking?" He proposed.

But there was no immediate response.

"It was an accident Jeffrey, I didn't think you would be naked on the bed when I got back, I just thought that... well, that... I'm sorry Jeffrey I didn't mean to embarrass you like that.

He did not respond. A few minutes passed and Judy was still at the bathroom door.

"I'll make sure everyone's out and the place is locked up. Again, I'm sorry Jeffrey."

The party was over, and for Jeffrey his relationship with these classmates would never be the same. For him, graduation was six weeks away and it couldn't come fast enough.

Scott A. Reighard

Chapter 10

Andrew was back at work early the next morning pondering the reunion invitation. While siphoning some leftover night shift coffee in the kitchen area he ran into his best friend on the force Sonny Bishop; a fireplug for a man whose solid frame complemented an enthusiastic love of life and liberty, not to mention steadfast principles. His brutal honesty at times could appear hurtful, but he always felt that it was better to be honest than not. "Honesty is a heckuva lot easier to remember than lies," he once told Andrew.

Sonny, a former marine, was, in many ways, like Andrew. He seemed to crave the excitement of, well, excitement, and although this was not a haven of the so called big city crime, the two of them realized this was where they wanted to raise a family. Both of them agreed, a slight forego of the street action for a more secure family setting was a palatable offset. Andrew and Sonny had worked together for nearly ten years.

After the usual small talk Andrew gave Sonny the scoop about the reunion and divulged a rare skeleton in the closet that carried the name Amy McMahon. She was Andrew's high school sweetheart. He explained how she was his first, and he was her first and that despite the love he has for Stephanie, Amy wanders into his thoughts now and again.

"Look, I think it's pretty normal to think about your ex's sometimes, but I wouldn't get too hung up on this, besides, that was a long time ago."

"I know, but it's not just her, it's the whole Florida thing," remarked Andrew as he poured more milk than there looked to be coffee.

"Bro, you got too much food in the refrigerator, it's time to throw some of it out."

The Reunion Reaper

Sonny noticed the milk pouring,
"A little coffee with your milk?"
"Have you ever had the night shifts coffee? Anyhow, I'm tryin' to get rid of some of this, believe me I am."
"Hey, we better get a move on it before Captain Hardass gives us that look of disgust.
Sonny patted him on the back as he continued.
You worry too much, it'll be fine. Go to Florida, get a tan, reacquaint with old classmates and get romantic with your wife while you're there."
"Trust me, there's no lack for affection in the romance department.
As they meandered down the hall Andrew acknowledged Sonny's advice.
You're right, maybe I should go."
Without batting an eye Sonny smiled, "I'm always right, I'm a US Marine."
"And modest too!"
"Hey, are we still on for our run tonight?"
"Yeah, but we go at my pace though, you younger guys are wearing me out."
"You got it ole man."
As the two of them entered the room they saw that everyone for shift turnover was there, including the captain, who, as Sonny claimed, glared at the two of them. With Andrew standing behind the shorter Sonny he simply pointed at him and indicated it was Sonny's fault they were late by mimicking the quacking like a duck hand gesture. Andrew smiled and patted his good friend on the shoulder as they took a seat.

Scott A. Reighard

Chapter 11

September 1981 – Singer Island, Florida

"What the hell are you doing? Let's go before the old bastard sees us with all this."

One of Andrew's new friends Mark Lambert whispered to him while in the Greater Gator convenience store.

"So, we're just walking out?"

"Exactly, like there's nothing suspicious."

The two boys, both juniors, were headed to the beach, with little money, yet very hungry.

"Don't you think it looks pretty stupid, not to mention obvious wearing a zipped up sweatshirt in September?"

"Come on, surfers and beach dudes always dress weird. Just don't act like anything is out of the ordinary. Just follow my lead."

The two of them walked toward the front of the store where the owner stood behind the counter. Just as they were passing Mark stopped.

"Excuse me sir. Jimmy you go on to the car, I'll be right there."

Andrew gave him a crossed look. Mark looked at Andrew and winked, "Go ahead Jimmy I'll be right there.

He turned back to the man behind the counter.

Yeah, hey can I see one of those Playboys you got there?"

The old owner kept the adult magazines behind the counter so kids wouldn't rip him off. The gray haired slender and overly tanned owner turned around to grab the September issue as Andrew quickly scooted out the door with a belly full of junk stuffed into his sweatshirt. Mark began to thumb through the magazine as the old man seemed to peak over the top glancing at the pictures or at Mark.

"Hey, you gonna buy it, or just fondle the damn thing?" he questioned with a pronounced Philadelphia accent.

"I just wanted to see if my old girlfriend was in there," and with that he tossed it back onto the counter, "maybe next month."

"Damn kids!" the old man commented as Mark punched at the door and headed toward his car. But the deed was done Mark Lambert had officially corrupted Andrew Keane. He convinced him to steal about three dollars worth of food. Andrew got a charge out of this, but probably felt like he had to do this more to impress his present company than to steal food like a starving homeless person.

They headed over to Singer Island Beach where they were going to meet the usual gang of guys. It was pretty much a ritual, every Saturday, the Pump House, Singer Island, bring your own guts and glory. Other than Mark and Andrew the usual gang meant Riley Bradshaw, Greg Madison, Paul Thurman, senior Steven Chambers and tagging along that day was Jeffrey Lewis.

School had just started back a few weeks ago and many of the kids were returning from summer vacation, except Andrew. When he and his family went on vacation they ended up in either Daytona, or Orlando, but many of his friends were headed up north to the Cape, Long Island, Montauk, or Martha's Vineyard for the entire summer. Andrew wasn't as lucky as most of these silver spoon kids, and he never even got an invite, which sort of told him he wasn't in their class, but the kid was one helluva an athlete, and when you are able to help your team win then there's a place for you at the table of elites. In this case it was the beach, and the guys would take turns jumping off the pump house into the cresting waves below.

The pump station was a large round structure built into the beach that was created to help drain part of the adjacent inlet. It had a large arm that would extend into the inlet, dredge sand, then pivot around and redistribute the sand it dredged on the other side of the jetty where it made a pretty nice beach and a large one too. Eventually some of that sand would get sucked out to sea during the winter months making the water deeper closer to the shore which was the optimal time for pump house antics; whereas in September most of the sand was still high meaning the water was shallow. In some areas you could walk out fifty, eighty, even one hundred yards off the beach and the water was only knee high.

Since the water level could be less than three feet on a calm day someone had to stay in the water below in order to let the person standing on the crow's nest of the pump house know when a wave was approaching. A simple thumbs up or a shout out gave the go ahead for leaps. It was all about the timing and you had to trust the guy below. If a mistake was to occur it could result in a broken leg or in one case the previous year, a kid broke several ribs because he slipped before clearing the jump area, fell onto the edge off the pump station and landed awkwardly in the shallow water below. Authorities posted **No Trespassing** signs, but that was more or less to alleviate the city of any liability. They knew kids were going to ignore the signs.

Some of the guys were completely crazy and would attempt to dive from the crow's nest, a distance of some twenty five feet off the water. Andrew was crazy, but not stupid and so he just stuck to jumping, cannon-balling, or jack-knifing into the water from the actual pump house roof, which was about fifteen feet off the water.

A couple of the guys that met Mark and him were just hanging out on the beach taking turns on a Bob Marley size blunt. Andrew wanted nothing to do with that, so he stayed in the water most of the time. He figured if there was going to be a bust he was not going to be one of the ones busted for something he didn't do. He could

The Reunion Reaper

understand getting busted for the Gator, Gator incident, but not this. He prided himself on being drug free, and so did his parents, besides a father working as a Florida DEA agent, getting busted for drugs would be the death knell for him, especially since his father often reminded him that he could make Andrew disappear should he bring shame on the family. His dad had a way with getting his point across.

Mark made his way up to the top of the crow's nest and was waiting for Andrew's signal. It was now Mark's turn to impress the judges who were still getting high on the beach. Andrew was standing in thigh high water as Mark stood on the crow's nest. He was waiting for the thumbs up sign.

Another wave approached, and Andrew gave him the thumbs up but Mark wasn't looking at him, he was scoping out a few girls walking toward the pump house area. The wave had passed. Andrew yelled up to get Mark's attention. Mark gave thumbs up as he whistled to the girls on the beach. Andrew yelled out, "NO!" but it was too late, Mark was off the crow's nest and on his way in to three feet of water. It would be a mistake Andrew could never forgive of himself.

When Mark hit the water there was only three feet of water, and his body was not in a good position as he slammed into the shallow water. Instantly there was a mad scream coming out of Mark's mouth. Andrew and Riley Bradshaw quickly swam over and grabbed him at once and dragged him to shore. Mark kept on screaming his leg was broken. Meeting Andrew and Riley on the shoreline were Jeffrey, Greg, Paul, and Steven Chambers, who was Mark's best friend of the bunch. Andrew was trying to console him, but it was useless. Steven came over and shoved Andrew out of the way calling him some pretty unkind names. The event would forever change some of the relationships.

Mark suffered multiple breaks in his leg and there was considerable hip damage that would require several surgeries. He would not be able to participate in sports again. Although it was an accident Andrew would live with the guilt of this moment for a very long time, and neither Steven Chambers nor Mark Lambert would ever find it within themselves to forgive Andrew.

Chapter 12

The Keane house was finally quieting down as Andrew comfortably positioned himself in bed. As he adjusted his position he thought about what Sonny had said about too much food in the fridge. Perhaps it was time to clean it out. He gathered two soft pillows for his head and a third to place between his knees. Sleeping on his side brought him some relief from the poundings he took playing lacrosse in college, as well as just being too physical in fun and games over the course of his life.

Within the last few years Andrew wanted to stay active and compete in something. Then he discovered triathlons, and he was hooked after a good friend enticed him to participate in a sprint triathlon. The sprint triathlons are not near as physically taxing as an Ironman Triathlon, but the workouts were still tough on his body, reminding him of his careless and physical ways, but it was well worth the pain he thought. So here he was dealing with some back and knee issues pondering a possible return to the Sunshine State.

"Andrew I am concerned about Ryan," announced Stephanie from the bathroom as she squeezed toothpaste onto her brush.

"What are you talking about?" he replied, finally discovering an agreeable position.

"Well, you know he's had this fever for a few days, and he's been coughing a lot."

"It's probably allergies; you know how this area gets in the spring."

"Well, I am taking him to the doctor's office tomorrow to have him checked out," mumbled Stephanie as she brushed her teeth.

"That's a good idea. He's a tough kid he'll be okay, they'll probably tell you to go buy some over the counter and be done with it."

Ryan, the youngest of the bunch, was a rough and tumble, five year old whose looks were more like his mother, but with actions more like his father. His ash colored hair and eyes, that sparkled like iced cubes in a blue dye were matched with a dangerous proclivity to test his jumping and tumbling skills at any turn.

She climbed into the bed and grabbed a magazine off the night stand, "I sure hope so."

"I know so, you worry too much. He'll be fine."

A few minutes later there was a knock at their bedroom door. It was Mary.

"Mom, dad."

"What is it dear?" responded her mother.

"I need some help on a school project."

"When is it due?" her mother asked, hoping not to hear the dreaded response.

"Tomorrow."

She had to say tomorrow. Cue Andrew, she thought.

"Mary, what have we told you about waiting until the last minute on projects and tests?" Andrew admonished her without altering his position, his voice sounding somewhat muffled by the pillows.

"I know, but my computer is acting up and I need to use yours."

"Well, if you wouldn't download so much crap onto your computer you'd –"

"Honey, what your dad is saying –"

"What I am saying is, it's eleven thirty on a school night and you —"

"Andrew honey, we're aware of that. Just keep it quiet for your father please."

"I will."

The Reunion Reaper

Andrew rolled his eyes. His daughter's procrastinating ate at him like a caterpillar on a fresh leaf. One thing Andrew prided himself on was organization. Every night he would get the next day's stuff ready to go. It didn't matter if it was for work, church, or the golf course, he had everything set out. As for his daughter she was more like her mother, procrastinating was an everyday occurrence. He tried to raise his kids with three elements in mind: discipline, organization and honesty. He figured if you had those three things you would be a good quality citizen in the game of life. This started early with his mother and father. They were pretty organized people, and from his vantage point as a kid, and now as a forty something he thought they did a pretty good job of instilling a value and moral system that was reflective of good honest people. Don't mess with success he would often say.

"You know if this situation would have happened to me you know what your pappy would have said, tough you know what, you should have gotten it done sooner."

"Andrew she knows that, just let her get her project done. Mary, I hope you understand what we mean when we talk about priorities."

"I know." Mary did her best to keep her answers simple. She knew when dad was less than happy.

"I know is not good enough young lady. Your mother and I have been through this too many times. You are a freshman in high school, and it's high time you start looking at things more responsibly."

"Yes sir." Mary turned and left the room.

"Doubtful," he murmured.
Stephanie rubbed Andrew on his back knowing full well that stuff like this irritated him, and so she leaned in real close, "Hey, she's learning—"

"Pretty darn slow don't you think?"

"Just don't be so rough all the time, she's a girl and your approach to her should be different than it is for Michael and Ryan."

"Yeah, well you know, a crack in the dam here, a crack in the dam there—"

"I know, the dam breaks, but this dam is pretty solid don't you think?"

Andrew hated being the bad guy, but he knew he had to take a hard stance from time to time. "Society will not shape and mold my kids," he preached. "That's our job."

He took solace knowing that his wife stood by him. It takes two he thought. It was tough enough in this day and age with a two parent household to raise kids let alone someone trying to do it as a single parent. He was thankful for that, and so was she.

The Reunion Reaper

Chapter 13

Staring at a computer screen and clicking on the desktop folder he created for mapping out his master plan, Jeffrey reflected on the two classmates already marked off the list Judy Barnett and Brandon Henniker. He was flying high at this point. It was almost like spin the wheel, and each spot had a name on it, but who would be next? He wasn't a random killer, he was a killer with a purpose, a plan, and he operated with great efficiency. All the pieces had to be in place before he would venture forward, and felt extremely confident that law enforcement, despite all of its new technology, didn't stand a chance.

As he stared at the list of his intended victims, he began to reflect on an unrelated job that took place in 2003. The mission then was whether he could take out a complete stranger, and this stranger gave him the perfect motive, he was an absolute scumbag. There was a feint sense of de-ja vu with this man because of a similar situation that happened to his father; therefore, he submitted himself to a test to see if he was actually capable of carrying out an emotionless crime.

The idea sprung while reading a newspaper article in the spring of 2003. The story chronicled how a real estate broker had just been acquitted of swindling some one hundred elderly couples of most of their savings in a fraudulent real estate deal. A seemingly common occurrence it seems. What was thought to be an investment in an elderly community was nothing more than a purchase of worthless desert. William Chapman made several million dollars from unsuspecting couples by promising them a gated community dotted with patio homes and a community area with a large Olympic size pool, a fitness area, shuffleboard courts and a community center, not to mention several tennis courts.

The judge ruled that Mr. Chapman was not liable because in the fine print there was a clause, a clause with no Santa in front of it, but a clause nonetheless. Although the judge took away Mr. Chapman's license to work in Arizona, it didn't make a difference to him. He could simply relocate to New Mexico or any other state for that matter and set up shop. Extorting money from unsuspecting old people and jeopardizing their retirement or inheritance was something that appalled Jeffrey and he felt he couldn't just let this guy walk around unaffected by the impact he made on the lives of many innocent victims. And so the mission was on, this guy needed to be taken out.

Thinking of Chapman and his swindling flooded him with memories of how his father had lost a lot of money by investing in some Florida real estate in northern Florida. His father invested heavily, and when the deal fell through the losses were so bad that it sent his father over the deep end and in the summer of 1995, Simon Lewis took his own life, but he made it look like an accident. He bled the brake line to his 1988 Mercedes. His decision was to drive too fast around a notoriously dangerous curve on South County Road in the southern part of Palm Beach Island. He lost control of the vehicle and crashed into the seawall doing more than seventy miles per hour. The investigation concluded it was an accident, finally something Simon Lewis could consider an accomplishment.

The family was able to collect on a lucrative life insurance policy. His father may have been weak, but not stupid. His father couldn't live with the idea of being practically broke, which would be excruciatingly embarrassing, plus his marriage was pretty much in the tank. And the young Jeffrey Lewis read the letter his father wrote to him just days before the accident. *People like me don't deserve to take up space. I've been a bad man and a*

The Reunion Reaper

terrible father. I've basically lost this marriage plus I'm a lousy investor. In case anything happens to me be sure to take care of your mom, and despite everything I love you. Burn this note if you know what I mean.

It was cold but to the point. His father had always been that way. Jeffrey had difficulty dealing with this confession, and after several weeks of going through all the usual emotions from the tragedy he decided to get out of Florida. The first thirty years of his life had yielded little. His mother had become a waste, either high or drunk, and he was in and out of jobs because of his disdain for authority. He needed to make a name for himself, away from all the distractions, and so he headed west as many wanderlust children seem to do.

His thoughts redirected back to the objective, the dark world of taking another's life. He located where William Chapman lived, a ranch just outside Tucson. Through some computer searching and scouting he knew that every Saturday morning Chapman enjoyed a lonely horse back ride around his ranch, most likely grinning ear to ear with the fact that very little of his own money paid for this five hundred acre sprawl. Somewhere deep into the property boundary a plateau pushed out of the desert ground marking the end of his property line; a most fortuitous hiding place.

It was a cool and dry Saturday morning with barely a cloud in the sky, and hiding behind a wall of rocks that ran adjacent to the plateau he waited for Chapman to pass by. Jeffrey was dressed in desert camouflage similar to those worn by the U.S. Military fighting in the desert, but he was far from being representative of the military. His head was covered with a boony cap, like those worn by Navy SEALS. He sported black shades to complete the ensemble. When Chapman was about twenty feet past he drew out his paint ball gun, but instead of loading it with paint balls he loaded it with ball bearings. He had to be close enough to get a good shot, and this was about as good as he was going to get. To draw him in that close he wedged a yellow silk scarf between two boulders, something Chapman would notice and possibly be curious about. Chapman took the bait and rode up, got off his mount and pulled out the scarf. He sniffed it to see if there was some sort of perfume smell, but there wasn't. *What a pervert.* He shoved the scarf into his saddle bag. Chapman tricked out his horse like some wrangler, or old western cowboy on the round up. He even had a rolled up blanket tied to the back of the saddle.

As he started forward there was an opportunistic shooting angle for Jeffrey. He aimed his weapon at Chapman's head and fired. All that could be heard was the thwack of the ball bearing hitting Chapman square in the neck. As he began to fall over the side of the horse, he wasted no time in smacking another ball bearing into the rear end of the horse. It quickly raised its front legs in a rearing motion and took off. Chapman's foot was stuck in the stirrup and so the horse dragged him for several hundred yards before finally coming to a stop.

After the horse took off dragging an unconscious Chapman he followed closely on foot. This was a pretty desolate area with the plateau as a beautiful back drop. He wasn't worried about being spotted. Just in case though he did what he could to maintain cover behind rocks as he followed the horse.

When the horse finally came to a stop he went over to check on Chapman. He was unconscious, but he was unsure if he was dead. He grabbed a rock the size of a football and proceeded to give one good bash to the side of Chapman's skull just behind the left ear. Surely there would be no doubt that he was now dead. The blow, which sounded like someone banging a coconut on the sidewalk, slightly startled the horse. He calmed it down so he could check to make sure Chapman was dead. He leaned in and

The Reunion Reaper

did not hear any breathing from the six foot one inch, two hundred forty pound man.

With leather gloves donned, he flipped open the saddle bag to retrieve the scarf. Feeling confident he stepped back, drew his paint ball gun and shot the horse in the rear again. The horse gave a quick rail and took off, still dragging the now lifeless body of William Chapman. As he watched the horse create a windstorm of dust he sang in a low tone *Desperado*, one of his favorite songs by the Eagles.

A week or so after reading the article about the death of Chapman, he saw a follow up story that indicated the coroner's report. It stated that Mr. Chapman most likely fell of his horse, and in the process of being dragged his head struck several rocks. The coroner concluded the blows to the head were fatal. *You're damn right it was,* he mumbled. There was no evidence of foul play. *That's why it's pure genius Dr. Phakar, or however you say your Pharkan name.*

The article would be added to the collection of many that he would store. Mission accomplished, the old people may not have gotten their money back but several probably relished in the thought that Mr. Chapman would no longer take advantage of people, and he was sure most of them would repeat the cliché, what goes around comes around. He snapped out of his flashback masterpiece wondering again, since he was keeping journal entries and articles, whether he should proclaim himself to be the Desert Vigilante or the Reunion Reaper? But it was back to the current game. The agenda was set for more victims, classmates from the class of 1983.

Chapter 14

The next morning Andrew woke from a good night's rest, although still struggling with the decision regarding the reunion. *Why is this thing bothering me so much,* he thought as he stood in a morning shower that felt soothing. He readied for another day on the job.

As he stepped out of the bathroom he was confronted by his wife.

"So what do you think?"

"About what?"

"About the reunion?"

Andrew was afraid of this; his wife was great at prodding him. For her it would mean a vacation back to Florida, a place she missed sometimes, but for Andrew it was a place he would sooner avoid. She was not too keen on moving to Virginia, but she understood Andrew's need to get out of a place that had changed so dramatically over the course of his years there. Andrew felt that Florida should have remained the way it was when he was a youngster, a place where tourists got eaten alive by mosquitoes, would burn as red as a vine ripe tomato, spend lots of money and then go back home.

"Honey?"

Andrew's thoughts returned from the Florida that was, "What?"

"The reunion!"

"Oh, uh..."

"Come on, we'll make it like a second honeymoon, just us, no kids." Stephanie stepped into the bathroom as they continued their discussion.

"Speaking of which, who do you think is going to tend to our three kids for a whole week IF we go?" Andrew began to get dressed for work.

The Reunion Reaper

"My mom can fly up here. She's retired and she would love it."
Stay in Texas he muttered to himself. Not hearing his muttering she continued, "Besides, you know how much she likes to see the kids."
And criticize yours truly. "What's that honey?"
"So we're going to have to pay for your mother's flight IF we go."
"Would you stop with the if we go please." She poked her head out of the bathroom looking toward their bedroom, "Hey, I got a great idea, let's check them into a local kennel, they'll get fed, cleaned up after—"
"Funny, I get the point thank you," Andrew heaved a heavy sigh, "Okay, I give, you win."
Stephanie beamed.
"Really? Come here my brave detective."
She threw out her arms and embraced him as he was just fastening the last button.
"Hey, I thought you no longer carried a baton… Oh yeah, that's not a baton."
"As much as I would love to I have to get to work."
"You know, wearing a suit is so much sexier than those silly Hawaiian shirts you used to wear with AGS.
"It was part of the job, you know, blend in," sarcastically adding, "kind of like these," as he pointed to his navy blue suit.
"Okay, so we're good for the reunion?"
"…Yes we're good for the reunion."
"Great, I'll check a few of the travel sites today at work and we can talk about them tonight."
"Just no real expensive hotels okay, we're working class people."
"Really?"
"You are such a smart aleck this morning." He said as he grabbed a silver and blue striped tie from his tie rack.

"I have a good teacher," she smacked him on his behind as he walked out of the bedroom. "Hey where's my kiss?"

"Sorry, preoccupied with the board interview today for Lieutenant." He leaned in to kiss her.

"Oh yeah that's today isn't it? Well, good luck, I know you'll get it."

"Yeah, but they need to know it too. All right, see you tonight!"

Andrew clogged his way up the stairs to grab his bagel and protein shake. He grabbed his lunch, went into the living room where Michael and Ryan were wolfing down some waffles while catching a few minutes of cartoons before school, "All right guys daddy's outta here."

Almost in unison, "Okay dad."

"Remember, concentrate at school, do all your work, I'll see you this afternoon. Love you."

"Love you too dad."

"Daddy!" Ryan stretched out his arms.

"Sorry bud," Andrew bent down to give his five year old a hug, "love you." Ryan began to cough. "Make sure mommy gives you your medicine, okay?"

He stopped by Mary's bedroom and tapped on the door, but the reaction was a bit different than what the boys had given him.

"Mary, dad's outta here."

"Okay."

"Have a good day."

"You too."

Andrew walked away from the door and whispered to himself, "nice talking with you honey, daddy loves you too." He was hoping that he wouldn't get a similar reception from the advancement board at the police station. It was a big day, and Andrew was going to find out very soon if his income and authority was about to increase; a much needed boost for a family with growing needs.

The Reunion Reaper

Chapter 15

Andrew showed up at the station by 7:15 and was quickly greeted by Lindsey Blankenship, a twenty eight year old brunette who had been working for the department just a few years. She was getting out of her car as she stopped Andrew. She gave him a hug, "Good luck today."

"Thanks." *That was awkward.*

Andrew liked Lindsey, and yes she had a pretty sweet body, even in a police uniform, but she was just something to look at, although it was pretty clear that she had a thing for him. She often commented on how she admired his work ethic. By all accounts, he was not as interested in her as she was in him. She kept jabbering away about going out with friends and how much she wished Andrew would join her some evening. *Yeah, I'm sure the wife would love that. Honey, I'll be hitting the town with three twenty something's, gonna be late.*

She continued her bantering as they entered through the secured entry to the public safety building. As he passed some of his colleagues, he was getting pats on the back, thumbs up, or well wishes. Andrew was well liked by most, and since this was a relatively small department everyone knew everyone's business, whether they liked it or not. Even if Andrew wanted Lindsey there was virtually no way it would stay hidden for very long. Andrew was not about to jeopardize a marriage, three kids, and possibly a career for approaching a woman's landing strip with his jet plane.

"Good luck Anj," responded Tony Moreno a ball busting New York transplant.

Andrew didn't care too much for Tony, but he was at least cordial with him.

"Thanks Tone," said Andrew with a right back at ya response.

Andrew felt like Tony was trying to bring too much of his New York to rural Virginia, and Tony was always telling these fantastic stories of how he did this or did that, but the worst was when Tony was talking about September 11, 2001 and how he was supposedly helping people down at the twin towers just after the second tower came down. September 11 was an event sensitive and personal to Andrew. He not only lost a fellow college lacrosse teammate in the South Tower, but his brother Sean, a Navy SEAL, spent months scouring Afghanistan looking for bin Laden.

Andrew decided to do a little investigating about Tony's 9.11 heroic claims and discovered that Tony wasn't exactly telling the truth and from that point on Andrew no longer trusted him or believed a word that came from his twisted mouth. Tony's deep set eyes bothered him too. They were close together and the eyebrows were thick and bushy. If he didn't know any better he thought Tony could have been related to one time mob boss Traficante. Andrew kept the findings to himself; he figured that sooner or later everyone would find out that Tony was full of New York butcher shop talk.

The board meeting was scheduled for eight a.m. so Andrew had time to inhale his bagel and chase it with his protein drink. His good friend Sonny was just passing by his desk.

"Hey, I was gonna call you last night but Haleigh had an episode and so Danielle and I were caught up with that."

"I understand, with three of my own I definitely understand when the little ones get sick. Ryan's battling this silly cough right now. Anyhow, what did you want?"

"Oh, I was just going to wish you luck and ask if there was anything I could do for you." Sonny grabbed a seat and pulled it closer alongside Andrew's desk.

The Reunion Reaper

"Nah, I'm good. I've gone over everything; the ball is in their court, if you will." Andrew forced the last bit of bagel into his mouth and chased it with his drink.

"I think you'll do fine, just tell them what they already know."

"Hey, nothing less," Andrew got up from his desk and smiled, "I'll see you after the execution," He joked as he tapped his friend on the shoulder.

"Just in case be sure to ask for one clean stroke of the axe, if they have to go twice there's way too much blood." Andrew just smiled.

Sonny loved his history. Both he and Andrew would spend hours discussing a variety of historical periods. In fact, they thought of becoming teachers, but they decided that criminals were easier to handle, literally, than high school students; at least they could handcuff a criminal.

Scott A. Reighard

Chapter 16

Leavenworth, Washington

The Leavenworth Echo, March 10, 2008. Bikers discover local man's body

Bikers discovered the body of Tucker Harrison earlier today near the Dead Bones Ravine. Mr. Harrison appeared to have lost his balance on the narrow bridge that crosses the dry creek bed some twenty feet below. Recently many dead and several cut trees have been placed into the ravine as a means to curb excessive erosion. According to local law enforcement, Mr. Harrison fell onto a broken and pointed branch that was sticking skyward. He was apparently riding alone. The last person to see Mr. Harrison said he was unloading his bike around 4 pm the day before. The biker commented that it was not rare to see Mr. Harrison that late in the day, for he liked to ride during dusk. Mr. Harrison was 40 years old; he was a divorcee with no children.

The day before

"Hey Mr. Harrison going for a dusk drive? Get it, dusk drive? Sounds like disk drive."

"Hey that's pretty good Shane, yes, I thought I'd get a ride in before I head out of town."

"What are you out to save now?"

"Those nasty oil creeps want to drill for oil on National Parks lands. I'm headed out to Denver to meet with fellow environmentalists about our plan to fight it."

"Well, good luck dude."

"You bet, thanks."

The Reunion Reaper

Tucker Harrison was unloading his Trek mountain bike off the back of his Subaru SUV. The sun was about an hour from permanently calling it a day in this region of the U.S. It wasn't spring officially yet, but the weather was cooperating. Tucker was one of those outdoor types who loved to ride and watch the shadows grow long as he weaved his way through a single track trail. He loved the thrill of that moment of last visual opportunity before it was mandatory that you flick on your head lamp, or if you desired more of a thrill you could just risk it and go 'rad black' as they call it out west. There were a few areas of the trail that called for extreme skill, especially in limited light, but Tucker had mastered this trail years ago in the daylight, and now seemed to revel in the challenge of a tough ride in the fading light. Tucker set off on the trailhead marked just off the area where the riders parked their vehicles.

The first part of the ride was a nice flat area where riders could establish some speed, zooming past trees that soon resembled towering picket fences. Then there were dips and curves that would force the rider to slow down, shift gears and manage the weaving snake shaped single track. After a quarter mile or so of these winding, sometimes switch back style turns and technically mastering them, Tucker was now headed for perhaps the most difficult part of the ride. Ahead lay a torrid uphill battle that challenged even the most hardened riders. It was ten minutes of pure hell, but the riders knew what waited at the end, a smooth meandering long downhill that would take them over two creeks, a crudely constructed bridge of one by sixes over a ravine, and finally a flat weaver that was about a quarter mile long. This particular track was not the most challenging of the tracks in the area, but it was enough to get a person's attention.

Dressed in red and black bike garb that matched his bike's color Tucker was slicing through the first part of the run and then settled in for the long uphill trek that required him to shift several times before finding a consistent pump that would take him to the top of the hill. He strode along, legs strong, chest slightly heaving under the stress of the uphill challenge, his eyes focused just a few feet ahead of the bike. Tucker was a seasoned rider, having ridden mountain bikes since his move to Washington State just a little over twelve years ago. His move was predicated on his love for nature and preservation, or perhaps the twenty-something he knocked up in Tampa, of whom he wanted no part.

On this late afternoon darting through the back trails of central Washington Tucker was enjoying yet another moment of peace, a sublime interface with nature and an insatiable desire not easily quenched. He climbed to the top of the hill without any serious chest heaving, but it was enough to raise the ticker a few notches. A deep breath and a quick view of the surroundings was the standard when reaching the top, but as for any rider, the cruise downhill was anxiously waiting. But on this one particular ascension Tucker had run into another biker who had obviously reached the same point from another trail that led to this same high point. There were several trails that meandered through the forest, and some intersected.

Of course this rider knew of Tucker's late day rides. Again, he had done his research. The strange rider surprised Tucker. Dressed in traditional biking garb, Lycra tights, and with a multi colored zip up Oakley jersey was Jeffrey. His helmet was a combination of blue and silver, not matching the green and yellow dominant colored jersey. Long hair lay on his shoulders and he sported a beard full enough to hide a hummingbird. Despite the setting sun he sported mirrored sunglasses that glared with an orange/yellow glow. Tucker could see his image from the reflection. Jeffrey was a walking spectacle of color, or in this case a riding spectacle.

The Reunion Reaper

Tucker looked at the stranger wondering why this guy who was dressed like rainbow sherbet was bringing so much attention to himself with the outrageous color combinations; then again this was Washington State. He just shrugged it off with an inner chuckle.

"Hey there, how's it goin'?" the stranger stated with a low undiscerning tone.

"Hey," Tucker responded.

"Sorry I startled you."

"Oh that's okay, I just thought I was alone that's all. Not often you run into someone at the top unless it's earlier in the day."

"Yeah, speaking of which, I'm kinda lost, this is my first solo ride up here."

"Yeah, I can't recall ever seeing you round here."

"I'm a little late today, I was hoping to get here earlier but I had a little car trouble just west of Skykomish."

"Wow, that's quite a drive for a short ride like this one," responded Tucker.

"So, you from nearby?" asked Jeffrey, but it was becoming clear that Tucker did not want to waste any more time than he had on the hill because darkness was looming and sometimes during dusk perception becomes a problem.

"Listen, I hate to sound rude, but we need to get off this hilltop. If you'll follow me I'll take you down to my SUV and then I can give you a lift to wherever you're parked."

"Sounds good, besides I didn't bring a sleeping bag, and getting lost up here would not be good." Jeffrey laughed with a snorting chortle. Tucker glanced at him with a weird look from the sound of his laughter.

"Yeah, that wouldn't be good. Okay, just follow me."

"Got it!"

The two of them clipped into their pedals and began their descent. Sunlight was now fading fast, the shadows were long and bountiful, and the trail was darkening with each passing minute. The stranger was trailing Tucker by twenty or more feet as they hunkered back in the saddle. As they continued the downhill portion there was a flat area that required the riders to traverse a creek. Tucker was shouting out to the stranger that the small creek was just ahead and that he should hang back. Tucker lifted himself out of the saddle and sliced across the small creek leaving a narrow rooster tail spray for the stranger to encounter upon his entry into the creek. Tucker always seemed to enjoy that moment, of being able to kick back a little creek water into the face of a trailer. Jeffrey seemed to glide through unfazed. He simply wiped his glasses and continued.

Back on the single track it wouldn't be long for the bridge crossing over the ravine. Riders often maintained the trails, and groups that were active in trail set ups, maintenance, working with local officials, and any other applications related to the parks, trails, or forest management, would build bridges, erosion barriers, and employ many other protective or nature related projects. It was important for activists to work in tandem with the officials because shutting down a trail was easily done.

Local bikers built the makeshift bridge that carried over a ravine. It was about twenty five or thirty feet in length and at the middle it was more than twenty feet above the valley of the ravine, a considerable drop that garnered the attention of every rider that dared traverse it. Most novice riders elected to hop off their bikes and simply walk across the bridge, but most riders in these parts were seasoned riders.

The sky had taken on a purple hue, but areas of the forest were quickly becoming blackened as Tucker and his trailing guest made their approach to the bridge. It got so dark that Jeffrey was forced to remove his sunglasses. He placed them into one of the shirt pockets normally designated for trail bars, or energy gels.

The hardest part about the bridge was not the bridge itself, but the entry. Because of the location of the trail in

The Reunion Reaper

relation to the ravine the bridgehead was a forty five degree angle to the right off the trail. All riders knew they had to slow down considerably, or subject themselves to careening off the bridge down into the ravine. Tucker was shouting out instructions to his trailer warning him to back off and slow down as they were just now about one hundred feet from the bridgehead. The stranger shouted back his understanding. Shadows were no longer a problem as the sun had completely disappeared. It was now twilight, that faint light that required strict focus. It was a point where the point where day gives way to night. Tucker knew the trail well and felt confident about his entry onto the bridge.

Just a few feet away now, Tucker tapped the brakes and geared down to approach the turn, as he did there was a sudden thud. Apparently Jeffrey was not back far enough, and with the fading light he rammed into the back of Tucker's bike sending him off the edge of the bridge. Tucker made an attempt to unhinge his shoes and bail off the bike, but like many riders who bunny hop obstacles he had tightened the screws to the point where it was extremely difficult to bail airborne. The bike turned sideways as Tucker's upper torso weight began to shift the direction of his fall. The nudge from Jeffrey jettisoned Tucker forward and this placed him over the craggy hillside area and thus his fall was more than ten feet straight down.

Initially, it looked as though it would have simply been a hell of a wipeout, but at the bottom of the ravine were clusters of dead or recently cut trees that had been cleared. Tucker struggled to gain some semblance of control but was unable to make the proper adjustment. He fell directly onto an awaiting branch that impaled him under his right shoulder and through his side. The branch pierced the rib and punctured his right lung. It was only a matter of time before Tucker would drown in his own blood. Jeffrey was able to stop in time before he went careening over the edge as well, and he looked down on Tucker, who was struggling against the branches deepening push under the weight of his one hundred and ninety pound frame. He was trying to say something to the image that looked down on him, but there was only a faint gurgling heard by any living organism within earshot. He looked up and his eyes grew wide at the surprise that the stranger made no effort to assist him, but at that moment Jeffrey removed his helmet and took off his wig.

"Remember me?"

Tucker looked at the stranger with puzzlement, his eyes watering from the point, his vision narrowing and fading. Tucker struggled to say a name but the gurgling drowned out any ability for even his own ears to hear it.

"At least I never poked my tiny tower into a tiny twat now did I? You pedophile freak! I should have known then you always liked the younger ones."

He laughed.

"I love the irony of this; the very thing you love has now taken you. Good riddance Sucker Harrison."

Again, Tucker could only look up, and as he finally figured out who it was he took his last breath. Jeffrey looking down on him and seeing his head tilt to the right knew this job was done, Tucker was no more. No more would little girls in Washington State, and who knows where else have to worry about Tucker Harrison seducing them, taking pictures and then posting them on child porn sites. Jeffrey looked with contempt in his eyes and he spat over the ravine as a mock gesture to his dead classmate. He calmly took out a headlamp from his back pouch, strapped it onto his helmet and turned it on. The little krypton bulb was about the only light seen as the sky had turned a charcoal gray and the forest was now completely black. He started to hum the Doobie Brothers hit, *Rockin' Down the Highway* as he mounted his bike and rode across the bridge, no longer needing to look down but only ahead. This task was done, and now it was time to move on.

Chapter 17

Journal date: April 7, 2008: Let's see, I just returned from the great Northwest, had an awesome bike ride, and oh yeah, relieved the world of an environmental pedophile.

How about two birds with one stone? Hot damn I'm on a roll. Well, it seems as though one less pedophile and extremist will no longer be parading about preying on little girls or supporting radical environmental laws. Tucker Harrison you were a pretty cool kid; I liked you back in the day. You taught me how to surf and enjoy the beauty that surrounded me, but man, oh man, did you ever change. I guess it's like they say, when you're in too deep, you don't know how deep you are or some BS like that.

Anyhow, you were in too deep you young girl seeking freak. I should have picked up on your desires when you chased that poor little ninth grader while you were a senior. You got way too much of a charge out of wanting to deflower the youngins' you sick bastard. I don't want to get off on a tangent, but let's just say that you, tiny dick Tucker had to go, you were using your position to corrupt little girls and environmental rationalists. I am surprised that you didn't recognize me; maybe I'll use the hippie look again.

Man, what I wouldn't give to see the expressions on people's faces when they hear of these classmates who are no longer with us; talk about a midlife crisis, they'll all be joining health clubs and watching their diets, or giving up their habits. Let's see, three down and who knows how many more. But the real question is, will he or won't he? To play or not to play, that is the question? I'm coming after you boy. I am genius, hear me roar!

Scott A. Reighard

Tucker Harrison, August 8, 1964 – March 8, 2008. Rest in, ah, screw that, burn in hell. Say hello to Brandon on your way by. Inferno level seven if you please

The Reunion Reaper

Chapter 18

Andrew entered the board room of the Roanoke County Police Department and grabbed one of the blue cloth covered seats at a small conference table. Surrounding him were portraits of former chiefs of police. It was a windowless room that looked like it didn't get a lot of use. As he circled the chair around the room his eyes fell on the portrait of the current chief of police Fairchilds. He thought about how much he liked having him as his chief and that he would be sorely missed after the retirement. No one could engage in more story telling than the old chief who had southern roots that went all the way back to the early days of expansion to the valley area.

Andrew was nervous, but this wasn't his first dance sitting in front of people who were going to have a tremendous impact on his career. He recalled his first interview with American Global Securities. He was a cocky 23 year old just fresh out of college, and he answered all their questions with a frankness and confidence they admired. He was hired a few days following that interview. Of course this was a different situation; here if you were rejected at the review you'd have to wait another six months before requesting the board review again. As he sat there waiting in walked Captain Hardy and Deputy Chief Wolfe. Yet to enter the room was Chief Fairchilds, who by all accounts, was late.

The two men took a seat as each greeted Andrew. Each of them dressed in their uniform of deep sea blue. Captain Hardy was a sturdy built man of five feet ten inches. His salt and pepper hair was full but kept relatively short; it appeared as though the salt was winning the battle with the fifty year old. He had a neat appearance for a man who was somewhat overweight at one hundred ninety pounds.

Needless to say he filled out his uniform almost to the point where a new size should be considered. It also did not help that his pale skin with gray eyes gave the impression of the coldness attributed to him. Conversely, Deputy Chief Wolfe was a tower of a man at six foot three inches and not an ounce under two hundred twenty pounds. His soft brown hair was neatly parted to one side which matched his deep brown eyes. His mustache offered a tint of gray, which seemed to say Deputy Chief Wolfe was older than he looked. He had the gift of gab, loving to talk about all things, especially politics.

"Looking good there Mr. Wolfe, you too Captain Hardy." Andrew offered.

"Nice try Andrew, flattery was a technique you should have used several months ago. Oh, and you need to get with it on the ass kissing, rumor has it you don't kiss ass." Mr. Wolfe wryly pointed out.

"Never have, never will. What you see is what you get I guess." Andrew smiled back, but Captain Hardy wasn't interested in the juvenile humor being bandied about.

These two men, who would have a pivotal role in Andrew's selection, each boasted more than twenty years of law enforcement experience. Chief Fairchilds had more than thirty. With the three men all born and raised locals, outsiders, like Andrew, felt the good ole boy network was still alive and well in these parts, but in reality Andrew was just too impressive to overlook. Tony Moreno maybe despite his New York experience, but not Andrew. He had worked his way up and had the respect of his peers.

Chief Fairchilds entered. His rural Virginia accent was obvious.

"Good mornin' gentlemen, sorry I'm late, early morning phone calls. I should know better than to pick up that phone this early. Anyhow, let's cook this bird, not you of course Andrew." Chief Fairchilds took a seat between Hardy and Wolfe. The older chief maintained a flat top cut that was

The Reunion Reaper

streaky white and his weathered face suggested it wasn't just his age that had taken its toll on the congenial man who loved his fishing and hunting. To match this was a voice that was gruff and sometimes raspy. His shape was more like that of a man who enjoyed three full meals a day plus an evening snack. Surprisingly, he looked evenly proportioned. His sense of humor and likeable personality made him a man where great sadness would be shared by all upon his retirement. He sat back in the executive style chair and rocked

"I'm sure this is all a formality. We like your style Andrew, you just need to answer a few questions for us and then we can go smoke us a big cigar." Then leaning in, "and then there's some blue gills waiting for my new rigs, if you know what I mean." Andrew smiled at his comments.

Captain Hardy was perhaps the only man in the room Andrew was worried about. Deputy Chief Wolfe was a hard working man who got along with everyone, and of course Chief Fairchilds was a man quite revered in this line of work and loved by the whole department. The chief was more laid back, he'd sooner talk to you about the Civil War than police business, but the old man was closing in on retirement. It's not that Andrew didn't enjoy working for Hardy but he wasn't called Captain Hardass for nothing, and nothing slipped by this guy; talk about a guy with his ear to the rails, he had a personal mental file on everybody at the department. The nickname came from the fact that he was a statistics kind of guy, a man who was always looking over reports for errors. He liked his quotas to be met, and he prided himself on his monthly reports to his boss. He kept to himself quite a bit, while Wolfe was more of a people person. The personalities were distinct. Wolfe was more hands on. He liked getting his hands dirty every now and again. Conversely, Captain Hardy barely left the office, and when he did his cell phone was attached to his ear often making any excuse to get back to the office. Unfortunately for him it was most likely that Deputy Chief Wolfe was going to be the chief's successor, although Hardy was keen on wanting to be the next chief.

"All right, let's see what we got here," barked the chief. "Uh-huh, yeah, that's good, oh, I didn't know that." The chief wasn't bothering to share what he was commenting on, a common custom of his. "Good day, you worked that case quick."

"Ahem," coughed Captain Hardy.

"Right, right, thank you Ben." The chief turned his attention to Andrew. "You know Andrew, some guys come in here lookin' for a promotion and despite their credentials there's just somethin' that's not workin' for me. I mean, they cross their T's and dot their I's, but some people just don't got that je ne say, whatever that French statement is, you know."

"Yes sir," responded Andrew with a respectful tone.

The chief continued, "You got character, you get stuff done. I like that about you, not to mention that you're a helluva detective. You got natural leadership skills and that's why you deserve this position."

"Thank you sir, I appreciate the compliments."

The remainder of the meeting was relatively short. There was laughing, and a few more stories by the old Chief. From the chief's comments it was obvious that the promotion was a lock. At the end of the meeting all the men stood up, shook hands and departed the room.

Standing just down the hall was Sonny.

"How did it go?" He inquired.

"Good, better than I expected."

"Good for you brother, listen, while you were in there Stephanie called, she said to call her as soon as possible."

"Thanks."

Sonny patted him on the back, "I'm happy for you Andrew, they made a good decision."

The Reunion Reaper

"Thanks, I really appreciate it. You should think about becoming a detective someday."

"No can do friend, I like my shift work too much, you know, no late night calls and stuff like that."

"Can't argue with that."

Andrew threw up his hands in a mock gesture to the higher power.

"Why did I have to be s-o-o ambitious?"

"Gotta go man," replied Sonny as he smiled and turned. "Way to go Brother!"

Andrew simply smiled as he ambled down the hall and into his office. He went over to his desk and promptly called his wife.

"Hey, what's up?"

"I forgot to tell you to pick up Michael and Ryan this afternoon; I'll be working late because of the doctor's appointment this morning."

"Got it, good luck with the appointment."

"Thanks honey, gotta go, I'll see you this evening. We're having leftovers okay?"

"Sounds good."

"Oh, don't forget Michael has baseball practice at 5:30."

"Should I put a load of laundry in for you as well?" Andrew sarcastically belted out.

"Aren't you the funny one, as a matter of fact yes. Listen, I gotta go, love you."

"Love you too!"

She forgot to ask about the review, but that's okay, she's got a lot on her mind, he thought. He was about to become the lieutenant of detectives, and that would mean greater responsibility, and some of the people he worked with would now be subordinates. It was an awkward situation to be in, but if this was the worst things could be for him then life wasn't too bad. He hung up the phone, looked around to see if anyone was looking, then he proceeded to do a fist pump like he just snaked in a twenty five foot putt. Things were going to change for him and the family, the problem was that the changes to come were one hundred eighty degrees from what he was thinking.

Chapter 19

Andrew picked up the boys at 4:30 at after care. Normally, Michael was in the fourth grade while Ryan was in kindergarten, the after care van would gather them up at school and kept them until either Andrew or Stephanie would pick them up. Mary, their ninth grader going on twenty would get picked up after practice or get a ride home from a friend's parent. Like her mom and dad, she was an athlete. She sported a neatly cropped strawberry blond hair-do that touched her shoulders. She had the same blazing blue eyes as her mother and stood five feet seven inches; athletic and beautiful were tough combinations for a protective father. She participated in volleyball during the fall season, and soccer in the spring. It could be a hectic schedule at times, but Andrew and Stephanie did a pretty good job of knowing who was picking up whom.

On this particular evening the mission was to race home get some food in the boys, pick up Mary, then it was on to Michael's baseball practice. Sometimes their lives moved at the speed of light, but Mary hated it when her father did this to her because she wanted to go home, relax in front of the television and chat with her friends. Andrew was obviously aware of this and he knew he could at least control the situation at times, so he would make her sit in his SUV and do her homework, or join him in watching her brother's practice. He and Stephanie tried to eschew the benefits of family and sharing time together, but she rarely understood either parent's logic. His thoughts on whether Mary paid attention to the benefits were that either way those memories would be etched in the memory of sweet thoughts or tremendous regret. Either way, she was going to do this whether she liked it or not.

Scott A. Reighard

On the way home Andrew asked Ryan how his doctor's appointment went, but five year olds might start out telling you something then have you thinking you're in the Twilight Zone by the time they finish. Andrew did his best to filter the information spewing from his five year old with a lot of uh-huh's, but he knew that mom would be the best source of information for the whole story later that evening. He, of course, was anxious to tell the boys of the good news of dad now becoming a lieutenant but he knew that Ryan was not good at keeping a secret, so Andrew thought he'd wait until later that evening to break the good news to everyone.

He was able to get the boys something to eat, pick up Mary, who copped an attitude, get Michael to practice, then it was home with still enough time for showers and a quick family meeting. When they arrived home Stephanie was on the phone.

"Yeah, I know what you mean. Uh, hang on Patrick I think they just walked in."

She placed her hand over the mouthpiece and whispered, "It's your father."

Andrew grabbed the phone, "hey dad how's it going?"

Andrew's father Patrick was a cagey, blunt and fastidious man in his mid sixties. He recently retired after working in some form for the government for thirty years, mostly for the Florida DEA. He was a kid from the streets. He climbed the ranks of his job with grit and determination. He was not one to sugar coat what he wanted to say.

"You know your mother and I aren't getting any younger down here."

"Really, with the way you act sometimes I thought for sure you were headed back to your childhood ways."

Ignoring his son's retort, "Listen, I wanted to know what your plans were this summer."

Nearly every summer the kids would visit Andrew's parents in Florida. They retired to the St. Augustine area. It was tough being that far apart from his parents, but Andrew felt he needed to be in a place where he was happy, and Florida no longer held that emotion for him.

"We really hadn't talked about summer yet, why?"

"Well, your mom's gettin' all sentimental and stuff and she wants to go see what's left of the family in Pennsylvania, so we were wondering if maybe the kids wanted to come down here with us on our way back home."

"Sounds like a great idea but let me talk with Stephanie to see what she wants to do."

"Okay, let us know as soon as you can because we need to plan our schedule."

His father then started on about his golf outing he had that day and Andrew was as cordial as he could be while trying to move around the house getting a few things done during the conversation. The boys were in their bedroom as Andrew directed them to the bathroom, "Hang on dad. Come on guys shower time."

He dug two towels out of the linen closet and tossed one to each of the boys,

"Sounds like you had a good game today."

"Yeah, you're old man still has some game left in him. So, is everything else okay?"

"Sure, things are good."

"Anything on your end?"

"Nope, not that I can recall right now."

"I see my son doesn't want to talk."

Shaking his head, "That's not it—"

"That's okay, your mother and I will just sit here and age a little more until you decide to call."

"Don't go tryin' to put that guilt thing on me you know I'm very busy these days with work and all the kids playing sports and stuff."

"I'm just messing with ya, you go tend to your family, but make sure you call your mother this weekend."

"I will, well listen, I better get these boys going or dad's gonna have to open up a can of you know what."

"All right, tell my beautiful grandkids that grandma and pappy loves them. Give our love to Steph as well."

"Will do, talk to ya soon dad."

His dad made one final pitch, "Call your mother."

"Good bye dad, love you too."

Andrew hung up the phone and completely forgot to tell his father about the promotion, and the reunion. *Oh well, I'll tell him this weekend when I have more time.*

After the boys had showered and everyone was settling in for the evening Andrew called the family together to inform them of his good news.

"Daddy's got an announcement to make—"

"We are going to Florida." Mary said.

"Actually, I was thinking more like a history vacation this year."

"A what?" Mary exhaled.

"Mary please," said Stephanie wanting to hear what her husband had to say.

"No, nice try though, this is not about a vacation." He stood erect as if for a portrait. "Ahem, you are now looking at the new Lieutenant of Detectives."

Stephanie stood up, "are you serious?"

"Would I joke about something as important as this?"

"No of course not," she embraced then kissed him.

"Wow, this is great news, kids this is great news."

A semi chorus of congratulations and good job dad followed.

"Does this mean I can get a cell phone now?" Mary inquired.

"I love teenagers they're so unselfish," responded Andrew as he glanced at his wife.

"This is not the time to discuss this Mary; like your father said no cell phone right now."

"God this sucks, everyone has a phone except me; I am such a loser."

Stephanie turned to her daughter and leaned in, "Hey young lady you are not a loser just because you don't have a cell phone, and if anyone tells you so they are not your friends. You got that? Now this is a big moment for your father, for us, could you at least not think about yourself right now?"

Michael offered, "That's okay dad I don't even want a cell phone."

Andrew smiled, "Thanks bud."

"Yeah, me too." Ryan suggested as Stephanie continued to glare at Mary.

"Sorry, congratulations dad," she offered sheepishly.

"Thank you honey," he said.

"So, is that it?" Mary asked.

"Is that it, what do you mean?" asked Stephanie.

"Are we finished?"

"Yes that's it honey you may return to whatever it was you were doing." Andrew commented with an air of sarcasm.

Mary got up, went over to kiss her father and bluntly repeated, "Congratulations again dad," and then proceeded to go to her bedroom.

"I think she was genuinely happy for me don't you think?"

Stephanie just shook her head in disbelief at what just came out of her daughter's mouth. Mary's age was a tough one, she was on the verge of becoming a woman, wanting independence, yet conflicted about her desire to be around her family that much. She especially felt uncomfortable when they went to church nearly every Sunday. She was unsure about a lot of things, and although she was a good student and athlete, she was still a teenager with issues, issues of which her parents tried very much to be patient.

After the meeting Andrew and Stephanie got the kids to bed and then headed to their bedroom where she and Andrew were able to discuss some private matters like finances and Ryan. The doctor told her that it was most likely an upper respiratory infection and he prescribed some medication for him. As for the finances Stephanie was wondering how the income increase would enable them to stop robbing Peter to pay Paul. Now, she thought, hopefully we will not have to tap into our savings so often. A savings account that looked a lot healthier a few short years ago, but with three kids and incremental raises the world was zooming by faster than they had imagined. They were two people trying to do their best in a world that seemed to push more and more demands onto families. As they concluded their discussion Stephanie asked, "Do you think we'll be able to do both the reunion and your parents place this summer?"

Andrew was preparing his clothes for the morning, "Well, the promotion will help, but I may have to put this one on my parents. They'll...wait, let me correct myself, my mom will understand that, my dad, I don't know."

"Oh well, we've got a few months and hopefully our taxes will help." Stephanie began to take off her make-up.

"I would think so," responded Andrew, "these last few years have been pretty good for us. We are very blessed"

"Yes we are."

Within a matter of an hour the house went quiet. The boys were in bed, Mary was in her bedroom hopefully working on school work, and Andrew was sliding into bed and Stephanie was just now able to sit down and relax.

The Reunion Reaper

Chapter 20

As Jeffrey closed out his computer and thought about Tucker being a pedophile and posting his pictures on porn sites, a certain young lady raced back into his mind. Soon after his father's death he moved west to get a fresh start, but it didn't take long for things to go sour. A few short frustrating years after his move west he was bored, lonely and felt he needed something new, enter Heather Downing, a prostitute working the streets of Tucson, Arizona.

After a few calls to her corner she became more than his usual, he wanted her permanently and he wanted her off the streets. A down and out, seemingly strung out Southern California girl, who he claimed was a product of permissive hippie parents, was a sexy leggy blond with a youthful exuberance and a habit to match. Trying to figure out a way to get her off the streets he decided to use his computer science degree and a new thing called the internet to devise a plan.

It was the mid-nineties and he felt the internet was going to be huge in terms of potential, so he gathered Heather and some of her friends and asked them if they would all take some pictures, separately and together, and of course, nude. He was experimenting with soft porn on the internet. To say he was in on the ground floor would be an understatement. Other than porn films, this was all new, and the curiosity of people's reactions would dictate whether this idea was going to be successful or drive him out of town. He predicted correctly, it became huge. Understanding man's depravity and throwing in the curiosity factor, he developed a "can't miss" idea, and he swam in the knowledge of this thirst that men wanted quenched.

Scott A. Reighard

Heather, who was about ten years younger than him, along with her friends were willing participants. It was fun they thought. The money started rolling in and horny guys and anyone else tuning in couldn't type in their credit card numbers fast enough. Of course the soft stuff could only last so long and with just a handful of girls it was impossible to keep the clientele pleased for long, so he decided to ratchet up the content and go hard core porn with some of the girls taping some of their sessions with their clientele. They blurred out the men's faces and any body marks or tattoos they may have had. They felt comfortable that they weren't so much as violating these men's civil liberties just their private parts.

Everything was going great for several years until sometime in 1999 when one of Heather's friend's clients happened to discover, not only the website, but what appeared to be him in the act. He sued the website, but he was unable to prove in court that that was him or his Johnson on the site. After the near legal disaster they decided they would rather pay male models to perform the acts. Jeffrey's thought was, what young man wouldn't want in on this?

After several months doing tapings with the paid male models Heather began to think differently about the agreement she had with him, she demanded a larger cut of the income. She threatened a lawsuit and to go public with the names of clients as well as the illegal tapings. He tried to explain to her that one, she was a prostitute and two, that if it wasn't for him, this never would have happened for them, and they'd still be walking the streets worrying about stiffs pulling a Jack the Ripper on them, or nutcases beating them up or something. This was safe for them he thought. She thought otherwise. Their relationship headed south months before her demands, so she had one of the young men hired as a male counterpart, probably her new toy for the web sessions, Jeffrey thought, who threatened to break

The Reunion Reaper

his arms and legs. He expressed to them that violence was not the way to solve things, and that he wanted to do what was right and just; little did they know that he had a plan.

Continuing his drift down recall river, he flipped on his thousand dollar stereo system and inserted Enigma who was known for their soothing synthetic and subtle electronica projections that were oftentimes accompanied by Franciscan chants. He hopped onto his couch and continued his thoughts on Heather.

He decided to meet with her and agree to her demands. He told her that he was willing to give her fifty percent of the cut, that he was hasty and irrational the last time they talked about the profit split, and that he didn't want any trouble.

Going over to her house on a night he knew the new stiff wouldn't be around, he surprised her with a new contract; and sure enough it contained within it the fifty percent profit split she demanded. She looked it over carefully and was happy that he decided to see it her way. He thought that they should celebrate and he pulled from his pocket some cocaine.

"Are you tryin' to take advantage of me or somethin'?" She questioned as she cozied up next to him on the couch.

"Of course not, I just thought a little celebration was in order, that's all."

"Cool, I haven't been doin' much of the stuff lately, but this is a night to celebrate."

"Besides, I was hopin' to make things smooth again between us. I know you've moved on and I'm happy for you, I understand." He sprinkled a line of cocaine on the table then organized it with an index card he had in his pocket.

"Really?"

"Sure."

"You always was my bottle a sunshine." She gave him a hug then proceeded to snort like a pig at the site of fresh feed.

As cool as one could be in this situation, he lured her in with the cocaine, and then faked snorting the stuff by distracting her and then quickly blowing it off the table. But she wasn't such a dummy, at least in her mind, "Hey, hang on, before I get more a this in me I want to sign the paper okay?"

"Absolutely, here you go!" He laid the contract out on the table, showed her the percentage split again just to make sure she understood it was going to be an even split.

"You got a pen?" she asked.

"Sorry, just brought the nose candy, but there's one on the side table there."

She reached for the pen and he smiled because he knew this would be the last time she would sign anything. She signed her name and he then signed his. After they each signed he removed the top copy to reveal a duplicate copy underneath. He folded it and handed it to her as a gesture of good faith. She accepted.

She moved in closer to him, "Do you wanna do it for old time's sake?" She put her hand on his crotch. "Ooh, just as I remember."

"Sounds great but I'll take a pass. You've moved on remember?" He slid away from her. He wanted no contact with her at all.

She snorted another line and within a few minutes she began to feel weird, almost nauseous. Suddenly she gagged and then threw up on the floor right in front of him. She didn't have enough time to react and get to the bathroom. She doubled over. The pain was excruciating as she was beginning to groan on the floor. It would only be a matter of time before her heart would explode with the arsenic acid laced cocaine. He watched her as she proceeded to fall onto the floor and roll into the fetal position. He asked her if she was all right, but she was basically non-responsive. He hung out for a few more minutes and waited until she stopped breathing. When it was over he grabbed the contract from off the table, cleaned up the area, and then quietly walked out the door singing, Eric Clapton. *If you want to hang out you gotta take her out, cocaine.*

This was his first venture into freeing himself of an albatross. At the time of this act the prospect of killing classmates and getting even was beginning to manifest. He was sad about having to kill someone close to him, but he was tired of being taken advantage of, a trend in his life that needed to end. Heather stood in the way of a good thing, himself and for that she had to be extracted from his life. After reflecting on this first job he suddenly realized how differently Heather and Judy reacted to the cocaine. *Interesting, oh well, as long as it did what it was supposed to do.*

Scott A. Reighard

Chapter 21

Sitting at his desk poring over paperwork, Andrew decided to put that on hold and call the Palm Beach Historical Society to inquire about the reunion. He spoke with Ms. Steinbach, a curator for the Society. She informed him that the reunion would take place at the world famous Breakers Hotel on Palm Beach. She also included that there would be a DJ banging out 70's and 80's hits, and a slide show that would display photos and other images from the school years of 1982-1983 to 1987-1988, as well as other events. Andrew was curious about his specific class to see who may have already committed to attending. He was thinking about Amy. She offered the list of names but missing were six people: Judy Barnett, Tucker Harrison, Brandon Henniker, Jonathan Snyder, Mark Lambert and Brian Morris.

"Well, we sent out invitations to everyone except for Judy, Tucker and Brandon."

"Why's that?"

"Oh, I'm sorry you haven't heard?" She paused, "they're dead!"

"What?"

"Yes sir, they're dead. Oh my, I feel so bad saying that. Strangely though, all of them passed away within the last year too."

"Wow, how?"

"I believe they were accidents."

"What like automobile accidents or plane accidents?" He began to scribble down their names.

She hesitated, "Well...I'm not sure if I should say this."

"Miss Steinbach, I am a police officer, you can tell me."

As if that means anything, he thought after stating that.

The Reunion Reaper

"Well...all right...Miss Barnett died of a supposed cocaine overdose. It was all over the papers. Then there was Mr. Harrison; he had a terrible biking accident, and apparently Mr. Henniker fell off a cliff while taking pictures out in Arizona."

Andrew just sat there his mouth agape. He was trying to be polite without being overbearing.

"How bizarre is that. You say these were accidents?"

"Yes sir, that's the news I got. I'm sorry sir I don't have any more than that." She seemed sincere about wanting to help him.

"That's okay, you said Miss Barnett, not Mrs."

"That's right, she and her husband divorced years ago. She still lives in the area. Oh goodness, I mean lived in the area. Their divorce was all over the local paper."

Andrew did not respond.

"Sir, is there anything else I can do for you it's almost my lunch hour."

"No, no, you go ahead...thank you for all your information."

"So before I go are you confirming your attendance?"

"Most definitely!"

Chapter 22

Andrew did not get much done at work as his mind got swept away in a sea of reflection on the news of his dead classmates. Later that evening when he and Stephanie had some private time he told her the news. She was shocked. It was hard to imagine that twenty plus years had gone by and no one died, then all of a sudden within a year three classmates were dead. Andrew gave her the names, whatever he remembered about them.

"Wow, how weird, and for them all to be accidents is really crazy."

"That's just the thing," as he plopped down on the bed, "you think these were just accidents?"

"Sure, you've heard of freak accidents, coincidences."

"Yeah, but three in one year?"

"It does seem a bit odd, but you said they were accidents. Did you ask if there were any investigations?" She offered as she began removing her make-up.

He had a far off look in his eyes, "Well, I wasn't exactly wearing my Sherlock Holmes cap, but I would assume there were." He removed his socks and tossed them toward the hamper. "You know I've been out of touch so long I don't even know what's going on in with these people's lives anymore, and I've forgotten more than I remember."

"Well, you've been away for a while now, that was a long time ago."

"It just seems pretty unbelievable."

"Yeah, I know." She looked at him from the reflection in her vanity mirror. "Andrew what are you doing?"

"What do you mean?"

"That look, the head slightly tilted back, eyes in a far off place."

The Reunion Reaper

Laughing at the silliness of her suggestion, "What are you talking about?"

"I've seen that look… it's that suspicious look, like that time in Florida when you thought the neighbor's kids across the street were stealing your golf balls from your paint bucket.

"Well they were!"

"Yeah, but to set up a camera was a little weird don't you think?"

"I had the evidence didn't I?"

"I guess, anyhow, that's the look I was referring to."

"Think about it though, three people, all of them accidents, and within a year. I mean, what are the odds on that? Well, you know what they say."

"Who are they?"

"You know, people. You've heard the adage." He began placing his fingers out like he was counting. "Once is an anomaly, twice is a coincidence, but three… is a pattern."

"Oh, I don't know about that, besides what can you do about it?"

"Who said I was gonna do anything about it, I just think it's a little weird that's all."

"Well, just don't get any goofy ideas."

"What are you talking about? I'm not gonna get any ideas, especially goofy ones."

She knew better, she didn't know this man for nearly twenty years not to know his characteristics, the circuits in his brain were already twitching, she knew it. She simply hoped that he wouldn't get too carried away with it.

Chapter 23

It was Easter Sunday and Andrew, Stephanie and the kids were all sitting in church at St. Andrew's where they attended mass on a regular basis. Father Flynn was delivering an inspirational homily about resurrection and salvation. Andrew always enjoyed Father's speeches, but he drifted into a daydream and started thinking again about Judy, Brandon and Tucker. He tried to remember if any of them were religious. *Funny time to be thinking about that,* he thought while gazing up at a crucified Jesus behind the altar. He didn't know their religious affiliations, or even if they had one, but he said a prayer for each and the thought of something foul couldn't escape his mind for anything. If something was foul regarding their deaths, he felt compelled to at least check it out, perhaps have his doubts put to rest.

Communion was about to get under way and Stephanie nudged at Andrew, who she thought was in prayer. Even though he was daydreaming thoughts of dead classmates, he amazingly, as if habitually, was able to proceed with mass and all the standing, kneeling, sitting, etc. Catholics like to exercise their faith during mass.

They all proceeded to communion, except for Ryan, he was too young, and had not had his first communion celebration, although Andrew was always mindful to just bite off half his communion bread and save the rest for Ryan when he returned to the pew. He wondered if they were keeping tabs upstairs. It was just a five year old who simply wanted to eat what everyone else was eating. No harm, no foul he thought.

Mass ended and they piled into the SUV as Andrew drove the family to their new ritual of attending brunch after Easter Mass.

The Reunion Reaper

The one thing that had changed for them after they moved to Virginia was when they lived in Florida it was almost a given that Easter Sunday would be spent with family, but over time things changed. His younger sister Deanna moved to Charlotte with her husband. His older brother Sean was a Navy SEAL and was stationed in Norfolk. When Andrew decided to move them all to Virginia they no longer had the family around, so it was just the five of them frequenting their favorite Italian restaurant as their new post-mass destination. Occasionally there were holiday gatherings, but those were mostly Thanksgiving or Christmas.

Never the less, without extended family it was still a good day, the kids all got Easter baskets, and mom got a little gift from Andrew, which was usually a new pin or perfume, but in this case it was, by making lieutenant, a diamond bracelet hidden in a box of chocolates. She thought that was one of the neatest things he had ever done for her. Stephanie, in turn, gave her husband a bottle of his favorite cologne and a box of his favorite dark chocolate, and no, the cologne was not in the box of chocolate. A simple man is happy with simple things.

The day was fairly cool for an early April day and after the Easter egg hunt with his boys and a few of the neighbor's kids, he decided to just relax and watch the final round of the Masters Golf tournament. As he watched Phil Mickelson strike a laser drive down the middle of the fairway he couldn't shake the idea of whether these deaths really were accidents or whether they were the master mind acts of a very skilled killer, or killers. *But why, who would want to see these people dead?* He questioned as he drifted off to sleep.

Scott A. Reighard

Chapter 24

That evening Andrew decided to call his father to discuss the situation with him. Since his father logged many years as a Florida DEA, he could still give him some good advice, or at least his thoughts.

"Hey dad, Happy Easter."

"Well did the Easter Bunny come to your house?"

"Of course, and he keeps stealing my money."

"Welcome to my world. With all you kids and grandkids I don't know how your mother and I do it?"

"Thirty years working basically covert for the government must have paid pretty well."

"Well, I wouldn't exactly say the government paid handsomely, there were many times I thought about getting out, and not just because of the danger either. Anyhow, let's move on, do you want to say hi to your mom?"

"I wanted to ask you a few questions first."

"What's on your mind?"

"Well, I don't know exactly how to say this."

"Oh this ain't bad stuff is it?"

"No, everything's fine here, the job, the kids, the wife, you know, just plowing ahead."

"Well then get to it O'Reilly starts in thirty minutes."

"It's Sunday dad."

"How do you know I don't tape it?"

"Because you've already asked me how to program your VCR. Besides, I told you how to TIVO your programs and you've asked me three times in the last month the process again."

"Well you can't expect me to remember everything you tell me."

"Uh, hey there cave man they've invented pen and paper in case you missed it."

The Reunion Reaper

"Don't be a smart ass. All right, move on, if everything is okay on the home-front what do you want?"

"Remember I told you about my twenty fifth high school reunion?"

"Yeah, you were thinking about how bad it would be if you didn't go and I remember saying that that is about as dumb as your—"

"Uh, thanks dad I remember what you said. No, here's the deal."

Andrew went on to explain the supposed accidents and how he thought otherwise. He commented that he had not been around these people in so long he hardly knew most of them anymore. He wasn't exactly too close to many of them either despite attending that school for six years; so much for the life long friends in high school cliché. There were only a few with whom he maintained a casual contact with and his dad was about to drop one of those names on him.

"You want my advice?"

"Of course, that's why I called."

"I thought you called to wish your mother and me a happy Easter?"

"Happy Easter, there you feel better?"

"Are you sure you're mine? Anyhow, I say you drop it."

"Drop it?"

"Look, I'm supposed to be the one with the hearing problem. I said drop it, it's not worth your time, and it's got bad written all over it."

"How can you say it's got bad written all over it? I have classmates that are dead dad, it's pretty hard to just drop it."

"Son, sometimes investigations are like mini-wars, there are so many variables, and they're especially tough when there's an emotional attachment."

"There's no emotional attachment."

"Ah, bullshit, you can't tell me that… I say drop it. You'll do yourself a big favor."

There was silence. His father continued, "You still there."

"I'm here."

"Look, I know you're a competitive guy, hell all my kids wanted to conquer the world at some point, and you were hoping I would say go for it, but sorry son, can't do it."

"I'm not disappointed. Okay, maybe a little, but I understand."

"Hey, what about Joe?"

"Joe who?"

"Damn boy you still got shit for brains? Joe the kid who works for the FBI, wasn't he a school buddy of yours?"

"Oh, you mean Joe Marketti? Yeah, but if I involve the FBI, then…"

"Yeah, go ahead, if you involve the FBI then what?"

"Well, if the FBI gets involved then that's it for me."

"So dad's advice fell on deaf ears."

Emphatically he shot back, "No." He switched the phone to his other ear. "I just want to satisfy a curiosity."

"Well, you know the ole sayin', curiosity killed the—"

"The cat, I know."

"Okay, but remember this, and this is thirty years of law enforcement warning you. You will be going beyond your jurisdiction, and all it takes is one bad screw up for you to lose everything you've worked for the last ten years or so, you understand me?"

"Yes, I'm aware of that."

"I don't think you are. Don't be a hero son, graveyards and bars are full of heroes. You got a good family, great kids. Don't do something that's going to jeopardize that."

"I won't you know that. They're all I think about, trust me."

"I know that, but I also know you. Hell it cost me a fortune to raise you. Listen, I still think you should call Joe and just talk to him about this."

The Reunion Reaper

"All right I will," said Andrew sullenly.

"Oh you sound like some kid who didn't get his candy. Now I don't want to hear anymore of this. Three people are dead and that is sad, but the sooner you talk to the FBI the sooner they can get crackin' on this case... Okay, enough about that did you see the Masters today?"

"Yeah, I was hoping for Mickelson to pull it out."

"You know what he's missing and Tiger's got?"

Andrew knew what his dad was going to say, but he had that kind of respect for a man who, for so long, was there when he really needed him. And now that his father was moving on up there in age he didn't want to seem in any way disrespectful.

"What's that?"

"Killer instinct. Tiger is more concerned about titles while Mick seems more interested in money."

Andrew didn't always agree with his father and they jabbered back and forth a bit as Andrew tried to defend that Mickelson, for all his talent, just wasn't in Tiger's league, and that maybe Mickelson, since he had a family and Tiger didn't, he could focus his priorities on that. Little did Andrew know that this conversation with his father would in some ways mirror what was about to be present in his life; the killer, a man with no family, and Andrew with a wife and three kids. Who was hungrier was soon to be tested.

"Well, maybe you're right. Anyhow, love you son, in the meantime, here talk to your mom I need to take a crap."

"Thanks for that information dad."

"I love you son, remember what I said."

"I will, love you too."

Andrew then spent the better part of twenty minutes chatting with his mom about family, the kids and life in general. He never mentioned his classmates. She told him several times how proud she was of his promotion. She also asked several times if everything was okay and he told her not to worry, but she did, that's what mothers do.

The Reunion Reaper

Chapter 25

A few nights after Easter, Andrew was sitting in his study counting out manila folders. He stopped at twenty one wondering if he should even put a folder together for Judy, Tucker and Brandon. He had done some Google searches and was able to locate some archival articles on their deaths. The articles were vague, and information was scant at best. *Maybe they **were** just accidents.*

Although it had been a long time he pulled a banker's like file box from storage. The box was marked *dad's stuff*, but it looked more like it should have said *the past dad can't shake.*

Picking out items one at a time and glancing at their importance he finally came to what he was looking for his high school yearbook. The book cover glowed with the school's colors of white and Mediterranean blue lettering. In the middle of the cover was a serene sunset shot that Brandon Henniker took a photo of while in the Keys over spring break. Above the photo was the school name Palm Beach Preparatory, and below it written on a banner were the words Semper Memoria Teneo with the school year 1983 below. A reflective smile creased his face.

Andrew turned the cover and on the first page inside the book was a well sketched pencil drawing of the school mascot a Mako Shark. Another smile and chuckle emerged as he entered memory lane.

He began flipping through the pages, first checking the senior photos. He had a good laugh and an 'ugh' moment when he saw his picture. Back then he sported a long wavy hair style as opposed to the short cropped cut he maintained these days. His sandy blond hair had been replaced by brown and flecks of white, although his wife argued they were gray. He also noticed that these days there were a few more lines around the forehead and the eyes. He marveled at how smooth and relatively unblemished his skin was then.

Looking into his own eyes, the eyes of a seventeen year old spoke volumes; for inside those eyes was a world waiting to be conquered, now it was just trying to be managed. Having seen enough of himself he continued on; whether it was disappointment in what he felt was possible for himself back then, or just content with where he was he flipped the page. Six pages over there she was, Amy, his first love. The bold brunette with piercing blue eyes shot feelings through his body, enough to make him feel guilty about Stephanie. Suddenly reality rang his ears as Michael was calling out to him to tell Ryan to stop writing on his homework.

"Where's your mother?"

"She went to the store," Michael shouted. "Stop Ryan... dad can I hit him?"

"Don't hit your brother." *Why didn't she say anything to me?* "I'll be right there." He glanced down at Amy's photo, "don't go away."

After settling the boy's conflict he went back to the yearbook. He harkened back to the day he met Amy, it was September 5, 1979. Although the two of them were freshman it was her first year there. He had already logged two years at the hallowed school. She had previously attended an all girl prep school.

She strolled into English 9 like Venus, except she was clothed in the school's customary uniform of a khaki skirt that draped below the knee and a sky blue short sleeved button down oxford. Needless to say he couldn't remember a single word Mr. Perkins said that morning. In fact, from that day forward he learned very little in class, and it had nothing to do with Mr. Perkins' teaching. The only time he half paid attention was when they were discussing *Romeo and Juliet*, and in a way he could sympathize with the story. He was a middle class across the inter-coastal commoner, while she was a Palm Beach socialite, a debutante no doubt. In a way he felt out of his league chasing this butterfly of a girl, in fact, he figured he had about the same odds of dating her as a midget had dunking a basketball. But he was determined to snare this butterfly, and in their junior year that opportunity arose as he came to her rescue like Rin Tin Tin.

Early in their junior year there was a party where Amy and a senior by the name of Larry Seibel was trying to fondle her nether regions despite repeated rejections, but Larry was the son of a legal giant in the area and pretty much felt he could do whatever he wanted. Andrew figured his father had more enemies than friends and his son was heading down the same asshole highway. He used to think these sordid types always seemed to take the same on ramp when their head gets filled with the self.

So here was Larry trying to go places he felt were a right rather than a privilege when in stumbled Andrew into the beach side cabana of Larry's family beach front home. On the couch were Amy and Larry. Larry had the upper hand so to speak and Amy asked for Andrew's help. Andrew jumped on Larry like he was a hungry shark on chum. He proceeded to pound Larry a few times in the head before Larry started crying and yelling out, 'uncle' or something like that. They left Larry laying there flailing away with a black eye on the floor. Larry was shouting that he was going to have his dad sue Andrew, but he just ignored the whining prick who just tried to take advantage of a girl.

He decided to escort Amy down to the beach for a walk in an effort to calm her down. The walk on the beach was as memorable as any he had of his youth. They sat and talked for hours watching the full moon glide over their shoulders across the night time sky. If merely walking and sitting with her on the beach was the appetizer Andrew was salivating at what the possibilities might be for the two of them. For the next two years they were inseparable. They were a cute couple, and despite the resistance of her parents the two of them, just like Romeo and Juliet defied their admonitions.

To this day Andrew keeps the ninth grade copy of *Romeo and Juliet* in his banker's box. On the inside of the book he "borrowed" from the school he replaced the names Romeo and Juliet with Andrew and Amy, not exactly Shakespeare-esque, but well enough for him. Sadly, three months after that party Larry was drunk and wrapped his BMW 2002 around a telephone pole, he was killed instantly.

Snapping out of his sojourn down memory lane at the sound of Stephanie closing the front door Andrew grabbed a legal pad setting on the desk and began jotting down a few notes on each person. He spent the better part of two hours scribbling down what he could remember of the characteristics, personality traits, attitudes and emotions about each person in his graduating class. Stephanie popped her head in.

"Hey sweetie what are you working on?"

"Oh, just some BS from work."

He was never a good liar.

"You sure about that?"

"Yeah!" He seemed to take exception to her questioning.

"Come on Andrew, I heard you talking to your father the other night about these so called murders."

"Look, before you get all freaked out, I don't know what to think right now. It just doesn't feel right Steph."

"Andrew honey you know how much I love you, but who are you to get involved in this?"

"The FBI is not going to just start running around the country on the whim of some guy who thinks these might be murders."

"Who said anything about the FBI?"

The Reunion Reaper

"I would think this would naturally be something they would have to deal with given the deaths occurred in several states." He said rather sheepishly. "Look, I just want to put together some information for them then I'll be glad to turn it over."

She knew he was stumbling with his response. "Other than walking away from your security position what have you ever walked away from?"

Andrew had walked away from something a long time ago, but this was not for Stephanie to know. From that experience he vowed to never quit on anything again in his life.

"Like I said, all I want to do is put together a little information for them and then I'll turn it over. Think about it, what could I do, I don't have jurisdiction or anything. I'm not stupid."

"I know you're not stupid, but I know the man I married, and when he sets his mind to something there's no turning back."

He smiled at her, "That's how I got you wasn't it?"

"Maybe I let you catch me."

"Yeah right, the way your friends felt about me, I earned every piece of you." He hesitated at that thought as she gave him a weird look, "I mean that in a good way."

"I got it. So you promise you'll turn it over and not go off on some wild goose chase?"

"I promise."

She walked over gave him a kiss and said, "I sure hope so."

So did he, but for Andrew this was the moment, the moment he instinctively felt convinced these were not accidents. Stephanie walked out of the room and closing the door behind her he breathed a heavy sigh. He was lying.

There was no way he was going to just hand this over without him first trying to pull a Maverick. He was about to start something he fully planned to finish. He had officially dismissed the wishes of both his father and wife. How that would come back on him he could only conjecture. The questions he had were many, but the main one was how he was going to try to conduct a murder investigation alone and from his home.

Chapter 26

Staring at the reunion invitation and sporting a grin that would make a beauty queen jealous Jeffrey turned his attention to the computer screen that contained information, statistics, particular likes and dislikes and employment or otherwise of his classmates, and as he scrolled down the screen he began to consider the next victim.

Under each of the victims information he had a journal entry; up to this point there were three, but there were several more to consider. He was pleased with his work. Everything had gone according to the script; conduct intensive background information, research, and then research more, devise the "accident" and set the time table. It was mid April and the reunion was another month away, and he couldn't wait. There was a need to hear how good he was and the reunion would provide him with that opportunity. What great timing for a reunion he thought, oh the discussions that will take place. He couldn't wait to get there and strut just like a proud cock would to his hens. He was anxious to hear anything that would reference the mastery of his work, but there was one in particular he was interested in hearing from. *Murders disguised as accidents, what a conversation that will make.* He would carefully plan his script.

He had his next target in mind, but knew that would have to wait until after the reunion. He marveled at how predictable people were, almost comparing them to animals; how they were so entrenched in their daily rituals. It just seemed too easy really. Conversely, he was unpredictable. He enjoyed showing up whenever and wherever, and he never got into patterns that someone could detect.

Scott A. Reighard

As he gazed at the embossed lettering of the invitation, he was looking forward to seeing some of these people, perhaps being a bit too nostalgic, he reminded himself that he was on a mission. A mission of: discovery, seek, and eventually destroy. The trick was to not be obvious to anyone's suspicions. The reunion would be an opportunity for him to give an Oscar like performance. Having put to bed any immediate thoughts of putting on his game face he considered tomorrow's plan. He was to go to the men's store and purchase a new suit for the reunion. He thought about buying a black suit but that would be too morose; perhaps a sharp pin stripe or solid navy blue with a light blue pinpoint shirt and a smart red and navy striped tie, and of course a pair of brown Sergio Brutini lace up dress shoes. Together the whole suit would command attention.

After nodding in approval of his choice of suit he wheeled his desk chair around and grabbed a book that lay on the table directly behind his desk. It was a book on serial killers. He flipped through some of the pages and wondered where they had gone wrong, well except for Jack the Ripper and the Zodiac killer. He admired these men but he was so unlike them. The only thing he wanted to keep in common with them was that those killers were never caught, at least for those particular crimes. He respected how the Ripper methodically went about his business, and how Zodiac fooled some of the keenest minds in law enforcement with his encrypted messages. He also liked the fact that they had cool names. That's why he gave considerable thought to publishing his masterpiece when all of this was done, from some distant shore of course. He didn't want the god forsaken media to play a role with his nickname, so he considered two names, the Desert Vigilante or the Reunion Reaper. To him there was nothing worse than some media prick that would ruin his beautiful work with some lame name. No sir, the names he came up with sounded dangerous and notorious like Jack the Ripper.

The Reunion Reaper

He put down the book and went into the bathroom. He stared into the gray eyes of someone who thought that all of this was about justice and ridding society of excrement. Then he went through a series of facial gestures as he ran through his mind the opening journal to all this madness. *There are times in a man's life where he must look to accountability and setting things right, and so that if he were to die in the blink of an eye he would know that he had dignity because he exercised his duty to do what he thought was right for self-preservation and not to die anonymously.*

Chapter 27

Andrew, Stephanie and the kids greeted Grandma O'Brien, Stephanie's mom at the airport. In a few days they would be headed to Florida for the reunion and grandma was needed to take care of the kids while they were away. It was mid-May and there was still the important matter of school. Shirley O'Brien was the traveling babysitter; since the death of her husband Stephen a few years back. She was always anxious to stay in touch with the grandkids. Stephanie was the youngest of three. Her brothers, Kyle and Randy still lived in and around Dallas. Kyle was an electrical contractor while Randy was struggling as a starving country musician.

Andrew cared very much for his mother-in-law as well as a mother-in-law could be loved, but he never thought that love was reciprocated; he would have accepted disingenuous love at that. It wasn't like a mother's love that is expressed implicitly as well as explicitly, hers was more or less through things she bought him for his birthday or Christmas.

The kids were excited to see their grandma as they greeted her with hugs and kisses. They enjoyed seeing her because she always brought them something, and most assuredly would take them shopping while she was visiting, whether out of guilt for living so far away or because she thought Andrew was so cheap. She made sure she got one day at the mall with them before getting back on the plane to head home. After the hugs and kisses she wasted no time ruffling Andrew's feathers.

"So, I hear you're not really happy about going to Florida," She quipped as Andrew was grabbing her bag from the baggage carousel.

The Reunion Reaper

He shot a quick glare at Stephanie, "What? I didn't say I wasn't happy, I just said I wasn't fired up to go back."

"But your parents live there."

"My parents live in St. Augustine, where we're going is no longer the same place it was."

She shot back quickly, "But what place is still the same?"

They all began to walk out to the parking lot as Andrew snapped back, "Look, I am not opposed to change it's just how anxious these developers are to rape the land instead of thinking about the impact they're going to make." Stephanie managed to squeeze out a diverting cough as Andrew continued. "Can we change the subject please, we're going and that's it, I'll get over it."

Andrew quickened his pace as Ryan had to nearly engage in jogging in order to keep up with his dad. Michael and Mary were giggling in the back.

"I'm sorry I must have hit a soft spot," offered Shirley with a slithering punctuation.

"Mother, leave him alone he's got a lot on his mind."

"I was just curious about him not wanting to go back to Florida that's all especially when his parents are still living there it's not fair to say that about them." She said rather quickly.

He turned to his pesky mother in law, "What? Say what about them?"

"Dad just chill out, she's just trying to get a rise out of you."

Stephanie stepped out and turned around to face them,

"Mary that will be enough from you… Look, mom just got here, can we at least make it back to the house without a major event please."

Everyone was quiet then Ryan spoke, "I won't say anything I promise."

There was a brief moment of silence then laughter. Ryan didn't quite understand because he was as sincere as a five year old could be, but it helped to calm the situation.

Scott A. Reighard

The trip home went better than the initial encounter at the airport. Of course Shirley was still probing Andrew for answers and Stephanie did her best to deflect them. There was some tension in Andrew's grip of the wheel and Stephanie placed her hand on his right knee as a sign to relax him, but it did little to mitigate his tension. Of course Stephanie didn't know the whole deal, it just wasn't the mother-in-law, it was everything that was running around in his head like an endless carousel: his promotion, the trip to the reunion, Amy, three dead classmates, a killer on the loose, and now a mother-in-law who was about to walk the rest of the way to their house. One good thing about going to Florida though, he wouldn't have to hang around his mother-in-law, and with that glimmer of hope his attitude improved.

The Reunion Reaper

Chapter 28

Andrew and his wife stepped off the Delta flight that had carried them from Roanoke through Atlanta and in to West Palm Beach, Florida. Both were casually dressed. Each had on khaki colored shorts. Andrew opted for a hunter green collared polo while Stephanie went with a sleeveless knit blouse that was shrimp in color. They blended in very well.

They sauntered through the crowded airport with each carrying a hiking pack as they weaved their way through a throng of Japanese tourists who were most likely on their way to Disney World. Andrew and Stephanie finally made their way to the baggage claim area, and still even more people for Andrew to gaze at.

Standing amidst the crowd of tourists, residents returning home and a gang of kids on a school trip, they waited as the carousel light went on and the baggage began rolling out. There was a sign of anxiousness on Andrew's face as he began to think about seeing old classmates, some he had not seen in nearly twenty five years. Standing next to his right watching the luggage slam into the rail area of the carousel his wife took her hand and began rubbing his back, smiling at him as they waited. She was pretty excited to be back in Florida and she was anxious to get to the hotel, relax and bask in the sun for a few days.

"That was a pretty good flight, don't you think?" She asked, "Honey?"

"Huh?"

"I said it was a nice flight."

"Oh yeah, well you know, Delta always seems to make you feel comfortable."

"Are you okay?"

"Yeah, sure, I was just thinking about seeing people I hadn't seen in years."

"I'm sure you're not the only one. I think it's exciting. To think that my twenty five year reunion is just two years away, wow how the years go by."

"They sure do."

Andrew spotted the two pieces of luggage they checked and he moved closer to the carousel to retrieve them. Grabbing the bags, he set them on the floor, pulled up the handles and began rolling them toward Stephanie; each of them grabbed one and walked their way out to snag the bus that would take them to the rental car location just down the road from the airport. Stepping through the automatic sliding doors it suddenly hit him. One thing that never leaves you is the distinctive Florida humidity. It briefly suffocated him, and suddenly memories of sweating his ass off for no reason came to mind. There was nothing like the feeling of having your skin in a perpetual state of moistness, such was the Florida humidity. They saw the bus sitting at the waiting area.

A soft breeze blew through the covered terminal, but it brought little relief as the day's temperature would reach eighty eight degrees with humidity to match. Andrew grabbed each bag and hoisted them onto the bus and they grabbed a seat near the back. As they sat down and waited for the bus to depart Stephanie smiled at him.

"Do you remember my first trip here?"

"Sure I do, it was your senior spring break."

"What a great trip that was."

"Sure was. I couldn't wait to show you off to my family."

Andrew and Stephanie had come to Florida twenty years ago. Andrew had already graduated from Roanoke College and Stephanie was closing out her career at the University of Georgia. Andrew was so proud to show her his old haunts. He took her to his first home, second home, schools, the beach he and his family would go to on most weekends, and he capped it all off by taking her to see some of his family. They fell in love with her right from the start. She was so full of life.

Finally, after five years of being together and feeling the sultry, sexy and smart young Texan had been fully vetted, he asked her for her hand in marriage. They spent a few days in the Palm Beaches then drove down to the Keys to enjoy the remainder of their honeymoon. Maybe that's why Shirley O'Brien had something against Andrew, he took her baby girl away from home.

This trip, however, was a much different one. For Stephanie it was a mini vacation, a chance to get away from the kids for a while, and to escape her job responsibilities, but for Andrew it was nostalgia mixed with anxiousness. Stephanie sighed, "Why did we ever leave again?"

Andrew sat there looking across the aisle at a man who looked like he was in businessman's hell, having to wear a suit while in Florida.

"All the changes you know that."

"I know, but you have to admit that it must feel good to return to the place you have so many memories."

"I guess."

Andrew had changed his attitude about Florida as the years passed. The place where he grew up had changed so dramatically. There was a population boom and developments crowded the once serene Florida landscape. Many of the Florida orange groves had disappeared because of the demand to build homes, shopping centers, golf courses and countless businesses. Areas that had once been clustered with woods now looked like a concrete maze of strip malls and parking lots. As the bus pulled out of the airport Andrew hardly recognized the area, there were hotels everywhere, and all the streets seemed to be two or four lanes wider than they used to be. The price of progress it seems.

The rental car business was just a few miles from the airport so there wasn't much time to ponder memories.

There was yet another line and it took them nearly thirty minutes to get their rental; *so much for rapid rentals* thought Andrew. Their hotel was less than five miles from the airport and not much said on the way there; Stephanie was too busy gazing at all the palm trees and art deco colored buildings and Spanish designed plazas while Andrew was in retro world evaluating the new from what once was. He didn't really care for what he was looking at. He decided to change his thoughts and considered whether he should actively engage his classmates at the reunion in a serious conversation with hopes of having some light shed on his suspicions, or should he just relax and enjoy the experience with old friends? Before he knew it Stephanie had to remind him of the hotel entrance.

Andrew parked the car in front of the hotel and they went inside. Each of them gathered their belongings and made their way through the lobby and onto an elevator that took them to the sixth floor where they would find their room 619. The room was nice and spacious, but it was a three star hotel room that was overpriced. Even his law enforcement discount which turned out to be no more than the senior citizen discount was ridiculous. The room contained a king sized bed along with a dresser, a night stand, and a desk. The only decent thing they offered for free was internet access, and HBO. Off to the left of the entry was the bathroom where Stephanie quickly checked it out.

"Wow, this is nice." She said.

"That's nice. How many sinks?" He asked as he hoisted the luggage onto the bed for unpacking.

"Only one, but the counter is pretty big."

"That's good!" responded Andrew. *I'm sure she'll hog it all up with her personals.*

He unzipped his suitcase and began to pull out his clothes to store in the dresser. He then removed his suit, the one he would wear to the reunion, and took it to the closet for hanging. Stephanie came out of the bathroom and went over to the window to open the drapes. The room overlooked the pool where Stephanie could see several sunbathers soaking up the intense Florida heat and sun.

"Come here honey, check out the pool."
Andrew slowly ambled over to the window.

"I guess you're looking to get down there as soon as possible." He said.

"I'd like to if you don't mind."

"No, of course not, just remember I'd like to get to the restaurant by six."

"That's fine that will give me about an hour to get a little sun."

"There's no such thing as a little sun in Florida. Look at those tourists down there, they do it every time. They think the sun is somehow going to disappear so they sit out there all day and get burned like a lobster and then complain about how uncomfortable they are. If they only knew what they were doing to their skin."

"Oh come on Doctor Andrew, a little burn never killed anybody."

"Oh yeah, you remember my Aunt Rose, when her parents said she was Irish she thought they said Osiris. She soaked up the sun like an immortal, well skin cancer made her mortal. Now when she goes outside, she looks like one of those old ladies who cover themselves from head to toe."

"Wow, so that's why she dresses that way. I never knew."

"Well, now you do."

He went into his personal bag to grab the suntan lotion he brought. "Here, lather up okay?"

"SPF 30?"
He pointed at her, "Remember Aunt Rose."

"But we're here for just a few days."

"It only takes one." He said as he stepped in close to her, "Remember Aunt Rose."

"Okay, okay. You gonna join me?"

"Well, I'd rather take a little nap if that's okay with you."
"You could nap at the pool."
"Nah, you know I can't nap in the heat."
"Okay, well you nap, and I'll tan."
"Sounds like a plan."
"Good, when you wake up will you come get me so I can get back and take a shower?"
"You got it," he said as he plopped down on the bed.
She looked down on him as he lay flat on the bed, "Hey, you're not going to be a dopey mopey on this trip are you?"
"No, why?" he said with eyes already closed.
"I don't know, it just seems that since we landed you seem unhappy."
"I'll be fine, I just need a little time and a nap. I promise I'll be better after that."
"Well who is going to rub on my SPF 30?"
"You're limber, you'll do fine."
"Or maybe I'll just find myself some twenty something hunk so I can tell the girl's some stories when I get back."
"Good luck." He said with sarcasm and a smile.
"You're too funny!" She slapped his foot.
She quickly unpacked the rest of their clothes and then changed into her new bathing suit, grabbed her new beach towel and headed out the door for the pool.
She leaned over and gave him a kiss, "Have a good nap honey."
"Thanks." He waited until he heard the door open, "Remember Aunt Rose."
"I will. You're such a stinker you know that?"
"And you love me for it."
"Yes I do."
Stephanie seemed to skip out of the room. Andrew got up from the bed and went over to the desk pulled out the chair and took a seat. He grabbed his computer bag and took out his laptop. He also took out the invitation to the reunion. He wanted to re-confirm tomorrow evening's

The Reunion Reaper

events. The drug store may have Preparation H, but Stephanie and the kids have Preparation A. He didn't care too much for surprises or not being prepared. The reunion was being held in the Venetian Ball Room at the Breakers Hotel on Palm Beach, a lavish hotel where the rich could flaunt their wealth, mingle, gossip, and conduct business. Andrew always felt out of place at places like that because he was neither rich nor desiring of such a lifestyle. Somehow he seemed to resent how rich people flaunted their wealth at times. He never could figure out why people would spend five hundred dollars a night to sleep in a bed that was no more comfortable than the one on which he was resting his feet.

He looked over the events of the party and saw that Senior Class President and valedictorian Greg Madison was to make the key address to the group of graduates from the class of 1983. Greg was a good friend of Andrew's back then, but nowadays he maintained only sporadic communication with him.

Greg graduated from M.I.T. in 1989 with a master's degree and then went on to the University of Massachusetts Medical School to earn his PhD in biochemistry. He currently was working for the CDC in Atlanta, Georgia as a chemical scientist. His work was more important than ever these days since the senseless tragedies of September 11, 2001. He sat there for a few minutes looking at the invitation as his computer was loading. *I thought they had high speed internet?* He continued thinking about the people who had mysteriously died and how everyone might react about this upon seeing one another. He then decided the computer could wait. *Maybe it'll be ready when we get back from dinner.*

He got up from his chair and went over to the window to look out onto a small section of a city transformed into a place he was glad he left many years ago. As he gazed beyond the hotel property all he could see were buildings and streets. Gone were the expanses of fields that were once adorned with clusters of pine trees, and open grassy fields. The road was now choked with traffic despite it being four lanes wider. Also gone were the days when cars could go flying down its small four lane road that seemed to cut a direct path from West Palm Beach to Riviera Beach. All the small businesses he had known had been gobbled up by the big franchises. Commercial was now the order of the day and this was something that was inexplicably eating at him. Man has always found a way to screw up a good thing he thought. *And Florida is wondering why they are going through the crap they are right now?* Man somehow finds a way to build yet destroy; a paradox with no viable end in sight, now that's frustrating.

As his eyes panned with disappointment he decided to look down toward the pool spotting Stephanie as she faithfully was rubbing lotion on her body. He thought, *she's right my attitude sucks right now.* He smiled. She had listened to him. He was happy that his wife would have an opportunity to get a little break from the hustle and bustle of the home life they left behind for a few days. A wry smile appeared that somehow had wiped away the haggard look in his eyes.

What a lucky man he was. Lucky to have a woman that was sensitive, loving, and yet a rock, and that rock was certainly capable of revealing a considerable resistance when it needed. He loved that about her. As crazy as it may sound, he loved it when they argued and that she stuck to her guns when she was right. Most of their friends thought the marriage would last a year maybe two, but Stephanie and Andrew were making fools of those who predicted that two such opposite people would simply give up easily and walk away. First of all, no one knew the depths of their faith and neither of them was known for quitting on anything they started, they were finishers, and according to

The Reunion Reaper

their marriage they were just getting started. He was lucky, and he knew it, but so was she. She had a man with deep principles, rock hard morals, and the determination that could frustrate the most patient. The beauty of the relationship lay with the harmony they were able to maintain. Sometimes it was soft and airy as an acoustic guitar with a light string accompaniment, while other times it was like Eddie Van Halen cranking out a screaming solo with Pat Benatar on vocals. Either way it was music, they liked it that way. Damn the torpedoes, full speed ahead.

    As he snapped out of his temporary drift he saw her adjust in her lounge chair. He thought how he had better get to his nap or he would have to forget about it. He closed the drapes and went over and pulled back the covers and slipped into the king size bed. The sheets were cool and the pillow soft, within a few minutes of laying his head on the down feather pillow he was out.

Scott A. Reighard

Chapter 29

Stepping off the plane that had just arrived from Dallas, Jeffrey was casually dressed in plain front khakis, brown loafers and a blue oxford with the sleeves folded to the elbows. His dark hair was neatly combed straight back with no discernible part. He was toting a small black laptop bag. He had the appearance of a business man returning home to see his family.

He looked around the familiar surroundings of Palm Beach International Airport, a place he knew well. He wasted no time getting to the baggage claim area to await the arrival of his luggage. This trip would be a conspicuous one. He would rent a car, get a hotel room at the Breakers, openly engage strangers in conversation, or sit in obvious places at restaurants. For a man who liked staying hidden from the scene, he made himself noticeable. Secretly he desired the spotlight, but he couldn't jeopardize his mission. There would be time for the spotlight. A killer had arrived, yet he gave the impression of someone looking for a little Florida sunshine.

His preference of vehicle was a drop top Mustang GT, although it was a drop off from his BMW Z3. With the top down and his medium length black hair, that he began to color a few years back when some gray hairs decided to pop up, was swirling in the circling air of the drive to Palm Beach. *What a rush this is going to be.* He entertained the idea of arranging an accident at the reunion, but reason outplayed vanity. As he directed his way toward Palm Beach, he tapped his fingers on the steering wheel and began to sing an oldie from his high school days now blaring out of the speakers.

"You take it on the run baby, 'cause that's the way you want it baby, then I don't want you around, dah, dah, dah,

The Reunion Reaper

dah something... you can kiss my ass pumpkin..."

It was *Take it on the Run* by R.E.O. Speedwagon. As he crossed the inter-coastal bridge leading to Palm Beach the air turned slightly cooler as he headed east toward the ocean. The Breakers location was right on the Atlantic Ocean. It was built in 1896 by Henry Flagler a wealthy railroad tycoon who partnered with John D. Rockefeller of the Standard Oil Company. Flagler was a key figure in the development of the east coast of Florida and he decided to make Palm Beach his home. The Breakers Hotel would be his grand creation, along with the establishment of the East Coast Railway. As he drove up the nearly quarter mile brick style driveway that was divided by a magnificent median that contained a golf course style green lawn to the hotel entrance he knew it was costly, but what the hell, you only have one twenty fifth year reunion, and for some of these people it would be their last.

He pulled up to the hotel and was greeted by the valet parking attendant who smiled from ear to ear. As the young man held out his hand for the turnover of keys he just looked at the kid like he was just another rich wannabe who wanted to see how the other fifteen percent lived.

"Thank you sir, here is your ticket."

"Thank you," he replied as he tipped him.

A concierge ran up to the car to retrieve the bag from the trunk.

"Nice wheels sir," the concierge remarked as he pulled the bag from the trunk.

Yet another, "Thanks, it's my son's, I stole it from him."

The concierge laughed, "Good one sir... my son's. So, is this your first trip to the Breakers?"

"Practically feel like I own it."

The concierge maintained his broad smile, "Great, well we try to make everyone feel that way here so I guess we're doing our job."

"We'll see." *Zip it schmuck!*

Scott A. Reighard

He walked into the two hundred foot long grand lobby of the hotel. It was a beautiful expanse of Italian Renaissance architecture. Although it had been through a few remodeling enhancements it rivaled the best and most famous hotels in all of Florida, perhaps even the world.

After he checked in he went up to his room unpacked his bag then immediately returned to the lobby hoping to see a classmate or two, again to be obvious and to flaunt stylish garb that shouted money. The hotel was not forthcoming with any names for him, so he decided to take a seat at one of the oak cushioned high back chairs positioned inside the lobby area. He figured he could wait and hope that some other schoolmates would be staying there. Time was of no concern since this was down time.

He was here, not only to see classmates and get their reactions on the killings, but also to get more information from them. This could be easily accomplished given people's pension to spill out chapters of their lives at the mere speculation that someone genuinely had an interest in them. Why are Americans so open? Maybe it's like this country he thought, we're open, we love wide spaces, we are optimists, and trusting. The paradox that is his mission, belying people's trust to get close enough to expel them from existence was contrary to his beliefs in some ways, he wanted to believe in people, but it was hard; too much disappointment shattered whatever optimism he could muster for humanity.

Snapping back from his side trip down philosophical lane he spotted a familiar face, it was the former Kathleen Walker with her husband. He watched as the two of them walked up to the counter to check in. The key was taken by the man accompanying her and when they turned to head toward their room he called out, "Kathleen? Kathleen Walker?"

She looked around; he waved his hand at her when her eyes fell in his direction.

The Reunion Reaper

"Oh my God! Jeffery Lewis, how are you?"
The two of them hugged as her husband looked on, "I'm good." He stepped back, "Wow, you look great."

"Thank you. Wow, look at you, you haven't changed a bit."

"Well, more than I care to say but thank you."

"Oh wow, I am so sorry this is my husband Brad."
Each man stuck out his hand to shake, "How do you do, I am—"

Suddenly a tray was dropped and a large crashing sound of broken glass echoed throughout the lobby area. "Well, there goes someone's whiskey on the rocks I'm sure." He said as the maitre d' began to pick up the pieces of glass.

They all laughed. "I'm Jeffrey."

"It's nice to meet you Jeffrey," responded Brad.

"Oh by the way it's Johnson now," she said.

"Right Johnson, I am so sorry about calling you Walker."

He responded with a curt smile.
"That's okay it's been a long time. We've only been married for seven years now…"

There appeared to be awkwardness to the moment given how long since they had seen one another. "Well, listen I would love to sit and chat but we were hoping to relax a little before dinner."

"Of course, of course how rude of me. Well, it was nice to meet you Brad; maybe we'll get the chance to talk some more tomorrow night at the reunion."

"Yes, I'd like that. It was nice to meet you as well."

The concierge loaded Brad and Kathleen's luggage and headed down the corridor that led them to their room. As they walked away he smirked at the thought that he knew her name was Johnson, and that she had been married for seven years and that they had no children. He knew that her husband Brad was an advertising executive for Frito Lay and she was a mortgage processor. They lived in a two thousand square foot home in Plano, Texas just off the

George Bush Parkway. She lived a pretty clean life it seemed, pretty loyal, a bit selfish though as indicated by the lack of children, but right now she was not a target. She was the kind of girl in school who innocently flaunted her upper middle class wealth and one who liked things her way. She was a pretty nasty soccer player in her day as well, and if you crossed Kathleen you would get the look, and quite possibly ostracized from her community of friends. His guess was that she wore the pants in the family. She had all the makings of a bitch, but not a dead bitch. She would likely see another reunion.

    Returning to his seat, he grabbed the local social scene magazine off an adjacent table as the maitre d' was finishing up his cleaning job. He decided to order a drink from the same maitre d' trusting he would not be so clumsy the next time around. He would sit for another hour sipping his Ketel One on the rocks not seeing anyone else he knew, but that was okay, work started tomorrow night, this was a night for relaxation and maybe an expensive escort.

The Reunion Reaper

Chapter 30

The hallway to the hotel was dark, it was apparent that some of the lights were out. Andrew could make out a faint light at the end of the hall by a door, most likely for the stairs. He was worried about Stephanie and that she may have fallen asleep at the pool. As he approached the door to open it he found that it was stuck. He gave it a few shoves then suddenly it flew open. His momentum was so that he had great difficulty catching himself and when he looked down he realized there were no steps only darkness. He waved his arms in a reverse wheeling motion to try and catch his balance, but someone behind him whispered, *good night dingle berry* and then he felt a push and went headlong into the darkness.

Shooting up into a sitting position waking from his nap Andrew felt a sudden heavy thump in his heart, the room was dark and it was strange to him. He looked around to locate a clock, and much to his surprise it was 5:12 pm. The dream was too surreal, but what did it mean, he questioned. He wished that somehow he would have been able to turn around to see the face of the one who spoke to him. He had slept forty five minutes, nearly a night's worth for a man who could snap to with just twenty minutes of nap time. After his heart settled he made his way over to the window and pulled back the heavy curtains. He looked down at the pool and noticed that his wife was gone; only the die hard remained. She was most likely making her way up to the room so he decided to take a quick shower, but the dream would play on his mind. Was it one of those weird dreams that can't be explained or was it a metaphor for what was about to be?

Stephanie returned to the room but he made no mention of the dream. After each showered and dressed they headed out to dinner. Andrew liked this one particular restaurant that, oddly enough, was one of the few that was still owned by the same family. He took her over to a popular Boulevard often referred to as restaurant row. He wanted so bad to savor the taste of a prime rib steak at Magellan's. Their motto above the doorway when you entered said,

We travel the world for the best in tastes and recipes.

According to Andrew they always had the best prime rib, and he had a hankering for a juicy twelve ounce slab of prime. Magellan's Italian Steak House was a great spot, expensive, but well worth it and the service was always superb. It had been at least fifteen years since Andrew and Stephanie had been there. Ironically this was the same restaurant he and his family enjoyed on his high school graduation day. So far the trip was bittersweet, there were times he would always remember, great times, but yet he continued to allow those memories to cloud the new place the Palm Beaches had become.

The two of them were seated and ordered a bottle of imported Italian Pinot Noir. Andrew ordered the twelve ounce cut prime, which he would later regret for stuffing himself, and Stephanie opted for a butterfly petite filet.

"I always loved the smell of this place; this is what a real steakhouse smells like."

"Yes, it definitely has that smell."

"You know, the first time I came to this place it was my thirteenth birthday. My parents always allowed us to choose the place and I wanted prime rib so we came here." Andrew noted as he sipped his wine.

"That must have been a special time."

"It was."

"Listen, Andrew, I know you like to think about those days, but you really need to stop harboring this newfound hatred of the place."

"I don't hate the place. I just hate what they've done to it."

The Reunion Reaper

"But that's progress."

"I know, but you just don't understand."

The appetizer of escargot that Andrew ordered arrived and he attacked it with a voraciousness that would make a dog jealous. He offered one to Stephanie but the look on her face was clear enough.

"Man, smell that garlic they always smother this in garlic."

"Remind me to not kiss you tonight."

"Awe come on, it's good for you."

"That's okay."

As Andrew scooped up the last escargot Stephanie approached him about the reunion.

"So, you must be anxious to see everyone."

"In a way!"

"Promise me you'll enjoy the party and not turn it into some fishing expedition."

"I won't."

"Yeah, you say that, but I know you. You always have this investigative nature you go into when you start talking to people."

"I can't help it."

"But you're always suspicious of people; you should just enjoy the conversation for what it is."

"I just think it's so weird how three of my former classmates are now dead, supposedly by accident..." He grabbed a sip of wine. "Something inside tells me it's someone from my graduating class."

"What do you mean?"

"It's just weird. Come on, think about it. How can three people who just happen to graduate together suddenly show up dead? I mean, what are the odds of that?"

"It's just a freaky coincidence, that's all."

"Mmm, I doubt that."

"Must we refresh this, we're on vacation, please try to enjoy it."

"I will." Again he lied.

Somehow she had a tough time believing what he said, but would hold out for a glimmer of hope that when the two of them got to the reunion he would focus more on reacquainting than investigating.

Dinner was excellent, and Andrew breathed a heavy breath knowing that he should have opted for a smaller cut, but he was not about to leave any bites of prime rib on his plate. Andrew reluctantly refused dessert, paid the bill and the two of them headed back to the hotel. This was the first night in a long time when there were no kids to put to bed, or worry about someone walking in at an inappropriate time and they planned on taking advantage of it.

The night air was thick with humidity and rain clouds began to tumble and roll in from the southwest. A few scatterings of heat lightning briefly lit the night sky on the drive back and Andrew's brain was as scattered as the heat lightning.

When they returned to the room he went over to the computer and the folder that contained files on those classmates who would not be joining in the festivities. She looked at him cautiously, and was relieved to see him shut it off. This was not a night for working it was a night for him and his lady.

As each of them got ready for bed, they took their turn in the bathroom searching for a youthful freshness and energy. They were acting almost like honeymooners. Andrew cupped his hands to smell his breath even though he had just brushed his teeth, and a faint smell of garlic lingered. He was pissed at himself for ordering the escargot, but man they were awesome he thought as he belched a distinct garlic flavor, *surely she would understand.*

Stephanie slid into bed, "I had a great time tonight."

"Yeah, me too."

The Reunion Reaper

As they lay there in the darkness both of them sensed that this was their night. She was hoping that he was thinking about this moment and not the reunion. On the other hand he was hoping that she wasn't thinking that he was thinking about the reunion because he wasn't. This was all about her. It didn't take long for both of them to focus their concentration on the moment and each other, and a very comforting notion swept through the two of them. Thoughts of the reunion would have to wait.

Scott A. Reighard

Chapter 31

The drive from the hotel to the Breakers was about a fifteen minute drive, but to Andrew it was one of the longest drives he had had in a while. Driving east on Belvedere Road, when he reached Flagler Drive he took a left heading north. The road ran along the inter-coastal waterway for miles. The sometimes winding road provided a beautiful view of the inter-coastal waterway with Palm Beach sitting across one of three bridges. Several glass buildings of many shapes and sizes that periodically decorated Flagler Drive reflected the majesty that was the Palm Beaches. It was a short drive on Flagler to where he needed to take a right on Royal Poinciana Way.

As they crossed over the draw bridge and onto the perfectly manicured island of Palm Beach, the royal palm trees that lined Royal Poinciana Way stood like towers one after the other while the frond branches gently swayed to the evening breeze that often swept its way through the island. Despite the neatness and cleanness of his surroundings Andrew's thoughts were still a mess. He couldn't recall having been this confused in a long time.

After he and Stephanie reacquainted themselves last night he prayed for some guidance, but apparently God wasn't listening. In the meantime he would have to basically trust whatever instincts he had.

"This is so beautiful in the evening light." Stephanie offered up.

"I used to love the sunsets we'd catch behind our house as a kid, more colors than a rainbow it seemed."

"We saw quite a few of those ourselves didn't we?"

"Yeah, we sure did."

Funny how he leaped back to his childhood to recall something he and I use to enjoy as we sat on our patio

The Reunion Reaper

overlooking the park just beyond the fence line, she thought.

Stephanie flipped down the visor to look over her makeup. There was a moment of silence, as if Andrew was saying a prayer internally.

"You gonna be okay?" she asked while gently circling the lipstick that gave off a sheen of '*kiss me you fool.*

"What do you mean?"

"You know, whatever you've been thinking about so much lately."

"Once I see everyone I'm sure I'll forget whatever it was you asked me not to do."

"Well good." She placed her lipstick back in her small purse. "I am so excited."

Andrew was putting together profiles on each of the remaining classmates, but that was about as far as he could go. The rest now lay in the approach he would make from here on out. One thing was for certain, soon he would know if he was on the verge of something worth chasing, or relegated to just another dog on a bad scent, a dead scent.

He had a plan but when the wife vehemently requested that he be on his best behavior he acquiesced, but was he only trying to pacify her? A major problem for Andrew was that he didn't really maintain close contact with the majority of his classmates over the years and it had been several years since he had talked with any. A few years back he spoke with Joe Marketti right after 9/11 because he knew Joe worked for the FBI. Joe graduated the year before in 1982. And then there was Riley Bradshaw a classmate of his. Riley was a financial analyst living in New York. About once a year he'd get a phone call, but it had been several years since their last conversation. Some in the class however remained close friends while he was moving on to other things in his life, and in some cases wanting to get as far away from these people as possible. Andrew was never the Palm Beach type. He just never felt comfortable with the whole atmosphere and because of that he did not have many friends from his school. Of course not all his thoughts were jaded, he was pretty excited to see Greg Madison, Riley, Paul Thurman, Adam Levitz, and of course his first love Amy.

Stephanie's nerves were of a different type. She definitely wasn't one of these high society types and she was worried she might say or do something inappropriate that might embarrass her husband. She had spent most of her growing years as a Texas two stepper and her style of association was different than this crowd. It wasn't uncommon for a good Texas girl to get involved in a good old fashioned "ho"down, but Stephanie often tried to take the high road when it came to conflict.

She had privately rehearsed her introductions and chit chat topics where need be. Tonight would be all about smiles, dancing, drinking, eating and socializing. Her last hope as he pulled the car into the entrance to the Breakers was that Andrew wouldn't ruin it by pulling a Columbo act on the festivities.

The Reunion Reaper

Chapter 32

Andrew pulled the rental into the valet area of the Breakers. He was quickly greeted. As he exited the vehicle, and grabbed the ticket the valet was holding, he walked around to other side of the car to open the door for his wife. She was dressed in a beautiful, yet simple evening gown that complemented her husband's navy blue suit with a stylish white pinpoint shirt that was finished off with a blue and white broad striped silk tie. They both walked with a confidence as they stepped through the elegant Italian designed doors and into the lobby area of the hotel. In front of them was a sign that directed them to the Venetian Ball Room.

It was 6:30 and the social was about to get under way. The first thing Andrew wanted to do was get him and his wife a drink to help them relax. He also figured the two hundred dollar reunion fee was worth at least a few free drinks before dinner. He and the wife kept it simple, he liked imported beer, she preferred domestic. Andrew began to spot some familiar faces. It was a little strange at first for Stephanie because she didn't know anyone, but she was an affable person. Andrew was not worried about his wife having a boring time. She was the kind of lady who knew how to make the rounds at a party even if she didn't know anyone.

Upon entering the Venetian Ball Room Stephanie's eyes lit up. One of the first things you notice when you walk into the Venetian Ball Room is the enormous paneled windows that look out over the ocean. Adorned with scalloped drapes that add to the windows character, there are double doors on each end of the ball room that take you to the terrace overlook. Chandeliers that looked like tiered candelabrum subtly lit the room. The floor was Italian marble with shades of jade, shrimp and white to add to the overall ambience of a Mediterranean feel. If you had closed your eyes and suddenly appeared in this room you would have thought that you were in an Italian villa on the Amalfi Coast

In front of them were fifteen round style tables symmetrically place where each could accommodate eight patrons. They were ornately decorated with tablecloths that represented the school's colors of Mediterranean blue and white. There were numbers for each table, and in the acceptance package that was sent to each participating member who paid to attend, Andrew saw that his table number was thirteen. Standing in the doorway Andrew looked to his far right and spotted the dance floor, and to his left against the wall and next to the exits for the rest rooms was the bar area. He directed Stephanie toward the bar.

As he glanced around looking for familiar faces, he noticed that *Back in Time* by Huey Lewis and the News from the *Back to the Future* movie was streaming out of the speakers near the dance floor. The song was a subtle reminder to all in attendance of a time where complications were few. A time when there were no cell phones, no internet, and a thousand channels to further distract a nation with ADD it seemed.

The first person he picked out was Greg Madison; he was there with his wife Sherry. He had not seen Greg in nearly twenty years. During their high school days both had spent a lot of time running around Greg's neighborhood shooting hoops or kicking around the soccer ball. When Greg went to M.I.T. and Andrew went off to Roanoke College they lost touch, but by chance a year or so after each had graduated from college Andrew received an invitation in the mail to Greg and Sherry's wedding. The wedding was the last time he had seen his good friend and skilled soccer and lacrosse goalie. He introduced his wife to

The Reunion Reaper

them. The small talk was underway as classmates ranging from over a five year graduation period got reacquainted. Andrew, Stephanie, Greg and his wife stood just off to the left of the bar area as each of them sipped their drinks, observed others in the room, listened to each other and talked of life.

"Greg was the smartest SOB in our class, not to mention a pretty good goalie."

"Thanks, you were a helluva an athlete yourself." Greg turned to his wife. "Andrew played lacrosse for Roanoke College."

"Wow, my Greg was too busy diving through biochemistry at MIT."

Andrew tipped his beer to her with a smile. Stephanie just looked at Andrew's reaction.

"So, it's been a long time there eh Andrew?" Greg offered as he took a sip of his rum and coke.

"Sure has been, a lots happened since then."

"You got that right. So, I hear you're a cop in Virginia now."

"Yep, about ten years now."

"Well, actually Andrew's been involved with law enforcement for about twenty years really. He's been with the Roanoke County Police Department for ten."

"Wow," Greg grabbed his wife's hand, "yeah, we're living in Atlanta these days."

"Greg works for the CDC, boasted Sherry."

"I went to the University of Georgia." Stephanie said.

"No kidding..."

As the three of them were chit chatting about Atlanta, Andrew glanced across the room to the entrance area and spotted a person who would make him nervous above all others, Amy McMahon. *This would be a good excuse to get away from Sherry and all her bragging.* Greg was most likely hating all the attention anyway. *Should I introduce Stephanie now, or will that look really contrived on my part?* He glanced over Greg's shoulder as he watched her walk. Stephanie and Sherry were too busy chatting it up for her to see her husband's boyish gawk at an old flame. And to make matters worse, Amy looked stunning dressed in a floral brocade dress that complemented the St. Tropez tan. Her hair was shorter but still dark. *Just as I had imagined,* he thought, *or did I just say that out loud?*

Amy was a bit heavier but was still beautifully proportioned. She looked like one of Clairol's cover girls. There was no doubt that he loved his wife dearly, but he couldn't prevent the resurgent flow of certain emotions that re-emerge when someone sees an old love for which there was no real explanation behind the break up. He tried to stay in the conversation with Greg but he was fumbling words like a politician caught without a teleprompter. When he finally gathered himself he was stunned to see that his wife still had not noticed his almost juvenile like stare at a former lover. He was now questioning whether he wanted to introduce his wife to her. He should be proud to introduce his wife to Amy; she was a beautiful fantastic woman who looked younger than her forty years.

He excused him and his wife from Greg and Sherry hoping to talk with them later. As he guided his wife across the room, he heard the unmistakable voice of Adam Levitz. He turned and sure enough it looked as though Adam was trying to hustle three ladies at once. A huge grin on Andrew's face captured the moment of instant recollection of when he, Adam, and Riley were trying to hustle three young ladies back in the day. Adam was always the cut up, joking his way into a girl's arms; it didn't hurt that the guy was from a pretty well off family as well. Being born in the right place and into the right family has its privileges, not to mention its influence. The six foot plus thin, well dressed Adam spotted Andrew.

The Reunion Reaper

When Adam spotted Andrew he stopped mid-sentence, and without missing a beat, "Ladies this man approaching you now is notorious, no, make that famous. He is the only guy I ever knew who, while surfing one day, jumped off his board and onto the back of a lemon shark that was swimming by."

The three women reacted with looks of shock, dismay, almost disbelief. Spotting yet another example of Adam's storytelling ability Andrew did not bother to object to the fabrication. The actual story was in part true, but Adam confused the jumping off part. Yes, Riley, Mark Lambert and Andrew were surfing one day, but Andrew jumped off his surfboard near the shore and gave the appearance of running on water as he headed to shore. Andrew fired back with a fabrication of his own.

"I would like to say that was brave of me, but did you know that Adam took a bullet for me?"

Again, there was utter shock and wide eyes from the ladies in attendance, even Stephanie at this point because she had no idea.

"That's right; maybe he'll show you his wound later on when it's more appropriate. It would be pretty embarrassing right Adam?"

Even Adam couldn't help but stare in wonder at Andrew's comments. Oh sure, he knew he had a scar, that if you looked closely enough, it gave the appearance of a bullet wound, but Adam knew full well the scar was from his poor attempt to jump a chain link fence, and his rear didn't quite clear it, and the top links took a little of his right cheek. It was a nice hole. For five minutes he jumped around like some hippie on LSD listening to Led Zeppelin. Everyone who was at the scene fell to the ground from laughter. Adam was a little heavier in those days, and when everyone had cleared the fence he feigned the suggestion of going to the very end of the fence to go through the gate.

Although he has the evidence to prove his courage, he also has it to endorse stupidity.

"So what happened?" One of the ladies of whom Andrew could not recall, asked him to tell the story.

"Oh I better, not Adam remembers it so much better than I do. I fell to the ground unconscious right after I heard Adam scream in pain." Andrew smiled at Adam.

Andrew then introduced Stephanie, to which Adam kissed her hand. The five of them stood around and chatted about the old days a bit, and the life they live today. Adam was an attorney who relocated to Tennessee because he wanted to be closer to Elvis he said. The other three ladies in attendance were brief attendees of Palm Beach Prep after Andrew and the rest had graduated. There was so much they didn't know or understand about the place. If the place were still there surely ghosts would be in residence, and oth the stories they would tell.

The night time festivities were getting under way. There were a lot of people to see and talk to, and for a brief moment Andrew wasn't even thinking about his other reason for being there. Right now he was having too much fun reminiscing, catching up with old friends, and genuinely having a great time. He patted Adam on the shoulder and with a smile cracked, "The multi-talented Adam Levitz, good to see you my friend."

"Actually, I am looking to change my name to something more dangerous." Adam grinned like the Cat in the Hat, and as Andrew walked away he said. "Beautiful wife Andrew, but then again I find that to no one's surprise."
Since Stephanie wasn't looking, Adam raised his eyebrow and tilted his head toward where Amy was seated. Andrew understood and mouthed, "I know," as he rolled his eyes.

"Talk to you later, right?"

"Most definitely."

The Reunion Reaper

Chapter 33

After shaking more hands and exchanging hugs than a politician on the campaign trail, Andrew was finally able to make his way over toward Amy's table, but on his way over to talk with Amy yet another familiar voice called out to him, Jeffrey Lewis. *Jesus, this is killing me, all I want to do is introduce my wife.* He hadn't seen Jeffrey in about seventeen or eighteen years. The last time he saw him Jeffrey was drunk at a local West Palm Beach night club, and he distinctly remembered that Jeffrey had his arm wrapped around a woman who was either a bouncer or a biker.

"Andy Keane, well I'll be. How goes the world my man?"

Jeffrey skated over to them like a used car salesman. The two shook hands and Jeffrey was quick to notice Stephanie, "I would say the world is obviously treating Andy Keane pretty well with a woman like this at his side."

Jeffrey was never shy, and so he grabbed her left hand and kissed it and imitating Pepe Lepeux said, "Mon cherie." Everyone got a good laugh as Andrew formally introduced her to Jeffrey.

He remembered that Jeffrey considered himself to be one of the school playboys. He loved to party and was not shy about his love for women and carpe diem. Everyone seemed to like Jeffrey. He was a lovable guy who just enjoyed life and living it to the fullest. So far it looked like Jeffrey's world was pretty good because he was still alive and he was a fairly wealthy guy; an inheritance as an only child, not to mention the fact he got in on the ground floor of the internet, will do that for someone.

"How did you hook this one Andy boy?"

Andrew hated being called Andy, but Jeffrey basically refused to abide by normal sets of rules, or Andrew's request at school, and after battling it for a few years he decided to give up the notion that Jeffrey would ever call him Andrew.

"With a fifty pound test and a lure the size of your wine glass there."

"Ha ha ha, good one my man, no seriously how did you get her down the aisle?"

"Well, to be honest with you it took incredible patience and lots of money."

Stephanie elbowed him in the side.

"Actually he got me incredibly drunk and the next thing I knew we were in a church confessing our love for one another." Stephanie chimed in.

Jeffrey raised his eyebrows at her comment, "And she's funny too." Jeffrey moved in close to Stephanie and suddenly she felt a little uncomfortable by his proximity. "So, what would it take for you to run off with me?"

"How's ten million?"

"I thought you were priceless?" Andrew said.

Everyone seemed to enjoy the light hearted banter and Stephanie's temporary tension went away.

"So what are you up to these days?" Jeffrey asked.

"I'm a police detective in Roanoke, Virginia."

"No kidding. How long you been at that?"

"About ten years."

"Wow, so you get a lot of action up your way?"

"Not exactly, but it's all good."

"Yeah, I hear ya." Jeffrey glanced over Andrew's shoulder. He was looking at someone in particular as he continued, "So, you being a cop and all, what do you think of Judy, and Brandon, and who was the other?"

"Tucker," Andrew responded.

"Yeah, Tucker."

The Reunion Reaper

"It's tragic." Stephanie grabbed Andrew's arm. Her indicator for not now, Andrew understood the gesture.

"They'll be missed."

"Yeah, I really liked them, we had some great times. Speaking of which," Jeffrey started to say something but was interrupted by Andrew.

"I'm sorry Jeffrey, but it's almost dinner and we haven't been to our table yet.

"Oh yeah, it's cool."

"We'll talk later."

"Sure."

Andrew decided that before they sit down they should approach Amy and get this nerve racking situation over. Jeffrey had his eye on someone else and sauntered over to her, only to receive a cold reception despite his compliments and adulations. The former Sharon Bloom was not thrilled to see Jeffrey Lewis. *Man, some people never forget the past,* he muttered as he walked over to his table.

Andrew took Stephanie over to meet Amy. Since this was not the usual class reunion it was not unusual to have people from differing graduating classes at the same table, and at Amy's table the classes 1983 through 1987 were represented. It never seemed to bother anyone as most of the people knew everyone anyway. Amy was alone. She had no escort it seemed. She smiled at him as they approached; she stood to shake Stephanie's hand and to give Andrew a hug.

"Amy, I'd like you to meet my wife, this is Stephanie, Stephanie this is Amy," he hesitated to say her last name because he wasn't sure she was married, but a quick glance down at the table name tag, "McMahon."

Both women exchanged cordials as Andrew took a large swig of his beer.

"I see you kept your last name."

"Well, when the divorce was final I thought I would change it back to my maiden name."

"Wow, sorry to hear about the divorce, any children?" Andrew inquired.

"Two boys, thirteen and ten, their names are Tyler and Alex; they're staying with their father until I return." She said as she glanced up at Stephanie.

"So you maintain a good relationship with your ex?" Stephanie glanced over at her husband, "Honey, I don't think Amy cares to get all personal with us here. I'm sorry Andrew can appear overbearing sometimes."

"Well I guess some things never change." She grabbed her wine glass and took a sip. "I don't mind the questions, I'm sure I'll hear worse tonight. Anyhow, to answer your question, Todd and I get along pretty well, we just couldn't live together you know."

"Tell me about it," Stephanie replied, at which time Andrew gave her the glance. "Oh just kidding honey, just making sure you were paying attention to **me**." Stephanie easily recognized Amy's mature and beautiful features, not to mention that womanly instinct.

"Well listen Amy, it was great seeing you, maybe we'll get a chance to talk before the night's out." said Andrew.

"That would be great," she said as she took another sip of wine.

Andrew proceeded to gulp down his beer glad that this encounter between the former and the current was over.

Amy watched as the two of them walked over to their assigned table. She watched as he pulled out a chair for his wife and then took off his suit coat and placed it on the back of his chair. *Still looking good,* she thought. She noticed his well maintained shape through his button down shirt. Social hour was coming to a close and Mrs. Steinbach from the Palm Beach Historical Society was approaching the podium. She directed everyone to their table, spoke a few words about the evening's events, and then asked

The Reunion Reaper

everyone to look on their table at the menu of choices available to them. This was Palm Beach and this was the Breakers Hotel with over one hundred years of experience, it was not about to disappoint.

Scott A. Reighard

Chapter 34

As the dinner portion of the evening got underway and everyone was at their designated tables the guest's chatted away and ordered dinner. The old days were the focus of conversation as well as current life. Easy listening music of the seventies and eighty's bounced out of the speakers as dinner arrived. Andrew was savoring his Steak au Poivre while Stephanie opted for the grilled swordfish with the mango salsa.

They were seated with the former Kathleen Walker and her husband Brad Johnson, Aida, from the class of 1984 and her husband Philip Truman and lastly there was Lydia Schwartz from the class of 1985. She explained to everyone that she was recently divorced and was attempting to take her husband Murray to the cleaners. She used the metaphor of hoping to have him starched and pressed; most everyone was wondering why she even bothered showing up, but then Stephanie figured she might be looking for the next schlep to walk her down the aisle.

The conversation at dinner was kept to a minimum. As all the guests were enjoying their savory meals the music switched over to light jazz. A slide show began to flash pictures like someone's screen saver of the school years 1982-1983 through 1987-1988 on a large screen that dropped down from a ceiling fixture. You could hear spotty laughter and occasional comments as the pictures flashed across the screen. Although Andrew was in the celebrating mode earlier, a little food and downtime provided him with the opportunity to refocus his energy on a most important situation. He was busy gazing around the room in between bites. He was hoping the killer was like a novice poker player who couldn't hide a flush hand. But then again, he pondered, that wouldn't be the case, this was Palm Beach,

The Reunion Reaper

champions of hidden agendas and false faces. There was considerable silence when pictures of Judy Barnett, Brandon Henniker and Tucker Harrison flashed near the end of the presentation. The pictures cast a pall on the place. As the pictures appeared and disappeared Andrew would have given just about anything to be a mind reader. Was there someone in the very same room who was relishing the photos as badges of honor? Was the killer even here he suggested.

At a time when everyone was lamenting the deaths of these individuals there was one who was looking on with pride. Jeffrey looked at the pictures and then looked around the room to watch the reactions of those in attendance. He wished he could have posted the pictures of the Arizona businessman and the ex girlfriend hooker just to show how good he was, but a certain brand of humility was the order of the day, besides it would have looked awkward. So he just glared at the photos just as the others yet never changing the countenance on his face. He did his best to look disconsolate, but underneath it all he was cheering the results. When the pictures disappeared there was still some silence, but within a few seconds the clanging of silverware against a dish could be heard. Most everyone was quiet not saying anything to each other out of respect for the dead.

Jeffrey attempted to break the silence at his table hoping to strike up a conversation about the terrible nature of how the three died, but everyone else at the table felt a little uncomfortable about talking about it, so he just went back to eating his dinner. It would take more mingling, but he did not want to arouse any suspicions, so he would appear aloof seeing if someone would bring it up. Someone would, Andrew Keane.

Scott A. Reighard

Chapter 35

After dinner Andrew grabbed his wife's hand and led her over to the dance floor. The DJ was slipping on Al Green's love song, *you ought to be with me.* They embraced one another on the dance floor as the smooth soul song swooned from the speakers. He could smell the sweet flowery scent of her perfume. She lightly rubbed his shoulders. They looked one another in the eye. Each seemed to be harkening back to their dating days. The two of them smiled and kissed. Andrew tightened his embrace with a strong yet loving tug. It had been a while since they danced; life, jobs, and kids often stood in the way of evenings that consisted of dancing, socializing with friends, or when they lived in Florida, drives to the beach at night listening to memorable songs.

"I'm having a great time," she said looking him in the eyes.

"Yeah, me too."

"Yeah?" She still wasn't sure about his desire to be there.

"Absolutely. I didn't realize how many friends and great times I had with this bunch."

"Well, I am glad that you are happy." She leaned in and kissed her husband.

On this evening they had the opportunity to recapture some of that early love they had several years ago as another song gently rolled out of the speakers and over the dimly lit dance floor. While breathing the words of Bread's *Baby I'm a Want You* into Stephanie's ear, Andrew's thoughts drifted.

As Andrew held his wife closely, he was trying not to think about the three dead classmates but then they had to show the slides of them and it all came rushing back in. Although he was glad to see everyone there was still a task

The Reunion Reaper

at hand. He whispered in her ear, she giggled. After several songs, dancing, whispers in the ear, and kisses it was time to mingle and reacquaint.

"Hey you two, goin' somewhere?" asked a tipsy Riley Bradshaw.

"No, just going to get our drinks and mingle," responded Andrew.

"Well I hope you were coming to see me next ole pal."

"Of course," he turned to Stephanie, "Honey would you be so kind as to grab my drink for me?"

As she walked back to their table she looked over at Lydia who was eyeing a few other divorcees. Stephanie couldn't help but chuckle when Lydia donned one of those come hither looks at someone who glanced her way but quickly shifted in his chair away from her direction. With beer bottle in hand, Stephanie walked over to where Andrew and a few others were seated and handed it to him.

"Honey, this is Paul Thurman, you already met Greg and Riley," receiving his drink, "Would you like to sit with us?"

"Sorry too much testosterone for me, I think I'll go find some ladies who'd be willing to reveal y'alls dirty little secrets."

A few of the men laughed at her comment. They liked her style, sassy, beautiful and smart. Stephanie left the men to grunt and squeal.

"Damn Andrew how did you manage to land that bird, she looks like an older Jenny McCarthy?" questioned Riley. Andrew blushed. "I mean that in a good way."

"I was thinking that myself, but I couldn't remember her name," responded Paul.

"I gotcha, but why does everyone think my wife is some sort of animal tonight?" he asked.

"They're all animals it just depends on their classification," Paul belted out.

"I'm a lucky guy what can I say?" Andrew responded.

Scott A. Reighard

"He's whipped I can see it in his eyes," said Greg as he took a large gulp of his draft beer.

"Look who married the first girl he fell in love with or had," retorted Andrew.

The whole table exploded in laughter.

"She's a good woman my Sherry." Greg said as he glanced around to find her.

The music faded into the background as the table of men discussed memories of school, the girls they all dated and the challenges of today's society. Each shared their current occupations, families, kids, and some talked of their divorce. Suddenly there was a noticeable shift in the style of music that interrupted this testosterone filled go around.

The D.J. switched over to disco. Some of the wives anxiously came in search of their husbands as Cheap Trick proclaimed *I want you to want me.* Andrew sought out Stephanie. They really enjoyed dancing. It was one of the things that attracted her to him. They were boogying down as K.C. and the Sunshine Band asked everyone *to shake, shake, shake.* There was a whole lot of shaking going on as the throng of dancers increased. There was barely an open spot on the dance floor. The disco reminiscing was in full swing. The atmosphere was hyped and happy. Over the course of the next thirty minutes Donna Summer, ABBA and the Bee Gees shook the elegant ballroom. The segment was closed out by the Village People as they encouraged young men to go to the YMCA. With sweat beginning to bead on most foreheads and with moistness beginning to form in the formal suits or dinner dresses of those boogying down, it was time to replenish lost fluids.

Several of the guys reclaimed their pre-disco table and a few others decided to join the now growing table of men, Dominic Bevacqua, Jeffrey Lewis and Adam Levitz grabbed a chair and the chatting continued. Adam and Jeffrey were tossing cut ups back and forth, just like the old days. It was not a surprise to hear two Jews calling each

The Reunion Reaper

other out with ethnic jabs; something lost on a society so obsessed with political correctness. But it was all in fun as each of them laughed at each other's comments. But one subject stopped the laughter and a serious tone replaced the levity of friendly insults. Andrew, although he tried, just couldn't do it. He had to bring up the accidents. Everyone was quiet for a moment then Adam spoke up, "Way to go Keane, you could ruin good sex with your sudden analytics."

Paul quickly followed, "Accidents my ass, somebody knocked these people off. I mean think about it, three of our classmates in less than a year? Come on, no way, if that's coincidence then the tides must be changin' or something."

"I agree," Jeffrey chimed in, "they're all too convenient, but who would do this?"

"You know who's missing tonight?" questioned Riley, "Lambert, Wyatt and Morris."

"Well, Hank is living in Washington, so he couldn't make it," chimed Dominic.

"Do you still talk to him? I haven't talked to…well, hardly any of you in twenty plus years," responded Andrew.

"We talk every once in a while. He's happy, love's his fly fishing."

"I heard that," injected Adam. "Hey Dominic, you remember all those times on your boat? Man, those were some good days."

"Yeah, they sure were. I still get out as much as I can. In fact, if any of you get up Orlando way, you're welcome to go out and carve the lake with me."

The conversation began to drift away from the accidents, but Andrew didn't want to sound like Hawai'i Five-O Dan-o, so he hoped someone would re-engage.

"I'll definitely look you up Dominic. Anyhow, seriously do you think Lambert and Morris are capable of something like this? I mean, these look to be pretty clever murders. And those two weren't exactly subtle," asked Jeffrey.

Thank you Jeffrey, thought Andrew.

"It's possible; everyone knows Lambert was a crazy bastard." Paul threw out as he grabbed his drink.

"And Morris was just one messed up dude," added Greg.

"He hated all of us by the time he graduated," Paul claimed, then looking over at Jeffrey, "You weren't exactly cozy with everyone either."

Jeffrey quickly replied, "Hey, what's in the past is in the past. I spent at least four years with most of you guys, why, you're all like brothers to me." *You prick.* Jeffrey smiled then tipped his drink to Paul.

Although engrossed in the conversation, there was someone Andrew occasionally glanced at, Amy. She was chatting it up with a few people at her table. Andrew wondered whether he should be feeling guilty about having the only two women he truly loved in the same room. He decided to finally say something, "but don't you think the killer, if there is a killer, would want to be here tonight?"

"I don't know," said Riley, "maybe he just knows who or what he wants."

Andrew couldn't help but be curious at the odd statement.
Adam responded, "You people, I'll tell you what, I'm packin' heat these days and if anyone gets around me and looks any kind of suspicious, BANG."

"Whoa, take it easy there Dirty Harry." Greg said as he threw both hands up like a stopping gesture.

"I was just kidding, but I do pack heat, I'm a lawyer, the law sure as hell isn't going to protect me," said a smiling Adam. "By the way," as he reached into his pocket, "here is my card." He proceeded to hand everyone in attendance his business card.

"Hey, who's ready for another round?" asked Riley, sensing a slight tension beginning to build.

The Reunion Reaper

As Riley made the run to the bar to grab beer for everyone the rest of them sat there absorbing what Riley had just spewed out. When Riley returned the conversation had shifted, at the request of Greg. They went back to discussing their victories on the field as well as off. Andrew's focus drifted off so much he was beginning to think he was ADD.

To Andrew one thing was certain there was a killer on the loose and by conversation's end everyone at the table had injected his own theory. One other thing that couldn't escape adding to Andrew's list was the fact that Mark Lambert's name kept popping up, along with Brian Morris. Both of whom enjoyed their moments in the spotlight. Whether it was Brian, who enjoyed popping his .22 caliber pistol at fish from his boat, or Mark's desire to make sure everyone could see what he was doing. Andrew wasn't a dummy, he knew that sometimes the most likely person was not always the person, but you never rule anyone out. One other problem that developed for Andrew as the evening progressed, he had more questions than before he arrived.

Chapter 36

For almost an hour Andrew sat and listened, looking for something, anything really. He began to think he was looking obvious so he excused himself and meandered his way over to the bar. He ordered a Harp beer and as he took a sip a long forgotten classmate bumped her hip into his.

"Hey there!"

Andrew looked surprised, but he was unsure as to who he was looking at, "Hey there, how's it going?"

She looked at him and then jokingly said, "Forgot your secret pal?"

Andrew looked at her confused.

"Andrea, Andrea Pruitt."

He seemed relieved, "Oh wow, you have changed."

"Well I was a freshman when you graduated, I don't blame you for not recognizing me."

"It's just been so long you know?"

"Yeah, I understand…So wow, a cop huh?"

Andrew didn't want to be rude, "Actually I'm a detective now."

"Sorry, well congratulations."

She ordered a rum and coke.

"How did you know I was a cop, err, I mean, a detective?"

"Oh, I stay in touch with some of the alumni and I heard that."

"You keep in touch with old classmates?"

"Yeah, I was always a busy body, you know, wanting to know what everyone was up to. I was the one who worked with the historical society to put this together."

"Oh that's cool, appreciate you doing this."

The Reunion Reaper

"I had a lot of fun, besides, I've been thinking about putting together a Facebook site in order for everyone to join in and stay in touch."
"Sounds like a great idea!"
"Well, I haven't done it yet, but I was hoping to get everyone's contact here and then spread the word."
"Well I think that is a great idea."
She took a sip through her thin red straw.
"Andrew, I was wondering, what do you think of the whole Tucker, Judy and Brandon deal?"
He took a quick look around them.
"Well, I'm not sure, but I must say that I am a bit bothered by the whole situation."
"Me too! I am worried there will be more."
"What makes you think that?"
"I don't know, call it women's intuition. Besides, I talked with Judy pretty regular and she never gave me any indication she was back on the snow blow."
"Well, people can be pretty deceptive."
"Yeah, but we met for lunches sometimes and I would know if someone was using, and I can say she wasn't using."
"When was the last time you saw her?"
"About a month before she died."
"Look Andrea, I would love to talk to you more about this, but this probably isn't the place. Why don't you give me your number and I'll call you when I get back to Roanoke."
"Okay, that's cool."
"But I can't make any promises though. Legally I shouldn't be doing what I am doing."
"Oh, I got it. I promise I won't tell anyone."
She wrote down her number on a napkin. Andrew looked around them and figured no one was within ear shot to hear their conversation. As he walked back over to the table of friends, he tried to act as if he never talked to Andrea Pruitt.

Chapter 37

After what appeared to be nearly an hour the men figured that if they didn't find their ladies, those who had dates that is, knew they'd be sleeping alone tonight, so they scattered. The only two to remain behind were Jeffrey and Riley, each were single; they would hit the bar.

Andrew went searching for Stephanie and eventually found her outside the ballroom standing out on the ocean terrace that overlooked the ocean. She was standing alone against the waist high stone wall staring out at the ocean. He snuck up behind her and whispered in her ear, apologizing for being away from her so long.

The ocean reflected calmness yet a slight breeze brushed them with a cool stroke. The salty smell of a low tide in the light breeze permeated their senses. She wasn't angry with him but confessed that some of the people in attendance were really snobs or bitches. She felt as though many looked at her in disapproval. Andrew explained that was often the attitude of those who either have money, or have parents who have money. It was natural for them to feel superior and look down on people. He explained that these society types either, know it all, have it all, or want it all. Since he was from the other side of the inter-coastal he was looked down upon by many at the school, and that's why he really didn't care too much to remain friends with many of these people after graduation. He attended the school in order to get a good education and play sports, period, not make life long friends. After sharing a few more horror stories from his past they just seemed to stare out at the ocean relishing a moment they hadn't had in a while.

The cool ocean breeze continued stroking itself against them like an invisible painter's brush. She had a slight chill and so he wrapped his arms around her, and kissed her neck

The Reunion Reaper

as they stared out at an ocean cooperating with their moment, calm shimmering and peaceful.

"It's so beautiful isn't it?" she offered.

"Yes, it is," *yes it is.*

After a while they decided they should return to the party, although they didn't mind the peaceful one on one time. Just then a few of the guests came tumbling out to the terrace laughing as they juggled drinks in their hands and singing *I ran so far away, I couldn't get away* by the Flock of Seagulls. Surprisingly they were in tune. Inside the music had returned to the wild songs of disco, only this time the floor appeared to be filled with dancing idiots, most of them adversely influenced by liquid sensations. There were at least three guys imitating the John Travolta dance move from *Saturday Night Fever.* As Andrew strutted mockingly onto the dance floor with his wife she elbowed him at his attempt to imitate with the others.

The evening was approaching a time when many had to summon a second wind. The reunion was in full blown party mode. After several dances and a hideous attempt at the *Electric Slide,* Andrew excused himself and told his wife that he was going to the bathroom and then to the bar for another drink. Stephanie returned to the table and toweled off the beads of sweat. She looked around and saw Lydia schmoozing up to a guy who hopefully had money because he sure didn't have looks; Stephanie giggled at her fascination with Lydia.

Several minutes had gone by and Andrew had not returned to the table. Again, more and more time slipped away and so she went in search of her husband. It was difficult to locate him in a sea of people on the dance floor or near the bar, so she tried looking outside, but he wasn't there. Suddenly she had the look of worry on her face. She spotted Sherry, Greg's wife and asked her if she had seen Andrew, she hadn't. She decided to return to the table to see if he had returned.

Outside the ballroom area where the bathrooms were located, Andrew ran into Amy. He lost track of time as their conversation continued.

"So, are you happy?" Andrew asked Amy. *Are you happy, what kind of question is that?*

"As happy as can be expected I guess. I got two great boys and a good job, so yeah I'm happy." She smiled at him as they looked each other in the eye.

"Yeah, kids are great, my three mean the world to me..." *Searching, searching, what do I say?* "Anyhow, you really look great."

"You too." *Really good in fact.* Amy couldn't help but think.

Andrew had completely forgotten about Stephanie sitting there all by herself. It was quiet in the hall as they continued their conversation, but it was soon broken up when Jeffrey rounded the corner and spotted them.

"Hey Andy boy, how's it goin'?" Jeffrey slapped him on the shoulder, "Amy."

Both of them acknowledged him. "Gotta piss man, talk to you later."

"Jeffrey and his subtlety," Andrew said.

She giggled, "Yeah, exactly."

"You always had a great laugh you know that?"

"So wow, a cop huh?" She blurted in order to avert the compliment Andrew just made. *He's had too much to drink, focus girl. Besides, he's married.*

"Yep," He lifted his pants and snarled his face imitating Barney Fife, "so don't go gettin' frisky with me or I'm gonna have to arrest you."

"I always knew you'd be successful."

"Well I don't know about that."

"I'm sure you're a great father and husband as well."

He shrugged his shoulders with humility, "I try."

There was a brief silence.

The Reunion Reaper

"Listen, I'm really sorry about the whole break up thing, I was a real ass wipe about that." Andrew took a step closer to her. They were less than a foot apart.
Her shoulders slumped, "it's okay." He put his hands on her shoulders.
"No it's not, I did you wrong. I should have been more of a man about it."
"It was a nice letter though, very thoughtful."
"You don't have to say that. Anyhow, I was wrong and I'm sorry. I walked away from something that didn't need or deserved walking away from.
There was a slight pause.
"Or something like that."
"Hey, we both knew it probably wasn't going to last."
"If I've learned anything from that experience it's that I vowed to never walk away from anything again."
"Look, we were young, naïve, whatever else goes with being young. I don't hold anything against you Andrew."
He put his head down, "You were always so good at understanding."

He pulled back before he did something that was creeping into his mind. She dug into her purse for a business card.
"If you ever want to talk about anything... I mean, I think we can still be friends." She said, handing him the card.
"Absolutely, no harm no foul I always say."
Andrew grabbed the card, placed it in his pocket and embraced her with an affectionate hug, then kissed Amy on the cheek. What the two of them did not know was that someone was listening in on their conversation. Jeffrey smiled broadly as he opened the bathroom door and re-emerged. When he came out of the bathroom he saw that someone else was observing them.
"Uh oh, the missus," Jeffrey whispered to Andrew then pointed down the way.

Scott A. Reighard

Standing at the edge of the hallway with a perturbed look was Stephanie. She had seen her husband affectionately hugging then kissing another woman.

The Reunion Reaper

Chapter 38

Despite Andrew's Irish genes he always felt he never had the luck of the Irish. What was an innocent goodbye hug was seen as a deceptive act went into damage control mode with the wife and quickly.

"I am so sorry Andrew," said Amy.

Quickly he turned back to her, "It's not your fault this was all innocent. She'll understand once I explain everything to her."

Jeffrey was standing behind them and pumped his fist with encouragement, "Good luck Andy boy." *You're gonna need it.*

Andrew dashed up the hallway in search of his wife. Jeffrey took the opportunity of being alone with Amy to toss her a come on line but she was not in the mood for his antics right now. She walked away from him. Jeffrey seemed to take it all in stride.

"What?" he threw both hands out at his side, "two single people a party, let's get it on girl." He smiled then thought to himself, *you and Andrew, it should have been you and me.*

Andrew re-entered the ballroom and weaved his way around tables and people before finally catching up to his disgruntled wife. She had gone back to the table. At this point in the reunion many of the patrons had consumed several alcoholic beverages, which most likely meant that emotions seemed more the order than reasoned logic. Andrew and Stephanie had their share of alcohol as well. He did his best to explain the embrace, but was he ready to tell her the truth, the whole truth, so help him God?

"I'm ready to go if you don't mind." She demanded.

"Come on Steph it was an innocent embrace that's all."

"Sure, down a darkened hallway away from everyone."

"Oh my God you gotta be kidding me."

"Do you know how embarrassing that is for a woman, not to mention a wife no less?"

"I understand you're hurt, but you have to believe me, you are the only one in my life, it was a goodbye hug and nothing more. Why would I be that obvious at a party of old friends and basically in front of my wife?"

"Isn't that what they teach at the academy be most suspicious of those right under your nose? I guess I wouldn't make a very good cop."

Andrew grabbed a chair for her to sit in. He then grabbed one for himself. "Honey, it meant nothing. Okay I saw her." *Be careful.* "It was nothing okay? Please, don't let this ruin a great night."

God you are such an ass sometimes. "She's the only reason you came isn't it, oh and your murder theory of course. You had no interest seeing these people other than your suspicions of them."

"I think you're being irrational Stephanie. Come on, you know me better than that."

"Do I? Anymore secrets there lover boy?"

There was a brief silence as Andrew looked around the room to see if anyone saw them. The only person to notice was sitting at the same table, Lydia. She simply shook her head in a motion of disapproval and pursed her lips to Andrew. He attempted a sheepish smile.

"You know what you're right, let's go before this turns into one of those moments for us. I am not going to try and convince you of something you can't be convinced of changing. You think I'm scum and right now maybe so, but if you think that I came all this way just to hug Amy McMahon, or to rekindle some long ago relationship from twenty some years ago you're out of your mind. As far as the other stuff, definitely, I'll take whatever I can get at this point." He stood up. "The way I see it, you can, either walk

The Reunion Reaper

around with me and say our goodbyes, or I can do it myself."

Her arms were folded as she was half turned away from him.

"You know what, I've changed my mind, we should stay, let's test your theory." She waved her hands at him with a shooing motion, "Go ahead Kojak, go to work."

Andrew was pissed. He shook his head and leaned in.

"Fine, sit here and wallow in your conspiracies, I'm gonna do what I need to do."

She readjusted in the chair as he walked away and then turned around at the table to grab her beer. "Asshole!"

"They're a real prize ain't they girl?" Lydia offered from across the table.

Perhaps it was good they separate right now at the party. Although they were pretty good communicators something not being communicated was the shadow stress each of them carried on this evening. She of the outcast and not knowing people, and he of the dead classmates and search for a killer, not to mention his first love showing up and looking very good.

Andrew felt bad about leaving his wife sitting there, but somehow he felt she would manage, as long as she didn't do some stupid spiteful thing just to strike back at him. *She's had way too much to drink.*

As he drifted across the ballroom seeking out friends he began to laugh when he noticed the song playing over the speakers. It was, *Torn Between Two Lovers by Mary MacGregor. Ah the luck of the Irish,* he chuckled to himself.

He stumbled onto a handful of guys Riley, Sam, Jeffrey, and Paul. Jeffrey pointed at him as he approached, "Oh man that must have been awkward."

"What?" asked Paul.

"Ole Andy boy here was puttin' the love lock on Amy when the wife spotted them."

"It wasn't a love lock you schmuck I was just basically hugging her goodbye."

All the guys almost in tandem, "Right!"

"Hey you've seen and met my wife, at least two of you pecker-heads tried to hit on her as I recall."

"Relax, we're just messin' with ya," Sam offered.

"Well, it's just not a good time to joke about this all right."

"Okay, okay," Jeffrey said as he patted Andrew on the shoulder. "So, as we were saying…"

For the next hour Andrew talked with his friends and bounced around the room like a kid on an Easter egg hunt. He was seeking anybody and everybody. He was asking stupid innocent questions trying to bait people into talking about private matters, or to give off any indicators of suspicion, and he wasn't ruling anybody out. Occasionally he would look around for his wife, and sometimes he would see her laughing it up with someone, or talking with another. She was good he thought. He was damn proud to have a woman like her indeed, despite her assumption. He also saw Amy engaged in conversation with a graduate from 1985.

After the talking dissipated Andrew began to wander around in search of his wife. It was getting late. He had talked with so many on this night and tried to retain all that he could. He had not had as much to drink as he led on, and this enabled him to retain more information. As he stood near the dance floor he watched in the distance as Riley asked Amy to dance. Suddenly a hard hand fell on his shoulder. It was Jeffrey.

"Hey, sorry about that back there. I guess I got a little too wound up."

"It's okay, you can't help yourself sometimes."

"You're right, so how goes the night my old friend?"

Andrew had no idea that just one foot away from him was the killer. He smiled at Andrew awaiting his response.

The Reunion Reaper

"Pretty good. It's been really good seeing everyone. Well, except for Judy, Brandon and Tucker."
Jeffrey put his head down, "I hear ya, just a damn tragedy man... Hey, we could use another beer. Jeffrey grabbed Andrew's bottle and went to the bar while Andrew watched Amy and Riley wiggle and jiggle to Kool and the Gang on the dance floor.

Returning with two beers, "So how long you gonna hang out here in Florida?"

"A couple a more days I guess. Stephanie really wanted this to be more than just a reunion trip."

"I don't blame her. I love this place. In fact, I was thinking of moving back here."

"Hey Jeffrey, I hate to be rude, but I better go find my wife before she thinks I forgot about her, again."

You already did you dingle-berry. "I gotcha. Hey, he said as he reached into his pocket, "here's my business card. If you get anything on these killings or just want to talk give me a buzz all right."

Andrew accepted the card. "Okay, you got it. It was good seeing you too Jeffrey."

"You take care now, and good luck with everything." *You're gonna need it.* They shook hands. Jeffrey smiled at him as he watched him walk away.

It was after midnight and some people began to call it a night. Andrew felt pretty satisfied with his contacts and conversations but still had no idea as to a possible suspect, maybe he was digging in the wrong place, but then again, most of these high society types could keep their gender from you if they wanted. So many of them are well schooled in the art of putting on the false face but bearing daggers in their hearts, Andrew considered as he couldn't help himself from drawing on yet another Shakespeare

Scott A. Reighard

reference. Trying to uncover a suspect was going to take quite a bit of luck. For Stephanie and Andrew this night had ended on a sour note, but for the killer it was only the chorus in a song he was writing and composing.

Chapter 39

After leaving the reunion Andrew decided to take a drive north on County Road. The road runs the length of Palm Beach Island as it winds from ocean view then down to where homes line either side of the road, and then back to ocean view. This lazy serpentine pattern meandered for several miles until the end of the road at the Palm Beach Inlet. Perhaps the drive would air out all of the tension before they got back to their hotel.

Andrew always remembered the advice of his grandfather, "Don't go to bed angry; go to bed by making it right." He wanted to make it right but when you are at the center of the storm that is a woman's hurt and anger there isn't a whole lot to do except to wait for forgiveness. As he drove past the myriad of million dollar homes, most of which were protected with high walls or hedges, he attempted to jump start the conversation.

"So, did you have a good time?" as he glanced her way.

"Sure."

"Listen, I appreciate you uh, you know."

"Of course Andrew playing the dutiful wife I think you want to say."

"That's not what I meant, I mean using your great personality to get along with anyone really."

His comments were like a black seal on a field of snow, "Don't Andrew, don't pander me like that, it's not very attractive."

As they passed where his old school was located, but had since been replaced with million dollar properties there was silence when she couldn't wait any longer, "So do you still love her?"

"Amy?"

"No Mother Teresa, of course Amy. Boy, put you men in a gotcha box and you trip all over yourselves." He glanced at her with a distorted eye and a raised brow.

"No, I don't love her. What's the matter with you?" He waited a few seconds for a reaction but Stephanie just sat there. "I did though, a long time ago."

"I see," Stephanie, eyes fixed forward on the road, began searching for an appropriate question although perturbed that her husband would be so forthcoming, but then again she always admired his honesty.

"What about tonight though, did it stir any emotions for you?"

Andrew gripped the wheel tightly and paused. *Tell the truth, what the hell, damn the torpedoes full speed ahead.*

"Some, but not what you would think. In some ways it was putting to bed some old nightmares."

Stephanie wasted no time pouncing on the Freudian slip, "I'll bet."

"What I meant was… it actually deepened my love for you." He quickly added, "And no I'm not pandering, because seeing her reaffirmed my love for you." She turned her eyes toward him as the wind through the windows tossed her hair like a soft blow dryer. He continued, "You are the only woman in my life, period. I love you beyond description. I would die for you without hesitation you know that? You are the only woman I want or will ever need, and that's the truth." He looked over to her.

He felt that he had acquitted himself, but it would be his wife who would actually be the one to judge if what he said was enough.

They always felt theirs was a relationship built on an absolute trust. They had always been honest with one another on things that really mattered. But did he really want to come clean on all of his past?

Andrew coolly carved the rental car around the famed Kennedy compound property that sat ocean-side on North

The Reunion Reaper

County Road as the road was now running along the ocean once again. The bright yellow moon looked down on them as it had no worries of clouds to obstruct its view of a couple trying to figure out whether this was a real crisis or an invented dramatic episode that would end with a sobering night's sleep.

Andrew completed the tour of Palm Beach by driving to the edge of North County Road, the most northern point of the island that overlooked the inlet that split Palm Beach Island from Singer Island. He got out of the car and walked to an area where a gate had been installed. He patiently waited as she finally stepped out of the car and with a deliberate walk to the gate, stood next to him. They gazed at the reflecting moon's glowing image off the water. High tide was making its way into the Palm Beach Inlet. As she stood leaning against the fence Andrew shifted over and got behind her. He wrapped his arms around her then gently blew on then kissed her neck. He could feel her shiver in his arms as he whispered, "I would never do anything to hurt you."

Although he wasn't completely in the clear, he knew this couldn't hurt. Plus, he couldn't gauge if she was making more of this than she should or because he had created the situation. Either way he felt cornered and so he would oblige whatever game she was playing, if in fact it was a game. Not wanting him to see her expression she turned her head to the side and smiled. She loved this man and was silly to think he would throw away a great marriage with three wonderful kids all for a high school sweetie. She was a jealous wife for a moment and she allowed it to get the better of her. She turned back to him and kissed his cheek. The look in her eyes said it all. She felt bad for being so melodramatic about this, "I'm sorry, I should have never doubted you. You know how much I love you."

He smiled and returned the kiss and as he embraced her he pointed out the pump house across the inlet where he and his buddies used to jump off, and the memory of Mark Lambert seized him yet again. He was hoping that Mark would have been at the reunion in order to bury the hatchet of their rivalry and discontent. A hatchet Andrew apparently buried deep in his own psyche, of which guilt still navigated its way around now and again. Because of the debilitating injuries Mark would not be able to share in the state lacrosse championship or the great year they had in soccer. Andrew was sad that by the end of his senior year Mark contemplated dropping out to attend another school, but his parents weren't about to be embarrassed or harassed by rumors. So, despite the desire to gather information for an investigation or the anticipation of seeing an old girlfriend, this trip had a third agenda for Andrew, closure. He wanted closure with everything because he was unsure if he would ever see or want to see these people again.

The night however, would end on a good note. The ride back to the hotel felt a lot shorter than the one he had taken several hours prior. *Whew,* he thought, *at least that's over, but now what?* Little did he know that he was about to enter into a new gut wrenching, marriage testing, ego busting situation.

The Reunion Reaper

Chapter 40

Returning from the reunion, Stephanie looked a little more tan; whereas Andrew was brain wracked. Encouraged by his brief talk with Andrea, he wanted to call her as soon as he could.

After settling in at home, unpacking, hanging out with the kids and eating pizza for dinner, it was time to conduct a follow up. Andrew snuck away to his study and got busy with calling Andrea. His encounter with her at the reunion gave him some encouragement, but he knew the deck was stacked given his lack of resources. In one respect it was folly to even entertain such an endeavor, but no one knew Andrew Keane better than he knew himself. Perhaps it was ego as well.

"Andrea, hey, it's Andrew Keane."

"Hey there, good to hear from you. Did you have a good time at the reunion?"

"Yeah, it was great. It's funny, I was telling Stephanie that I had forgotten more than I remembered, and it was great to hear the stories again. When you hear about those days you realize how much fun we had."

"Yeah, even though I was four years younger than you guys, it's pretty amazing how so many of us could be friends no matter what class we were in."

"That's a good point."
Andrew was fiddling around with his computer as he stayed in the conversation.

"Listen, I hope you didn't get the wrong idea about my approach at the bar."

"No of course not, you have legitimate concern, and as I said, it is a pretty curious situation."

"Yeah, it's really sad though. I don't know if you remember that Tucker and I dated back in the day, and when I heard about his death I was stunned."

"Well, I'm going to look into this and see what I come up with."

"What's your plan?"

Unbeknownst to Andrew someone was listening in. Jeffrey decided to hang out in Roanoke, take in some local sites and take a drive on the Blue Ridge Parkway. He was anxious to see if his little trick on Andrew would work. Based on what he heard at the reunion there was no doubt that he felt Andrew would jump in with both feet. Settling in sitting in a rental car a few houses down, he could hear most of what Andrew was saying.

Turn toward the mike you oaph, what you got your head buried in a pillow?

"I don't want to say too much right now, but it's about flushing out those of whom it would seem would be incapable of pulling this off. I mean, if these deaths are murders and not accidents, you would have to say that whoever is behind this is pretty clever."

You got that right. I am a genius and little do you know how good I am. Damn, who is he talking to? I should have bugged the phones.

"How can I help?"

Suddenly Andrew had a crazy thought. She approached him, she's asked about his plan, and she wants to know more information. Could it be? Could she be a front for someone else?

"You still there?"

Andrew snapped to, "I'm sorry, just got distracted, what did you say?"

"How can I help?"

"Well, I don't know what to tell you right now. You said you keep in touch with a few classmates, so maybe you could just talk to them and see what they have to say. But you have to remember not to say anything about me checking into things, it's just conversation."

"I gotcha. I was looking to put a Facebook site together and hopefully get a lot of former friends and classmates join in."

"That sounds like a good idea. Let me know how that goes."

"Hey, do you remember Mark Lambert?"

"Yeah, we were pretty good friends until he had that incident."

"Oh yeah, I remember that."

"Man, he never got over that did he?"

Who never got over what? Nah, there's no way they could be talking about me.

"Anyhow, I heard a while back that he was arrested for domestic violence."

"Really?"

"Yeah, he got a divorce and then moved away. I don't know where, but I do remember back in school how he talked about how much he hated everyone at school and that he wanted to leave and go to another school, but his parents wouldn't have it."

"Yeah, he wasn't fun to hang around with at all."

"And he hated Tucker especially. After I heard this from him Tucker wanted to kick the crap out of him, but I told him it wasn't worth it."

Who in the hell are you talking to Andy Boy?

"Wow, that's a good story."

"Yeah, so maybe start with him."

"Hey, gotta start somewhere. Well listen, you've been a big help, I really appreciate it Andrea. I will stay in touch."

Andrea…Pruitt? Hmm, interesting.

Scott A. Reighard

Chapter 41

A week passed since the reunion and Jeffrey was back at his safe haunt plotting his next mission. He eavesdropped on a pretty significant conversation between Andrew, and what appeared to be Andrea Pruitt. He didn't know what to make of it, and would look into that in due time, but right now there was another matter to tend to. The timeline was closing in for the next job. He had to get to work.

He reflected on all that he heard and saw at the reunion, how some of them made him absolutely sick, and how others made him feel like he felt twenty five years ago, wanted and happy. In his hands was a file on his next victim, a female, attractive, single and ripe for the taking off. He tossed the folder on the desk and reclined in his lounger.

He took out his remote control and clicked on his stereo to listen to some music, music he liked to refer to as inspirational because it gave him the ability to quiet his mind and allow the demons to foment their plan. He clicked on the CD of classic rock and Foghat's *Slow Ride* began to rumble its way out of the speakers. As he listened to the lyrics he slipped into a distant memory of the time when this song made him feel high as a kite.

As a kid in high school he fantasized about having sex with women while certain songs played. And just as luck would have it he got an opportunity his senior year.

He was able to coax Sharon Bloom to his car to share a little blow and a snifter of vodka. A deadly combination, but teenagers are invincible right, so bring it on he observed. It was yet another Palm Beach party where the liquor flowed like water from a fountain and drugs were as accessible as if the pharmacist were there personally to deliver.

The Reunion Reaper

The two of them stumbled off to the street and into the back of his Saab. He jammed the key into the ignition, turned on the radio and the music began to bounce around the roomy car. Both were high sitting there laughing at nothing basically, but he wasn't as high as he let on. He looked at this bleach blond bomber whose chest could rival that of Sophia Loren or Racquel Welch. She kept flipping her head around as she laughed and he felt that was the sign to move in. Ever so subtle he kissed her on the neck. She didn't resist. He then kissed her on her ear and placed his hand on her knee, again no resistance. Becoming bolder in his approach he whispered sweet words in her ear wherein she laughed at the coolness and tickling his voice gave to her ear. He took his left hand and placed it on her right breast. Once again there was no resistance. He was becoming excited at the prospect that he could bed one of the hottest girls in the school.

Although she was perceived as one of the biggest sluts in the school, he didn't care one way or the other. He was not about to let go of the opportunity to have this high school queen feel his scepter. However, what he didn't know was that he was not her type. Soon he would find out.

There was some slobbering smooching going on as well as some touchy feely, but after a few minutes she decided to curb the advancements. For a bit of blow and booze she thought what she allowed was enough. Apparently he didn't get the message. To his surprise *Slow Ride* came screaming over the radio. He placed his hand in her crotch just under her skirt, she grabbed his hand and told him to stop, but something had happened to him. He felt compelled to move forward regardless of what she would say, and so he continued his assault. He pushed her flat on the back seat and placed his body weight on her. He kept telling her that she really wanted this and that she needed to relax and let it happen. She tried to resist, calling him names that sorely angered him, but she was well out of it and basically unable to resist. The words of the song rang in his ears, *slow ride, easy...slow ride, sleazy*. She was a sleaze and was about to get hers he thought. He placed his hand over her mouth as he completed the assault on this drunk and high teenage girl who was in the wrong place at the wrong time. As the song came to a close it was mission accomplished. She lay there crying. He tried to console her but it was pointless. He then threatened her that if she told anyone about this he would make her disappear.

He figured that she was so high that she wouldn't want to tell anyone fearing embarrassment. After all, she came to his car knowing full well what was going to happen. She wanted it, he thought. He opened the door to tell her to get the hell out of his car. She stumbled away, tears in her eyes. He composed himself, pulled up his pants, jumped into the front seat and drove off.

Ironically, the song from the CD seemed to end as did his journey back in time. A simpering smile appeared on his face as he reclined all the way back lying nearly flat. His eyes were closed as yet another vintage song rolled out. It was *Lunatic Fringe* by Red Rider. He laughed at the title as the song began its synthetic whistle and guitar intro, within a few minutes he drifted off to sleep unable to hear the end of the song.

For the next few weeks he would complete the reconnaissance on his victim as well as rehash the information he already obtained. With Andrew now involved there was an adrenaline he hadn't felt since his first job, but he knew he needed to be extremely cautious; Andrew was not to be underestimated. With several more names on the list it was not a time to slip up. His next victim lived in Florida, so did Andrea. He had to be quick and fast on this one, there was little to no room for error. The first real test he thought.

Chapter 42

The next day, Andrew was back at work and several of his colleagues mocked him for not coming back with a tan.

"Must a stayed in the hotel room the whole time huh killa?" joked, Tony Moreno, the former NYPD.

Andrew laughed at his comment, "Yeah, something like that," as he continued his walk into his office.

Since the reunion, he had been poring over all the information he gathered there. Did he have something, or nothing? He wanted to work on a profile, but of whom? One thing he felt certain was that the killer was very professional, detail oriented, had incredible resources, and was very careful; not to mention appearing to be an enigma disguised in a labyrinth of schemes, which made it extremely difficult to focus in on just one or two people.

He entered his office and closed the door. It was a simple office with the basic generic look of a desk, some filing cabinets, a few chairs and a bookshelf. On his desk was a portrait of the family. He glanced at it thinking, *am I doing the right thing here? Am I about to make you sacrifices in all of this?* He leaned back in his executive style chair, swung his chair around, and gazed out over one of the few good features available to him as a detective for Roanoke County, an office with a window view that had a clear shot of the nearby mountains. He could see the star that sat on top of Mill Mountain, which was located in the downtown area of Roanoke. The star stood ninety feet tall and at night was lit with the colors of America. He flipped back around to face his desk and began shuffling through his mind objectives and goals, as well as paperwork that had piled up since his absence.

Now, Andrew never considered himself to be the greatest at solving puzzles, but he felt that with a little help and luck he just might be able to pull this off. He needed a little reassurance and perhaps that could come in the name of Joe Marketti of the FBI. He had to consider how much he should say to him. Despite being an old and trusted friend, Andrew knew that Joe was an ethical by the book kind of guy.

Andrew leaned forward in his chair and picked up the phone then quickly hung it up. *What am I going to say? Is this a good idea?* He had already talked to Andrea, but this was a fellow law enforcement official. Before he picked up the phone again, he would wait and talk with someone who these days was about as close a friend as he had, Sonny. Even though he was at a considerable disadvantage his gut didn't care about jurisdiction or evidence; it said that he should advance the theory that these were not accidents and that he had a responsibility, no, a duty to his classmates to get to the bottom of this. He had many questions, the family and the legality of it notwithstanding, but he also couldn't avoid the obvious, where was he going to get the time and money to work on this? He knew that not everything was going to drop on his doorstep; he was convinced that he was going to have to go places, but how? The savings was watched by his wife closer than Fort Knox, plus he would have to take time off in order to conduct this venture. His mind was swirling, so much so that he didn't even hear Lindsay Blankenship walk in.

"Andrew, are you okay?"

"What? Oh yeah sure, I was just thinking about a few things."

This was not what he needed right now, a horny twenty something to go along with all the other immediate matters present in his life.

"I just got back from my parents in Johnson City, Tennessee, so how did it go in Florida? I would love to go there, it's so beautiful. I mean, the beaches, getting tans and all, and then the late night party scene. Like, I watch these shows on South Beach that must be, like, really wild you know."

I don't need this right now...How did she ever get through the academy? Suddenly Lindsay's voice faded into a droning sound for Andrew. She was a pretty little thing, but *God could you just shut up and take a breath for a second?*

Hatching a brilliant getaway idea he politely excused himself to the men's room figuring there was no way she would walk in there, or would she?

He took a seat on a toilet in one of the stalls and just sat there pondering his dilemma. He was going to have to talk to his wife about this idea of him wanting to move forward with an investigation, and he was going to gracefully ask her for her patience, and then money from the savings account; however, one thing still loomed large, his job and the ramifications of his actions. Andrew loved a challenge and this was certainly one of them, but these complications would have to be considered. Only time and a few conversations would tell, and he was one that hated for things to wait.

Someone walked into the bathroom banging the door against the door stop startling him from his stupor. He walked out of the stall and past Ben, a fifteen year veteran.

"Hey Andrew, how's it going?"

"Good Ben thanks."

"How was Florida?"

"It's still there. Just kidding, it was great."

As Andrew opened the door to leave, Ben cleared his throat, but Andrew missed the hint.

"Damn, he didn't even wash his hands."

He shuffled his way back to his office, Lindsay was gone thankfully. Before calling Sonny he logged onto his work computer. He pulled up a confidential site dedicated to law enforcement. After his talk with Andrea and the mention of Mark Lambert, he decided to do a little illegal digging. He knew that using his work computer for personal purposes could bring him some serious problems, but this is all he had right now. He grabbed his pin drive and did a little search on Lambert.

After doing a quick, albeit, illegal poke into Mark Lambert's life, he called for Sonny on the radio. They agreed to get together for lunch.

Andrew met Sonny at a bistro café in SW Roanoke, which happened to be Sonny's patrol area. Andrew talked a lot about the reunion, old acquaintances and then proceeded to go through all of his concerns about the idea of moving forward from this point. Sonny had no real answers for him, but he did have one question. Why didn't Andrew want to talk with the FBI about this, let them do their job. In some strange way Andrew couldn't explain to Sonny his desire to pursue this solo; that it was something compelling him to move forward. Sonny was a good friend, but there was no way he could understand the certain relationship Andrew had with such a small contingent of people, who at this point were going down one by one.

"Well, you sound as though you are bent on doing this, just know I've got your back on this. If there's anything you need just let me know."

Sonny assured him of his secrecy to this and his commitment to his friend.

"Well listen, I really appreciate your input. This is one tough decision."

"Yes it is. You just need to figure out where this falls on your list of priorities and if there will be a point of no return or a point of enough is enough."

"Yeah I guess, but time's tickin' and I need to decide, like yesterday you know."

It was time to hunker down and advance this, or consider the words of his father, *Throw up the ole hail Mary or punt.*

The Reunion Reaper

Chapter 43

Jeffrey was back, yet another landing at Palm Beach International Airport, but this time he was low key. There was work to do. There would be no drop top Mustang or parading through restaurants or bars, and no late night escort girl. He was on a mission and needed complete focus and anonymity. Occasionally on these jobs he would disguise himself, but he really preferred to be himself, it made it more special when the job was done and that he was not hiding behind some mask like a bank robber or terrorist. Of course, a stealth warrior almost unseen was how he felt at times. It was a high he snorted with defiance. There was no greater joy in killing someone and then being able to walk away leaving no clues, or even suspicions. The only element that was missing was the credit. In some way he wanted to drop hints or clever cryptograms for law enforcement, but at this point this was the way he wanted to play his game and he held the clock, the rules and with any luck, the outcome.

He had scoped his next target, done his homework, and now it was time for his exam. It was a female, yet another who spurned his advances. What was wrong with these women he thought, he had money, he was smart, had a cool car, and decent looks, after all he had seen far uglier guys date some knockouts, so what was it that made him a pariah with his female counterparts in his graduating class? He was a typical teenage boy who desired to nail these girls like a frog nails flies, but he was mostly relegated to fantasy and television and books. In fact, it wasn't until his junior year that he finally lost his virginity despite his claims to have already bagged at least a dozen girls by that time.

Scott A. Reighard

His first was a freshman, new to the school that he was able to charm and get high at a party; his calling card it seemed. He bragged on that girl like he just climbed Mount Everest; most everyone thought he was pulling their leg until she withdrew from the school. No one knew what came of her, but there were rumors he got her pregnant and her parents did not want to face the humiliation. He simply bragged it up. Yep, he sure had style, and feelings.

Slipping through a wooded gate, he stood in a darkened area protected by hedges and away from a spot light that shimmered off a rectangular shaped pool he waited for his opportunity. Glancing through a window he could see the side image of a man parked on a recliner in front of the television. He quickly shuffled up to the house. He ducked below that window and moved to another window that was partially shaded with wooded Venetian blinds. He was able to glance through the side area to see his target. She had just emerged from the shower and was wrapped in a light bath robe that dropped to the length of mid thigh. Her hair was wet and so it was darker than the bleached blond most people recognized. She disappeared behind a wall, presumably to a closet. He waited for a few minutes, perhaps hoping she would disrobe giving him a brief moment of rising joy, but when she returned she took a seat at her vanity table and began fiddling with her hair.

He decided there would be no show so he slithered his way around to the side of the house where there was a door that led to a garage. *People are so stupid,* he thought; *they make it so easy.* The door was unlocked and he slipped into the garage area unseen. Dressed in dark clothing he was sweating profusely. Oh the sacrifices one must make to get the job done. In addition to the dark outfit he donned a long brown beard that looked more like Grizzly Adams. His hair was colored the same as the beard so it looked very natural, but he had his hair shoved into a hair net so as not to leave anything behind other than the poison. With his gloved

The Reunion Reaper

hand he checked the handle on the door that led to the kitchen, it was unlocked also. He smiled.

He slowly pushed the door to peak inside. He knew where the hubby was and where the victim was, but there were two rug rats he had to consider, their kids. He couldn't hear anything except for the television blaring out an automotive commercial, so he just opened the door enough that if someone were in the kitchen they may think it was simply a brush of wind through the garage door spacing that opened the door. He peaked inside and could see that no one was in the kitchen. It was dark enough for him to slip in unnoticed. The only drawback to this job was that he was hoping to guess correctly. If what he was looking for was not where he had hoped, then he would have to re-gather and wait for another opportunity or forget about this one altogether.

He stepped into the kitchen without a sound. He could see flickering of lights from the television bouncing off the wall of the living room. Suddenly he saw a moving shadow; a figure whose shadow grew larger with each passing second. Someone was coming into the kitchen. He backed up and almost backed into the door he had just entered through, but he sidestepped the disaster and slipped back into the garage. Since he had to do so quickly he was unable to close the door completely. He ducked down behind the family mini-van. He could hear a female voice.

"Honey, did you mix my drinks like I asked?"

"Yes, they're all ready to go, and your energy gels I put in your bag."

"Thank you."

There was a brief silence, then he saw light shoot into the garage.

"Honey, where are the kids?"

"They're in Blake's room playing a game I think."

"You think? Oh, and please remember to close the garage door completely."

He heard the door shut and was hoping that he didn't hear the clicking noise of someone locking the door.

After a few minutes of silence he was back at it again, checking the door handle, peaking into the darkened kitchen, tiptoeing up to the refrigerator door. He glanced into the living room and saw that the man had not moved. He glided back to the refrigerator, opened the door and pulled out one of the drink bottles. He pulled from his pocket a vile and poured in some of the liquid. He closed the cap and placed it back on the shelf. As the refrigerator door was closing he could hear the sound of a recliner closing.

"Honey, you still in the kitchen?" There was no response, "Honey?"

Jeffrey quickly slipped out into the garage as he heard the footfalls of flip flops on the ceramic kitchen floor. Slumping behind the mini-van again he waited for silence. When he felt it was clear, he ducked out of the door, slinked down by her window again and tried to get a peak, but she was fully clothed and packing a small black bag. Mission accomplished, he hoped as he calmly made his way through the gate that he had previously compromised only minutes before.

The Reunion Reaper

Chapter 44

Sharon Bloom was a girl who had good looks and a pretty sharp brain, but several areas where she lacked cover girl completeness was her love for partying and eating. She was a heavy set girl who could have had the boys kicking down the door if it weren't for the additional weight she was carrying, drawbacks to a society insatiably desiring image.

After she graduated from college at a hefty two hundred and ten pounds she decided that enough was enough. She had partied and eaten so much food that she looked in the mirror one day and saw a woman who looked ten years older than she was. She made a dramatic change. She started running a few miles a week, heaving like her next breath would be her last, but she persisted. After several years she eventually was running upwards of fifty miles a week. Over the course of the next three years she went from two hundred and ten pounds to one hundred and thirty. She had a breast reduction in the late nineties so her new body from the neck down wouldn't resemble the capital letter P, but most of the weight loss came by way of her newly committed fitness lifestyle. At age forty two she was now down to one hundred fifteen pounds. During her change of life period she found a younger guy who became not only her workout partner but her life partner. She had found true happiness. Happiness that was about to come to a dramatic end.

Ever since Sharon's early thirties she began to participate in charity runs, 5K's or 10K's. She also participated in a few sprint triathlons. An admitted bad swimmer she was pretty solid on a bike and excellent on the run. A triathlon was being held on Singer Island the first weekend of June and Sharon was competitor number 341. As the competitors made their way down to the beach a final goodbye to her husband Ralph with a kiss and a hug, as well as hugs from her two children, Blake who was eleven and Maggie, eight. Donning her pink swimmers cap she jogged down to where the waiting swimmers anticipated the gun for the start of the race.

The gun sounded and several hundred swimmers raced into the water and started their vicious swimming strokes that would take them out to a buoy where they would make a right turn to another buoy and then a right back to the shore. Sharon always liked staying to the outside trying to avoid the kicks and slaps of fellow swimmers. She was on the outside kicking and stroking her best to stay in a straight line heading out to the first buoy.

Standing on the shore in disguise, Jeffrey watched as Sharon methodically rotated her body allowing each arm to slice into the water at a precise angle providing the least amount of resistance. Standing in the background he glanced at the family, they were all cheering her on even though they knew she couldn't hear them. It was just a matter of time he thought before her strokes would cease and like a lump of clay she would sink.

He watched as she continued her strokes. She began to labor a little bit. The family didn't really see this as a problem given it was her worst event and each of them seemed to mouth words of encouragement to her. Her strokes became more labored as she almost seemed to stop in the water. She began to wave her hand, a signal to boats nearby that a swimmer needed assistance. Sharon was laboring terribly now and her husband seemed to sense that something was wrong and he began a torrid running pace to the water's edge. She was probably a hundred yards or so off the beach and it would seem imprudent for him to go after her, so he stood on the shore yelling to any boat that would hear him. A boat spotted her waving her arms as suddenly she went under. When her husband Ralph saw her go under he dove into the water and began to swim out to

The Reunion Reaper

her. Others in the area began to notice that something was terribly wrong, but Jeffrey just stood there and watched a desperate husband swim to his wife's aid.

    A few minutes later Sharon was retrieved out of the water and CPR was administered. Ralph was laboring badly and the boat swung around to pick him up as well. When they hoisted him into the boat he disappeared from view. He was hunched over on the deck hugging his now dead wife. Within a few minutes the EMT van pulled up onto the beach as the boat crept closely to the shore. The triathlon had nearly come to a standstill. Swimmers were still stroking their way around the buoys as others emerged from the water as they completed the swim portion and were making their way to the transition area between the swim and the bike. The race continued on though as race officials tried their best to inform everyone that a swimmer was having difficulty and was now being taken to the local hospital; little did they know that she was already dead.

    As the van pulled off he felt confident that she was gone, and even if she was alive there was no way the finger could be pointed at him. He was able to sneak onto their property and place the strychnine in her competition drink bottle while her husband was just one room over watching television, but surely no one saw him.

    As he saw the van drive out of site, he decided he had enough and was ready to get out of there. He felt pretty comfortable the poison had worked. Sharon Bloom had competed for the last time. He would be able to read about it over the internet within a day or so. Mission accomplished. Although he was anxious to get out of West Palm, it was time for a quick check up on the ever nosy Andrea Pruitt, and then it was on to Roanoke to see what ole Andy Boy was up to.

Scott A. Reighard

Chapter 45

Andrew had no answers to a very complex situation, so after returning from lunch with Sonny he needed time to think, so he decided to close his office door. Hesitating, he picked up the phone and called the Federal Bureau of Investigations in Washington, D.C. in an effort to contact a high school chum Joe Marketti who had been an FBI agent for the better part of twelve years now.

Back at Palm Beach Prep Joe was a respected student. He was a three sport athlete who was quick, agile and surprisingly strong for his five foot nine inch frame that was built more like an action figure. His brown hair and brownish skin was consistent with a demeanor that projected toughness, and a stubbornness he attributed to his mom. He was a scrappy Italian who could mix it up with anyone. Andrew loved going over to his house because he could always smell his mom's Italian cooking. Joe's father worked for the Palm Beach Sheriff's Department, but was fatally killed in a drug bust when Joe was a senior in high school. Since then he had spent his life in the pursuit of justice. Although his father's killers were brought to justice or killed in other busts, he was still a guy on a mission.

After graduating from college in 1985 he went to work for the Florida Highway Patrol, but his true calling came in 1995 when he was accepted into the FBI academy. In 2003 he was brought to D.C. and placed in the Counterterrorism Division. In 2005 he helped to foil a terrorist plot where terrorists were planning on setting off a delivery truck bomb full of explosives near the wharf in Baltimore during a Baltimore Orioles game. The predicted number of dead would have potentially been in the hundreds, possibly thousands, but Joe wasn't the kind of guy who was looking

The Reunion Reaper

to have his face on FBI monthly. He was modest, efficient, and most of all a dedicated law enforcement officer.

Andrew's call was redirected to the office of Counterterrorism and after a few more number key prompts, he was finally able to talk to a human being. He asked for Joe and was told to hold. After a few minutes a familiar voice could be heard.

"Joe Marketti, Office of Counterterrorism, this is a non-secure line and this call may be monitored for quality control, how may I help you?"

Andrew decided to play a little prank by disguising himself as an old lady's voice, "Yes young man, is this where we can report a possible crime?"

"This is counterterrorism do you have suspicions of a terror event?"

"Well, my husband wants to blow up the New York Yankees."

Sensing this might be a whack job he adroitly said, "I see and what evidence do you have of this ma'am?"

"Well, he keeps saying those damn Yankees I wish they'd all just go to hell."

"Is your husband a Red Sox fan ma'am?"

"No, he's an Atlanta Brave fan."

"I see, and he wants the damn Yankees to all go to hell, are you sure he doesn't mean the New York Mets?"

"Why's that?"

"Cause they lead the national league east by eight games and the Braves are under five hundred at this point."

Unable to maintain the prank any longer Andrew broke out with laughter, "I knew I couldn't fool you."

"Is this who I think it is?"

"Your mom made the best friggin' meatballs man."

"Andrew Keane, what's shakin' bacon?"

"Tryin' to keep from fryin' Brian."

"Well I know what you mean jelly bean."

"Ain't that the truth Ruth?"

"Okay, I'm outta rhymes you win. Wow, it's been a while, so what do you want slacker?" enquired Joe.

"Well, I would say this is part social call, part serious BS call."

"Come on man I work for the FBI I don't need more BS, you know what I mean?"

"Sorry, but it is pretty serious."

"All right give it to me, your brother hasn't gone off the deep end has he?

Andrew's brother had been through several missions in Afghanistan and Iraq as a Navy SEAL.

"No, Sean is just fine, did you know he's retiring next year."

"No kidding, how many years?"

"Twenty eight, can you believe it, the guy's only forty six years old and he'll retire with full pension."

"Well being an academy graduate will do that for you."

"Says he's gonna buy one of those big RV's and travel the US."

"Don't blame him, it's an awesome country."

"You got that right."

"Listen, Andrew I would love to rally with you on the old times, but I have a meeting in about ten minutes so you gotta be quick. Sorry man."

Andrew understood. He went on to explain as much as he could in ten minutes. Joe was concerned about Andrew's intent to do this on his own.

"Any idea who you think it might be?"

"Nah, I just started putting together some files on everyone," responded Andrew.

"Okay, well here's a quick analysis, but I'll need to give it more thought. What you have is some guy who is probably pissed off at something or some people. It might be one of those childhoods where he was abused, overly coddled, something out of the extreme. He may suffer from Narcissistic Personality Disorder or NPD as we call it, but

The Reunion Reaper

in this case the guy wants to remain anonymous, which doesn't sound like NPD. Anyhow, like I said, I gotta give it more thought."

There were more questions from Andrew and although he was hoping to hear better answers or even ideas from his old high school chum, Joe essentially left him with some heady advice.

"Hey Andrew, you gotta be low key on this man, what you're doin' is illegal so don't get caught doing any foolish stuff all right?"

"Yeah, okay."

"I'm dead serious my friend."

"I got it, low key."

"All right, good luck. Hey, take down my private cell number and feel free to call me anytime all right."

After jotting down his number, "Okay, I really appreciate it Joe."

"Go nail this guy. My money is on Mark Lambert, he was a friggin' nutcase."

"You know a lot of people have been saying that."

"Sounds like a good starting point."

"Hey Joe one last thing, aren't you worried this call may have been recorded?"

"Didn't you hear the message? It said this call may be monitored for quality control. Quality control at the FBI?"

"All right, be cool."

"As my ex-wife's heart."

"Good one," as the phone on the other end clicked.

Scott A. Reighard

Chapter 46

Ah, Roanoke, Virginia. Sounds weird, but you're growing on me. I must be going soft. He exited the small aircraft at Roanoke Regional. It was a beautiful southwest Virginia day; temperatures were moderate and spotty clouds mitigated the heat.

Jeffrey sauntered through the terminal carrying a duffle bag in one hand and his computer bag in the other. His hair was still the color of brown that he colored while in Florida as part of his disguise, but the beard was gone. He was wearing baggy khakis and a navy blue polo that was not tucked in.

Perhaps the star city was growing on him, but he couldn't find it within himself to keep from laughing at such a ridiculous nickname for a city in SW Virginia. *Like this place was L.A. or something,* he thought. *Where's the action? I'll bet they don't even get a dozen murders a year around here. I might match that myself.* As he exited the airport to catch a taxi he flipped on his sunglasses and was anxious to get to his intended target, the home of Andrew Keane, but first a hotel, a shower and a trip to the local outdoor store for some supplies.

He was excited about the listening devices he planted in Andrew's house just after the reunion while the mother-in-law took the kids shopping, and it had already paid dividends. Andrew was talking, and it was time to ramp up the game content with more dead bodies and misdirection. The game was providing him with an adrenaline he hadn't experienced since cocaine, but he gave that up for something more satisfying, vengeance and vanity. Well, he always had the vanity. He oftentimes wondered why he didn't start this earlier, but he always figured himself for a

The Reunion Reaper

late bloomer anyway, besides the maturity level wasn't there.

With all he had done in his life up to this point he couldn't believe he somehow made it past forty. All too often he had engaged in dangerous behavior, and as time carried on a spark remained lit in his mind that dwelled on his youth. He was tired of being outdone, or outwitted, but no more. It was his turn to shift the field of play, a kind of home field of advantage, but he was not willing to share the rules of his game which gave him the needed edge. And here he was a self proclaimed genius who was playing a dangerous game, but to him well worth it.

He checked into a hotel in the northeast section of the county and stuffed down the Subway sandwich he bought on his way to the hotel. In order to maintain a slim look, he would always carefully consider his diet choices. A mirror was always a welcome friend. He would often sit in a mall and watch the weight of America transform before his eyes. What a fat lazy nation we have become, he would mutter. Every chance he got he'd look at himself in the mirror and wonder why it was that people were satisfied looking like walking manatees.

Later that afternoon he walked to a nearby gas station and called another taxi that would take him to where he would rent a car that he would pay for in cash and under an assumed name. He had his shopping list, again, leaving nothing to chance. He did his shopping and waited for the right time to go pay Andy a visit. His plan was to hide out in a wooded area just across from Andy and his ever happy family's house. *Ugh!* he thought *a truly happy family is all a myth*. He was curious to hear Andy talk about the case to anyone, his wife, friends, whomever. The bait had been set, and an unknowing playing partner went for it hook, line and sinker.

Boy you have no idea what you are about to get yourself into.

Scott A. Reighard

Chapter 47

Andrew traipsed through the door of his home from a long day at the office and a sobering conversation with an old friend. The house was quiet which usually meant someone had practice or a game. He hoped that he didn't forget either Michael's soccer game or Ryan's T-Ball. There was a note on the counter from Stephanie, she took Michael to soccer practice; Ryan was also with her. Mary was at a friend's house. Andrew guessed she was at her best friend Courtney's house.

He decided to buzz the Lafferty's to see if she was there. He spoke with the veteran high school teacher as to the whereabouts of his daughter and how the classroom was treating him. John indicated the girl's had gone to a lacrosse game. Also, his comment on being a teacher these days seemed to capture the essence of his profession. "They're definitely a different breed right now that's for sure." Andrew couldn't disagree. Their conversation ended with Andrew inviting John and his family over for a cookout.

Well, with the wife and kids gone he thought he'd take advantage of some quiet and personal time to go for a run, but there was a greater calling right now, the run would have to wait.

He went over to the refrigerator to see what the wife had left. Usually on practice night it was leftovers, which seemed to be at least two nights a week this time of year, not including nights there were games. Andrew bobbed his head up and down looking in all areas of the fridge trying to find something that would please his palate but nothing was calling his name, and when in doubt he always went to the cupboard of cereals and glanced over the eight to ten boxes of cereal they would keep. Andrew always joked

The Reunion Reaper

about how much cereal they kept in the house likening it to the show *Seinfeld,* where Jerry always seemed to have boxes and boxes of cereal of which Kramer his neighbor would always come over and "borrow". He pulled the Honey Nut Cheerios out and grabbed dad's bowl, the biggest one in the cupboard and nearly filled it with cereal. He poured the milk and invariably a few cheerios were able to escape the bowl but not for long, he bent down near the counter and like a vacuum cleaner sucked up the strays. He was a bachelor for about an hour, and rather than plop down in front of the television, he decided to rummage through the mail and go to his computer.

Flipping on the light to his study, or so he thought it was his study; it was more of a universal room really, he saw various toys strewn about. For Michael and Ryan it was another room to build forts or play with their Hot Wheels. For mom it was a room for paying bills. Mary only used it when she needed to use the house computer. For Andrew it was his walk in the woods, or his seaside sanctuary. He would close the door, put on some light music and lose himself in whatever it was he was working on. The study exuded peace and serenity. When you entered the room through a deep maple colored door you saw to your right a medium oak colored office desk with shelving overhead neatly tucked into the corner.

On one of the shelves was Andrew's toy, a stereo where he could stack CDs and listen to his music for hours on end. The room boasted a four file cabinet, a book shelf, and in another corner a large brown toy chest that held several of the boy's toys. Off to the left of the desk was a window that looked out over a wooded area that extended far beyond Andrew's house. During this time of year as the sun approached a higher angle the sun would shoot through the room providing Andrew with an almost transcendental feeling. Sometimes he would just glide his executive chair over to the window, sit and daydream. Although it had been a while for that because his life had become increasingly busy.

With the house empty it was time to discover NPD, a disorder he knew very little about. At first he thought it was pretty harmless, everyone had a bit of narcissism in them, but to kill?

"Son of a bitch," Andrew commented as he looked at the keyboard. "She has got to keep a better eye on these kids."

On several of the keys were brown smudges almost covering the letters; he was hoping it wasn't what it looked like, but with Michael and Ryan anything was possible. He moved his face closer for a sniff.

"Okay, it's just chocolate." He went into the bathroom, grabbed a few wipes and proceeded to wipe down the keyboard as the computer loaded.

He was able to finally make out all the keys as he typed in his password. He hated being secretive, but he was more worried about the boys getting in to the computer and accidentally deleting files or worse, so he kept a password. In this case it would work well because he wanted to keep an electronic copy of his work as well as some hand file copies and he didn't want his wife snooping around. Although they had briefly discussed his involvement with the case, she was still pretty clueless as to his commitment. He was able to keep a lid on things, but he knew it wouldn't last. The immediate question looming was when to notify the wife of his doings and how deep into this case he was going to get. He knew she wouldn't approve of all of this, but when the time was right he would tell her the truth the whole truth and nothing but the truth so help him God. God help him indeed.

It was going to be a busy night, so he wasted no time. He double clicked the internet icon and within a few seconds his homepage popped up. Andrew wasn't swept up in all the new technology, but he did like the fact that he could be on the internet in seconds if he needed to; the plus

The Reunion Reaper

of technology in a world gone mad for it. He often muttered to himself.

Before looking up his homework for the evening he decided to check his email. He had about thirty messages. He cursed himself for having filled out an online survey, and now it appeared as though every company related to the survey had his email. He skipped down to one he spotted from his father. His dad sent him another joke, but unfortunately, as in most cases, his dad was still learning how to attach messages, or forward for that matter; this one came up empty, the only words typed in the message saying, "*funny one about elderly couple on vacation.*" Andrew could only assume it was funny. He hit the delete icon. *Sorry dad.* He zipped through deleting the rest of them, but there was one very interesting one with the subject, "Murder, murder will out!" Andrew recalled the line from Shakespeare's Macbeth; ironic, because he had an earlier flashback episode about the very same play. He quickly shuffled through his memory if he had a specific conversation with someone at the reunion about the play, but he came up empty. Perhaps this was just some sick worm or virus that some bored computer geek had sent anonymously, but tempted by the subject line he reluctantly opened it. He didn't know the addressor, it was just a bunch of gibberish, but as soon as he opened it he knew it was legitimate. It was an email from him.

Well, well, well, aren't you the brave one taking a chance on opening a strange e-mail. I'm guessing you're reading this now so I'll just say what I have to say. I received some information where you think the deaths of your classmates were not accidents. Well, duh! I also heard the reunion was a sappy gathering of morons and sluts, so it's no surprise that you were there. Now look, I'm sure you have a thousand questions, and as much as I'd like to answer them, I am going to have to decline at this time. But I can imagine what some of them are, let's see, hmm, is he

Scott A. Reighard

a classmate? Is he a nut? How did he get my email address? Why is the sky blue? Okay, I'm thinking of a number, how many should it be? Hey, here's something interesting, for each death here on out I will attribute that death to you just for playing my game. What a sport I am. You can thank me later.

I also heard that you are a pig in poke a poke Vagina. Great, a Podunk cop in a Podunk town. What is Roanoke anyway, it sounds like it should be the name of a sewer company or something. I heard it used to be called Big Lick; lick what, balls? Anyhow, I am absolutely dying to see if you decide to play my game. So, if I guess correctly I can pencil you in for adversary dumble-dick in my game. Oh, and you're off to a great start the number is now four, poor Sharon Bloom, "You bastard," Andrew remarked, *and five is just around the corner.*

Oh, and forget about trying to trace this email, I've covered all my bases. I'll be in touch. Good luck dingle-berry.

Andrew felt like someone had just hit him in the chest with a sledge hammer. He couldn't believe what he had just read. The dingle berry reference from the dream now had created a weird affirmation of what he was about to get himself into. Over and over he kept asking himself why the killer would contact him. How could he have been made aware of his curiosity? Andrew was coming down hard on himself, but he was always that way. He felt that mistakes should be based on effort not stupidity. He was outmaneuvered on this one, bishop to C3. It felt like check mate already and the game had only just begun. If this investigation was a marathon, he was already trying to close a ten minute lead with just a few miles left in the race.

Again, he tried desperately to recall conversations he had at the reunion; unfortunately his mind was pummeled with thoughts of the Amy McMahon slash wife situation that popped up like a dead body that washed up on shore.

The Reunion Reaper

He needed better instincts. At the reunion, he had talked with a lot of people about a lot of things, and so he had no clue as to who this mystery e-mailer could be. Could the killer have been at the reunion and is simply downplaying this as a diversion, or did the killer talk with someone who went and discovered that his questions stuck out like a skunk at a perfume party? Disgusted and angry he hit the reply button and typed in a few choice words.

I've got news for you I am a lot closer to you than you think. You better be awful sure about number five because I will be on you like a seasoned hound on a fresh scent. Guys like you are too dumb to succeed that's why you pick on unsuspecting people. Rest assured I will be on you before you know it. .

He hit the send button, but just as soon as he hit the send button he heard a ding, an email transmission was coming through. "Damn it!" The message he had just sent came back; the email address was undeliverable. He printed off the email message as well as the email address and jotted down that he needed to check with the IT department at work the next day. To Andrew this was a good news bad news situation. The bad, Sharon Bloom was most likely dead as the message indicated, the good news was that he had a glimmer of evidence and it came right from the mouth of the killer.

Scott A. Reighard

Chapter 48

The next day Andrew visited the IT department at work which quickly informed him that it was nearly impossible to trace certain email tracks. Dejected, he went to his desk and made another phone call, but this one was to the Palm Beach County Sheriff's Department. He recalled that Sharon still lived in the area although he didn't really talk with her the night of the reunion. He needed to know for sure that the email the previous night was legitimate. But why would the person lie about killing someone? Or for that matter tip it off? After several nauseating messages and what seemed to be endless waiting, he began to wonder if anybody worked at the sheriff's department. Finally a strong deep throated male answered the phone.

"Homicide, this is detective Olsen."

"Yes, detective Olsen this is Detective Keane of the Roanoke County Police Department in Roanoke, Virginia how are you today?"

"What can I do you for detective?"

"Okay uh, I was wondering, have you all run across a death within the last few days or so of a female, about forty years old, bleach blond hair, about five feet eight?"

"A five foot eight bleach blond forty year old in Florida, hmm, which hour of the day are you looking for?"

Sensing his sarcasm, "Well, what I mean is have you all discovered a female fitting this description as being deceased?"

"Look, as much as I'd really like to help another badge I am going to need a little more than that."

Andrew decided to go with yet another lie. "She's my sister and about a month ago she took off to Florida with this loser and I am worried about her health. She mentioned Palm Beach County."

The Reunion Reaper

"I'm going to have to put you in contact with missing persons, hold on."

Andrew tried to get him to stop before putting him on hold but it was too late. Some recorded message was bragging about how well the Palm Beach County Sheriff's Department was working to reduce crime in the county. Finally a female voice with a pronounced Jersey or New York accent picked up, "missing persons."

Andrew went through the same song and dance but got nowhere. No forty year old five foot eight bleach blond had come through missing persons so she abruptly said, "Hold for homicide please."

"No, wait." Andrew tried to be quick with the response, but apparently her finger was faster. *Holy crap, a man would have better luck getting struck by lightning.*

"Homicide, detective Olsen."

"Hey, detective, Lieutenant Keane again."

"No luck with missing persons I guess?"

"Nope, it's just you and me. Listen, I would really appreciate it if you could check into this for me. Her name is Sharon Bloom."

"Well, I don't have that kind of information at my disposal as we speak, give me your number and I'll call you with what I come up with, good enough?"

Andrew was somewhat disappointed because he figured there would be no return call, "Sure, I guess that'll work." Andrew proceeded to give him his direct line then hung up.

Scott A. Reighard

Chapter 49

After a job well done and enjoying Andrew's torture, not to mention spying Stephanie, it was time to head home. In the airport he spotted a billboard with a picture of the Caribbean. He looked at the poster and considered that when this was all over he would go to Jamaica to write that best selling tell all serial killer novel. He quietly slipped back on the plane under yet another alias.

He loved Jamaica. He used to go there as a kid with his parents. They would spend a week nearly every year in Montego Bay and he would love it when they took him to Ocho Rios and to the world famous Dunns River Falls. You could literally climb these falls. The water was a gently flowing oasis of cascading waterfalls that resembled more of a tiered fountain someone would have in their courtyard.

Unfortunately for him it had been a long time ago; their last trip being the summer of his junior year in college. Soon after that the family's losses in several bogus real estate investments put a cramp in their jaunts to the island. About a year after his father committed suicide he suggested to his mother they go back to Jamaica as a fitting tribute to his father, but his mother, who changed quite dramatically after her husband's death, refused to take him and so for twenty years or so he had not returned to a place that really made him happy. Soon he hoped to return there, for his father and for himself.

Caught in a momentary flashback also made him think of his mom, perhaps it was time to pay her a visit. It had been many years since he saw her last. She didn't like his onetime girlfriend Heather or the business of the internet with which he was involved, and there were several other personal issues the two had with one another, but he was

The Reunion Reaper

feeling a little nostalgic and last he heard his mother was not well.

So in the meantime it was back to the old homestead. The flight was smooth, the drive home reflective. He would commit to his usual journal entry and begin work on his next target.

Journal Date: June 15, 2008: The Bitch Ain't Back

What can I say, life is good. No, life is great! Man, I came so close to getting caught, that was way too exciting, yet almost too stupid as well. I have got to remember to stay cool right now. This is too easy, but now since I have challenged the wonderful Andy Keane let's see if dip-shit has any smarts at all. I can't wait to start messing with his mind. Welcome to my game Andy boy.

Okay, let's see, Sharon 'I'm a complete bitch witch' Bloom, so beautiful yet so insecure. I really wanted to look you in the eyes and call you for the be-autch you were. I give you credit for cleaning up your sleazy reputation and getting your life on track, the weight loss was a good idea. However, you just couldn't shake the bitch out of you. I loved how you purposely went out of your way to avoid me and not introduce me to your husband at the reunion. God you were such a cunt. I told you not to tell anyone about our special encounter and you had to go and tell lies about me, but you should have also been cautious in revealing the heart condition you had since childhood, I have a very good memory. I've waited twenty five years bitch to repay you for your lies. Think about why the hell you got in my car you slut. Who's the guy who always had the blow you were begging for? Me, you bleach headed bimbo.

Scott A. Reighard

You see, you've made me angry again and I don't want to get that way. Okay, let's shut this down. You're gone, I'm here, who's laughing now, huh?

Sharon Bloom, December 22, 1965 – June 10, 2008. Nothing more to add, she's ashes to ashes, dust to dust.

The Reunion Reaper

Chapter 50

Cruising through the website for the Palm Beach Post newspaper Jeffrey located the article he was looking for, *Local woman drowns competing in triathlon.* When he finished reading the article he was somewhat subdued. What should have been another feather in his cap and a proud moment became reflective examination. Like his master blue print everything had gone the way he planned, and by all accounts he should have been elated, but somehow there was a void. He needed to find out what that void was. Yeah, the whole vengeance thing that gnawed at him like a hunger as well as ridding the world of excrement was noble in his eyes, but there was a void nonetheless. There was no one to share his joy. He wanted to advertise his work, but was too smart to do something so stupid. His only light was Andrew, a man he pretty much hated all through school, but the good actor he was and still is made Andrew out to be some sort of friend. This prick, who was elected senior vice president, was awarded the most congenial in the senior superlatives, and who won the heart of a woman he so dearly wanted, fell into a trap he cleverly set. Yes sir, Ole Andy Boy was about to get crushed.

Things had definitely become more interesting. He knew there was a competitive fire in Andy since their high school days and there was only one way to find out how engaged he would be. A killer, who had thus far, killed with impunity, finally had a playing partner and that was a dangerous thought.

The new game was on and that sent a charge through him that he hadn't had for a while. So far the plan was going along swimmingly, but there were no accolades or anointments at this point, but someday there would be, but right now he needed some aspect of commentary, even though Andrew couldn't give it to him in words, it would be through actions. Andy would be a playmate, someone he could give fits to, baffle, demean, and downright embarrass.

The genius of his work was the fact that what he had hoped for actually happened. He picked up the large file that contained some of the most intimate items and background on classmates that would make the background analysis department of the C.I.A. jealous. It took several years to amass all this information, and the only real roadblock was maintaining up to date information. He looked over the next target.

He began to prepare himself for his next act. He knew this was a game of chess, and the key was to stay two to three moves ahead of your opponent. The recent email to Andy hopefully caused a reaction. He knew Andy wouldn't turn away from a challenge such as this.

"Game on schmuckatelli!" He announced to his hollow home. Despite his excitement for the change in mission he needed to update his information on the next victim. Also, he felt compelled to see his mother. Despite the rift in their relationship she was mom, and he needed to see her and try to free even more demons from the past. The next target acquisition would have to wait for now.

Chapter 51

Around three in the afternoon Andrew was sitting at his desk when the phone rang. He was completely surprised to hear the voice of Detective Olsen of the Palm Beach County Sheriff's Department.

"Man, I have to admit I didn't think you were going to call me back." Andrew said.

"Well we continue to surprise people all the time. Listen, I have some information on the person you were asking about."

"Great, go ahead, I'm ready." Andrew zipped open his leather bound zip binder he specifically dedicated to the case.

"Well it's not exactly great. Sharon Weismann, the former Sharon Bloom drowned competing in a local triathlon event."

"You're kidding me," he said scribbling down the information.

"I don't kid about deaths detective, but I do have a question for you."

Andrew shifted in his seat, he knew what was coming.

"You said this person was your sister and that she was running from someone or to someone. Well, she was married... happily it seems, with two children, and has always lived in Florida... I find that odd don't you lieutenant?"

Andrew was now in the unenviable position of having to explain himself to a fellow law enforcement brother.

He stuttered a nervous laugh. "Uh, yeah, listen, I know what I told you, but it wasn't the truth."

"No shit, you want to tell me what's going on... Keane is it?"

"I'd love to, but you gotta understand I can't."

A heavy breath sighed into the phone receiver. "Look...I don't know if you're trying to hide something from your boss or wife, but this smells like week old fish, you know what I mean? So, like, were you involved with this woman?"

"No, absolutely not...All right, my chips are on the table. She was a high school classmate of mine. There was some concern about her welfare and I was just checking into it."

"Well, it seems a little odd that you would inquire into the status of an individual who suddenly shows up dead, and then lie to a sheriff's deputy."

"I know it looks bad, and I apologize for the deception, it wasn't meant to...um, indicate my involvement or... Anyhow, I was just conducting an investigation due to a tip."

"Someone tipped you off to her missing or death?"

"The implication was death, but it was via email. Listen detective, I would love to explain all of this to you, but I just lost a classmate, and I'm in the middle of an investigation and what I'd really like is your understanding right now."

"Well, I hate to break it to you but Mrs. Weismann, not Bloom, died of an accidental drowning due to a heart attack. Are you saying this was a homicide?"

"A heart attack?" Andrew said as he was feverishly writing down the information.

"Her husband Alfred Weismann disclosed that information to us upon the initial investigation."

"Have they done an autopsy?"

"We're still waiting on the report, why?"

"Detective, I need to ask you a favor."

"You're kidding right?"

"No, I am one hundred percent serious. When the autopsy report is final could you call me?"

"Look, I've been in law enforcement for the better part of twenty years and I can spot a dirty hand job when I see it,

The Reunion Reaper

what you're doing is illegal, and I am not going to put myself in the firing line of your bullshit. You want an autopsy report you fly your ass down here and request it yourself. As far as I'm concerned this conversation never took place. You got your information. Good luck detective."

The phone went silent and soon followed a dial tone, "Damn it." What was simply between him and a few close trusted individuals was now out there to a complete stranger. He had made blunders before, but this one was careless.

As he sat there he pondered whether he should do as the detective suggested and fly back to Florida to gather his own information? Was this all an act of folly, or was he serious about the whole idea of seeing this thing through? Andrew had come to the proverbial fork in the road, but without a compass. If there was a time to back out now was the time, but another classmate was dead, and he feared more to come.

It seemed like there was no choice, he had to go. The question was how he was going to get the time off, and more importantly convince his wife he needed to return to a place he had come to loath.

Scott A. Reighard

Chapter 52

That evening Andrew snuck into his sanctuary and called his father. If there was one person whom he could trust to speak bluntly and lovingly at the same time that man was Patrick Keane, the man who metaphorically wore six shooters on his hip because that's how you got it, straight as could be. He and his father traded pleasantries and his dad sensed that all was not right, so he jump started the conversation with his usual crack.

"Well it was nice talking to you son, take care now."

"Come on dad."

"Son if I wanted silence I'd get me a cat, I don't expect you to be that way."

"I'm sorry, should I break out my journal book for you and start reading?" Andrew offered sarcastically.

"You still keep one of them piss ant journal books?"

"They're not piss ant, you should consider one yourself. I figure with your age and all the stuff you have to say you'd want to write things down."

"Shit, I barely leave your mother a note when I go out somewhere, why would I keep a journal, besides it's your job to take all this in, you know for posterity purposes."

"You know what you're right dad. I have too much time on my hands not to be writing down your wisdom and sage advice."

"Don't be a smart ass. Now you called me, so what do you want?"

"I'm sorry I'm just wound a little tight right now."

"I'll say, the last time we talked you sounded like you were talking in Morse code. My guess is you're still workin' this case and you're tryin' to keep it hush hush."

"So how's the golf game?"

"The golf game's fine, speak."

The Reunion Reaper

"All right here's the deal."

Andrew proceeded to bring his father up to date with all the information he had at this point, but his father was most intrigued by the fact the killer contacted him.

"I told you to turn this over to the Feds, but no, you're too damn stubborn aren't you?"

"Dad, if I wanted to fight over my involvement with this I would simply talk to my wife, I am asking my father for his advice."

"I gave you advice you didn't take it. Now you want more?"

"Did you think I was going to take that initial advice?"

His father paused, "No, I know my son too well, but listen you got yourself in one helluva pickle here. You screw this up and about the only thing you're gonna get is a low grade security job."

"I know the consequences dad," more emphatically now, "what do you think I should do?"

"Well, if you're gonna do it, do it. Stop peddling around testing the water, jump in, and get all wet."

Andrew was tapping his pen on the desk as his father continued.

"I think you should come to Florida and start sniffing around like a hound dog. You can't keep sitting back while this guy runs around. Besides, you know things and if the Feds get a hold of this that makes you as culpable as him for the killings."

"Wait a minute, did you just say I could be as culpable as the killer?"

"Hell yeah…look… you are the only one who has even sniffed a scent of these killings, if the Feds get a whiff of this and find out that you knew something and…"

"Okay, I got it dad."

"Listen son, the more he kills the less credible you become and the more emboldened he becomes. You got to chase this bastard down and get him quick.

His father knew how to hit the right buttons to motivate his son.

"He emailed you, so he knows you're on to him, he's probably got an erection right now knowin' that someone is with him on this."

"Dad you know I love you, but you gotta be kidding me."

"Son, this is nothing to kid about, this guy is playin' a game with you and you better figure out the rules something quick. As much as I hate to say this, but knowing your determination here is what I think. See if you can get a leave of absence and then start bustin' your ass to get this guy. I say if you come up empty within the next few weeks and don't have it figured out then call your buddy at the FBI.

There was a brief silence.

"You with me on this?" his father inquired.

"Yeah, I guess."

"Hey, ain't no guessin' on this son, you gotta killer out there who probably won't stop until you confront him. He thinks you're an idiot right, I mean, from the email he sent you. Go back into everybody's history as far as you can. Maybe this is out of revenge for something, or worse, to get his kicks. Either way you better get hustlin' on this or it'll eat you alive. Based on all that you told me he's pretty good at what he does?"

"I guess."

"And there's no real pattern, everything seems to be a different set of situations and circumstances?"

"Pretty much."

"So it's gotta be something in his moves. You gotta anticipate his move."

"I've already made files on everybody and I've been trying to collect more background but it's not easy, I haven't seen these people in years. I did get some information at the reunion."

The Reunion Reaper

"Well that's a start. Did you get a bead on anyone at the reunion? Was there any feelings you got about someone in particular?"

"Well there was one, but he really doesn't strike me as a guy who could do this."

"Hey, first rule of investigatin' is, don't rule anybody out, you know that. It could be some granny everyone thinks is nice because she bakes cookies for everybody then all of a sudden everyone starts dyin' because she laced the cookies with rat poison or something like that."

"I understand that dad, I said I thought he seemed unlikely but I didn't rule him out."

"Okay, okay. Well, is there anything you need me to do?"

"I don't want you involved in this dad."

"Hey, look who you're talkin' to? I'm already retired, who's gonna give me shit about this?"

"One illegal action doesn't need to be followed by another. I'll take care of this myself."

"Well, if there's any information you're lookin' for or whatever you know to call me right?"

"Yeah sure."

"That didn't sound too convincing."

"I will I promise, if I need anything from you I will ask."

"Good, do you want to talk with your mother?"

"I'd rather wait until this weekend. I need to talk to Stephanie about me heading down to Florida."

"All right, I love you son, good luck."

"Love you too dad, give our love to mom."

"Will do, talk to you soon."

Andrew hung up the phone and sat there for a few minutes. It was time to confront the gauntlet known as Stephanie Keane.

Scott A. Reighard

Chapter 53

Stephanie was sitting in the living room scanning one of her women's magazines. Michael and Ryan were downstairs going through their football card collections and Mary was over at a friend's house. Welcome to summer at the Keane house. The light of a beautifully sunny day looked like it refused to go away as Andrew adjusted the blinds in the living room. Andrew took a deep breath and asked Stephanie if she had a few minutes to talk.

Andrew began bluntly, "Sharon Bloom is dead," as he plopped down on the recliner.

"Wow, how did you find that out?" she asked.

"I got a call from the Palm Beach County Sheriff's Department today."

"What did they tell you?" she put her magazine down.

Andrew was running his hands through his hair, "They said she had a heart attack while swimming in a triathlon."

"Wow!"

"Yeah, wow," there was a brief silence, "the detective said she had a heart condition from childhood and that most likely is what caused the drowning or the heart attack."

"I recall that she was the one at the reunion that was a bit snobbish and showy."

Out of nowhere Andrew seemed to imply, "I don't know how he did it, but he is good."

"What are you talking about?"

Andrew raised his head to look at her, "You know what I'm talking about, what you think this was another accident?"

"Well you said she had a heart attack while swimming and that she had a heart…wait a minute, why did the sheriff's office call you?

The Reunion Reaper

Andrew deflected her question momentarily by getting up and walking over to the window looking out over the woods across the way. It gave him a few seconds to think.

"Andrew."

Andrew continued to look out the window.

"I called the other day to ask a few questions about Judith and we got to talking about the school and he dropped the news about Sharon."

"So I guess Andrew Keane is bent on solving this case."

The third person was always a sure sign of disapproval.

"Stephanie, please not now." He turned to her. "Another classmate is dead. Do I just sit here and hope that no more show up dead?"

"Why you though?"

"Why not me?"

"Because you are a Roanoke County detective not the FBI... come on Andrew you're smart enough to know that you are treading on dangerous ground here."

"I know, but I have the confidence to know I can do this."

Stephanie said something, but Andrew seemed too distant with his thoughts, until she blurted, "Are you ignoring me?"

"Sorry honey, I was just thinking, I need to go to Florida."

"You what!" she said not believing the words her husband just uttered.

He walked towards her, "just listen to me for a second before you say anything.

Stephanie crossed her arms not wanting any part should Andrew attempt to embrace her.

"I just want to go and interview her family."

"And where will that get you?"

"I don't know, they may have had some suspicions, or they might be able to provide me with some information that would lead somewhere."

She reached out and grabbed his hand.

"Andrew honey you know I support you in all you do, but I think you are taking this too far, and we can't afford you just flying here or there, and who knows what other expenses there'll be."

"What do you mean Steph?"

She smiled trying to relax the tenseness in her body.

"Did you hear me? You are a Roanoke County Police detective not the FBI...I mean, you could be jeopardizing your...our future."

"You don't trust that I can do this," he said, becoming agitated with the direction of the conversation. He pulled away his hand.

"I trust you I just don't believe this is something you should be involved with."

Andrew looked down on her, "I can't just let this guy get away with this; I have to do something."

"Please lower your voice. Look, I know they were your classmates and you're hurt, angry and protective, but you can't just haul off and throw yourself into this."

With grit in his voice and a clench of his jaw he said.

"I can do this Stephanie."

"Why does it have to be you, why can't you just call the FBI or something and let them take care of it? Won't it be reward enough that this guy will be caught?"

She made a lot of sense and he knew it, but there was so much that she didn't understand. She didn't know about the email from the killer, or the connection he still maintained with these lost individuals. She wouldn't understand that he was compelled to do this.

"You don't understand. I just can't.

He shrugged his shoulders and threw out his hands, "I just can't," as he walked out of the room.

Stephanie sat silently as she listened to her husband mutter a few choice words as he went downstairs. A few minutes passed. She decided to pursue the conversation further. She walked downstairs and into the study where

The Reunion Reaper

Andrew was sitting pointing away from the door in his high back office chair. He was staring at a picture on the wall that projected a scene with a small sail boat in a rather calm and quaint lake surrounded by mountains, long shadows and beams of sunlight indicated that it was the setting of a spring day given the array of flowers that were in bloom. It was a setting Andrew preferred and needed at this point.

"If you go and don't turn up any solid information will you turn everything over to the FBI?"

He did not turn to look at her, "I can't make that promise."

"I see, and what will you do about the time off?"

"I'll go when I get my three days off later this week."

Andrew worked four twelve hour shifts. He didn't really care for the longer shifts, but this was law enforcement.

"Your sons have ball games those days."

There it was the guilt trip; use the kids as an excuse for her not wanting him to pursue this.

"It's just one weekend they'll understand, daddy's got business to attend to."

"And the money?" she asked.

"We've still got plenty of money in the savings from our taxes, I can work some overtime and put it back later on."

He still sat with his back to her. The test of wills was on.

"Well it seems like you've got it all figured out and your mind's made up, so go Andrew, go catch your killer."

Stephanie turned and walked away. He could hear the sounds of her steps as she returned to the upstairs part of the house. Her steps were not the usual soft toed one's these seemed to say that he was so stubborn sometimes. He knew he had made her angry but he had to do this, to at least try anyway. Deep down in the bowel of his inner desire was a gnarled ball of emotion. There was the reality of all that was evident in his life: wife, kids, a great job, and then there was this, dead friends, a killer testing him and the challenge. He swung the chair around and pulled out the files on his classmates.

Scott A. Reighard

Chapter 54

A few days after their heated debate, Andrew booked his flight and the following day would head back to a place for which he thought he was finally done. He thought the reunion would bring him closure; instead it opened old wounds and started new bleeding.

He was going to work on Mark Lambert and Brian Morris as his first leads. It wasn't much, but it was a starting point. Sonny offered to do some more checking on the two. Andrew denied his request saying that he couldn't jeopardize any body else's career.

Andrew slogged through the door dreading his relationship with the wife right now. Stephanie still wasn't saying much to him. He understood the silent treatment, but he wasn't sure if it was an attitude that indicated anger or disapproval. She was his mate and he wanted to tell her more, but he felt she might try to undermine his motivation; motivation that was part anger, part challenge and yes, part ego. A woman's reasoning is so much different than a man's he pondered as he laid his keys on the counter.

He just had to move forward and quickly. After dinner and some time with the boys he returned to his familiar haunt the study, then the phone rang and it was a surprise voice on the other end. He did not recognize the number from the caller ID.

"Andy boy how's it shakin'?"

"Jeffrey Lewis, what's going on?"

"Sorry to bother you, but I've been giving this whole death of our classmates some thought."

"Yeah me too"

"Well, I did some checking on Alan Gordon, you remember we talked about him at the reunion."

"Yeah, and…"

The Reunion Reaper

"Turns out the guy's been in Europe the last six months workin' on his daddy's business."

"So I guess that rules him out given Tucker and Sharon have died in that same time period. How did you get that information?"

"Whoa, whoa, whoa, did you say Sharon?"

"Yeah, Sharon Bloom, well Weismann now."

Good boy Andy, I see you are hot on the trail of an elusive killer.

"Oh my God, what happened?" asked Jeffrey.

"Apparently she drowned while competing in a triathlon. Did you know she had a heart condition?"

"No way, drowned huh?" *You should have seen it Andy, perfect execution.*

"Yeah, this guy is good Jeffrey I don't know how he does it." *I know, I'm a genius.*

"So, how do you know she was murdered?"

"I don't know sounds too convenient to be an accident." *Convenient, I worked my ass off to get to her.*

"Is there anything you need me to do?"

"I appreciate it Jeffrey but I don't need to involve anybody else in all of this."

"I don't mind."

"No really I can't have others getting involved in this."

Oh sure, you got Andrea involved, why not...oh wait, I am involved.

"All right, but just let me know if I can do anything for you. Speaking of which, I got this information by calling Alan's dad's business."

"Oh yeah, good call," responded Andrew. *You hillbilly ding dong.* "Hey, it was the least I could do... by the way, I got a name that might be of interest, Rodney Adams."

"I got someone too, Mark."

"We talked about him at the reunion, what makes you think him?"

"I don't know call it gut instinct I guess." Jeffrey's thoughts couldn't help but intervene. *Your instincts suck idiot.* "I'm headed to Florida tomorrow to check on some things."

"Oh yeah," Jeffrey questioned with intrigue.

"You said Rodney Adams, why him?"

"Look, everyone knows he was a flamer and he was teased by a lot by people, maybe he just snapped. Notice he wasn't too chummy at the reunion."

"I guess, but wouldn't you think that if he was the killer he'd try to buddy up rather than make himself isolated even suspicious?"

"Maybe he thinks everyone feels these are just accidents as reported."

"Well, I don't know about that, I think the killer knows someone is on to him?"

"You think?" *I sure as hell hope so, things were getting boring.*

"Just call it a gut feeling."

You're gut feelings suck.

"All right, well good luck. Keep me on speed dial, you have my number right?"

"Well, I really appreciate your help Jeffrey."

"Hey it's the least I could do." *LOL you BFI.*

"I'll let you know what I find in Florida."

I already know but go waste your time and money. I've got more work to do.

"Okay, and hey, don't forget about Rodney, supposedly lives in Atlanta."

"I'll check into it."

"Talk to ya later Sandy Andy."

After hanging up the phone, Andrew immediately pulled out the file for Rodney Adams. It was funny that Andrea also mentioned that Rodney did not return any of her emails. Could Jeffrey be serious, was Rodney Adams capable of killing? Homosexuals weren't really known for

The Reunion Reaper

being serial killers. Other than Jeffrey Dahmer he was not aware of homosexual killers other than the garden variety domestic violence he came across now and again, but like his father said, never rule anybody out.

It was strange though how Rodney always seemed to look at people with a sideways glance. It seemed like he was always suspicious of people, and now here it was that Andrew was suspicious of him, maybe. Rodney's sister Carrie always protected him. Although Rodney kept his sexuality a secret it was pretty well known that he was either a homosexual or highly effeminate. Even Andrew had taken some cheap shots at him from time to time, words he now wishes he never said, but as it is said, you are hung by the tongue, what you say cannot be taken back.

Andrew fought through the clouds of images and words in hopes of recalling valuable memories of that evening at the reunion. He was trying to picture Rodney as he made his rounds and how he seemed to avoid the table where Andrew and his friends gathered. He was alone Andrew remembered that much, and he recalled that when Rodney danced he danced with his sister. That was odd, very incestuously weird. Andrew would do as Jeffrey suggested, he would keep that name in the back of his mind, but first things first, Florida and the investigation into the death of Sharon Bloom and the whereabouts of Mark and Brian.

Andrew finished up his packing and went upstairs to tend to the boys in getting them to bed. Summertime was always tough, the boys wanted to stay up late, but Andrew was a stickler for keeping them on a schedule. He and Stephanie had relaxed their bedtime but they seemed to fight it every night. Stephanie was finishing up a load of laundry as he went in to tell her good night. His approach was cautious and he thought that he would give her some words that might make her feel better.

"Hey, I'm going to bed," he said as he approached to kiss her.

"Okay, sleep well."

As he leaned in to kiss her goodnight he sensed her continued disapproving feelings of his chase. He needed to say something to make it right.

"Listen, if I come up empty in Florida there's only one other lead I want to follow up on. If that all comes up empty I'll give up the case and hand it over."

She pulled back from his embrace, "Are you just saying that to get out of the dog house?"

"No, I mean it. If things don't work out I'm done."

"Promise?"

She had to ask for the promise. "I promise," he kissed her again.

"Well, I think that's a good decision."

As he walked out of the laundry room she smiled. Her husband had made a good decision, but the only thing troubling her was, what if he does come up with evidence, what then? As she grabbed a towel from the dryer and snapped off the lint she was left with several questions. She didn't want failure for her husband, but she couldn't help but wish he would come up empty. Was that what a loyal wife should ponder?

Chapter 55

Andrew was back on a plane headed to Florida. After arriving, picking up his rental car and checking into the hotel, he spent the remainder of the day questioning family and friends of the former Sharon Bloom and spending time at the office of public records. He wanted to get as much information as possible on his classmates. He visited the Palm Beach Historical Society to get more information there as well.

He went to the Palm Beach Post and tried to dig up archival articles on whomever he could. Something he should have done more of during the reunion visit he thought. He had already searched the website news locations for the Daily Courier of Prescott, Arizona and the Leavenworth Echo of Leavenworth, Washington regarding the deaths of Brandon and Tucker. Of course he avoided the Palm Beach County Sheriff's Department. No need to bother them he thought.

The next day he went searching for the elusive Mark Lambert. The information he obtained at work was older information, and the resident at the address he pulled did not know of a Mark Lambert. He tried the Palm Beach Historical Society, but they had the same address and nothing else. It was a dead end. However, Andrew remembered that Steven Chambers was one of Mark's best friends, and he was able to coerce the information from the historical society.

Steven graduated in 1982. Andrew was nervous about the call because of the beach incident that occurred with Mark, and since Steven was pretty much Mark's best friend he wondered if that was still an issue. He called him at his office.

"Steven Chambers."

"Hey Steven, it's Andrew Keane."
"Well I'll be. How are you?"
"Good, good. So, a big time CPA in Jersey huh?"
"Yep, life's good. So how are you doing these days?"

Andrew and Steve exchanged a few pleasantries of family doings and current goings on then Andrew got to the point.

"So, why the chime old friend?"
"I have a few questions for you if you don't mind."
"Go for it."
"I've been working on contacting some old classmates, you know, getting a little nostalgic I guess."
"I hear ya, go ahead."

Andrew took out his legal pad and flipped to a page he had dedicated for Mark.

"Well, I've just about contacted everyone except for Mark.

There was a pause on the phone, "Steven?"
"Yeah, sorry my secretary just handed me something. Mark Lambert, ooh wow, man I haven't talked to him in years."
"Do you know where he might be?"
"Maybe, the last I knew of Mark he was in Lauderdale working odd jobs."
"Odd jobs?"
"Yeah, he's all messed up man."
"What do you mean messed up?"
"Ever since high school, well, let me correct that, about five or so years after graduation he was working at the Port of Palm Beach. His dad got him a job as the supervisor of cargo inspections. Man some of those older guys who worked there a long time were pissed you know, this young guy taking a more experienced guy's job."
"Yeah…"
"Anyhow, Mark didn't last very long. As you know he had a limp from that pump house accident."

The Reunion Reaper

Andrew's head dropped. "Don't remind me."

"Hey, that's water under the bridge. Mark should have waited man. He did that jump a hundred times. If he wasn't lookin' at those honey's maybe he'd still be hangin' with us. Besides, there's no point in hangin' on to anger like that. Anyhow, sorry."

"No that's okay, you were saying?"

"Well, long story short, he left the Port and went down to Lauderdale some where. Someone said he started getting strung out with drugs and stuff. Left behind a wife and two boys."

"I wonder why the report didn't give me that information?"

"What?" Steven asked.

"Oh, it's nothing, just another unreliable source. So, when was that?"

"I don't know, mid-90's I think. I've been up here since my days at Columbia and the only time I get down that way is when Ida wants to see the family."

"Ida?"

"Yeah, my wife. She's got family in Naples."

"I see, so that's all you have on Mark?"

"Sorry man, you want more you gotta talk to his ex Cindy."

"You mean Cindy Pearman?"

"Yep, the one and only."

"I know they dated the last few years in high school, but they got married?"

"Yep, but you might not want to talk to her though, mention his name she goes ballistic."

"What for?"

"Oh she hates the guy, with the abandonment and all."

"Yeah, probably not good then, well listen Steven I really appreciate all your help."

"No problem. Hey, if you locate him let me know okay? I know we're not exactly friends any more but it would be nice to hear from him."

"Okay will do. Well, take care of yourself."

Steven hung up the phone. Well, one thing was for sure, if Mark wanted to disappear he did a pretty good job of hiding his identity and information. He circled the sentence he had written down, strung out with drugs and stuff. Could it be possible the guy did a turnaround and became a killer? Or did he just continue to get strung out? One thing Andrew didn't want to contemplate was more time in Florida than necessary. His flight was leaving the next day, so he spent the better part of the day on the phone talking with Lauderdale Police and the Broward County Sheriff's Department. What he found made him able to close the book on Mark Lambert.

Mark was arrested in 2003 for drug trafficking and sales. He was serving ten years in the Broward County Jail. Although he was sad for Mark, he was glad for himself. He was able to definitely cross off one person. But in some way he was bummed because his instincts had failed him. He thought of calling Steven to let him know, but there's no need to spread someone's misfortune.

Before he headed over to a familiar place he called Andrea, but all she had to say was that most of the people who contacted her were from her graduating class. He thanked her. She told him that she would keep her ears to the rails.

Since this was his last night there, he did something he hadn't done since his days in Florida. He went to the local convenient store he ripped off as a junior in high school called the Greater Gator, which oddly enough it was Mark Lambert who corrupted him that same day Mark had his accident. He bought a six pack of imported beer and drove over to the beach. He knew it was illegal to have bottles and alcohol for that matter on the beach, but he did it anyway.

As he sat on the beach at Singer Island he reflected back on childhood days. Days spent at the beach with family and friends, or challenging his buddies to talk to the hottest girl on the beach, if she was not with some guy of course, but even the hardiest of guys like Mark or Tucker would feign reasoned advice and challenge themselves to talk with girls who were there with their boyfriends. How they would wait to see if the girl would wade into the water alone, and then like a killer whale on a helpless seal plunge in for the impossible. Andrew laughed at the thought of how many times they almost got into fights with the jealous boyfriends, or how they would all laugh when they saw the couple arguing after the encounter.

As he chugged a beer he smiled, those were the days he thought, innocent fun, just raising havoc for the sake of raising havoc, but never intending to hurt anyone. However, it wasn't long before the smile ran away from his face when slamming him like one of Greg Madison's dodge ball throws the thought of his dead classmates re-emerged. It made him angry to know that perhaps one of his own old friends could be doing this. He had found information, but it was not the helpful kind. His gap in contact was too great to capture in such a short amount of time. He figured the killer had better resources as well as a closer relationship with them. Sometimes he felt like he was staring at a sheer wall with few or no karabiners, and a rope being manned by the killer.

He always seemed to be left with more questions than answers. And what about the promise he made to his wife, was he going to keep it? He had never broken a promise to her before and he had to consider how important this really was to him. Maybe she was right as the alcohol seemed to be affecting his emotions; maybe he should just turn this over and be done with it. Who cares if the killer contacted him and basically called him an idiot? Was this a situation of wanting to do the right thing, to seek justice, or was this more about him versus the killer being the driving factor? No way, people are dying, he thought. This is about bringing another killer to justice.

He mulled over these thoughts and many others as he polished off his third beer. Then he remembered something his father once told him, don't allow your pride to control your reason. So the initial instinct of a real suspect failed, so was he going to just quit? He knew he was operating with limited resources, whining or lamenting on it proved worthless.

He concluded his saunter down nostalgia boulevard as he witnessed at least the fourth couple quietly sneaking around the beach for a private spot as he got up to leave, and then like some flash of brilliance he realized there was no moon out that night, perfect for young lovers he pondered. The only moon that would shine that night would be the hind ends of young lovers bucking like wild horses. He felt that he had accomplished at least something in Florida and would have a lot to absorb in the coming days, especially the promise to his wife.

Chapter 56

Wanting to conduct the follow up to Atlanta Andrew called Stephanie to tell her that he would be taking a minor detour in Atlanta. What he didn't tell her was that he was already there and making his way out of the airport to rent a car. She seemed more than happy to remind him that he made her a promise. *Yeah, yeah, yeah the promise.* He tried to convince her that his flight had to stop in Atlanta anyway, and that this wouldn't take more than one more day. Of course she grilled him about work, the kids and responsibilities. *I gotcha, I'm a terrible husband, how do you live with me, blah, blah, blah?*

She was angry that he was lying to his boss and that he would be missing a couple days of work. He tried to tell her that he had some things figured out, but she didn't seem to be in the mood to hear of his progress. Not wanting to argue with her he told her his flight was about to take off and that he would call her.

"I know honey, like I said, I'll be home tomorrow, maybe even later this evening. I'll call you okay?"

"Remember what you promised. By the way Michael scored two goals in his soccer game and Ryan got three hits in his T-ball game."

Ouch!

Scott A. Reighard

Chapter 57

The flight from Atlanta to LaGuardia International Airport took longer than expected as the flight encountered seasonal weather of unpredictable thunderstorms. Jeffrey was dressed casually in blue jeans that were complemented with a black polo shirt and loafers. On top of his black mane of colored hair were rectangular shaped wire rimmed sunglasses as he stepped off the plane and into the terminal. It had been a while since he saw the inside of this airport, but very little had changed. It was cold, metallic and full of tortured souls. Of course he was not to be included in that throng of people he was so much better adjusted than them. There would be no one to greet him that day for he had decided to surprise his mother with an impromptu visit. That was his method of operation anyway, so why change things. He figured that she would have been against his coming if he had called her in advance.

It had been several years since he last saw his mother and he was nervous at what her reaction might be to seeing her boy show up unannounced, but he needed to see her for reasons he really couldn't explain, but felt it was time to see her. Standing in a line of many to fetch a cab he looked around to see a place that had long since been a familiar place.

As a child, he and his mother and father would frequent this airport on their way to visit family in the summer. He grabbed a cab to Camden, New Jersey where he would seek out the residence of his aunt Delores or Aunt Dee as he called her. His mother had been living with her for the last five years because of failing health, besides she refused to stay in a hospice or elder care facility. From his memory his mother was a two pack a day cigarette smoker and rarely turned down alcohol or drugs, and so after years of

The Reunion Reaper

abuse the toll was evident. His Aunt Delores was a widow and welcomed the company, but she maintained strict rules regarding his mother's habits. One, there was absolutely no smoking in the house, and she limited Barbra, his mother, to a half a pack a day. Unbeknownst to Delores was the stash of cigarettes she kept hidden, and two, alcohol was limited to one drink per day and that was after dinner.

    The cab pulled up to the white cottage style house Aunt Delores and his mom called home and he saw that there was no car in the driveway. Despite this he paid the cabbie then ambled up to the door and knocked. There was no response. He wrapped again, still no response. He figured they were out and so he decided to sit on the front stoop to await their return. While he sat there he considered what he would say and wondered what kind of reception he would get. What would her condition be like? Would she even recognize him?

    He rehearsed a few lines and for the first time in a long time he was actually nervous. Gone was the ebullient confidence, or the brash wittiness of a clever on your feet thinker. This was a son, a lonely son hoping his mom would embrace him with the love he had so long desired from her. Conflicted as he was he ached to forgive her. Maybe age has changed her he thought. Oh sure, she loved him as a son, but it wasn't the kind of love he had hoped for. She was a selfish woman who thought more about her social standing than managing a house and one child. She was too selfish to have more children despite the urging of her husband, his father who seemed to cherish him so much, but now that man was gone taken by his own hand, too weak to face the reality of failure.

    He would sit there for the better part of an hour until Aunt Delores' white Buick LeSabre pulled into the driveway. In the passenger seat was a woman somewhat hunched down, looking quite aged. Delores quickly recognized the strange man sitting on her front stoop. As she seemingly hopped out of the car she had a broad smile, "Shaggy, is that you?"

Many in his family called him Shaggy, adopted from the old Scooby Doo cartoon. This was a seemingly appropriate nickname as a kid because he not only resembled the shaggy haired character, but he too seemed so aloof when it came to caring about anything. He smiled and rose to his feet walking over to the car. His aunt quickly grabbed him and hugged him like a child hugs a teddy bear.

Aunt Delores was a thickly built woman who despite the build looked healthy. Her reddish hair now had streaks of gray, and her smile warranted a Colgate commercial. She was a few years older than his mother, but she looked fifteen years younger. Delores opened the back seat door on the passenger side and pulled out a walker as he opened the door for his mother. She looked up at him and said, "Well if it isn't my long lost son, come to see your mother die have you?"

She was quickly interrupted by Delores, "Now Barbra, be nice I'm sure Shaggy came a long way just to see his mother."

"It's okay I kind of expected it," as he helped her out of the car he attempted to hug her, but the hug was not equally reciprocated. He offered her the walker.

The three of them made their way to the house where he helped his mother up the steps of the front stoop. He went back out and grabbed his bag and set it near the front door in the living room. The small home was clean and cozy, but there was the unmistakable smell of moth balls that gave it that odd smell of boxed up clothes. The floor was carpeted and the furniture looked old, but well maintained. Jeffrey had a brief flash of recalling this exact look the last time he was here as a senior in high school. The walls were decorated with pictures of family. He glanced at them but

The Reunion Reaper

didn't care to reminisce or try to absorb the placid looks of those on the older black and white photos.

Aunt Delores ambled into the kitchen and began to prepare lunch. He stood in the living room watching his mother scrape across the floor and into the kitchen. It wasn't long before he joined them at the urging of Aunt Delores.

He looked at his mother as she sat across from him at the kitchen table. She was fumbling through her purse as he looked on with dismay and disappointment. Gone was the vibrant dark haired slender beauty of younger days. The face that once maintained high cheek bones with soft blue eyes was now a saggy lined and weathered visage he almost couldn't recognize; the cigarettes, alcohol and years of make-up had taken their toll. The flowing strands of shiny black hair were replaced with cold gray, and the posture had dipped considerably, yet despite all this she was still mother, a person he would always love regardless of her physical or mental state. Of course he was too vain to ever allow himself to get into the same condition as his mother so he limited his intake of alcohol and did away with drugs completely; indulging in them that is, but he was certainly not opposed to using drugs for advantageous purposes. He was clean and sober maybe, but he was a maniac killer with the smile of a Gentlemen's Quarterly cover boy.

As they sat and ate a lunch of soup and French bread most of the questions were being asked by Aunt Delores. She was so happy to see a nephew she hadn't seen or heard from in years. She was hopeful he would come around more often. He filled them in as much as he could admit to. Of course there were the killings he failed to mention. He was proud of his newfound accomplishments, and in some way he wanted to share this news with so many, but in good time he thought, all in good time. And so he answered the questions with smiles, laughter and some glances toward a mother who barely raised an eyebrow to him during the whole of the conversation. He felt compelled to lean over and pat dry her chin that seemed to catch whatever broth couldn't be slurped into her mouth.

When lunch was complete it didn't take long for his mother to comment on her daily rituals.

"It's time for one of my smokes Delores," as she proceeded to sound like a cat coughing up a hairball.

"Yes Barbra your post lunch smoke. Shaggy would you please unlock the door there for your mother so she can go out on the back porch?"

He got up to unlock the door then held it open as she shuffled her way out to smoke. She pushed her walker along the dark wooden floor. His aunt installed a couple of tennis balls on the front legs of the walker to prevent her from making drag marks. As he watched her awkwardly lift and shift herself outside he decided to remain inside to gain some insight about his mom from his aunt. She shared with him his mother's debilitating health and her curmudgeon attitude toward so many people and things. But as his aunt explained that after his father committed suicide and when her husband Sheldon died they only had each other. She was willing to tolerate his mother's ways for the sake of having someone around. He could see the sincerity in her eyes and hear it in her voice and he wondered how she could have come from the same screwed up family of which he was a part. His mother was a selfish vain woman. In some deep avenue of his soul he wished that Delores had been his mom and that Barbra would play the role of the screwed up aunt, but it wasn't so. He decided to go outside to talk with his mom.

She was hunched over in a padded patio chair and was flipping her ashes anywhere she pleased. The weather was warm but she still wore a light sweater. For a woman who had just turned sixty five she looked eighty. Her bony fingers clutched the current lifeline and happiness of her

The Reunion Reaper

existence as she stared out into the serene setting of a well manicured lawn of colorful summer flowers, and a garden. The yard was divided off into halves. One side resembling a country club lawn while the other half was dedicated to a lush garden of zucchini, squash, tomatoes, peppers and herbs. Aunt Delores maintained the energy of a forty year old. She kept busy by maintaining a garden, not to mention her brisk daily walks. Conversely there was his mother. The only thing she planted was her very self in front of the television for most of the day. The serene setting didn't do much to curb his mother's attitude either.

"So how are you mother?" he asked as he grabbed a seat.

"I'm great, just look at me, don't I look great?"

"Absolutely, you look the same as I remember."

"Look son you shouldn't have come all this way to see me, I'm dying you know."

"Aren't we all? I mean, at some point right?" he tried to calm the tension, but it wasn't working.

"Why are you here? Why have you come all this way?"

He hesitated and then spotting a fly that landed on his mother's shoulder of which she was oblivious to, he swatted at the fly.

"What are you doing?"

"There was a fly on your shoulder. Anyhow, I came here because I was thinking about you and dad a while back and the vacations we used to go on. Weren't they great? I wish you and I could go on a vacation back to Jamaica."

"I don't like to fly anymore."

"Well, what I meant was, I just thought it would be nice I didn't say we definitely would go."

"Simon's been dead for almost twenty years now."

"Actually it's been fourteen."

"What are you some damn time keeper or something? I said almost twenty years, did I say twenty? No, I said almost twenty."

Somewhat agitated with his mother's nastiness, "Okay fine whatever you say, I didn't come here to argue over dad's death anniversary."

"Jesus, you see this is how you were as a boy always arguing with me. You never questioned Simon, but when I spoke it was always some witty comeback or smart ass comment."

He just sat there and began to wonder why the hell he made this trip. The woman hadn't changed, but he was doing his best to maintain a good attitude.

"I'm sorry mother, in fact that was one of the reasons I came back, to apologize to you for some of the ways I treated you back then. I was wrong."

Although he didn't necessarily mean all of it at least it sounded sincere. She seemed to ignore his apology.

"Simon was such a weak man, he was a coward for taking his own life you know that don't you."

"I just think he was afraid of failure, that he failed us."

"Oh he failed me all right, but he didn't fail you did he, he left you a hefty sum."

There was a brief silence as she glared at him.

"I…I just think he was afraid."

"Of what," she barked back

He hesitated then looking out into the yard said, "Your habits."

"My habits, what the hell are you talking about?"

"Come on mom everyone knew you had some drug and alcohol issues, there was no way he was going to just hand over the money to someone who might—"

"Might what, go ahead say it, snort it up my nose?"

"I wasn't going to say that."

"The hell you weren't. So why are you really here, to show me how Simon's money has made you a nice wealthy man, while I waste away in friggin' Jersey?"

She began to cough badly, almost hacking, obviously irritated with the subject of the conversation. He considered

The Reunion Reaper

putting his hand on her back and rubbing it hoping to calm her but he just sat there watching this old woman's body convulse with each cough.

"I don't want this to be about money...I still love you mom, I want us to spend some more time together, since dad's death we're all we have."

And then his mother dropped a bomb shell, "Simon was never your real father by the way."

There was a considerable pause.

"What are you talkin' about?"

"Forget it I shouldn't have said anything."

"Forget about it, are you crazy? You just tell me Simon's not my real father and expect me to just forget you just said it?"

She shrugged her shoulders and dropped her cigarette into a canister Delores kept for her. "It was a long time ago."

He had fire in his eyes. The woman he loved and looked up to had just slapped him with a huge surprise, "I'm listening."

She told him the story of how she met and had an affair with a married man, a man by the name of Abe Lippman, a probate attorney.

"You mean Abe Lippman, the attorney in West Palm?"

"He's the one, he's your real father," almost with a cold churlishness to her tone.

He sat in complete silence as she continued, "Simon always loved me despite knowing you weren't his. He was a proud man, he wasn't about to let the family or community know that he fired blanks, and so he married me and took you for his own.

Still not a word, he sat in utter shock, she continued, "Well if you're not going to say anything."

"You had an affair with a married man?"

"Newsbreak, it's not the first time that's happened you know."

"But you said Simon loved you, and you had an affair anyway?"

Again she shrugged her shoulders, "I was young and probably a little coked out at the time Abe and I, you know…" She looked at her son as his head hung low against his chest. "Oh don't give me that innocent little Johnny look, you were nearly a strung out teenager yourself. You can't tell me you did some things you now regret."

He leaned in real close to her. "Well, I didn't make a fucking baby mom."

He got up from his chair and walked toward the door leading into the house. She turned to him, coughing again, "Where are you going?"

"Away from this insanity," he flung the screen door open.

"Go ahead, run like they all do," she said as he slammed the door behind him.

That woman is out of her mind. He passed by his aunt who was sitting watching her daily soap opera.

"Shaggy what's wrong honey?"

"I'm outta here Aunt Dee."

"Wait, talk to me."

He stopped briefly only to pick up his bag, then pointing toward the back door, "She's a lunatic Aunt Dee how can you live with that?"

"She's been through a lot Shaggy, she loves you, she really does."

"Yeah I can see that. I've been living a lie Aunt Dee, for forty years I have been living a lie."

"She shouldn't have told you that it's true, but now that you know you need to forgive her, she was in a bad way then you know."

"Forgive her? HA!"

He turned toward the door, "Shaggy please wait, don't walk away without making peace, please God don't go."

The Reunion Reaper

"It's too late Aunt Dee, I shoulda never have come here..." He paused by the door. "I'm sorry for placing you in the middle of this, but sitting on that porch is a wacky screwed up woman, you'd be best served to put her away where she belongs."

He stomped out the door with bag in hand and emptiness in his soul. A tear trickled down his aunt's cheek as she saw him jump down the steps and quickly make his way down the street. She could hear Barbra muttering some words as well as expletives through the door. "Oh just shut up woman, you've ruined enough lives as it is already. God forgive him."

Scott A. Reighard

Chapter 58

Andrew's plane touched down in Atlanta. He rented a car and headed north on the I-75/I-85 interchange. The address he located for Rodney Adams was on Georgia Avenue, an older area in downtown Atlanta that over the past years had undergone some major changes. He wasn't exactly sure what he was doing but he thought at this point he would take a stab at finding anything that would either further his investigation or put it to rest, especially given that Mark Lambert was no longer a part of the equation. Perhaps just talking with Rodney would shed some light on something, anything really.

It had been a while since he was in Atlanta, other than being at the airport, but the place was familiar, this was where he met the former Stephanie O'Brien his wife. She was a college student at the University of Georgia. The two of them were set up on a blind date by his college mate Ralph Sherman who was from Atlanta. Ralph's girlfriend happened to be best friends with Stephanie. They spent a spring weekend in 1988 getting to know one another as they bopped around Atlanta. Stephanie was a junior at UGA studying Marketing and Business. He claimed to his friends it was one of the best times he ever had with a woman, second only to that night on the beach with Amy. Although he had a few girlfriends through college none were really serious long term relationships. Stephanie was different. She was so vibrant, exciting, beautiful, athletic and smart. She was the complete package and although he wasn't thinking about being serious about relationships at that time he couldn't help but stay in contact with her and eventually establish a long distance relationship.

The ride from Roanoke College to UGA took about six hours and he made it quite often after their initial date.

The Reunion Reaper

After graduating, she moved to Florida and subsequently moved in with Andrew. They eventually married in 1993.

Andrew passed Turner Field and took the downtown exit to locate Georgia Avenue. As he slowly drove down the street he spotted the house he was looking for. It was an old Victorian style home that looked to be yet another of the many recently remodeled homes in that area. He drove past it to the next street made a U-turn and then parked on the opposite side of the street a few houses down from Rodney's. He reached over into his dark blue backpack where he kept his leather zip binder and began rummaging through the file to find Rodney's information. *This is silly Rodney doesn't fit the mold for a serial killer. Despite all the crap he's been through surely he wouldn't resort to murder.* But as he went through his file he did see where Rodney had a few bouts of domestic issues in his life. There was an incident in a Florida bar.

One night Rodney and a few of his friends happened to be partying at Le Chez, a bar owned by one of his friends. On that particular evening Rodney and another man were involved in a dispute over a previously shared partner. No physical blows were thrown but the fight finally came to an end when Rodney reached behind the bar and grabbed his friend's handgun. He pointed it at the man's private area and threatened to destroy a close member of the family.

Although Rodney didn't shoot him, the man pressed charges, but those charges were later dropped due to the fact the man was involved in a male prostitution sting. There was local media coverage and the bar, which turned out to be a front for the male prostitution business, was closed.

Rodney also had a major falling out with his father several years back and that precipitated the move to Atlanta. For the last few years there was no recordable information on him. He was not gainfully employed which could lead someone to assume that he had a lot of time on his hands. And since no one really talked with him at the reunion very little was known about Rodney Adams since his foray into the media spotlight.

Andrew sat there for a while just looking for signs of life. There was an older cobalt colored Mercedes Benz parked in front of the house but he wasn't sure it was Rodney's. Several cars had passed by as well as a few walkers, some with dogs while others just seemed to be enjoying an early evening stroll. Despite it being early evening it was another steamy day in Atlanta. He didn't want to look suspicious despite the fact that he had the car running and the A/C blowing, but as he zipped up the binder he felt it was time to do something soon.

He got out of the car and slowly paced toward the house. He looked it over, glancing around to the back of the house as well as up and down the street. He walked up the steps to the front door and wrapped on it several times. He knocked again yet still there was no response. Out of curiosity he placed his hand on the door knob and it was unlocked. He slowly opened the door and stepped inside. He called out to see if anyone was in the house, but there was no answer. He took a few more steps in and called out Rodney's name; still no response. He walked around the first floor checking out the living room and the dining area. Despite the home being a Victorian model on the outside, the inside was very contemporary, almost cosmopolitan. In the kitchen however he discovered something surprising. On the counter there were several baking items and it looked like someone was in the middle of cooking. The oven was turned off but there were several pans containing cake batter that looked like they should have been thrown in the oven. This doesn't look good he thought. On a side table near a back door were business cards. *Adams Catering Service* they had printed on them. Rodney was a caterer. *Is it any wonder there wasn't any gainful employment listed for him, but you would have thought that*

The Reunion Reaper

he would have passed out his business cards at the reunion? He continued inspecting for signs of life, and instinctively placed his hand on his weapon.

Leaving the kitchen, he once again called out Rodney's name. He was trying to think what he would say should Rodney or whoever else lived there suddenly appear. *I'll just say I was in town and wanted to see a few classmates on my way back home, no harm no foul right?*

He came back to the front door area and looked up the stairs that led to the second floor. He tiptoed up the wooden steps until he came to the second floor. He spotted a bedroom door open just down the hall from where he was standing. *What the hell am I doing?* He debated whether to proceed, but curiosity and instinct took over.

He walked down the hallway and peeked into the bedroom, he saw someone lying on the bed looking as though they were asleep. He pushed the door open and then saw something he did not expect. Lying on the bed wearing only a black thong with hands and feet bound with rope to the bedposts was the body of Rodney Adams. His mouth stuffed with what looked to be a sock or something.

Andrew could not conceive how bad this was for him or worse yet, for Rodney. He had just discovered a dead body and the question was should he report it or just get the hell out of town? He knew that what he was doing was illegal. He moved closer to the body hoping to see anything that would indicate cause of death. Suddenly his heart seemed to pump out of his chest as he heard the sound of a car door closing.

He looked out the window and spotted a Caucasian male in his thirties getting out of a car that he parked right behind the Mercedes. The man was carrying a few grocery bags. Andrew's eyes grew wide. *Please go next door. Come on go next door. Shit.*

Not wasting any time he bolted down the hall and down the steps as quickly and quietly as he could. Thankfully the man was slowly walking up to the house as Andrew reached the bottom step. He remembered a back door just off the kitchen and he headed that way.

Once outside in the backyard he glanced around, there was no one was around. He snuck around to the side of the house. He was sweating profusely and it wasn't the Atlanta heat causing that sweat. His legs were shaky as well. The young man had just walked into the house. Andrew's eyes were darting around hoping no one was around to see him. He did his best to walk calmly down the street to his car. He was feeling lucky yet unlucky at the same time. He took a few seconds to compose himself before driving off. As he started the car he gripped the wheel like a shaken teen grips the bar of a thrill ride at the fair. As he drove by the house he swore he could hear the sound of a male voice yelling out in horror at just discovering the body of his lover.

Chapter 59

Andrew spent the better part of that evening in his Atlanta hotel going over what he discovered only hours earlier. He paced back and forth and drank enough water for a camel as he considered the prospect that his prints, and any other evidence that would be discovered at the crime scene, not to mention how he would explain it. He was in a quandary and knew he had screwed up, bad.

He plopped down onto the side of the bed and stared at his reflection in the television screen. He should have never checked the door to see whether it was locked. He struck the bed in anger at his stupidity. He felt at this point he had no choice. After a few hours agonizing over his dilemma, he picked up the phone and called the Atlanta Police Department to ask for directions. He thought it best to be up front, sort of, and tell them what he discovered. After all, he didn't know how bad things were and by playing the wait and see game might not work out to his benefit. While driving to the station he thought about his luck, and briefly questioned his abilities. Were the screw ups a result of being unlucky, or were they more about feeling the pressure to capture a killer? He went to school for a lot of things, but operationally there were things he needed to know as an investigator, especially given the unusual circumstances of this bizarre run through what seemed to be Andrew's Adventures in Wonderland.

He drove down to the central station located at Ponce de Leon Avenue and notified them of who he was and what he had discovered. The dispatcher called detective Martin, who was currently at the scene. She informed Martin that there was someone confessing to being at the crime scene then fleeing. *It wasn't exactly fleeing,* Andrew muttered to himself.

Following standard protocol they placed him in a holding cell despite showing them his law enforcement credentials, but he understood a man was dead. He would have done the same thing.

Andrew sat quietly. It was late, and Andrew was tired, in more ways than one. When the detective released him from his holding cell and sat him down next to his desk Andrew proceeded to tell detective Martin all he could short of giving away the fact that he was conducting an investigation. If Andrew was a good liar he needed to be the nonpareil for the Atlanta Police that evening as well as the following day. They insisted on holding him until all the information he provided was verified. Some of the initial information coming out of the case showed that the time of death was estimated between ten o'clock in the morning and noon, and since Andrew's plane did not land until four that afternoon he could not have been at Rodney's house earlier that day. Rodney's partner also explained that he was at work all day and that he called the house around noontime to ask Rodney about dinner but there was no answer.

After satisfying their questions and checking on his credentials, Andrew was free to go. Charges for unlawful trespass were dropped against him because he was a fellow officer. That was the good news for Andrew, the bad, how he was going to explain all this to both his wife and his boss.

The following day after discovering Rodney Adam's body he was finally back on a plane and headed home; in the meantime he had missed work, not to mention the fact that his wife and family were extremely worried for him.

On the plane ride home, he wondered if this case was really meant for him to solve. The haunting thoughts were that Andrew was in need of evidence, but was he sick to consider his bad luck while classmates were dying? This most recent event was the first death that was actually a

The Reunion Reaper

homicide. Had the killer changed tactics? Had he run out of ideas? He would keep a watchful eye on the Atlanta investigation. Perhaps they could be the one's to break the case. In the meantime if Andrew was keeping score bad luck was kicking good luck's butt right now.

Andrew returned home to Roanoke but not to the open arm welcome he had hoped for. Of course he couldn't help but consider that his marriage was becoming strained. For the time being he was able to keep the investigation a secret from his work place and much of it from his wife also, but he felt things were falling apart and that perhaps it was time to turn over the case and come clean; to free himself of this albatross growing heavier with each failure. The weight of time, money and relationships was getting to the point of doing severe damage to his lifestyle. He made a promise to his wife and he was going to keep it. He had failed. He was unable to turn up any credible evidence that would take him forward in the case.

After a cold reception from his wife despite his reassurances to her that he was done with the case, he made sure to spend some good time with his kids that evening. Guilt has a way of motivating a man, so he played Yahtzee and some card games to pass away the evening hours. It's not that he didn't spend time with the kids, he did, but at this particular time it was a way to save face with an upset and confused wife. He was not looking forward to returning to work the next day. He most likely would have to explain not only his absence to his superior, but why the department received a phone call from the Atlanta Police Department.

Scott A. Reighard

Chapter 60

The flight back home was one of reflection, anger, and very sobering. Jeffrey examined who he had in his life and it was basically no one. He lost his father, or the person he thought was his real father to suicide, he lost his long time girlfriend by his own hands and now he had lost his mother to complete whacks-ville. In some weird way he wanted to kill her right there on the spot for lying to him all these years. For the first time in a long time he felt as though he wasn't in control. For a man who had designed, made the rules, and dictated the pace of play, he was the victim of the curve ball; and deadly accurate by a mother who felt no remorse. Confusion crept in like an early morning fog. He didn't know what to do. Being home provided him with the atmosphere he needed right now.

He felt the urge to fly down to Florida to see Abe his real father, but he had only known him to be a probate attorney and nothing more. How exciting could that be he questioned. Better yet, how awkward would that be? Did Abe even know he fathered a child? *The guy's a probate attorney, he oversees estate planning. How could my mother be attracted to such a dolt? Maybe I was adopted and she was just bullshitting me yet once more*. But she wasn't, he was Abe's boy and that was that. How interested could he be in his life, Abe never once took interest or knew anything about the young man he fathered to a married woman. He was a bastard child. His journal entry would be one of anger and hatred, and of planning.

That night back home was a quiet one. There would be no clever hyped up music to get his juices flowing instead it would be a night being comforted by the Eagles and a little Bob Marley. He needed to erase the trip that was the opposite of what he had hoped. As he banged the keys on

The Reunion Reaper

the keyboard he created his journal entry, but it seemed to ramble on like the lyrics to a Bob Dylan song. He had to focus there were still other lives to add to his misery list. After the journal entry he decided to email the only friend he felt he had, yet ironically, the man trying to hunt him down. He was crossed about communicating with Andrew, but felt getting back in the game would ease his ill thoughts of a hosed up domestic situation. He needed to talk with someone, despite the fact that this was a one way communication. The email was simple:

Hey boner! I say that because your detective skills are about as stiff as they come. I'm sorry, I know you're tryin'. Hey you know what you and I have a lot in common, we are both competitive, we love life and we wish only to make things right. It's too bad that there are those who come along and screw it all up for us. I was a happy kid, or so I thought. I had a lot, I was lucky, but you know, without a parent's love it's pretty much a false existence and one day you look in the mirror and the person you see is not who you think it is. Oh well, like Macbeth said, life is but a walking shadow, a poor player who struts his hour upon the stage and then is heard no more, full of sound and fury, signifying nothing, or something like that. What is it with Shakespeare that sticks to you like someone's discarded gum on the bottom of your shoe? Is that what we are poor players shouting from the tops of our lungs hoping to be heard? How sad I guess. Oh well, you know what, game on shit-dick, if I am just a poor player strutting my hour upon the stage I plan on stealing the scene.

As he weighed the intent of the message by re-reading it he paused, wondering if he was revealing a vulnerability, a weakness that might spell doom when the job is yet unfinished. He looked it over and decided to save it to the rant folder. He saw the email as a sign of weakness. Weakness is for the undisciplined and those who wish to be seen as such for sympathies sake he thought. It was time to get back to work. The recent events had ushered in a different kind of anger and more determination as well. He would make those people, who relish in other's pain, pay for their crimes, even if it was a mother, or those who stand idly by and do nothing for those reaching out to witness what it is like to need someone yet have no one when it counted most. It was time to get back to work. He would write a different email for Andrew, but send this one.

The Reunion Reaper

Chapter 61

It didn't take long for Andrew to get the word that Captain Hardy wanted to see him. Andrew knew it was coming. For most of the morning he stayed in his office trying to avoid as many colleagues as possible and get caught up on paperwork, which had grown considerably. One of the captain's assistants Rita called Andrew to let him know he was to see the Captain. He wondered what took him so long, probably to make him sweat no less.

He slowly approached his office door. He tapped lightly on the open door.

"You wanted to see me Captain?"

"What do you think?" Captain Hardy retorted as he was shuffling through some papers.

"I guess you know about my run-in in Atlanta."

"Have a seat Andrew we need to talk."

Andrew approached the captain's desk and grabbed a seat. Sitting there he felt like Gulliver from *Gulliver's Travels* when he was lost on Brobdingnag. He was feeling pretty small given that he not only was blowing this case, but getting into legal trouble as well. He had to cautiously and with great thought answer the captain's questions.

"So how do you like being a lieutenant so far?"

Great start, ask me if I want to keep this position right?

"Things are going well, I am really learning a lot, and again, I really appreciate the opportunity you and the chief gave me." *There, was that brown nose enough?*

"I see, how do you think you've performed so far?"

Damn El Capitan really wants to send me to the gallows I can just feel it, no wonder they call him hard-ass.

"I think that I have proven myself quite well sir. I'm not behind on any of my work."

"Well in all honesty*,"* *here it comes*, "we are quite pleased with your work, but as you know I got a very disturbing call the other day about one of my officer's. Now I want to protect my people as much as I can as long as I have good information. Why don't you tell me what happened in Atlanta?"

Andrew told Captain Hardy basically the same thing he told the Atlanta Police. How he was on his way back from Florida from seeing his parents about wills and such, and then on a brief stopover in Atlanta seeing an old high school chum. *I sure hope he buys that one.* Of course it was a lie and he hated to lie, but right now he thought he was saving his twin cheeks and was getting ready to turn over the case anyway so once again his favorite thought emerged, no harm no foul. Sure he failed, but the odds were really stacked against him. So he bails on what seems to be an impossible situation, at least his job was safe and he was ready to get back to work on what he should be working on.

After he was done Captain Hardy commented, "All right, if what you are saying is the truth then we have nothing to worry about. I suspect you're anxious to get back to work."

"Yes sir, definitely." Andrew stood up, "is that all sir?" Captain Hardy simply waved his hand at Andrew and went back to the paperwork on his desk.

Andrew was making his way out of the room when the captain offered, "Andrew, this is a small police force, we hear and see things, I hope you're making good decisions."

"I am sir. My first priority is to this job, after my family of course."

"We'll see."

Andrew walked out and could swear he felt a moistness he hadn't felt in a region of his body in a long time. *This is a small force we see and hear things,* he repeated to himself. Surely Sonny hadn't said anything?

The Reunion Reaper

Returning to his desk he placed a call to Sonny who was not at work that day. He left a message. Andrew would have to wait to find out if one of his best friends opened his mouth to co-workers about his extra-curricular adventure.

Scott A. Reighard

Chapter 62

That evening after work Andrew was back home. The boys were running around in the yard and Mary was prepping for a night out with her friends. Andrew had stopped off at the grocery store. Knowing he was still in the dog house; most likely chained to the back with little or no wiggle room, he cooked his wife her favorite meal, a strip steak with a loaded baked potato and steamed asparagus. Andrew would have preferred chewing on the bottom of his shoe rather than eat asparagus, but he was willing to take one for the team that night and down a few stalks of the vegetable that looked like a blade of grass on steroids.

Stephanie knew what her husband of fifteen years was up to, but she played along and when he reiterated that he was going to turn things over to Joe at the FBI that following Monday she was glad to hear it. He didn't want to quit on this but he weighed the options, his obsession or risking his family and job? It was a pretty easy decision really.

After dinner and cleaning the gas grill, Andrew was out in the yard kicking the soccer ball around with the boys. The evening was hot but dry. His neighbor Jeff had just cut his grass and the fresh sweet woodsy smell of newly mown grass was in the air, not to mention the lightning bugs that danced here and there, glowing like neon green bulbs that flicked off and on. The night descended quickly and the mosquitoes were letting everyone know they were out for blood. Afterwards Andrew got the boys ready for bed then sauntered into his study. He wanted to package everything up and send it to Joe. He fired up his computer and was going to print off some things he had typed, as well as some of the articles he saved from the deaths. He would try to hand over as much information as he could for Joe.

The Reunion Reaper

While he was on the computer he jumped online to check his mail, and sure enough there was another email from the killer. The subject line read: *This Bud's for you.*
He reluctantly opened it trying to understand if he enjoyed the pain of being belittled or whether he was just plain curious; either way he read what the psycho had to say.

The devil went down to Georgia he was looking for a soul to steal, he was in a bind cause he was way behind he was lookin' to make a deal. When he came across this dumb shit working on a case and screwin' it up, well the devil jumped up on a hickory stump and said boy let me tell you what.

Aare you related to Barney Fife? How in the world did you get a badge, let alone work for that security company in Florida? You are boring me. Please tell me I'm not working with a retard. GIVE ME SOMEONE WORTHY! Hey, doesn't Joe Marketti work for the FBI these days? He was a pretty smart guy, unlike you, you one tooth Neanderthal. Damn, maybe I should leave bread crumbs to my front door for you. You are such a loser! You apparently have the detective skills of a deaf, dumb and blind squirrel. You couldn't find a nut if it dropped on your head.

Okay, here's the deal, once again I am about to show you how smart I am and how dumb you are. I am going to kill another classmate within, oh let's see, forty eight hours, that should give you enough time to wallow in the pity of your pathetic life. Oh, and don't get stupid and try to call people because I just might go Postal you backwoods hick. You must be wondering, who is this genius that is toying with me like the Greek gods toyed with meaningless humans? You know what's funny, what you're doing is illegal and if the authorities find out you'll not only lose your job, you just might end up behind bars. Here you are after me to put me behind bars yet here I am in control. Oh, and what to make of your wife and kids, hmm, what to do, what to do? Should Andrew continue to give chase or concede? Gee, I don't know Batman. Well, regardless of what ding dong does, oh that's you by the way, someone's goin' down within 48 hours. Okay, so read this real slow so you can understand okay? What soars through the sky but doesn't flap its wings?

Andrew was just about to hit the delete button but he couldn't shake the threat. He was going to kill someone within forty eight hours. Looking at his watch and the time the email was sent, he figured he had about forty two hours to catch a killer. But what about the promise to his wife, and the hints his boss dropped on him at work? People's lives hung in the balance however, and this dilemma was unlike any other he had in his life. Again, there was only one person he could really go to in dire situations. He picked up the phone and called dad.

When his dad answered the phone Andrew's tone was sobering, his dad noticed. Andrew briefed him on everything that happened in Atlanta and that he made a promise to Stephanie and that his job might be in jeopardy. His dad listened to a son who was hurting and this ate at him, but his son created this situation and he had to make a decision.

"So I'm guessing things aren't going that well."

"Dad, are you going to help or constantly play devil's advocate?"

"You have how many dead right now?"

"Five…I just feel that I should have made more headway at this point."

"What about those leads you talked about?"

"One is dead, and the other is in jail."

"That does make it tough. Son, let me tell you a little story."

Great, Andrew thought.

His father then went into a story about a case he worked in the mid-70's. It was a story about this elusive guy who

The Reunion Reaper

was breaking into these hotels in Florida and stealing tourist's money, jewels, etc. and he was slipping every trap his team set up. Finally they nabbed the guy by mistake because he had a fetish for young boys who worked at these hotels as cabana boys. They set up a sting for the cabana groper and when the guy was nailed for trying to grope an undercover agent posing as a teenage boy he was taken into custody. The amazing thing was he confessed to all the robberies but pleaded that we not publicize the cabana boy incidences because he was married and had an image to protect.

"I'm sorry dad, what's the point here?"

"Well, other than being a damn good story the point is, his emailing you is most likely a diversion. I told you this guy is just playin' a game with you. Don't get trapped by all his crap. Just do what you need to do. I always taught you about distracting your opponent and now you're allowing this asshole to distract you. If you want him, he's gonna have to come to you it seems."

"You think so?"

"Hell yeah, this guy's definitely playing a mind game. He knows somehow that you're on to him and he's trying to keep you off balance. Don't fall for the bait son you'll get hooked every time."

"So what do I do about the next," Andrew looked at his watch, "forty hours? Stephanie thinks I've given up on this Holy Grail search and my boss is hoping that I am making good decisions."

"Well, sounds like you have forty hours to find this prick."

"And Stephanie and the job?"

"You worry too much about that, your wife understands. Oh they have their ways, but ultimately they understand. And as for your job, well, you're a cop."

He knew what his father meant, but his father didn't have to face a resolute Irish woman who, when lied to, becomes a different species, or to a boss who was worried about his newly appointed lieutenant.

"You know son, the bottom line is whether you feel you owe these dead people something, and potentially the rest some form of protection. It's a tough place you're in, but you're there and you have to make a decision. I will not try to influence you one way or the other. Pray about it, and talk reasonably with Stephanie, she'll understand."

Andrew thanked his father for all his advice and input and as he said goodbye his father left him with one last thing to consider, "Don't do it because you feel guilty about the deaths of your classmates, do it because it's the right thing to do, it's all about good and evil son, and you are good people, very good people. I love you. Good luck."

"I love you too dad, thanks."

Andrew hung up the phone and leaned back in his chair. He closed his eyes and tried to imagine how Stephanie would feel, and what this might do to his place at work. When he rolled back up he looked over at his clock and didn't realize how late it was. He looked in on Stephanie and she had fallen asleep with the television on, their conversation would have to wait until tomorrow. In the mean time it was going to be another late night and an early morning because he had to go to work the next day, but he had no choice. It was time to put up or shut up.

The Reunion Reaper

Chapter 63

The hour had quickly passed as Andrew sat in his study looking over the yearbook, files on classmates, and articles he found on the internet relative to the victims thus far. There didn't appear to be any sort of discernible pattern to the killings, at least Andrew didn't see one. He called Andrea again, who was now becoming his Huggie Bear, so to speak, but she was on vacation. The only thing he really had at this point was that the victims thus far were from his graduating class, and so his thoughts turned back to the internet and he began to Google several classmates just to see what he could find.

After what seemed to be an hour of absolute futility on the internet search engine and sometimes getting diverted with "irrelevant" material, Andrew had one of those a-ha moments. He remembered his conversation with Jeffrey Lewis prior to his going to Florida. He thought that it was odd that Jeffrey not only called him, but mentioned Rodney Adams as well. A strange coincidence or a lead, Andrew didn't know. He grabbed his pad and found the number he had jotted down for Jeffrey.

Dialing the cell number Jeffrey gave to him, Andrew heard several rings before the voice of Jeffrey Lewis chimed in.

"Hey, this is Jeffrey. I am currently out of the country right now. For some reason I cannot get cell service across the pond on this cell phone, besides I am vacationing on the Amalfi Coast so leave me alone. Anyhow, leave me your information and I will get back to you as soon as I get back to the states. Ciao!"

"Great!" Andrew hung up the phone, deciding not to leave a message.

He was disappointed that he couldn't talk with Jeffrey, and at this point was a little confused as to what he believed. An egocentric maniac was playing him, he couldn't talk to anybody in the professional arena about this, and within a matter of hours another classmate was going to die. It would be yet another rough night's sleep for Andrew.

What Andrew didn't know was Jeffrey was still at his home and he watched as his phone buzzed on the kitchen table. He glanced at the number and saw that it was an incoming call from Virginia. He checked for a message but the caller didn't leave one.

"I wonder what that was all about? Maybe Andy was looking for some advice."

First he smiled then laughed out loud unable to contain his brilliance with any modicum of humility.

"Don't you just love it when you have someone exactly where you want them to be?"

He took a slow sip of the smoothie he just made.

"He's got to be going crazy. Well, if he bought the Italy message then I probably bought at least two weeks of complete cluelessness from dick-weed. Lord have mercy this is fun."

Time to visit someone who just can't seem to keep her nose out of people's business.

The Reunion Reaper

Chapter 64

Standing in the break room at the department Andrew was trying to shake off the drowsiness as even a third cup of coffee wasn't enough. Perhaps it was mental exhaustion from a case heading nowhere, and from the fact that he appeared to be driving an investigative car stuck in neutral. He was gassing it like crazy but he wasn't having much luck with the drive train. Time wasn't on his side either as he needed to find another gear, even a little luck. He slowly strolled his way down to his desk, and as he sat staring at the paperwork on his desk, just shook his head. *This is too much right now.* As he stared Sonny approached him.

"Congratulations!"

Looking confused Andrew gazed up at him, "about what?"

"It's been three months there honcho."

"Three months for what?"

"You mean you don't know, lieutenant there big guy, it's been three months."

"Oh yeah, feels good, break out the beer and nuts."

Sonny looked at him strangely, "All right what's goin' on?"

"Sorry, there's a lot going on right now."

"So what's up?"

"This case is kickin' my butt man."

Sonny grabbed a chair and sat down next to Andrew's desk, "talk to me bro. I'm not Catholic but come on, Father Bishop is here. Don't you say something like forgive me father for I have—,"

"Sinned," Andrew raised an eyebrow, "It sure seems like that."

"I wouldn't necessarily call it sin."

"Well, besides being detained in Atlanta, a wife who is giving me the cold shoulder, a son with a mysterious cough, a father who has hinted I'm in over my head, and oh yeah, a killer who thinks I'm Barney Fife, life's pretty peachy right now.

"And your problem is?" Sonny waited for Andrew's reaction, but all he got was one of those, you're funny as all hell looks. "Okay, maybe I pushed too far on that. All right, so it sounds like you got a lot of issues right now."

"I'm just venting I guess, It'll be all right." Andrew ran his hand through his hair and let out a big yawn. "I've been in tougher situations in the past. The bottom line is I need to catch this guy, and fast."

"You'll get him, just stay positive."

"I just don't have the resources."

"So let me help you."

"I appreciate it, but I just can't jeopardize two careers."

"Can I share something with you." Sonny inched closer to Andrew.

Sonny told him another story of his days in Iraq during the first Gulf War. He told him that his platoon, just after a sand storm, got separated from other platoons and that their communications went down during a sand storm. They were leery of any kind of unsecured communication because if the Iraqis were listening they could hone in on their location and all hell would break loose he explained. Maintaining radio silence they ended up having to resort to an old style of communication and within a few days, they were able to rendezvous with the other platoons. His point was, if you don't have what you need, you need to make the best of what you have. Andrew understood the point but still seemed to be in a daze about the dilemma of his personal, as well as, professional life.

"Look, don't worry about Hardy right now he's just upset he got passed over for deputy chief."

"Sometimes I wonder why I even jumped into this though... I should've listened to my wife and father."

"I know why, you have a protective nature about you and this violates that... element of you I guess."

The Reunion Reaper

Andrew stared with a puzzled gaze, and then offered, "So you think I should keep going?"

"It's not about what I think or want, it's what you want or think is best. I've known you for a long time now and I've never known you to back down from anybody or anything."

Andrew began scribbling circles on a desk calendar, his tone becoming more agitated. "You're right, and this bastard... sorry, has made it so personal you know."

Andrew tried his best not to use profanity in front of the ex-Marine who used to use profanity as adjectives but now was a devout Christian man who desired to distance himself from the troubled youth that was. The Marines gave him perspective and something to live for, and they didn't mind the creative language bouncing around the tents and foxholes he would say, but that all changed when he met Danielle. He wanted to be a clean ex-Marine. There would be no more tattoos, or profanity. The only things he wanted to maintain were the toughness and grit they taught him. Andrew continued, "This guy is toyin' with me and I can't gain an edge. I just can't figure out which classmate could be capable of this?"

"Well, one of them has a warped sense of reality."

"I guess. What I do know is that I have got to catch this guy soon, or I'm toast." Andrew failed to realize that he already said something to that effect, but Sonny wasn't about to remind a tired and stressed friend of redundancy.

"I've already lied to my wife more than I care to. I told her that once I got back from Atlanta that I was going to hand over everything to the FBI, but I just can't you know, I just can't."

"Then don't. Look, you're hurting yourself with all this questioning and confusion. Either do it or don't do it. Think about this though, let's say you put it on a shelf is it something you will regret later on? I gotta go, but think about the consequences of not acting. One of our platoon mantras was, keep moving forward and never retreat."

Sonny stood up, patted his good friend on the shoulder and walked out. Andrew just stared for a few minutes. He knew his friend was right, but he sure hated the thought of the battle that would take place, not just between him and a psychopath killer, but between him and Captain Hardy, and the biggest one of all, his queen Stephanie. After Sonny walked out a few minutes later there was another knock at the door. This time it was Deputy Chief Wolfe.

"Hey, need to talk to ya for a minute."

Great... and the hits just keep on coming. Sorry Tom Cruise, just had to steal that one from you.

The Reunion Reaper

Chapter 65

After a semi-confession to Deputy Chief Wolfe, of whom he made yet another promise to be off the case within a few days, he knew he stood at the door to zero hour. He finished out his work day, which consisted of interviewing victims whose homes were broken into in an affluent community. So far five homes had fallen victim to what was turning into serial break-ins. Meanwhile, on the killer front, when he got home he decided to play a hunch and follow up on Brian Morris, who vaulted to the top of the list after Mark Lambert dead end. Information he lifted off yet another illegal search at work, he discovered that his last known address was in Maryland, and that he worked for a real estate auction broker.

"Garrison Auction Associates."

"Brian Morris, please."

"I'm sorry Mr. Morris is out of the office, would you like his voice mail."

"Uh, could I ask you if he'll be back today?"

"Mr. Morris is attending an auction out of state and will not be returning until next Monday." Her voice had a quick tempo that suggested annoyance with the caller.

"I see, listen, I'm a high school buddy of his and I was just trying to reach him, any idea where the auction is taking place?"

"I'm really not supposed to give out that information sir;" Sounding more like a CEO rather than a receptionist.

"Well I don't think the whereabouts of an auction he's attending is a matter of national security. Please, he's an old friend." *Come on lady show a human side for Heaven's sake.*

There was a slight pause, "Las Vegas. It's in Las Vegas. Is there anything else sir?"

"Does he have a cell number that you could give to me?"

"I'm sorry sir, we can notify him of your call, then he can…"

"I got it, call me."

"Will there be anything else sir?"

"No that's it, you've been so helpful… *you* have a great day okay?" There was a sudden click. "Thanks, I will too." He said to a now dead phone line.

Well, it certainly made things more interesting, Las Vegas. He looked at his watch. He was losing time. From all that he gathered at the reunion, he couldn't think of anyone that lived in Vegas. Well hopefully it wasn't going to be one of those, what happens in Vegas stays in Vegas situations.

He went back to the email the killer sent and read it over a few more times. He was analyzing the supposed riddle when it hit him, an airplane. But what does that mean? Someone will be flying? He'll be flying to kill someone? Then it hit him, someone who flies. Paul Thurman.

Paul was the only classmate he knew who had his own flying license. He was definitely happy to broadcast that information to everyone at the reunion too. Since he was the owner of a popular fitness magazine in Florida he traveled around promoting new gyms, or attended health science and fitness seminars. Had the novice detective made a breakthrough? He returned to his files and picked out Paul's file. He called his cell phone. Paul picked up.

Andrew was quick to explain his suspicions because the 48 hour promise was down to thirty some hours at this point. At first Paul was skeptical, but when Andrew gave him some insight into the last two murders and the killers riddle, Andrew had his full attention. Andrew couldn't tell him who it was, but he figured the killer would try something very soon. They hatched a plan, a brilliant plan; one that would trap a killer by his own doing. Andrew was happy his old friend was willing to cooperate.

The Reunion Reaper

When Andrew hung up the phone for the first time in a long time he donned a smile. He booked a flight to Fort Lauderdale for the next morning knowing the wife would throw him deeper into the dog house, but as Andrew looked at it, the dog house is as bad as it gets anyway, and since he was already there, it didn't matter at this point. He thought about what his father and Sonny said, "She'll understand."

When he was done with his work he leaned back in the office chair and threw his legs up on the desk. It was finally game on. He was feeling more upbeat over what had just transpired. He was pondering scenarios when Stephanie knocked on the door. They had not really spoken all that much since his return. She was hurt, he knew it, but a sense of duty trumped a happy wife right now.

"I just wanted to know if you were going to eat?" she asked.

He plopped his feet on the floor and sat up straight in the chair, "Of course, is it ready now?"

"It'll be ready in about ten minutes."

"Great, just call me when it's ready please."

She turned to walk away and without turning back she asked, "Are you still on this chase, I mean, case?"

He paused for a moment attempting to draw on something diplomatic or appropriate, unfortunately nothing was there so he gave a straightforward response, "Stephanie, I know you don't approve, but I'm into this pretty deep, and as we both agreed to earlier on we don't quit on something we start. If this places me in the dog house well then I'm willing to live with that right now."

"More like the poor house." A sharp retort from a suspicious wife no doubt.

"I can't continue to live with my classmates slowly being picked off one by one. He's going to kill someone else by tomorrow and I'm taking a wild guess as to who it might be. Hell it could be me for all I know."

"How do you know that?"

"Know what?"

"Don't play dumb Andrew, you just said, he is going to kill someone by tomorrow, how do you know that?"

"He's been emailing me." He hated confessing, but maybe now she'll believe in him and know that these are murders, not accidents.

She stood silent for a moment, deciding to look off, not at her husband.

"How many times has he emailed you?"

"A couple."

"Have you responded?"

"Yeah, but he seems to have made it so it's just a one way communication."

"Well, don't you think it would be a good time to turn over all of this knowing what you know now?

He hesitated and glanced over to his computer.

"I just don't think I can do that?"

"Why? Andrew's ego too big to let someone else solve this?"

"He's contacted me Stephanie. If I turn this over, he may stop the killings."

"What a novel idea that is."

"Come on, you know what I mean. If he stops he goes away maybe never to be found."

"And how long does Andrew fumble around and lose classmates while his ego gets stroked by all of this?"

Stephanie didn't pull any punches either.

"Thank you for your confidence, but I will catch this guy. I'm taking a chance on someone and I have already booked my flight to go back to Florida."

"You just don't get it," retorted a curt Stephanie. Andrew smiled at the crass nature of her comment, "I am the only one who can do this."

"Of course what was I thinking?" She said as she turned to leave the room.

The Reunion Reaper

"I leave in the morning. I should be back in a day or two."

"Just make sure you update your frequent flyer miles 007."

She turned to walk up the stairs and he asked her to stop. "Just in case you think I'm just winging, I think Paul Thurman is next. That's why I have to go. I just talked to him a little while ago and he's on board with my plan."

"Well Magnum P.I. would be proud of you." She heard Michael yell out that something was boiling on the stove. "I have to finish dinner."

"Your support overwhelms me, thank you." He finished off sarcastically.

Once again he had to listen to the heavy steps his wife made as she returned upstairs. She sounded more like a German storm trooper that stamped heel first. There were definitely better days in the Keane household. Andrew muttered some choice words. He didn't have time to consider what his wife just said about his ego. In his mind this was about doing what's right. Regardless, the flight was booked, the clock was ticking, and once again, Florida came calling.

Scott A. Reighard

Chapter 66

A few days after the threatening email, taking care of a few other personal issues, Jeffrey decided to pay a surprise visit to Roanoke. *This is too good* Jeffrey said to no one in particular. *Way to work Andy boy, unfortunately your compass is pointed in the wrong direction.* The day was losing its fight with the oncoming assault of darkness as he lay camouflaged in the woods across from Andrew's house listening in on the Keane household. He wanted to see firsthand how his game opponent was faring. He knew this was cheating to some degree but certainly something he was used to. He was chomping on a sandwich as he was listening in. He loved what he was hearing. First there was a phone conversation to locate Brian. Not a bad guess he muttered. "Brian's too stupid to pull something this brilliant," he offered to the birds in the trees. "And what an idiot husband, the guy's got five kids and he's never home. Way to go Brian."

A little while later he heard Andrew on the phone. "It's got to be Paul," he mumbled. *Oh there is definitely impending danger for Paul you doofus, the plan is already in place. Good job amigo, you finally solved something, a riddle.* But the real charge came when he listened in on the conversation between Andrew and his wife. Things were not well; Andrew's world was in a tumult. *Oh this is good, you tell him Stephanie.* Maybe Jeffrey had a little Irish blood in him, because the only one having any luck at this point was him, even if he was cheating.

He waited until complete darkness to gather his stuff and head out to his parked rental. He had an early flight the next morning. Ironically, it was to depart an hour before Andrew's flight to Florida. Andrew was so close and had no idea.

The Reunion Reaper

Chapter 67

Andrew took an early flight out of Roanoke with a short layover in Atlanta. As he sat in Atlanta memories of Rodney and his last traveling side excursion raced back in. He was praying that he was right about this. He really needed this one to be right. The money was getting thin as well as people's patience. Also, while he was in Atlanta he ventured a call to detective Martin of the Atlanta police, who was investigating Rodney's murder. Although the detective was aloof in his responses, he did say that no one was on the immediate radar at this point, and the only piece of evidence the Atlanta Police Department had was the sock in Rodney's mouth laced with strychnine.

Andrew recalled the reports he saw on Judith and Sharon, and ironically both of them contained traces of strychnine in their systems as well. Andrew didn't know how that could help him other than knowing the killer had his preferences of techniques and methods. It seemed like there was a pattern established by the killer, and Andrew felt like an absolute heel. Here was the killer's calling card, something the FBI might be able to solve more quickly given its vast resources, yet he remained selfish, or stubborn. *Am I doing more damage than good? Was dad right?*

Andrew made it into Ft. Lauderdale by late morning. He rushed out to pick up his rental car then made his way over to a parking area close to where Paul would be taxing his plane upon arrival. Paul had talked of flying back to Lauderdale after a brief meeting in Tallahassee that morning and was scheduled to arrive sometime after noon. The plan was that Andrew would sit in the car, not make any physical contact with Paul just in case the killer was watching also, and then follow him for the day. The killer mentioned within forty eight hours and had up to this point kept his promises. If that were the case by that afternoon something was supposed to happen to Paul, or to someone for whom he had not predicted.

Paul had been flying planes for about five years since becoming chief executive of his own company. His one dream was to fly planes. A few years back he bought a Cessna Mustang and was an experienced tropical weather flyer. A pilot in Florida had to be a seasoned pilot. Summertime was the worst time to fly because of all the thunderstorms that appear out of nowhere. Most pilots would simply fly around them, but occasionally Paul Thurman tackled a storm or two. He was a tough guy who enjoyed challenges and he wasn't afraid to approach anyone, which gave him an air of charming likeability.

The morning skies were favorable as Andrew waited patiently for his friend. And he waited. Then he waited some more. It was closing in on one in the afternoon and his friend's plane had not arrived. Losing his patience yet gaining a hunger he could barely stand, he ventured into the airport to see about possible bad weather in northern Florida that may have delayed their encounter.

He decided to grab a quick sandwich and a drink from one of the many dining facilities in the airport. He saw that the weather was good for flying but as he guzzled down his bottled water he saw flashing on the screen at one of the many televisions throughout the airport that CNN news was reporting that a small plane had gone down over the Gulf of Mexico. Instantly his heart seized him and began to beat so that his chest physically bulged in and out at the thought of the impossible. *No way,* he thought, *there's no way, how could he know?* Shaking his head and almost talking out loud for those around him to hear he moved closer to the television hoping to hear what the newsman was saying. There was no real time information made available, only that a small plane had gone down and that information was

The Reunion Reaper

sketchy. Andrew didn't know whether to sit there and watch the television or go back out to his car and hope that Paul's plane would soon round the corner of the terminal and come to a stop. They agreed that there should be no communication and so he was crossed about violating that agreement. He decided to return to the car and turn on the radio stations hoping someone would be broadcasting this information.

Time slowly moved on and still the information was not what he had hoped for, the news reported that the plane was a small plane and speculative reports flooded the airwaves. First it was thought to be a small Jetblue airplane, or Allegiant Air, or that it was a private plane that may have had as many as eight passengers. "Jesus, why don't they just wait until they know for sure instead of putting out speculative information?"

Hours passed and there he sat sweating every possible way in a rental car that was now becoming more useless to him, as was the whole trip for that matter. The forty eight hour window had passed. Finally at about three he decided to call his friend's cell number, but there was no response. He waited for another hour, but his gut was telling him that Paul's plane was the one they were talking about. He was lost. How could this have happened he questioned.

In some lurid manner he respected the cunning of the killer, he knew that somehow he was behind this and yet he had no answers. He now knew the mastery and cunning of this psycho, and that he had masterfully planned things so well. But the lingering question was how he did it. How in the world could he know that Paul would be in Tallahassee? Andrew's emotions were one of confusion. He pounded at the steering wheel, frustration now a regular emotion in his life. He decided that staying at the airport was futile, so he drove out of the airport and got a hotel room for the night.

He called Paul's cell repeatedly, but there was no response. Most likely his friend was lost and that night while sitting in yet another lonely hotel he wept. He felt about as empty as anyone could feel. For he not only felt for his friend and prevent his death, but feeling horribly responsible for it as well. He was losing hope and confidence. Even though he had predicted correctly about Paul possibly being the next victim, little good did it do him, the killer was one step ahead, almost as if he knew Andrew's thoughts.

To ease some of his pain he phoned Andrea Pruitt. He got a family member instead.

"Hi, I'm an old school friend. Is Andrea there?"

There was a considerable pause.

"Hello?" Andrew continued.

"Yes…I guess you haven't heard. Andrea had an accident while on vacation."

Immediately he felt a cold emptiness in his chest and a sudden sweat consumed his body.

"Oh, is she all right?" He was hoping the gut feeling was wrong.

"She's…she's dead."

Andrew nearly blurted, "You have got to be kidding me?" but he refrained and said, "From an accident you say?"

"Yes sir, it was a diving accident in the Bahamas."

With a sweating head, a head throbbing with confusion he respectfully said, "Please give my condolences to the family on the loss of a wonderful person."

"Thank you. Would you like us to send you funeral information?"

Andrew gave her his information then slowly hung up the phone. He sat silent for a very long time trying to make sense of all that was going on around him. In one minute he was ready to pack it in, the next minute he was more determined than ever to find who was responsible for these senseless murders. He would take those thoughts to bed.

The Reunion Reaper

Chapter 68

The following morning Andrew turned out of bed. It was another toss and turn kind of night. Stun and confusion were still present. He couldn't believe the audacity of the killer. In some weird way he had to credit the killer with his ability to perform so many spontaneous accidents. He was sick to his stomach. He grabbed the remote and immediately turned on the television figuring there had to be more news on the plane crash. The day before was beyond belief.

As he sat there on the edge of the bed he began flipping through the early morning news shows, growing more and more frustrated as saw that NBC was covering aging tips for the independent woman, while CBS was having a segment on alternative BBQ's to the traditional dogs and burgers for the fourth of July, and ABC was whisking some young couple off to Cabo san Lucas for the wedding of a lifetime. He decided the cable news networks were locked in to basically everything there was in the news so he flipped over to look at the slow scroll on the bottom of the screen as news flashed away. Nature was making its morning call, so he upped the volume on the television and rushed into the bathroom to take care of business. Afterwards he decided to make some coffee, there was no news yet. Sitting in a high back chair sipping coffee with eyes glued to the television, the scroll continued and finally there it was: *Two dead in single plane accident over the Gulf of Mexico.* The scroll continued to roll out some information. *FAA authorities claim Paul Thurman, CEO of Tropical Media and co-pilot George Palmer were heading to Ft. Lauderdale when Thurman radioed that he was having engine problems.*

A huge sigh heaved its way out of Andrew as his eyes welled up. His good friend would be added to the list of those gone. His head sunk into his chest and he began to swing it from side to side in disbelief. Aside from the sheer sadness of the event he was equally furious. Why do some celebrate with a warped sense of gratification the death of another human being, he questioned. In one day he lost two friends. Unfortunately for Andrew an old adage crept in like the Cheshire cat, two steps forward and one step back, but in the case of Andrew it seemed more like one step forward and two steps back. Going in reverse on a murder investigation is a sure sign of an eventual cold case. He wanted to tear his t-shirt from his body or kick the holy shit out of a wall. *Yet another waste of time and money, I hope you're listening up there 'cause I'm shouting as loud as I can.* There was nothing he could do sitting in a lonely hotel room, so after he calmed himself, he called his wife to give her the news. He checked out of the hotel, yet again, empty handed.

His flight back home was one wracked with confusion and despair. However, as he flew out of Atlanta he was reminiscing on Rodney and then thinking about Paul and Andrea. Suddenly he had a thought. A thought he would explore when he returned home.

The Reunion Reaper

Chapter 69

Journal date: July 5, 2008: Who's in the Cockpit Now?

I am flying this plane, I am running this show. I am dictating this ride. Holy Frikkin' Shit! Insert huge laugh here. Just what the doctor ordered! Whew, I didn't think the game would give me this feeling, but it really feels good. Oh Andy boy are you in trouble, there's no way you can keep up with me. God what an idiot! How in the world did you ever get that beautiful woman, become a cop, or stay alive up to this point in his life?

Okay, to the business at hand. I just had to get some things off my chest. Paul "the Thurmanator", what you don't know Pauly Boy is that you were basically a dick to me. You were such a man of honor to the ladies though weren't you? Mr. Good guy, you protected the unprotected, ran your little stupid magazine that offered fitness, health and nutrition for four to ninety four year olds, married your college sweetheart, but worst of all you were a friend to that idiot that couldn't catch a mouse in a two by two room with fifty mouse traps. Well, as they say, who is piloting this flight now my friend? Huh? Certainly not you I can say with certainty. You should never trust a mechanic who doesn't speak English. I can't believe you didn't recognize me. Oh well, adios mi amigo. Time to email the daddy of the dumb.

Paul Thurman: September 1, 1964 – July 2, 2008.

Scott A. Reighard

Chapter 70

Journal Date: July 5, 2008: A minor distraction.

Andrea, Andrea, Andrea, you just couldn't keep your nose out of people's business. Seems like our little busy body asked the wrong questions. I have to admit you are, err, I mean were, pretty clever. How keen it was of you to remember the embarrassing party and how you had just talked to Judith weeks before her death knowing she was off the blow. Oh, and the little ditty about my penchant for keeping an enemy's list was over the top, you had to go. I couldn't take a chance on you and Andy boy striking up the ole tag team on me. This was supposed to be about my graduating class, thanks for throwing a monkey in the wrench wench. By the way, you really should check your dive tanks better, funny how the wrong ingredient can turn oxygen into a toxic inhalant. I have to admit that was pretty smart on my part to put it together so quickly. Then again telling me you and your significant other were headed to Bimini wasn't such a good idea. Never throw a mad dog a bone and then expect it to leave it alone. Ruff!

Oh where oh where has my Andrea gone, she's gone to meet the maker, maybe.

Andrea Pruitt: Born, who cares when - June 28, 2008.

The Reunion Reaper

Chapter 71

Andrew returned home yet again empty handed but not empty headed. On the flight home he couldn't get a certain thought out of his head. It was something he repeated to himself; he's been one step ahead since his involvement. Although it seemed far fetched he decided to contact the department's surveillance squad. He wanted them to come out to his house to survey every square inch possible, without Stephanie's knowledge of course.

To his surprise they discovered there were three listening devices installed in Andrew's house, one in the study, the kitchen, and the other in their bedroom. He was right about the gut instinct he had that his house was bugged, but when, how and by whom? How much had this guy heard, he questioned. It was odd how the killer mentioned some things about Roanoke.

Now it all seemed to be coming into focus, the killer was near, but how close? How was he able to get in and install the devices, and when did he install them? Just then anger emerged when he blurted, "Son of a bitch invaded my home." His thoughts quickly turned to his wife and kids. All at once he felt vulnerable. The team was just finishing up as Andrew walked a few of them outside. How was he going to explain this to his wife, and how was he going to justify this act from the department?

"Thanks Tom, Nick, I really appreciate what you did for me today?"

"We'll send you our bill," replied Tom.

Rather sheepishly Andrew asked, "So the Captain won't know anything about this right?"

"Not unless someone talks, no one knows we came out today."

"Again I really appreciate everything you did for me."

"It's no problem, but you owe us a keg on this one."

Andrew smiled, "no problem."

Nick looked around, "Can I ask a question though?"

He asked Andrew who would want to bug his house and Andrew did his best Fred Astaire, but in some way he knew he should have just told them the truth, in many ways they were like him, they would have understood. Unfortunately Andrew was confused between truth and lies these days, a place he rarely visited before this case.

When they left Andrew commented that he needed to take a long look in the mirror, he had lied more in the last month than he had the last ten years. He felt terrible. The killer was turning him into something he did not like. Suddenly he came up with a brilliant idea. He ran back outside and stopped Tom. He asked him the strangest thing, he asked him to reinstall the listening devices. Tom looked at him like he had three heads, but at Andrew's insistence, occasional begging and eventual bribe of a free lunch at a local eatery, he agreed. It was no longer about to be a one way communication. He would hold conversations for the study that he was hoping the killer would hear in order to set the trap. He had to appear just as the killer wanted, stupid and out of his league. The problem was convincing the wife of the same.

After Tom installed the devices, Andrew only had to figure when the killer would be around again. He was unable to ask for a surveillance team and so he called on one guy he could truly trust Sonny. He was going to ask his friend for a lot, but this was a crucial time and an opportunity looked to be in the offing. Somehow he knew the killer had his itinerary in his back pocket and Andrew was about to give him an itinerary that would lead him right into Andrew's waiting handcuffs. Andrew was finally excited about the possibilities, finally something had broken for him. The killer made a mistake by treading on his property and by dropping what seemed to be innocuous

The Reunion Reaper

comments in emails where those comments turned out to be pretty incriminating ones at that. It was time to set the trap and wait.

Scott A. Reighard

Chapter 72

With a smile as broad as Lake Erie, Jeffrey mused over the fact that he was holding Andrew out like a puppet. He took out what seemed to be his last contact and that gave him great pleasure, plus he had a renewed sense of purpose. All of this gave him the ability to put his mother and family issues on the backburner. Perhaps this was his way of dealing, or not dealing with a reality he should otherwise deal with. Back in a familiar place he was sitting in his window seat on a flight headed to Roanoke via Cincinnati.

During his layover in Cincinnati he decided to head to Laptop Lane, an internet style café located within the airport, surf the net a bit, email some friends and give Andrew something to chew on. He was a people watcher so he sat near his departure gate facing out into Concourse B so he could look at passersby.

As he looked at a mother trying to control her son who wanted a toy, from the nearby gift store, he began to consider what he would say in his email to Andrew.

Let's see, what shall it be today, he pondered. *Who should I compare him to, Dudley Do Right, Underdog, or Deputy Dog? I wonder if he has made any headway in my supposed absence. I'll bet he's pissed that I got to Paul before their little reunion in Lauderdale.*

He tapped out another email to his new best buddy and titled it: *Never fear, Underdog is here.*

Hey Underdog, I'll bet that's how you feel right now because I am just kicking your dog ass all over the place. How sweet it is. Hey listen to this I was thinking about you the other day when I was on the crapper and I said you know what Andrew needs a break.

So here is my special of the day, as he glanced at a daily special white board sign from an eatery at the airport food

The Reunion Reaper

court area called the Grove, *I apologize about giving you just 48 hours, but I thought you were smarter than that, so here's the deal. Another one goes down in, oh let's say, a week. Good enough for you? I am so confident in your ineptitude that I'll bet within the week you are no closer to me than you were with Paul, too bad about that, huh, seems you can never trust a mechanic these days. Surely your wife knows what an absolute idiot you are. You've got less than a week, see you later schmuck.*

The Underdog message wasn't his best effort but he only had about a fifty minute layover and the fact that he was headed to Roanoke yet again he was hoping to hear what new pathetic ideas his boy toy had. He loved listening in and with this most recent email he was hoping to further enrage him to say even worse things. The banter may have been one sided according to Andrew but this killer was able to hear some of what Andrew had to say about his nemesis, and he loved it. Although, he would rather eat sand then listen in on sappy conversations between Andrew and his wife or with the kids, or long talks between Andrew and his daughter about the importance of focusing on school work. Right now these were not sappy conversations between Andrew and Stephanie, they were more like snappy retorts from an angry wife and confused husband. Of course he never really got to experience sibling rivalries or unconditional love, and he never really received the attention he wanted as a child. Even though Andrew's relationship seemed to be in the crapper it still dwarfed his. He pained to listen to Andrew's happy life while his seemed to be stuck in a perpetual state of redundancy, still listening in served a needful purpose.

His flight was about to begin boarding so he shut down the laptop, threw away his empty drink container and made his way down the concourse to his gate. Once again, dressed in his Polo khakis and mesh polo shirt, this one grape colored with a yellow logo, and Sebago shoes, he sauntered like he hit triple 7's at a Vegas slot. He smiled at a few of the ladies he passed, winked at a few kids and bought the morning addition of the *New York Times* because at that particular moment he was too happy, he needed an edge and that paper seemed to give him just enough to want to kill someone.

The Reunion Reaper

Chapter 73

Later that evening when Stephanie and the kids got home, Andrew decided to wait until after dinner to discuss with her what was going on; he tried to avoid talking business, finances and other sensitive issues in front of the kids. He debated whether to tell her about the devices to begin with, but then figured the wrath of her finding out after the fact would be too much to bear. He also knew she would be angry because his meddling induced the killer to install listening devices, plus her natural instinct would be to think that somehow the kids were in jeopardy. Andrew would do his best to assuage his wife's worries, but he would understand her reaction when it reared its ugly head. He was just hoping it wouldn't be one of those Irish outbursts she was capable of from time to time. It was time to be truthful about something.

Andrew took Stephanie into the laundry room and sent the boys outside to play so he could give her the news. Of course his first comment was that she and the kids were not in danger, at least he hoped that was the case. He told here what he discovered.

"Jesus Andrew when is enough going to be enough?"

"What are you getting so freaked out about?"

"Well, the fact that you're out of control on this. I mean, what's going on?"

She stood square with him with arms folded.

"I'm trying to solve a series of murders Steph and I don't need your badgering okay. You think I want all this?"

"I went those devices taken out."

"We can't do that right now."

"Why not?"

"Because if we do he'll know we're on to him."

"Isn't that the point?"

"He's going to have to get close enough for these to be effective. We need to keep them for a while."

He tried to keep his voice down as he glanced outside to see if the boys were trying to listen in. There was a brief silence. He knew this moment would come, he just wished he could predict the killer like he could predict his kid's motives.

"I think you've lost it Andrew I really do, I mean, you're approving the use of listening devices in our house. Do you hear yourself?"

"You don't understand how important this discovery is."

"This is just too much. I'm tired Andrew and the kids sense something is wrong between us."

"So you tell them dad's just doing his job. Look, it's not easy I know, but I can't quit on this Steph, I can't."

"I mean come on Andrew, you can't possibly tell me that you can do all you're doing and be effective."

He took a step closer to her emphasizing his defense. "I can be plenty effective. Haven't we known each other long enough to trust what we're capable of?"

"Of course, but you're conducting a murder investigation God knows where, and with little or no resources, not to mention straining the savings."

"I'm aware of that thank you."

"What is this some sort of competition for you? I mean, aren't your triathlons enough?"

"People don't get killed in triathlons—"

"Oh yeah, what about that woman, Sharon was it?"

He waved his arms out to his side, "And that should reinforce your support for me. Can't you see this is about some maniac who is playing me for a fool and killing classmates along the way?"

"Is this more about your classmates, or more about you?"

"What the hell is that supposed to mean?" He barked.

"Andrew honey, I feel bad about your classmates, I really do, but I don't see why you feel you have to be some sort

The Reunion Reaper

of savior here." Her eyes welled up, "what is compelling you to the point of straining everything you've worked so hard to get?"

Andrew was angry with her lack of understanding, but at the same time understood her hurt, and in some deep cavity of his mind he really couldn't answer her honestly because he did not know what was compelling him to this point either, but he urged her to understand his reasons.

He closed his eyes and tilted his head skyward and exhaled. "Stephanie, this is about my classmates and regardless of how you feel I have to do something."

He wanted to add more, to let her know how hard he was trying to balance it all, family, the job, this case and their relationship, but now was not the time to seek a sympathy angle, besides, in walked Michael.

"Mommy is everything okay?" She walked over and hugged him.

"Everything's fine honey daddy and I are just discussing some really important issues right now."

"Yeah bud, we're almost done okay? Hey, why don't you go up and find a movie or a game and I'll be right there."

Michael left the room and they closed the door.

"Well, I guess nothing's going to change your mind so what's your plan?" she asked.

He told her that Sonny was going to provide surveillance for him so he and the family would give the impression that everything is normal in their habits and daily activities.

"And when does all this surveillance begin?"

"As soon as Sonny agrees to start," but he left out the part where he was supposed to say that he hadn't even talked with Sonny about it yet.

Her husband had been through a lot and she wanted this all to be over as soon as possible as well, and to say that she agreed with this plan meant to say that she hoped this would finally end the strain of these events for her husband

and for her as well. The conjugal nature of their relationship had been strained like never before, their dialog was short and to the point and their private encounters virtually nonexistent. To catch a killer at this point was first and foremost.

Stephanie took a deep breath and exhaled with a heavy sigh, "Well, I hope this is it. You feel absolutely confident the killer will return because of these bugs?"

"The guys from the department's surveillance team said that if someone wanted to hear based on the devices used they would have to be less than a hundred yards or so, so he'll have to get close. I feel pretty confident he'll come back. He's an arrogant SOB and likes to play games. I've got a gut feeling on this. He wants to know my steps and I plan on giving him a lot to digest."

She shook her head in despair. "I don't know Andrew, my emotions all over the place right now."

"You just gotta trust me okay?"

"I trust you, but a killer capable of anything?" She raised her brows.

He stopped short of embracing her, "I want this guy so bad Steph."

"I know… I know." Her arms were still folded.
He hesitated, wanting to say something that would relieve his wife's anxiety and worry, but he just couldn't muster up the words at that moment.

"I gotta go, Sonny is waiting on me."

As Andrew made his way out to his vehicle he told the boys he was leaving for a while. He gave them both a strong embrace. Michael was somewhat suspicious, Ryan oblivious to the sincere nature of the hug.

"Dad, what about our game?"

"Oh man, Michael I am so sorry, dad just has to meet a friend, it's really important okay?" He gave him an even stronger hug. He felt like crap doing this to his son.

"It's okay I understand, you have an important job."

The Reunion Reaper

What a kid, so understanding at such an early age.
"I love you guys."
Both responded in kind.
"Now make sure you listen to mom, I might not make it back before you go to bed so make it easy for her okay?"
Both responded to their father's desire.
"You're good boys, daddy loves you."
As he walked to his SUV he did something he hadn't done since his days in Florida working in the dangerous yet exciting global security business, he looked around suspiciously yet as nonchalant as he could. He was trying to remember which neighbors drove which cars or SUV's or trucks. All the way to Denny's he kept one eye on the road and the other in the rear view mirror. He wasn't paranoid, just hopeful, hoping that someone was tailing him.

Scott A. Reighard

Chapter 74

While Sonny was waiting on Andrew he gave in to the urge and ordered a famous Denny burger and a shake. Andrew arrived as Sonny seemed to be in ecstasy over the burger. He slid into the booth.

"Sorry I'm late I had to clear the air with Stephanie before coming here."

"It's cool, do you want to order something? I didn't know if you were going to order anything, so I just got you a water."

"Thanks, I'm good. Looks like you got your hands full." Andrew quipped.

"You got that right, gave in to a guilty pleasure and I'm lovin' every minute of it."

"So you asked to meet me here on purpose, God, what ails you man?" Andrew joked.

"You know what, in 1991 while I was in the sandbox it seemed like ages before we had a real burger you know. Ever since this has been one of those guilty pleasures." He suffocated another huge bite.

"Well just make sure you say five Hail Mary's and all's forgiven."

A waitress was standing over them and asked Andrew if he wanted something. He just ordered water.

"Can you say them if you are not Catholic."

"I'll say them for you."

"Thanks, so what's going on?" Sonny asked.

Andrew explained that he needed someone to spend a couple nights a week parked down the street from Andrew's house to keep an eye on all activity that might be headed Andrew's way. Sonny jumped at the chance to help his friend. There was only one way onto Andrew's winding

The Reunion Reaper

road, which dead ended about a quarter mile further down from his house.

"What do you think about watching the street a couple nights a week for say a week to start out?"

"I don't see that as a problem, I'll just tell Danielle that I'm working a case, she'll be okay with what I tell her."

"I don't want you to get into trouble over this, you can back out."

Sonny responded with a matter of fact tone, "Hey, a friend needs me, she'll understand, I'll just cancel my Bible class this week."

"Oh man, I hate for you to have to do that; speaking of which I need to get the kids back on our scripture studies again. Since this case and all the other stuff going on I barely have time for my regular job let alone the family and scripture. You know what, Mary got a job at the mall, and it took me three weeks to know about it."

"Well, you've got a lot going on right now."

"That's why I need to find this killer and soon."

Sonny approached him reassuringly, "Look, if this bug device stuff is all his work he'll screw up, and when he does we can nail him."

Andrew and Sonny agreed that they would begin the surveillance the following evening. Yeah, it was a long shot, but that's all Andrew really had right now. He was just glad he wasn't sitting at a Craps table in Vegas betting the house on his assumptions. He reached across the table and grabbed Sonny's forearm, "Look, I've dragged you into this and you could get into a lot of trouble for being complicit, you can back out you know."

"A marine never leaves his fellow soldier high and dry."

Andrew smiled, "Man I am glad you're my friend and not my enemy."

"Maybe those who hate us so much should think the same way."

Sonny was sensitive about how the United States was perceived around the world. He thought most of it was more ignorance than ideology.

"I hear ya my friend, these are weird times, but that conversation will have to wait," said Andrew as he grabbed for his water.

"I'm sorry I just get pissed about a lot of stuff out there."

"It's all right man I understand, I feel the same way. Sean tells me stories all the time." Andrew suggested since his brother was in the Special Forces and sometimes would hear some real horror stories from him.

They finished their conversation and Andrew waited on Sonny to finish his meal before leaving. With fingers crossed the plan was set and most of the pieces were in place, the only missing piece was a killer being in the right place at the wrong time.

The Reunion Reaper

Chapter 75

Another pseudonym another hotel, this was his life right now, but he was okay with that. So far Jeffrey was up to six classmates. He had been consistent with his messages and threats. Andrew jumped in as predicted, and he was close to finishing his ultimate goal. His mission on this trip to Roanoke was to gather more feedback from Andrew, and to have Andrew realize how vulnerable he was. He would tell Andrew about the listening devices, but not yet. He loved cornering Andrew, but wanted to take the game in a new and dangerous direction. He moved the focus of victims more toward those Andrew was well associated and he mulled whether the next victim should be female or male.

He had done a lot of surveillance and research on Carrie Adams and Greg Madison, but they just didn't fit the profile he was looking for. Although he knew Andrew and Greg were close in high school. So far the listening devices had worked as he was able to intercept Andrew's plans on two occasions and beat him to the punch. He was hoping to do it again.

The strange thing about all of this was he had been a friend to Andrew for several years, and it wasn't unnatural for friends to be competitive with one another but this was a new spin on the whole aspect of competition. Perhaps it was some bitter enmity, or paradoxically they were alike. They had competed on so many levels; both of them were funny and engaging, but it was pretty clear that Andrew was the more athletic one, the one voted as senior class vice-president, and the one to win Amy McMahon's heart. It was fitting and expected that Andrew would stick his nose in this mission. He couldn't have created a better scenario than the one that basically unfolded before him, Andrew, so courageous, so confident, was now a vulnerable shell of his former self. He had bludgeoned him into a state of near supplication, and that made him feel good. He was the master of this show, and was now wondering how he was going to bring it to an end. The unfortunate circumstances for the most recent victims were that they were victims by association not to mention his maniacal ego.

He knew the Underdog email would piss off Andrew but he wanted to send him another ambiguous email. He chuckled as he typed away. When he finished the email and hit send he looked at his watch and decided this was as good a time as any to head over to his usual hideout near Andrew's place. From earlier trips he knew Andrew would most likely be home sweating over information, trying to get out of the dog house with the wife or trying to piece together a puzzle with no discernable pattern. He was hoping yet again to eavesdrop on a conversation between Andrew and his wife, a woman with whom he had now become fixated. He especially liked the athletic shape she maintained for a woman in her forties. The strong features of her face up close were tempting aspects to a mind diseased.

On earlier visits while Andrew was at work and she and the kids were home, he would sneak up close to the house and dare the whole situation of getting caught. Sure, he had the listening devices but he wanted to see her up close. From his earlier days in the porn business he was used to watching. Although he never caught Andrew and his wife in the act he did fantasize about being with her. Other than the occasional bar slut he would come across he had to rely on funds to get his rocks off.

He entertained the idea of finding a way to get rid of Andrew, but he had more pressing matters right now. It was about destroying his ego, crushing his confidence, or shaking the very fabric of his existence. It was not a time to incense him with threats about his family or tease him

The Reunion Reaper

about the desirable nature of his wife. He figured he had a few days to hang out and he most certainly would take advantage of his opportunity. This time he brought along a small video camera and when the time was right he would record Stephanie Keane, inside the house or out, and he would listen to intimate conversations. It was time to get to work.

Chapter 76

Andrew returned home being ever vigilant as he drove down his street. He didn't notice anything odd; in fact, he thought that it would be difficult for someone to park on his road because it was so winding, and there was barely enough room for two cars to pass by without tearing off their side view mirrors. He considered how the killer could not park his car nearby if he intended on listening to them? If he didn't park on the street then he would have to walk a long way through the woods in order to get close enough to Andrew's house. A house that sat more than a mile deep into a mile and a half street that ended near a wooded area.

He knew that Sonny could easily spot someone parking a car and then walking down the street. He also knew the killer wasn't a dummy, but did the killer know that he found the devices? These and a hundred other thoughts clouded his mind as he pulled into the driveway and entered the house through a side door. He was immediately greeted by Ryan his five year old.

"Hey buddy, shouldn't you be in bed by now?" As he bent down to pick him up and then kissed him on his forehead.

"Mom said I could wait for you. Dad, are you going away again?"

"Why would you ask that?" Andrew questioned and hoped Stephanie hadn't put him up to this.

"I don't know, I just want you to stay home with us, you've been gone a lot."

"Well hopefully soon I will be home more." He placed him back down. "Daddy's working on a pretty important case right now."

"Are you after a killer?"

The Reunion Reaper

"Have you and Michael been shuffling through dad's private stuff in the study?"
With a sense of guilt, "Huh-uh, we don't touch your books or anything."
"Well I hope not."
Stephanie walked into the room. She looked at her husband with a serious look as Ryan started coughing again.
"Okay there little one time for bed. We need to give you your medicine then you need to brush your teeth."
"What about Michael?" he asked.
"Don't you worry about Michael you just worry about Ryan, now come on," quipped Stephanie.
"Listen to your mother, please." Andrew stated as he glanced at his wife.

Stephanie and Andrew walked Ryan to the kitchen for his cough medicine. But she had a look of contempt on her face that said back off I got this. Ryan's cough continued to persist despite all efforts to give him just about everything that was available. Stephanie had become more worried in recent weeks and wanted to take Ryan to Charlottesville for further testing. The University of Virginia's Children's Hospital maintains an impeccable reputation in the area of pediatrics. They hadn't had much time to discuss such an important subject because in truth Andrew was consumed by several other issues that continued to race through his mind like the Daytona 500. He felt horrible about not being able to help his youngest child, a feeling that haunts a parent. He often prayed that God would transfer the cough to himself in order to take it away from his son, but apparently the big guy hadn't thought it necessary yet, or just wasn't responding to a man whose faith probably needed a tune up at this time. He had neglected his scriptures lately because the plate of his life had runneth over with so much going on. His faith was strong but sometimes, as in this moment, it was being tested. Maybe the cough was a sign of his neglect for his son, yet another conundrum of whether God was pulling the strings on all this. Regardless, he knew his time lately had been strained, but hopefully soon all this would be over.

"Maybe it's time we get him to Charlottesville." Andrew suggested.

"I've already made arrangements. We're going next Tuesday."

"I gotta work that day, couldn't we get another date?"

"You want UVA to schedule around us?" She asked with a conjectured tort to her face.

"Yeah, I guess not. Well, I'll just take off that's all."

"You don't have to, my mom was going to fly up Monday and go with me."

"And when did you hatch this plan?"

She looked him in the eye, "When you were sitting in the Atlanta jail."

Damn she's good at this.

"Well, how come you didn't tell me this earlier?"

"Uh-gee Andrew because you were too busy saving the world I guess." She finished with a smirk, at which Ryan interrupted, "You're trying to save the world dad?"

"Not quite bud," as he patted his son on the head, then with a look of disparage toward his wife. "This isn't the time or place to—"

"Exactly!"

Andrew urged his son to go back upstairs, "Well I'd still like to go." He suggested.

"Fine, but you and my mother in the same car for several hours. I don't know."

"Why does that woman hate me so much?"

"That's not fair my mother loves you."

He just gave her a sideways glance.

"Well I want to talk more about this Charlottesville trip."

"It's already settled."

She changed the subject.

The Reunion Reaper

"How did it go with Sonny?"
"Good, he'll start tomorrow night."
"I hope this works," she muttered.
"What," he asked.
"Nothing."
He hated when she did that.

Andrew left her and went to the kitchen to grab a bowl of cereal and took it to his study. He went up to the boys' room kissed Ryan good night and told him to remember to say his prayers. Michael soon followed. Mary was out bowling with some friends. As he watched Stephanie finally get Michael to his bedroom, he tried to recall when he last saw his daughter. Sitting in his study in complete silence he reasoned on all that was going on around him. It was like some bizarre show where he was moving in slow motion, yet ironically everything was whizzing by at a rapid pace. At times he felt invisible to his family. He felt bad as he wrestled with his conscience. But then, like some weird incident he thought about a story Sonny had told him about his time in Iraq during the Gulf War of 1991.

He said there was a moment when one of his men in his platoon was shot and that his fellow marine was no more than three feet away from him when he dropped. "Imagine, three feet between life and death," Sonny said to him. For a few minutes Sonny said he lay there looking at his dead friend, but the bursting of shells being fired brought him out of his stupor. He had to move on. Andrew had to move on. If there was a best part about this was that for the family there were no casualties, and hopefully in his view only temporary bruises of neglect.

He began to consider the plan he and Sonny hatched. He was hopeful that this could be it, the moment he had been waiting for, where a killer is caught and justice prevails. In the minutes it took for the computer to boot and for him to log on, he came across Paul's file. Things had happened so fast that he didn't have time to look it over, or close it out; a truly painful event that was getting old. He stared at it for a moment then opened it up to gaze on the picture he had of Paul inside.

"Goodbye my friend. I don't think I'll ever understand why, but I'm gonna get this bastard I promise you that. Take care of him Lord."

He closed the folder and placed it with the others who had gone before him. It was a stack that was getting way too high.

His main page popped up and he saw that he had eight new messages. Staring at the screen he grabbed the mouse, adjusted it over his mail icon and clicked. His instincts proved correct there was another email with the title of *Underdog*. As he read he made a few passing comments at the content. This did not sit well with him as once again someone who was now appearing to be almost omnipotent was demeaning him again.

The Reunion Reaper

Chapter 77

After reading the Underdog email, Andrew's mood was mixed. The killer was degrading him yet again and his wife earlier that evening gave him the third degree, but on the other hand a friend was willing to listen and offered to help. Andrew always considered himself to be a glass as half full kind of guy, so he was not about to be deterred by the condescending nature of a killer whose life appeared to be in despair to react like this. Either that or the guy was looking to be a contender for the next comedy reality show. But this certainly was no laughing matter. As he sat there pondering the phone rang with the caller ID as US Govt. He picked it up and slumped back in his chair.

"Well, have you captured a killer yet?"

He was shocked to hear Joe Marketti's voice on the other line.

"Well, I'm close."

Joe didn't pull punches, "How close, like I'm hot on his trail and apprehension is imminent, or I'm closer to the moon?"

The latter was probably the most accurate assessment, but something Andrew was becoming quite good at was lying.

"I'm probably days within getting this guy."

"Three days or three hundred days."

Sheepishly he said, "Somewhere in between."

"So did Mark Lambert pan out?"

"Not exactly, he's in jail" Andrew deadpanned.

"No surprise there I guess. Got any hard leads?" Andrew paused.

"No not really."

"That's okay, sometimes we know who they are and they're still a bitch to catch. Remember Eric Rudolph, took us years to get that guy."

"Yeah, this is a lot tougher than I thought."

"Well, it's not exactly C.S.I. is it?"

"I don't watch that stuff but Stephanie likes it though, but I know it doesn't work that way."

"Look, you know I'm your friend and I want you to know that I am rooting for ya, but you gotta do something quick Andrew, I have to officially say that a federal agent has been made aware of a series of murders across several states and that is dangerous for both of us."

"I know, I know. I do have some good news."

Andrew explained in short detail all that he had. Of course he failed to mention the listening devices or the Atlanta incident beyond the fact that he knew Rodney was dead and the Atlanta police were investigating it as a homicide. He hated to lie but in reality it clearly looked like he was a member of the Keystone Cops and he was screwing up in every possible manner, but he was trying to avoid giving the impression of incompetence. One thing he did divulge was the emails and the contents of some of them. Again, Joe was short to the point.

"Looks like you got a real son of a bitch who now looks to have it in for you."

"What do you mean?"

"The emails. He's trying to take away your focus from the case and put it more on pride. It's the old watch this hand while I slap the shit out of you with the other."

"Distraction, it's funny you say that because my dad mentioned that as well."

"Looks like he knows a thing or two."

"And he's not afraid to share it either."

"Okay, so you lay a trap, you just might get lucky. If not, I would contact everyone in the class and let them know what's going on. Put a little fear in everyone. Now I know

The Reunion Reaper

this may sound like panic mode, but the killer will most likely be pissed you're not following his protocol and from there he just might make his mistake."

"Listen, I appreciate you keeping a lid on this."

"No problem, but not for much longer you catch me?"

"Yeah I gotcha."

"Hey, you're running out of time you know. You gotta put a squeeze on someone."

"Okay, I got it."

"I'm dead serious, this is federal obstruction, and we could lose our asses on this."

"You've got us on a secure line right?"

"Are we ever?" Joe quipped.

"I'll get him Joe."

"You better, you're my friend but this goes beyond friendship."

Andrew understood completely.

"Talk to ya soon okay? Remember, call everybody, start goin' against the grain, it's time for him to put up or shut up."

"Yeah me too, got it, thanks."

When he finished talking with Joe, he thought about what he had said about calling everybody. He wheeled around to his computer again and was about to close out his email to look for everyone's number he had on file when he was surprised to see another email. The killer was becoming either more brazen, or more comedic because this email subject line had the title of a song *It's me again Margaret,* from the Ray Stevens song about a man obsessed so much about a woman he even spends his only call from prison on her. He clicked on the subject to open the message.

What do you say Goober, how goes it on the hickory farm? I gotta admit you have a nice little town. I apologize about the sewer reference earlier, it really has some charm to it, this opposed to the big town I live in. Oops, did I just

Scott A. Reighard

give Elmer Fudd a clue? Well, since there are hundreds of cities in the U.S. with large populations I wouldn't call that much of a clue. Okay, how about this one. I'm thinking of a number between one and a million, if you guess the right number I'll give myself up. Oh wait, you can't contact me, too bad, so sad, I had a doozey of a number too. Get it, number two? Come on get in the game, how are you going to be famous if you keep dawdling around like this, it's pretty pathetic you know that? I told you earlier that another goes down in about a week. Oh, and I will even leave you a tangible clue that would enable you and me to actually make contact. What do you think about that? Come on L'il Abner, I'm running out of nicknames for you. Speaking of which, you remember the Batman show don't you? Man was that a great show or what? I loved how the Joker and the Riddler kept getting away from Batman. I always hated that guy who played Batman he was such a bad actor. Somehow I see a parallel path here don't you? Okay, here you go Jessica Fletcher see if you can solve the clue of the next dead classmate.

But there was nothing else written after the last sentence. There was no clue. Was this a calculated move on the killer's part to make him guess completely, or did he inadvertently hit the send button before finishing his message? He closed that mail and looked for another email but there wasn't one. He opened the Underdog one again, and decided to print both emails to look for something within the messages that might indicate something, perhaps another riddle or some cryptic clue to a classmate. The killer had never done that before. Andrew questioned whether this was a change in tactics. Was he now leaving encrypted messages within the email? For the next thirty minutes this drove Andrew crazy. Like a forensics expert analyzing a murder scene he meticulously examined the messages. Did it have something to do with comics or

The Reunion Reaper

cartoon references, L'il Abner, Batman, or even Jessica Fletcher for that matter?

After coming to a dead end he rubbed his eyes, grabbed the files on his remaining classmates and started going over each one again.. "What the hell am I doing? How in the world am I expected to recall things that happened more than twenty five years ago, and with who? This is pointless, just guess you dumb ass that's about what you've done up to this point anyway." He was at an end, the possibilities were nearly impossible to calculate. But he couldn't get rid of the fact that the killer said it would be another one within a week. Whatever the killer's intent it was working, conversely for him there was nothing working. His head whirled like a merry go round. Andrew was a mess following every scent out there. He needed to take a deep breath, throw out the garbage the killer had filled his emails with and attempt to, once again, climb into the mind of a killer. Yet again, it was not going to be an easy night's sleep for Andrew.

Scott A. Reighard

Chapter 78

This was becoming a familiar theme for him. Jeffrey had camped out near Andrew's home and heard some very interesting conversations. He waited until it was dark to snuggle into his usual spot. Across the street from Andrew's house was a wooded area where there were no houses. It was sandwiched between Andrew's street and a street that was about a quarter of a mile on the other side of the wooded area. On his first trip there a few months ago he scouted the area during the day and set out markers for himself so he would have his bearings at night. He did his research by mapping out the terrain, as well as the access and escape route should he need it, although he thought that unlikely.

One thing that Andrew and Sonny did not take into consideration was that the killer just might walk through the woods to get close enough. They didn't think about it because the woods were thick and the nights were very dark due to the fact there were no street lights nearby. Only someone with a working knowledge of the woods could navigate its unpredictable terrain.

Jeffrey saw an SUV approaching Andrew's house. It was Andrew's. He watched as he parked his vehicle and walked through a side door into the house just off the driveway. He listened intently as greetings were heard from father to sons and then husband to wife. The night was warm as he lay there listening and looking up at the stars. There was only a little activity as he switched his channels from room to room hoping to hear something of value. Occasionally he would hear murmurings, but mostly it was the boys, especially Ryan with *Michael stop*. "Just clock him one kid, he'll stop." He was so glad he never had kids, what a pain in the ass he thought. He switched over to the

The Reunion Reaper

kitchen only to hear Andrew and Stephanie discussing Ryan's coughing situation.
Andy, Andy, Andy, you gotta be home more often, what are you doing running around trying to find a mastermind? ...Yeah, you gotta go to Charlottesville what's wrong with you? ...Ooh, good one Stephanie that got 'em. Man I like this girl.

He continued to smile and comment as the conversation ended. *Who's Sonny,* he wondered?

The kitchen went dead so he switched over to the study. He could hear clicking sounds like someone at the keyboard of a computer. There was a moment of silence and then the words "I got your underdog right here you smug bastard. I'm a lot closer than you think." A chuckle emerged as he heard the lamentations of a man clearly frustrated at reading his most recent email.

Hours went by as he listened to voices that would fade in and out from where he had planted the devices. He got a kick out of thinking how Andrew would interpret his emails. Listening to any information that would give away plans Andrew was making regarding his investigation was his main purpose for being here, plus he loved the idea of the proximity of his location to a man desperately trying to catch him. *If he only knew I was right across the street.*

Chewing on some jerky, he could hear that Andrew was talking on the phone. He did his best to try and figure out who it could be he was talking to. *Maybe it's a friend at the force or someone in his family.* He could only hear Andrew's voice. He did not know it was Joe Marketti on the other end. "Yeah right," he commented. When he heard Andrew mention to the person on the other end, "I'm probably a few days within getting this guy." He was kicking himself for not bugging the phones, but he still was able to hear enough.

There was a click of the phone and more banging of computer keys. *I wonder if he's reading the next one,* he

- 309 -

asked himself. There was considerable silence for a while, the only sound being a printer. There were occasional shuffling sounds, but nothing discernable. Finally he heard Andrew mutter a few expletives as he seemed to be turning off the computer. He looked over and saw the study go dark. He turned his attention to other areas of the house, but there was nothing worthwhile. For the remainder of the evening he sat comfortably against a tree. He carried a small mat to sit on plus provisions in case he got hungry.

As the night got quiet he stared up at the stars mulling the game. He was feeling somewhat ambivalent though because he knew the game would have to end sometime, but how would he end the game? *Kill Andrew, or should I leave him to live with his failure?* Staring up at the stars he noticed a streaking light zip across the sky and then disappear, *a falling star, just like Andrew, about to crash and burn.*

He clicked back over to the bedroom where Andrew had now entered. He was surprised that much wasn't said as he knew both Andrew and Stephanie were in the bedroom. He smiled. "A wreck, he's an absolute wreck," he whispered to himself. It wasn't very long before he decided to get out of there and get back to his hotel for a good night's sleep something of which Andrew was unfamiliar with these last few months.

The Reunion Reaper

Chapter 79

Andrew was busy trying to catch up on some things at work when he got a call from Captain Hardy. He was asked to stop by his office as soon as he got the chance, which meant now. Andrew was trying to figure out what it could be that the captain wanted. Did he receive a call from Florida, Georgia, or someone who had a complaint he thought? He was losing track of all his stories, facts, and other information jamming his brain. He was walking on eggshells enough he didn't need another headache or burden. He tapped on the captain's office door.

"Come on in Andrew."

Captain Hardy was sitting behind his desk reading through a few notes.

Doing his best to be relaxed he tried a little levity, "Top of the morning captain, I'm sure you're wondering why I called this meeting."

Not looking up, "I never heard that one before, sit down."

Andrew just smirked at the captain's lack of a sense of humor and took a seat. The captain continued to flip through the papers he had in his hands while Andrew just casually looked about the office. He noticed a picture on the wall he had never seen before, it was a picture of Captain Hardy and Frank Beamer the head football coach for Virginia Tech. The picture looked to be fairly recent. Captain Hardy was dressed in his formal uniform while Frank Beamer was in a business suit.

Again, Andrew was trying to keep the moment light, "Hey, you and Beamer huh? Where did you take that?"

"The Hotel Roanoke, it was a benefit for the Virginia Policemen's Association."

"Wow, too bad he can't keep his own team policed."

Captain Hardy looked up at Andrew over his bifocals, "I'm a VT grad."

"You are? I thought Deputy Chief Wolfe went there." Andrew faked a laugh. He didn't need more screw ups than he had already encountered. The captain tossed up an eyebrow at Andrew.

Obviously embarrassed, "sorry about the whole policing the team thing, I was just joking… I knew you went to Tech. In fact, I believe Deputy Chief—"

"You can stop now."

"Yes sir."

The captain put down his papers and adjusted himself back in his seat. He breathed a sigh, took off his glasses and then leaned forward placing both arms on his desk.

"Andrew, I just want to ask you one simple question, what in the hell are you doing?"

"Sir?"

"Don't sir me. You know exactly what I am talking about. I thought you were done with your solo chase for some killer of your classmates?"

How in the world did he find out? I never told him this. Did I tell him and not remember?

"Andrew!"

"Yes sir."

"I asked you a question."

"Did I tell you that's what I was doing?" Andrew attempted to turn a question into a question hoping to confuse the captain. A vain attempt at that.

"I told you it's a small force, we hear things. Besides, your work around here the last few weeks has been less than stellar. You have yet to crack the break-ins in SW. Do you know what it's like to get calls from rich people who want things done now? And they always mention lawyers. Now…" The captain removed his glasses. "What do you have to say?"

The Reunion Reaper

Andrew sat there feeling like the little boy who just broke the neighbor's window. What should he say? Who gave him up? He knew it wasn't Sonny.

"Look captain, it's complicated, you need to put yourself in my shoes just for one—"

"First off it's not complicated and I don't want to wear your shoes. All I know is that you are violating more laws than I can think of."

"But captain—"

"Now, I have no choice but to give you an ultimatum." He pointed his finger at him as he continued, "give up the case or face suspension and possible charges of federal obstruction."

Andrew pleaded, "But I am really close to—"

"You're right, you're close to jail that is. Look, I feel for your classmates, but this case ain't for you. Now do as I say or the mud's gonna get real thick if you know what I mean."

Andrew had no immediate response. He was in a rough spot. He felt that he was actually making some headway and now he was being told to put on the brakes. He had that deer in the headlights look.

"Now I got things to do here, you go on back to your real work, you got that?"

"Yes sir."

Andrew stood up and slowly strolled out of the captain's office. As he made his way back to his office he saw a familiar face, Tony Moreno.

"Yo Andj, what's shakin'?"

Andrew didn't respond he just ignored him and continued his walk.

"Whatever! We'll do lunch sometime," Tony replied sarcastically to his being snubbed.

The remainder of Andrew's day would be muddled with confusing thoughts. He knew that he had to think about his future as a Roanoke County Police Detective and

as a father and husband to people who were relying on him. In some circles the gig was up so to speak. He could no longer continue this elusive chase.
Damn, this is like one of those repeating nightmares.
He laid his head against the back of his chair and raised his head to the ceiling boring a hole through to the heavens.

"Come on, there's got to be something. I mean, am I the guy for the job or not? Why all these tests? I need your help, please."

It was a plea, but was it too late? He didn't solve it in time. Six people were dead and a career was potentially on the line, not to mention a marriage. He had failed.
Later that day his office phone rang, it was Sonny.

"Hey, are we still on for tonight?"

"Sorry to tell you but someone ratted me out and Captain Hardy threatened me to quit the case or he was going to suspend me or charge me with some obstruction BS."

"Really, I'm sorry to hear that brother. Well look, I already told the wife I was going to be out so I'll be at my post at nine."

"You really don't need to do that, it's over man, it's over."

"Nothing is over until we say it is. Was it over when the Germans bombed Pearl Harbor?" Sonny was trying to put a light spin by using the John Belushi analogy from Animal House. Andrew tried to laugh. "Come on man, let's give it a night or two, nobody will have to know except you and me okay?"

"You're really okay with this?"

"Heck yeah, let's do this, what if we get 'em then it's really over."

"All right, but I sure hope no one else finds out."

"No one is going to find out, I'll be there okay?"

"Okay. Sonny, thanks for everything so far, you are a true friend."

"Ooh rah, so are you brother."

The Reunion Reaper

Chapter 80

If the killer was around or coming around the bait was set; Sonny would be positioned near the entrance to Andrew's road looking for anything suspicious while Andrew would attempt to keep things as normal as possible. He and Sonny had a system of texting one another should a situation arise.

Andrew's bedroom window had a front view to his property as well as the street. He could peak out of the corner of the blinds and see a hundred feet or so in either direction of the street. He felt nervously confident that it was just a matter of time before the killer would arrive. He was praying the killer would make a mistake to finally end, what seemed to be an endless chase. He was tired, broke and falling out of favor with just about everyone. *If only I had a dog surely it wouldn't hate me right now.*

Perhaps the killer was most likely feeling a sense of invincibility and would make a mistake he pondered. "Pride goeth before a fall," he mouthed. First it was the listening devices and now the conflicting messages. Was the killer losing his focus or becoming more brazen than ever? He could feel that something was going to happen and soon, and it better, or else he might be the new security guard at Wal-Mart.

The family had just finished up a delicious meatloaf with mashed potatoes dinner and Andrew decided to play a game of Yahtzee with the boys; one of the family favorites. It would be an evening for some much needed relaxation, if it could be called that. Andrew had to assist Ryan with most of his rolls during the game, after all how much could a five year old figure out about strategy in a game that talked of three or four of a kind, or trying to understand what the word Yahtzee actually meant? Playing a game of chance was more the norm lately, so Andrew was more than comfortable rolling the dice. Rolling off a four of a kind certainly wasn't the cure to what ailed him, but it was at least a little ointment on a burn that penetrated deep into his conscience. Game one would go to Michael who proceeded to dance around the kitchen knowing he had defeated his dad. They would play five games at the urging of Ryan who so much enjoyed shaking the dice in a vicious manner inside the circular cardboard dice shaker that came with the game. Andrew had a pair of eyes looking out for him at the end of the street and felt comfortable about that while Stephanie sat in the living room, glad to see her husband being a father.

Despite all that was going on he decided to not think about the case. He genuinely needed a free night. The study would get no visit tonight. The hour was getting late and it was time for the boys to head on into bed. When that feat was accomplished Andrew sat with his wife and suffered through her evening television shows. He always hated those cop shows that appeared so unrealistic to him, but for some reason she enjoyed the drama. He had indulged her on this evening in hopes that she would look favorably on him or perhaps that he was as transparent as cubic zirconium. If I could just read her mind he thought to himself. She in turn was wondering what her husband was up to.

It was now just after eleven as Andrew and Stephanie were catching the news when his cell phone vibrated, it was Sonny. He was letting him know that Mary in a car full of friends was headed down the street. He returned a thank you message and asked if he had noticed anything unusual. The return message was a negative. It was late and he was having a tough time staying awake, and despite being off the next day he needed all the sleep he could get. Mary walked through the door and Andrew felt comfortable with going to bed at that point. He was always nervous if he went to bed and his daughter was not yet at home. His sleep

The Reunion Reaper

was easily disrupted by the slightest noise, common of a parents worry sleep. He kissed his wife, kissed his daughter and then slumbered off to the bedroom feeling good that Sonny was down the street ever vigilant, ever the Marine.

Scott A. Reighard

Chapter 81

It was a pleasant clear evening as Jeffrey made his way through the woods and plopped down in his usual spot some one hundred and fifty feet or so from Andrew's house. The humidity was low but the mosquitoes were busily buzzing the ear tower. He doused himself with deep woods OFF, turned on his earpiece, and removed his video recorder from a small bag.

He pondered the idea of squatter's rights. This was becoming almost a habit, but he felt this part of the game needed to come to an end. He too was plotting. Victims seven and eight were ripe for the taking off, so this was like intermission for him, but the final act was coming soon.

As he sat patiently he rooted for Michael in the Yahtzee games and waited to see how many times Stephanie would pass in front of the living room window so he could record her movements. He watched as Mary got dropped off by her friends from an evening out at the movies. He recorded her movement from the car to the house. His biggest disappointment was that the dialog was limited.

Jeffrey wrestled with how much longer he would stay, but this just seemed to be too much fun. It was better than television drama, but he never watched television that much. As he glanced down at his watch he saw a truck pull up to the house. He did not recognize it. A man got out of the driver's side. Perhaps it was a young man calling on Mary. *This could be interesting.* He saw a stocky built individual with a determined walk head toward the front door. He was carrying something in his hand. He continued to roll the camera to see who would answer the door. It was Stephanie. The man stepped inside. He was unable to get a view of the man's face but he quickly shot the camera toward the vehicle he drove. It was a Dodge truck with

The Reunion Reaper

Virginia plates, but he couldn't make out the plate because it was too dark and the picture was fuzzy because it was beyond a clear viewable zoom.

   A few minutes later the man emerged and Andrew was with him. They were standing in the doorway but the front light was not on so it was difficult to get an image of the two, but he knew that one was Andrew and the other possibly a friend or fellow cop. If he could just get a little closer he could get a better shot. *I wonder if that's that Sonny guy.* He moved quietly forward to get a better look for his camera as they continued their conversation on the front stoop of the house, but in the echo of the woods there was a snap. He had stepped on a fallen branch. The sound echoed through the woods and quickly Andrew reached inside the doorway and flipped on a switch. Unbeknownst to the watcher in the woods Andrew had long ago installed a flood lamp system that lit up the woods across the way like the Roanoke Airport runway. He had missed a detail, but then again he never suspected that Andrew would figure out the listening device scheme. He tried to take refuge behind a tree but Sonny was quick to spot the image and jumped off the stoop and headed toward his truck.

  "I gotta a flashlight in my truck."
Andrew quickly responded, "I got him." He reached inside to grab the flashlight that hung on the coat rack. "I knew you'd come in handy one of these days."

   Something Jeffrey hadn't planned was now happening. He was on the run with two very determined individuals on his ass like wolves on a wounded deer. He weaved his way around trees, occasionally stumbling. A shot of adrenaline gave his body a chill and his heart was racing like a nervous amateur playing golf with Tiger Woods for the first time. Andrew and Sonny were closing in flashlights darting around the woods like spotlights that beam to the heavens of the night time sky at a debut movie gala. Bodies swiftly darted and dodged the natural landscape that could easily hospitalize an unsuspecting adventurer.

"I got him over here." Shouted Sonny, fixed on a moving mark.

The Marine training instantly kicked in as he jumped and leaped over obstacles like those during boot camp days. Andrew's triathlon training came in handy as well as he swiftly moved his forty plus frame through the woods. Sonny's flashlight beam bounced around the landscape. Andrew knew these woods somewhat, but not great. He did realize one thing, there was a road that ran parallel to his that was just beyond the next thick set of trees, and most likely a waiting car for the man on the run.

"The road is just beyond those trees we need to…" Andrew had tripped over a medium size branch that lay crossways across the path. He went down in a heap.

"What?" Sonny shouted back, but there was no immediate response.

Jeffrey's adrenaline was at a fevered pitch as he could sense the ex-Marine and Andrew closing in on him. He had a lead, but it was quickly evaporating. He was hoping one or both of them would encounter a branch that would clothesline them. He was glad he mapped out and traipsed through these woods several times because if this had been the first time the chase would have ended with his apprehension. He swiftly maneuvered his way around as he heard someone shout, "The road is just beyond those trees we need to…" and he heard nothing more, only the pounding of his heart or his feet upon the ground; there was no time to debate which.

Andrew was able to get back to his feet as he cursed the branch and his inability to see it. Once again he gave chase, but with a noticeable limp. They were running out of real estate. If the killer got to the road he could get to his car, or at the very least find some place to hide in the neighborhood. It's not like they could call for back up

The Reunion Reaper

either. It would be unlikely that Captain Hardy would understand two Roanoke Police Officers acting like mavericks and without the authority to do so, especially after his talk with Andrew.

Sonny was getting closer when suddenly his right foot disappeared in to a hole. His leg straightened like a rod as he went down with a heavy thump and a groan. The flashlight flipped out of his hand and was now shining back at him. He knew that he had hyper extended his knee. He was able to hop up and continue hopping after the stranger in the woods. Any other man would have laid there writhing in pain, but Sonny was no ordinary man. Sonny could see that there was only about fifty or so feet to the street as both he and Andrew had unfortunately lost ground. Ironically during this chase, two local guys got dumped while a stranger zipped and zagged to his vehicle.

Jeffrey had escaped. The car sped off and neither Andrew nor Sonny was able to get a fix on the plates. They only knew the make, a late model Toyota Avalon. Sonny was limping badly now as the effect of the hyper extension began to settle in and Andrew hobbled with a bruise on his ankle. They had failed.

Chapter 82

Both Andrew and Sonny were heaving from the adrenaline paced chase as they watched the car speed off toward the highway of Interstate 81.

"Son of a bitch," Andrew shouted then turned to Sonny.

"Are you okay?"

"Yeah, found an inconvenient hole that's all." Responded Sonny as he began to rub his right knee, "You?"

"A downed branch got me... Damn it, we had a great chance." Andrew slapped his leg.

"It was a Toyota Avalon," Sonny responded as his breathing was heavy and deep. "I didn't get the plate but it's an Avalon I'm almost positive."

Andrew was drenched in a blanket of sweat as he looked around the neighborhood, it was eerily quiet. "I guess he'll probably high tail out of town now."

"Did you recognize him?"

"Just looked like a thin frame with dark hair."

"Yeah, that's about what I got too. It's pretty dark in those woods even with our flashlights."

"Why didn't I think of that when I discovered the listening devices?"

"What?"

"The woods. In order for him to listen, he would have to sit nearby in a car, or..." Andrew pointed around him, "here."

"Listen, there's a chance that's a rental he's driving." Sonny observed as he started limping back toward the woods.

"Well, it's doubtful we'll get anywhere tonight with it, besides I-81 is just up the road. He's probably headed that way." Andrew said.

The Reunion Reaper

Sonny stopped and began to rub his knee again. "Do you think we should call some of our guys to be on the lookout for a white Avalon?"

"Sounds great, but technically I'm off this chase."

"I have Caleb's number on my cell, he's working over this way tonight."

"Ah what the hell, go ahead and call it in when we get back."

As they limped back to the house each of them seemed to lament the lost opportunity. Andrew cursed their luck. Andrew felt there was one thing that was for sure, the killer knew Andrew was on to him. *Now what's he going to do? If he had to bug my house, perhaps he's not the cocky and brazen psycho I take him for.*

As they hobbled up the driveway Stephanie was standing on the front stoop, the flood lights still glaring out into the distance of the woods. Both were limping as she quickly made her way to the street to greet them.

"Are you two okay?"

"Yeah, we'll be fine. He got away Stephanie. We were so close."

Sonny limped over to his vehicle then sat inside to call Caleb and a few other patrols on duty.

"Well, I guess we blew it," remarked Andrew to Stephanie.

"Did you get a look at him?"

"Not really."

"What is Sonny doing?"

"He's calling a few guys working tonight. The guy was driving a white Avalon."

Stephanie could only look and wonder if this could get her husband in trouble.

"So what about Captain Hardy and what he said?"

"I'll worry about him later."

As she helped her husband walk toward the house Sonny came limping back toward them.

"I gave them your number."

"Thanks."

"So now he's got you involved I see."

"Stephanie, your husband is doing the right thing. He'll get him, be patient."

"I'm trying."

Andrew glanced at Stephanie.

"Well, I'd better get home before Danielle gets too worried."

Sonny patted Andrew on the shoulder as he limped past him. "Sorry Andrew."

"Hey, no need to apologize we gave it our best shot. I'll keep an ear out from our guys to see if they get anything."

"Call me if you do."

"You just get home to the wife and daughter. I'll let you know if anything comes of it."

"You sure you're okay to drive Sonny?" asked Stephanie.

"Been hit by worse Stephanie, nothing a little ice and a couple of Advil won't take care of."

"I appreciate it bud." Andrew said.

"Ooh rah!" Sonny grunted as he got into his truck.

They both watched him drive away as Andrew explained the chase. In the meantime she helped him inside the house and would get him some ice for his ankle. As she sat there looking at a man still sweating from the chase with an ice pack on his ankle, she asked herself if she was blunting his efforts. She was not happy with the recent events, but was now convinced that her husband wasn't on some phantom chase. She would re-evaluate her position and support for her husband.

Andrew figured if nothing crossed the radio that night he would take the next day scouring the area across the way, and contact car rental agencies. If the killer thought Andrew was as dumb as he assumed than surely he wasn't expecting Andrew to pick up on the listening devices or lay a trap.

The Reunion Reaper

In the meantime he stayed up for a few more hours, but no calls came in from anyone. He would fall asleep on the couch with his cell phone clutched in his hand. It would remain silent during the night.

Scott A. Reighard

Chapter 83

Arriving back at his hotel Jeffrey quickly made his way into his room. He was sweating profusely as he tossed the camera, earpiece and recorder on the bed and went into the bathroom to wash up. He had escaped. There was a sigh of relief, but oddly a sensation of thrill as well. He was actually chased and nearly caught, what a rush that was. He looked in the mirror at a face that was equally excited and afraid. This was too close for comfort, but then he wondered how Andrew could have figured that someone would be watching. *Did he find the listening devices or was this just pure luck?* Then he remembered the other guy saying, "I got him over here." Surely, this was planned he considered. They were waiting for me to show up. *Clever boy Andrew, it's about time you did something of note, I thought I was going to have to knock on the door*. He knew the wiretapping advantage was no more.

He finished washing up and walked over to the bed and plopped down. It was late. Things had now changed and he needed to get out of town quickly. So much for a few days in the Roanoke Valley he figured. I wonder if he or the stumpy guy got a look at me. Regardless, it was time to get on a plane.

Jeffrey laid back and stared up at the hideous popcorn ceiling that was so popular in older hotels. His mind was racing. Suddenly he popped up like a Jack in the Box. The scene, did he leave anything at the scene he questioned. A huge knot formed in the pit of his gut. For the first time in a long time a moment of anxiety flushed through his body. He always wore his gloves and covered up well, but what about other stuff. He couldn't take any chances he knew he had to do something that evening.

The Reunion Reaper

After returning to the hotel several hours later and thinking about the excitement of what just happened, he laughed out loud. It was more of a nervous laugh, but it kicked in a recall of sorts about the last time he ran from someone. It was as a junior in high school where he and a friend were sneaking around the house of Amy McMahon.

His friend Simon lived a few streets over from hers and he would ask if they could go by her house. He liked Amy, but she was dating Andrew at the time and so all he could do was gaze and dream. He liked a lot of the girls in his school, but Amy was different. She had a genuine innocent nature about her. She was athletic, smart, although a little awkward in her walk as she was nearly pigeon toed. It was almost sexy, especially when she wore shorts with sandals, her tan legs shimmering in the light of the sun. He never considered himself a stalker, just a curious boy with an active imagination, but others would call it otherwise.

So here were Jeffrey and Simon hiding out in the crocus plants waiting for Amy to pass by into her bedroom where cream colored shears shaded the window. If she turned on a certain light in her room it made a perfect silhouette to any onlooker that noticed. As she passed by the window of where they were hiding they watched. Her bedroom light went on and they proceeded to sneak around to her bedroom window to wait for a moment they could etch into their collective perverted memories.

On this certain occasion Amy's father happened to be in the backyard taking in an evening gaze of his own. He was an astronomy buff and was checking out a few constellations when he thought he heard a few voices whispering. Her father quietly snuck around the corner of the house and as he turned toward the side of the house where Amy's window was he saw two boys crouching near a large crocus plant. Suddenly they spotted the father standing there fists on his waist with that, you little shits, look on his face. Both boys did not hesitate to bolt out of the plant and scamper down the street. Mr. McMahon gave a little chase shouting expletives at them as they nearly tripped over one another getting clear of a man who could have easily knocked them out cold with a swift thump of his Popeye forearms chiseled from working construction for so many years. Soon after that incident Mr. McMahon replaced Amy's shears with heavy double sided drapes that could blacken a mid-day sun when closed.

    Jeffrey smiled as he recalled that moment and then was struck with his next great act. It was time to put Andrew in a box, literally. He had already done a little surveillance on this person, but wasn't serious about adding this person to the list of targets, but circumstances had changed. *How do you make a man wither like a flower with no sun or water? You go after his heart.* Plus, it made for good drama. The plan would further flower the next day as he would catch a flight to Atlanta and hang out there until he was sure all would go according to plan.

The Reunion Reaper

Chapter 84

The following morning, disappointed with the fact that none of the midnight shift officers spotted a white Avalon, he took to the woods and paced around looking for any evidence. He staked out a possible location as to where the intruder may have hung out and set out to find anything that could help him. As he limped closer to the area, his leg still stiff from the night before, there was the unmistakable smell of bleach. *No way, the son of a bitch came back.* He found various items lying about that he bagged for testing, but he knew that bleach was an intensive cleanser that could rid an area of mounds of evidence. He was anxious, yet restrained because he had been here before. Standing on the doorstep of a possible breakthrough only to be denied; however this time he stood on that doorstep with guarded optimism. Before he left the area he exhausted every possibility in hopes of finding something, anything that might lead him to the killer and finally end this continuous nightmare. Feigning the advice of his captain he moved on, driven by an obsession, or craziness.

The closest he got was that a Toyota Avalon was rented from the Hertz Counter at the airport by a man by the name of Jack Fortchen from Satellite Beach, Florida. Andrew asked to see a credit card receipt, but the man paid in cash was the response. Of course, he didn't expect anything less. The only other information he received was that the clerk thought the man had dark hair that was somewhat long, touching the collar perhaps. The clerk couldn't remember if the hair was black or brown, glasses or no glasses, blue eyes or green, but he said the guy made a few witty cracks when he heard what vehicle he was renting. He recalled the man asking if the vehicle once contained the remains of King Arthur. *Yeah, he's a regular funny guy isn't he?* Andrew requested that he inspect the car, but it had not been returned yet. He decided to find a little corner of the airport and kept the counter in view; perhaps catching lightning in a bottle he hoped.

After several hours, a full read of the newspaper, skimming through a few magazines and several cups of coffee Andrew was ready to go to plan B. He handed the clerk his card. The clerk agreed to contact Andrew but indicated that he would be leaving at five that evening.

Before he got to the station he stopped off at the County Building to see Chris, one of the local pathologists for the police department, and a good golf buddy of Andrew's. He dropped off all the evidence he gathered at the scene. Chris's comment about the bleach pretty much told Andrew he had nothing, but he would run the items through analysis. It would take days for Chris to come back with any kind of information for him.

Just what I need, more delays, thought Andrew.

Considering the description he and Sonny came up with, there were only two classmates in his graduating class with dark hair and slender build, Greg Madison and Jeffrey Lewis, although there could be a dark horse from another class entirely. He couldn't imagine either, and besides Jeffrey was out of the country, or so he thought. Although it seemed completely crazy to think of Greg or Jeffrey because they were considered good friends, could it be that one of them turned into a serial psycho? He knew both of them to be funny, sarcastic, and even a little edgy at times, but their disposition did not match that of a serial killer. He knew he was running out of time and was hedging his gut feelings against logic and physical evidence. He called the clerk a few times that day, but there was no information to be had.

The Reunion Reaper

The next day Andrew called the rental agency, but yielded the same result, the vehicle had not been returned yet; however later in the day airport security was provided information on a late model Toyota Avalon parked in the airports long term parking lot. The plates matched that of a rental and Hertz confirmed it was their car. The clerk called Andrew to tell him the car was found but there was no driver turn in. Apparently someone had simply parked it in long term parking with the key in the ignition. Hertz said a person walking to their vehicle noticed the key in the ignition and notified airport security. When Andrew came on the scene whatever evidence he was looking for was already vacuumed, wiped or brushed down. The cleaning crew said there was the unmistakable smell of bleach in the car. *Of course, luck of the Irish my ass.*

Scott A. Reighard

Chapter 85

Arriving at a familiar stopover Jeffrey sauntered once again through the Atlanta airport. He would need a few days to ensure himself that his plans would work in his favor. He was meticulous. He wanted this to be the final act where he would play the part of the director directing his cast. He would move Andrew here and there and then send him over the edge of reason and solution. Everything had gone rather swimmingly until a few recent hiccups, but this was no time to panic. Get to a hotel, map out the plan just like others before and move on he thought.

He would not rent a car this time, it was all about being invisible, so he took MARTA, the metro Atlanta transportation system to a hotel near the airport. He would walk down to a local diner and then hunker down in the hotel and plan.

He had his best friend with him everywhere he went, his laptop computer. A friend that facilitated his ideas and provided him with a means to communicate with those he wished to communicate with; a friend, to which he could get things off his chest. It would come in very handy on this trip for he had one more email to send to a distant friend, a friend who was on the hunt, a friend who was about to be greeted with a surprise of profound effect.

Settling into his less than desirable hotel accommodations he was simply glad the young clerk at the front desk accepted cash for the two nights. *Cocksucker will probably pocket the cash.* Sitting in his shit hole of a hotel room he tried to slide the defective desk chair forward to type up his other plan; again, being specific in his wording and process. While performing this he had a momentary reflective thought, *I guess we're getting close to the inevitable aren't we?* Time to make Andrew pay in

The Reunion Reaper

totality he keyed out on the laptop, as well as the scenario he was about to perform.

By night's end he had most of it figured; he just needed a time frame and for the victim to be in the wrong place at the right time. He was counting on Andy boy to be where he needed him to be. It had worked before, could it work again? It would not take long for the question to be answered. An unsuspecting phone call to the victim and a short conversation would seal the deal. It would take place in a few days. Now it was time to let ole Andy boy in on the plan.

Scott A. Reighard

Chapter 86

Andrew was stewing over his luck as he clicked his way to his email site. What idiots they were at Hertz to clean the vehicle, he thought. Perhaps it wouldn't have really mattered this killer was clever at covering all his bases. *He deliberately left the vehicle in long term figuring it would take a while to discover the vehicle. No need to check the airlines, I'm sure he's got dozens of John Doe Id's. I've got to make a bold move.*

It didn't take long for the move to be made. If this was a game of chess Andrew felt dangerously close to either losing his queen or getting cornered into check mate. Sifting through his email there it was, in the subject line, *Score one for the moron!* He smiled as he read the opening sentence. *So you have a brain after all, smooth move Vaseline. How did you find out? Did the lone brain cell kick in? Or was it that I left you such easy clues that a four year old could find them before you? I guess taking out Andrea was the kicker, huh? Well, good for you, but not for her right? Hey, a man's gotta do what a man's gotta do. Way to get her killed by the way. You should have left her out of it. This is between you and me – GOT IT!* He was tiring of this joker's comments, but he continued to read on looking for something important he could use to perhaps chase and finally end this.

Your wife is very sexy by the way, I wonder if you can satisfy her enough. I could take care of that for you if you'd like. Hell, make that if I'd want to I would. Do you know how many times I could have taken you out? You're like Opie when you leave the house man, all secure in your small town America feel with not a worry in the world. What a moron you are! Well, I'm about to fuck your world

The Reunion Reaper

moron. You know they say the fastest way to get to a man is through his heart or some dumb shit cliché like that. Well I am about to rip yours out. Hmm, which one though? Let's see, there's one girl on the left, and one on the right, which will meet with an unfortunate accident? The clock is ticking and time's running out dick wad, gotta go make things right. Screw you later!

Once again a one sided transmission with no ability to respond, but there was a way to respond, to try and bring this all to an end. It was time to shut this bastard up he thought. The question Andrew asked himself was what did he mean by a woman on my left and a woman on my right? Then it hit him, Amy. But did he mean that it was Amy, or was he coming after his wife. He had hoped that his family would have been able to stay out of this mess, but what if this most recent event pushed this guy into acceleration mode where he decided that he wanted to go out with a big bang? Could he be serious about his wife or was it all a bluff in order to throw him off the next potential victim, which he now assumed might be Amy? Was it like the previous email? Was there anything to it, or just another smoke screen? He couldn't take that chance. He called for Stephanie to come down to the study immediately.

Scott A. Reighard

Chapter 87

Andrew did something for the first time since working on this case he showed his wife emails from the killer. Perhaps it was his ego that prevented him from giving these to her previously, but it was time to let her know what kind of person he was dealing with. She sat in a chair adjacent to his desk. He sat down and wheeled his chair around to face her, then used his feet to wheel closer to her. He handed her some of the emails. She read them.

"How many more are there?" she asked.

"That's pretty much all of them." Andrew however would not go into detail about what some of the others said. He felt that these few would be enough, plus the most recent seemed to apply directly to her and that scared her. Reading the email gave her the creeps just knowing he was there in the woods. How many times she thought? How many times was he there looking at her, the kids, maybe even Mary a sweet young good looking teenage girl? It made her sick to think about those images. Her feelings were still mixed, but she also began to feel sympathy for her husband given the way he was referred to in the emails.

"So what do you think is next?" as she continued to read the emails.

"Well, I figured he'd run out of here given the chase by me and Sonny, but he could be pulling a bluff."

"What do you mean a bluff?"

"Well, he could make me think it's you and I stick around and he murders another with no fear of me chasing because I'm here with you. Or he thinks I might make a chase down to Florida and he circles back here for you."

"Florida? You're going to stay here with me right?" she questioned emphatically.

The Reunion Reaper

He hesitated with his response. She seemed annoyed at his lack of response.

"Oh I see, you think she's the target and so you're going to try and save her. Well, what if he does come back for me Andrew, if you're in Florida who will protect me, or the kids?" A look of concern quickly turned to consternation.

He grabbed her hands. "Look, I'm not going to leave you here unprotected, Sonny will be here and we will have the guys who are on patrol keep a watchful and attentive eye on our street, as well as over on Woodlawn. There will not be a minute that goes by that you won't have protection. I promise."

There was a brief silence, but then Stephanie couldn't help but wonder and then ask, "What if it is her, how does that make you feel?"

He was surprised by her question. "I care for every single person that's been killed Stephanie, but if you're wondering whether I have more feelings for Amy than the others well then I can't lie, of course." Then sarcastically, "Although I have to admit that I never kissed Brandon or Paul so perhaps my feelings for them have been skewed by that."

"You're such an ass sometimes, I'm serious!" she barked as she pulled her hands away.

"Jesus Stephanie a classmate might be on the verge of being murdered and you're concerned with how I feel about that? Give me a break please…no wait, give me more credit than that. I have been busting my ass trying to catch this guy I don't need a wife to further agitate the situation." He slid his chair back to his desk. She sat there looking down at the floor. He turned away looking at papers on his desk. He mumbled the F word, a sure sign he was extremely pissed.

"I'm sorry, you're right… I think the two of us have been through a lot these past few months. I don't know what I was thinking... I completely trust you." And then with a tone of exasperation, "I am just so tired with all of this you know?"

"I am too Stephanie, I am too. Sometimes I feel like a complete incompetent over this whole process that's why I didn't show or tell you everything. I should have listened to my dad and handed this over months ago to Joe at the bureau, but my stubbornness and ego got in the way. I got in over my head, and I've jeopardized my job as well as sacrificed my family."

She looked at a sullen husband. One who had been through hell trying to work on this case; a man dedicating his time, sacrificing his family, job and whatever else in order to do the right thing, she didn't need to be negative at a time like this. She got out of her chair and moved closer to her husband. She placed both of her hands on his shoulders and bent down just inches from his face. "You are most definitely not in over your head here; challenged yes, but not in over your head. You have done all you can up to this point and now it's time to finish it."

"What are you saying?"

"I think you should go to Florida, I'll be fine here with the kids and knowing Sonny and the guys will be watching out for me." She kissed his forehead. "I love you."

"I love you too…You sure about this?"

"Go catch this guy and be done with it."

She kissed him one more time and then started to walk out of the study.

"Steph." She stopped. "You're a good woman."

Turning around and smiling she responded, "And you're a good man Andrew Keane, I can't tell you how glad I am to be married to you." She walked out and closed the door giving her husband privacy so he could get to work.

Andrew quickly called Sonny and explained what he needed his good friend to do for him. He was all in on this one; all the chips were down he thought. Sonny never hesitated. He assured Andrew that he would have a few

The Reunion Reaper

guys who were on patrol in the area to keep a constant eye or at least presence around Andrew's house. Sonny would spend the next few nights in the woods under camouflage. It was his turn to be the hunter if the need arose and he was glad to serve his good friend.

Andrew then tried to contact Amy. He pulled her card from his file and called, but there was no answer at her house phone. He then tried her cell phone, but service had been temporarily interrupted. "What the hell, how can service be interrupted? Something's not right." Feeling powerless at that moment the only thing he could do was to go online and book his flight. He feverishly clicked away as he was becoming too familiar with navigating the various travel websites. The earliest flight was the next morning. There wasn't much else he could do that evening. He was hoping that he could get to Amy before him. All of these thoughts and those of his wife's concerns and neglecting his kids whirled through his mind as he packed his travel case.

When he was done he headed upstairs to do the guilt hang out once again with the boys who were busy watching their favorite shows on Nickelodeon. He plopped down on the couch between the two of them. The boys snuggled up to their dad as he wrapped an arm around each of them. Stephanie was in the kitchen writing out birthday invitations for Mary's sixteenth birthday party that they planned on having in a few weeks. Mary was planted on her bed chatting it up with a friend. It looked normal, but it wasn't. Andrew was about to confront something unimaginable within the next twenty four hours.

Scott A. Reighard

Chapter 88

Jeffrey had been here before but it was only to case out the home and its occupant just in case he would need to resort to this location and this particular victim. Initially she wasn't on the list because she was likeable, a good woman and a good mother to her two boys, not to mention that he still had a thing for her. She had tolerated a husband who for a long time verbally abused her. Perhaps he was killing some of the wrong people, but he quickly shrugged off those thoughts, this was an important moment. She wound up on the list out of necessity; out of misfortune really. He was targeting Greg Madison, but when he considered that Andrew was tightening the noose he decided for the big prize. Andrew had bested him several times in their younger years, but not this time.

On the surface there was a list, retribution in his eyes, yet underneath an untapped reservoir of hate that unfortunately spilled over to these recent unlikely victims, and he was not shy about blaming Andrew. In some edge of the universe darkness he was hoping it would go this way; Andrew Keane did not disappoint. He stood up to the plate and took his swings, albeit, up to this point striking out. He smiled as he thought about the fact that He had Andrew in the batter's box swinging haphazardly in this the case of the dying classmates.

He had already gotten to the house the day before and snipped the telephone line. He figured that Andrew might get wise and try to warn her so why take chances. He felt good and confident about cutting the line. It was a little after eight in the morning as she exited the house with her two boys.

They were headed off to their father's place and mom was heading off to work. He knew that she was a

The Reunion Reaper

pharmaceutical representative whose territory was Ocala, Gainesville and other smaller towns in and around these two larger cities. She would first drop off her two boys because it was their dad's weekend, and then she would head out to her first client.

She had stopped for gas near I-75 and he pulled his rental car into a vacant spot at the convenient mart. As she got out of the car he looked her over, she was wearing a taupe linen skirt that came to her knees and a white short sleeve blouse. By all accounts she was a classy lady; sexy, professional, yet vulnerable. Oh how he wanted her, but someone had beaten him to her. If only he were the one to discover her that evening being assaulted by Larry. Perhaps Andrew Keane did have the luck of the Irish. Times change and so do circumstances, even if they are manipulated by a mind that has seen better days. Regardless this was his moment, he needed to seize it. It was time to give back what he had received most of his life, disappointment.

She got her gas and was headed out toward the highway heading north on I-75. Today was a Gainesville day. She would make several client stops before a late afternoon hair appointment. He was careful to stay several cars behind but never out of view. He followed her around all day. Even while she got her hair done he sat and waited. He was a patient man. Following her throughout the day created an uncomfortable situation of second thoughts. Maybe he should hang it up, pursue Amy again. Surely circumstances were much different these days, she was a divorcee and he had money; *that makes up a lot of marriages in America, right?* He could pocket the six murders and begin a fresh new life. But what about the book and the legacy he questioned. It was a nice try but there was way too much depravity and loose wires in his brain. He thought more about revenge and hate then he did about love and all that goes with it. "Focus," he muttered to himself. As she headed home from a busy day it was time for him to go fishing and wait for the right moment when he could snap the line and hook his catch. That time was fast approaching.

She stopped off at the grocery store to pick up a few items and then headed home. He was so ballsy that he even walked in the store behind her and bought a bottle of wine; something to savor when all was done. He wondered if she even had the slightest inclination that someone was following her, watching her, admiring her.

When she pulled into the driveway of her home he drove past her house and parked his car near the end of the street next to a park. He got out of his car. He looked over at the park to see that several kids were playing on the swings, while others were running around playing some game of chase. Some were just sitting on the seesaw. He calmly sauntered down the street passing several houses before getting to hers. The only thing that could screw this up was if the boys were home or came home. He only wanted one kill today, not two or possibly three. He had everything planned except for the boys. He needed a little luck. He got his wish.

He knocked on the door and Amy McMahon answered. She was alone. She was shocked and surprised to see who it was.

The Reunion Reaper

Chapter 89

Andrew tried to contact Amy one more time before boarding the flight out of Roanoke, but there was no answer yet again. Who doesn't have an answering machine in this day and age he asked himself. He tried her cell phone but it was still temporarily out of service. He was now getting very nervous. He boarded the plane and while on the way to Florida he prayed and hoped that she was still alive. He knew time was of the essence because the message from the killer was pretty explicit. There was no doubt in Andrew's mind that Amy was the next victim. But he also wanted his wife protected just in case the killer doubled back, or never left Roanoke for that matter. *Am I doing the right thing,* he conjectured as the flight attendant asked if he would like a beverage?

The flight arrived in Sanford, Florida a few hours later. He rented his car, looked over the map he printed off from MapQuest, and was quickly on I-75 headed for Ocala and the home of Amy McMahon. Several times on the way there he tried to call her house and cell phone, but it was only the same result. He pounded the steering wheel in frustration. He had a bad feeling. He prayed that she would be safe, that no harm would come to her, but sometimes evil wins

He arrived at her place in the early evening. He saw her Volvo SUV parked in the driveway, or at least he assumed that was her vehicle as he pulled into the driveway. He walked up to the door and knocked, there was no answer. He knocked yet again, no answer. He decided to walk around the contemporary style home built in the late 1990's. There were ten foot high photinia hedges that bordered the property and there was a small entry way just off to the right of the house with an area decorated by a flagstone pathway that led to the back yard. He made his way around to the back of the house to try and look inside. He came to a door that led to an enclosed patio. He checked the handle. It was open. He stepped inside the patio area and made his way over to the sliding glass doors that led into the house. Through the window he could see the family room and dining room area but he could not see anyone. By chance he checked the handle on the sliding glass door and it too was open. He slid the door across its rail and called out her name as well as Alex and Tyler's, but there was no answer. He had a bad feeling in his gut. He nervously called out again, still no response.

   He stepped into the house and looked around. He saw that there was some food on the kitchen counter not yet put away. He kept calling out names as he slowly made his way around the house. He drew his Glock and held it close to his chest. Although it seemed a long shot if the killer would still be hanging out waiting for him to show up, he wasn't about to take anything for granted.

   He heard a feint noise coming from one of the bedrooms across the house. The sound was barely audible, but other than the pounding of his heart nothing else could be heard except for that sound. He again called out not getting a response. As he made his way to the bedroom he was trying to prepare himself for what he might see but that wasn't possible. The sound he heard was coming from the television inside her bedroom and as he looked inside his worst nightmare had come true. Tears instantly filled his eyes. Lying on the bed was Amy McMahon. She was dead.

The Reunion Reaper

Chapter 90

Parked down near the end of Seminole Way he watched as Andrew pulled into the driveway of Amy's home. He was taking a chance hanging around, but he just couldn't resist the reaction and aftermath of his latest triumph.

He watched as Andrew knocked on the door getting no response. "Go around back dumb ass I left the back door open." Andrew peaked into a front window, but apparently could not see anything, and then he watched as Andrew disappeared behind the high wall of photinia hedges making his way around to the back of the house. He pulled out a cell phone he purchased at the nearby Wal-Mart and called 911.

Calmly, he would report a disturbance of hearing a woman yelling for someone to stop and pleading for her life at 14358 Seminole Way. He told the dispatcher that he may have heard a gun shot when he passed by the house while taking a walk. He would sit there and watch two Ocala PD cruisers pull up to the house. One team of officers knocked on the door while the other team went around to the back of the house. A few minutes would pass and then emerging from the house and opening the front door for the other officers was one of the officers who had gone around to the back. He could sense a chill rushing through his body at the anticipation of what was going on inside the house. He felt like eating popcorn, the show was so good.

Had his plan worked? Could he have drawn it up any better? Was Andrew a stupid moth whirling by a spider's web unknowingly? He donned a smile wider than the Joker of *Batman* fame and tried to imitate Jack Nicholson as he uttered these words while Andrew was being escorted out of the home of Amy McMahon's in handcuffs, Andrew Keane just got an enema.

The Reunion Reaper

Chapter 91

Not only had another of Andrew's nightmares come true, but now he was accused of making it happen. He was taken to the Ocala Police Department on Pine Avenue, and despite showing them his badge and travel itinerary he was placed in a holding cell. A few hours later he was questioned by Detective Thomas, a twenty five year veteran of law enforcement. This was a situation Andrew had become all too familiar with and thus was caught between confusion and anger. Confused about how he was going to wriggle out of, not only this situation, but the entire case and keeping his job, but also explaining to his wife yet another blunder, he could only sit and wonder.

Anger stemmed from two things, one getting so easily entrapped in a psycho's plan and two not being able to see it coming, especially since the wiretapping incident, Rodney Adams, and Paul Thurman. He felt he would most likely have to come forward with everything at this point if he wanted to get out of this jam and get back home. As for keeping his job and quite possibly his marriage, that was another matter.

With a pronounced southern drawl detective Thomas questioned him, "So you're tellin' me that you jus' happened on the scene and the woman was already dead?"

"Exactly," He was in a hot spot no doubt, and although he was innocent, he needed to stay cool and think clearly.

"Now what made you go to her place to begin with?" the detective asked as he sat back in his chair and flipped on some glasses to look at a piece of paper an officer just handed to him.

Andrew heaved a sigh that was becoming an all too familiar act. In some way he knew he was busted in more ways than one, he decided to cooperate. He needed to purge

– to confess – to admit – not only his feelings, but in some Rod Serling fashion, his responsibility for this. He lowered his head and began to tell the detective everything he had on the case. He told him how he underestimated the killer's abilities and resources. He further explained that this was obvious a frame and he fell right into the trap. *I'm sure this will make for a good story for them. Let me tell you about this story of an incompetent detective from Virginia.*

"I'd say the feds are gonna love talkin' to you, federal obstruction, violation of jurisdiction, just to mention a few." Andrew's face displayed a tired despondency to the detective's comments as he continued, "I have here from the Atlanta Police Department that you were questioned about another death, of one Rodney Adams, and that you gave them a similar story."

"It's what I've been saying all along. He wire-tapped my house and was able to hear my conversations and my plans. He knew I would go to Florida and then..." Suddenly Andrew stopped talking. He sat back in his chair and a crazy thought entered his mind.

"You were sayin'?" asked the detective.

"Detective, I know this sounds absolutely crazy, but you gotta let me out of here."

"You're not going anywhere until we get this all figured out."

"But you don't understand I have to get back home to check something out."

"You ain't goin' no-where you hear?"

"But..."

"Ain't no buts about it, you're here until we say you ain't here no more, you got that!" declared the detective.

Andrew just jammed his body into the back of the chair in disgust. He finally felt he had a breakthrough, one he couldn't share though. He just wanted to get back home, go through his files and hope that this hunch would finally put him on the right track. Instead he was sitting in a place he'd

The Reunion Reaper

rather not be, but he had no choice. As detective Thomas rose from his chair to walk over to the water fountain, Andrew sat and gazed out at a very stale looking police department that could have used some renovations. He briefly considered making a run for it, but a more reasonable mind prevailed, and so he sat in thought as to how he could get out of there and back home as quickly as possible. He prayed that this recent revelation was correct. Perhaps there was a little luck of the Irish in him yet, but first he had to get out of that police station and out of Ocala.

Scott A. Reighard

Chapter 92

Andrew spent the night in a cold holding cell of the Ocala Police Department with two drunks, one of whom spent half the night embracing the lone steel toilet, and a man who claimed that he was assaulted by his wife, not the other way around as reported. He also spent part of the night holding back tears for Amy. He felt responsible for her death even though he didn't pull the trigger. Had it not been for him he thought, she would not have been in the crosshairs of a crazed killer. He needed to sleep but the conscience preempted the necessity.

Andrew wanted to be out of there and on his way home, but the Ocala Police weren't exactly finished with him yet. He was not anticipating the call the detective would make to his captain especially since their last conversation was basically a directive telling Andrew to get off this case or else; it looked like or else was pulling ahead in the race that Andrew had hoped would have been over at this point. He was swimming up stream and he knew it.

The station was preparing for the shift turnover as Andrew was startled by the loud clanging of a steel door. He barely slept, if at all, and his eyes were burning. The previous day had been exceedingly long and the night even longer. He looked down at his watch and realized that it was after eight a.m. The first thought to come to his mind was of his wife and kids. For all he had put them through all he had to show for it was now sitting in a ten by twelve holding cell. The thoughts he had the previous night would become moot if he was not given the opportunity to act on them. He was in a jam. The killer had outsmarted him in every area and was able to trap him into a very compromising position. He was pissed. He just wanted one more chance before being hung out to dry and that is the

The Reunion Reaper

way things seemed to be headed. He couldn't believe how tired he was. His brain felt like a bowl of jell-o, or a jumbled word search. As he tried to gather more of his faculties despite the horrible night he was about to hear even worse news.

One of the morning officers who just came on duty escorted him to detective Thomas's office. In the office were detectives Thomas and his partner detective Price. He was told to take a seat. He didn't like the look on either of their faces. He was a cop, he knew that look. It was one that did not bode well for the accused.

Scott A. Reighard

Chapter 93

Logging onto the Ocala.com website and checking out the newspaper link Jeffrey smiled as he looked at a byline that claimed, *Virginia Officer Involved in Local Woman's Death.* He read and chuckled at the article that talked about how Andrew Keane, a police officer from Roanoke was being held without bond in the Ocala Detention Facility and for questioning in the death of an area pharmaceutical sales representative Amy McMahon. Could it have worked out any better, he thought. He also read where Andrew Keane was being questioned in connection with a similar style murder of an Atlanta man just a few weeks prior. He had done it. He giggled at the sheer genius of his ability to manipulate someone like a hunter manipulates his prey. Andrew followed the scent like a hound dog on the chase.

"He was so obedient that Andy, and predictable, just like most of humanity."

As he finished the article he backed his chair from the desk and swung his feet up onto the desk and crossed his legs. He created a small rocking motion with his chair and began to wonder his next move. Was this it, game over? What could top this though he thought? Surely he would be placed on the same pedestal as other great serial killers of the past like the Ripper and the Zodiac who were able to evade capture. Was it time to take that vacation to Jamaica and write that best seller of the infamous Reunion Reaper? He was glad to finally see Andy go down, but it was bittersweet. He knew Andy would be absolved of guilt due to a lack of evidence, but his trip through hell was guaranteed, not to mention his reputation forever tarnished. Should he let him wallow in misery, or end it with one final mission? Was it time to cash out his hand or put all the chips on this thought of bringing Andy to a final end?

The Reunion Reaper

Perhaps add Andy to the list? He would mull over this new idea.

He smiled broad and shiny at the thought that Andy's life would change forever, and with that it was time for his journal entry.

Journal: July 28, 2008: Don't fear the Reaper!

Well, I have to say game over I guess. What a glorious day this is. I'll need a few weeks before I figure out the final chapter though. Oh well to the current business at hand.

Dear Amy, how gorgeous you looked even after a long day's work. I have to admit that I really, really, really hated this one, but I had to make a choice. Enter a sigh here! Unfortunately you were a victim by association. A long time ago I told you Andy boy was no good for you and that one day he would leave you. I would have hung around and married you and we would have lived happily ever after. I just wish you would have understood more about me before you decided to deny my desire to be with you. Oh, and was I right about Bradley? What a moron asshole of a man did you marry there? Irreconcilable differences my ass he couldn't keep his Johnson to one woman. You lived with that far too long. Woman you are strong, but you always were, and that's why this one was so tough. I'm sorry I had to make it quick, but I knew Andy was on his way to try and save the day. You have to admit that I was clever to use the same model and caliber weapon as Andy's private handgun. How did I know? You see, when I bugged his house in poke a poke Virginia, I saw a bumper sticker on his son's dresser that said, "Keep out or meet my friend, Glock." Oh and then there was a .40 caliber bullet along with some change sitting in a dish tray near his bed. It is amazing how much you can learn about someone when you break into their house. Anyhow, sorry about our final encounter, I never wanted it to be this way, but he made me do it.

You know what, here's what I am going to do for you. A beautiful woman like yourself deserves a dedicated man and so here is my promise to you, whether they convict Andy Keane or not. I am going to find a way to kill him for you. By hook or crook I promise you that I will lay to rest the man who has caused you so much misery for so long. I love you Amy McMahon, and yes my dear, don't fear the reaper, for it is only I.

Amy McMahon, December 12, 1965 – Forever in my thoughts.

The Reunion Reaper

Chapter 94

The following day, Andrew was taken from the detention facility back to the police station. He was escorted into an office and was instructed to take a seat. *Yet another seat and more questions to answer I'm sure.* Andrew raised his head to the ceiling. *Hey big guy, I could use a little signage right now. I know I haven't been the most diligent of your disciples but you are always with me. I could use some help if you don't mind.* As he waited he couldn't help but close his eyes due to the burning sensation he was continuing to have with his eyes. He was not getting much sleep and the last conversation he had with his wife on the phone the night before was not one most couples would care to have. With his eyes closed he could hear the turning of a door handle and feel the wind of the door as it was being pushed through and around. He was startled to hear a familiar voice.

"Well, I pretty much figured that you'd either end up in jail or suspended, I guess my first inclination was right."
Shocked to see his father standing there along side a man he did not recognize, "Dad what are you doing here?"

"Trying to save your ass that's what," he said as he took a seat next to him. Another man walked around the desk and sat down. Andrew must have been so tired that he didn't notice that in front of him was a desk plaque that indicated the man he was looking at was the chief of police for the Ocala Police Department, Chief Dickey.

"What's going on, I don't understand why you're here, when… wait, how did they know to call…"

"Damn son you lost all your faculties or something? And you look terrible by the way."

"It's been a long few days, no wait, a long several months how about that." Andrew looked at the chief, "I'm sorry chief, all of this is my fault and I take full responsibility, but I really need to get home."

The tall thin man who looked younger than his age swayed back in his high back leather office chair, "We'll have to see about that, what do you think Patrick, should we let him go home to his family?"

"Well he sure needs them a whole lot more than they need him right now."

Andrew just sat there in disbelief as to the nature of the conversation between these two elder men. Finally, exasperated by it all, "Will someone please tell me what in the hell is going on here?"

His dad turned to him, "Son this is Carl Dickey, he's the chief, we go back a ways. He called me last night when he got news they had some cop from Roanoke named Keane sitting in a cell who was conspicuously attached to a crime scene."

"I already told them the story of how I couldn't have murdered Amy McMahon because she was already dead when my plane arrived in Orlando—"

"Yeah, yeah, yeah we got all that. The problem is son, you, as I predicted, have become entangled in a web that is not easily broken from."

Andrew now seeming to plead, "Look, I know it looks bad on the surface, but I think I am really close on this. If I don't nab this guy I'll turn in my badge and take whatever punishment is meted out."

His father slid back in his chair and sat upright, "Wow, that's a pretty bold statement coming from a man who has yet to solve anything about this case. I told you to turn it over to the FBI son, why don't you ever listen to me?"

"We've had this conversation, you wouldn't understand…"

"The hell I wouldn't and now look at you. Carl there has to decide whether to pursue charges or to allow you to return home to face your captain. Damn boy, I've gone in

The Reunion Reaper

deep for you before but now you've really placed me in a bad way."

"Hey, I didn't ask you to come down here."

"No you didn't, but you're my son and I have to protect you just like you'd protect Mary, Michael and Ryan, am I right?"

Andrew just shook his head in agreement.

"Andrew I can let you out of here and pass this off as some friend who came to visit an old school friend, but we know a lot more than that. From what you explained to detective Thomas this guy has claimed seven victims?" offered Chief Dickey.

"Yes sir and I need to get to him before he gets to eight."

"Well hang on there Sherlock. The stipulation is this, we have evidence, albeit planted by someone other than you, but it's not that simple." The chief leaned forward. "I'll let you walk out of here, but you tell your captain that you're done with all this and that you'll hand over everything to the FBI today. Your father says you got a buddy up there in Washington."

"Yes sir, but he's in counter-terrorism."

"I don't care if he is in to counterfeit-ism; you call him and give him what you got."

Andrew sat dejected not really knowing if it was frustration or sheer exhaustion. *Maybe they're right; I've done most of the leg work.* But he lamented the thought that all it was going to take was one phone call and he'd be off the case, perhaps all of this in vain, feeling an even deeper sense of responsibility.

"So all I have to do is call the FBI give them all I have and that's it?"

"That's it son, do what they ask and this'll all be over. I'm sure Carl could talk to your captain up there and smooth things over with him."

There was a brief silence when Andrew finally capitulated, "All right, I'll do it. As soon as I get home I'll call Joe and give him all I have and send him my files."

Chief Dickey had been here before when someone promises to do something, "Uh, let's say you call him now tell him all you know."

"Call him now?" Andrew questioned.

"Yep, or you don't go anywhere."

Andrew didn't want to call Joe right now because he had a gut feeling and really wanted to close this out himself, but the gig was up, it was time to turn it over and get rolled over. Chief Dickey slid the phone around and pushed it toward Andrew. The chief also tossed a bag onto the table that contained all of Andrew's belongings. Andrew reached into the bag and pulled out a small memoranda type booklet. He flipped to Joe's number. Reluctantly he picked up the receiver and dialed the number he had listed. He reached Joe's number but was only able to leave a message. He left a message for Joe containing important information as well who he thought the killer might be.

Andrew's father sensed that Andrew wasn't exactly telling Joe everything, but a wily father understood a determined son. He decided to keep his mouth shut.

"Is that good enough?" Andrew asked, hoping the chief would allow him to go.

"Patrick what do you think, do you trust him enough to follow up on this when he gets back home? Because if I call his captain and ask for leniency he better do as I instruct or else I may extradite him back here and introduce him firsthand to Sparky." The chief was alluding to the nickname for the Florida electric chair that was known to set people's heads on fire.

"He'll do the right thing Carl."

"I'll do the right thing chief, you can bet on that."

The Reunion Reaper

"That's what I'm afraid of, a man with the same DNA as Patrick Keane saying he's gonna do the right thing. Get 'im out of here Patrick and talk to him good you hear?"

"I'll give you a call later on this week Carl. Thanks for what you're doing, if this had been Miami I don't think Martinez would have been as forgiving."

"Martinez is too much of a politician. Folks say he wants to be the next governor."

"Maybe, you should run Carl."

"There ain't enough alligator wrestlers left to support me."

Both of them laughed, but Andrew was a bit agitated by the good ole boy chit chat.

"Uh guys, can we save the chit chat for later I need to get on a plane, and sooner than that, call my wife to let her know the good news."

"Patrick did you ever tell him the story of how Sparky lit up that triple murderer in '88?" indicating Andrew should be more patient and understanding with someone who just let him off the hook.

"I'm sure I did but he's got his mom's selective memory if you know what I mean."

The two elder men just laughed as Andrew tried to decipher what they were talking about.

"Now look, all bullshit aside, we got us a homicide, and if the statement you gave to Detective Thomas pans out I think that would serve you well, you get me?" The chief was sure to look Andrew in the eye when he said that.

"Yes sir, I'll make sure Joe gets everything."

The chief wished them both luck. Patrick gave the chief a hearty hand shake and pat on the shoulder and Andrew did likewise, although the chief did not feel so inclined to reciprocate the kindred attempt by Andrew. Andrew turned toward the office door, but his father looked back at Chief Dickey. The old friend winked and gave thumbs up to a father who was doing his best to protect his son.

As soon as Andrew got out of the chief's office he called Stephanie to let her know he was out and headed home. The conversation did not go the way he had hoped as she dropped on him the dreaded words, "We need to talk when you get home." Andrew pried for more information, but she was getting as good as him when it came to leaving people in the dark. She loved her husband dearly and wanted so much for this to be over, but she too was at wit's end and in a brief moment of light hearted thinking considered that her husband clearly lacked the resources and perhaps the natural gumption for all of this. *Oh well, not every artist is a Renoir* she pondered as the conversation came to an abrupt end.

"So how is Stephanie with all of this?" asked his father as they walked out of the police station.

Andrew paused, "Well, let's just say that she is reacting typically of a woman who doesn't have all the information she should."

"Son, do you know why your mother and I have lasted forty five years?"

"Because you have a large schwantz?"

"It's not just that," commented his father at Andrew's obvious poke at the malignancy of man's continuous fascination about manhood. "It's about communication. We have always been good communicators. If you don't talk to your wife they start to think two things, one you don't love them anymore, or two you are hiding something from them which makes them lose trust in you."

"We communicate plenty, I just couldn't sit her down and explain all of this to her, besides, there's a lot of this she wouldn't understand—"

"Ah, that's bullshit and you know it. You need to be open with your wife. You'll feel better about it, trust me. Be open and tell her the facts, and if she feels a certain way understand it, but let her know you've got to do what you've got to do"

The Reunion Reaper

"What about you, some of your jobs were covert and top secret, did you tell mom about those?"

"Your mom knew the racket I was in, it was dangerous for all of us, but she was one tough woman and she still is. She knew I couldn't tell her everything, but I always told her what she needed to do just in case."

"In case you got killed."

"That's right, and she was well prepared for that God bless her. Now look, this ain't about me or your mother, it's about you and your family. You do the right thing as quick as you can you hear?"

"I will, I promise."

"I can't cover your ass in Virginia."

"I got it dad. Thanks for bailing me out."

One thing about the Keane family was that whenever someone said to do the right thing that meant sticking to your principles and values. Oftentimes when the Keane clan communicated, there were code words or implied understandings, and his father knew that his son was not done and that doing the right thing meant he was still on the case. This was his deal to close. Nothing against Joe and the FBI, but he wasn't about to simply pass this off.

"Now don't forget, your mother and I want to see those kids before summer's gone."

Andrew waved and acknowledged his request, but he had something more important right now to tend to. As he pulled the rental car out of the lot to head back to Orlando for a long awaited flight home he rolled down the window and asked his father for one more favor.

Scott A. Reighard

Chapter 95

Despite her anger for her husband, in some strange way Stephanie felt sorry for him and was not about to abandon him in a time of need, but there were some things she was going to say considered as tough love. She was carrying a considerable load for the entire family while Andrew conducted this mad chase, and for what she thought? Was her husband vainglorious? He seemed so much to be a humble man, yet who knows what stirs in the mind of anyone really? These thoughts she questioned as she drove to the airport to pick him up. The boys in the back seat were anxious to see their father. She had picked herself up from her self pity about this whole ordeal and decided to confront and solve, not only the strain that had developed in their relationship, but a conclusion to the lunacy of endless chasing.

Andrew looked like he'd been through a military interrogation where he was denied sleep for days, the eyes said it all. Michael and Ryan ran toward their father as he emerged from the concourse to the family and friends waiting area. To the boys dad was on a work related trip. Ryan had asked Andrew a few weeks back if his daddy was a spy for the government. He missed his boys and his daughter, and he was missing his wife. He was gone just a few days but by all accounts he had been gone for the last few months. He was both excited and nervous about seeing his wife, part of it being his inability to shake the words she left with him at the end of their conversation, *we need to talk*.

There were hugs and kisses and a short drive home. The boys were asking a thousand questions it seems about what dad does while he's away, but Andrew skirted their questions by asking them questions of how they were

The Reunion Reaper

filling their days and what new things they were into since the summer was nearly halfway over. During the entire drive home he must have gazed over at his wife a half dozen times, she kept her eyes forward, occasionally laughing at some of the things the boys said, or commenting on their summer activities.

As Andrew pulled the SUV into the driveway and everyone clamored to the house. Andrew stopped Stephanie before she headed into the house.

"Listen, I know you said we need to talk, but I was really hoping to get some much needed sleep, I feel like I haven't slept in a week."

She looked at a man who looked rather haggard and said, "Sure, it'll do you some good I think, and give me more time to think as well. I'm just glad you're home."

Of course the boys wanted to play catch or go swimming with dad, but Stephanie deflected their wishes by letting them know that dad needed some sleep first. Andrew slogged into the house and directly into the bedroom where he quickly shed his clothing in favor of something more comfortable. He hit the bed like he had just been hit with a bat from behind. He was in a comfortable bed, finally. He would sleep through that evening and into the next morning.

Scott A. Reighard

Chapter 96

The next morning Andrew's energy level had shot up dramatically as though injected with a can of MonaVie energy drink. He had slept for twelve hours and had a wild dream that was extremely surreal. One he didn't know whether he should share. It had a similar theme to the dream he had in the hotel in Florida, but this time he was chasing someone through a fog laden forest. The image turned to look at him but he couldn't see the face, the fog growing thicker. Suddenly the dream shifted to him sitting in the back seat of a car. The car was being driven somehow, but with no driver. He was able to leap into the driver's seat just before the car crashed into a large cement wall. He didn't know how to interpret his dreams, but he at least paid attention to potential messages they may offer. Could it be a sign that despite a potential crash this case would somehow be able to be saved?

He was up before everyone and was cooking breakfast as Ryan was the first to come traipsing into the kitchen followed by Michael. He made them pancakes. His mindset was one of anxiousness and nervousness. He was finally excited about having a real substantive angle that he wished to share with his wife, but he was nervous about how she would take his newfound excitement and the intent of her desire to talk. He could hear her making her way up the stairs.

The boys were chomping away at their pancakes, "Hey, make sure mom and Mary have some, I'm on the last batch here and these are dads."

Stephanie shuffled her way into the kitchen.

"Good morning sunshine," he said with a smile, a kiss and a cup of coffee.

The Reunion Reaper

"Good morning," she responded as she went over to the table to kiss both boys. "Is Mary still asleep?"

"Yep, I went in to wake her up but she told me to go away," replied Ryan with a dejected tone.

"That's okay honey we'll get her up in a little bit. She has a funny way of expressing herself sometimes. In fact, some people have a tough time of expressing themselves period." An obvious jab at Andrew's withholding of information to his wife. Andrew only glanced over his shoulder at her implication as he flipped the final four pancakes. "Now you and Michael finish your pancakes and go get some clothes on for the day your father and I need to talk."

Uh oh, and on an empty stomach, surely she's crazy.

"Honey, eat some pancakes," he offered.

"I will. I just want to finish my coffee first."

As Andrew completed his daddy's home breakfast duties he sat down with a stack of home style pancakes and a steaming cup of coffee. Stephanie forked two pancakes from the remaining stack he had made that were staying warm under a large Tupperware container. It was conspicuously quiet. She methodically poured her syrup around the pancakes and then in a zigzag motion over the pancakes. Andrew watched and seemed to infer that she was sending him the message that he was skirting around things and zigzagging from the truth, or was it his guilty conscience that simply interpreted her syrup gyrations as such?

"Well aren't you the energy bunny this morning."

"You don't know how bad I needed those twelve hours of sleep."

"Yeah, I guess all of us are in need of good sleep these days."

"I know honey, you're absolutely right, and I am so sorry for having put you through all of this."

"I got a call last night." She said matter of fact.

- 365 -

"Oh yeah, who was it?" He said as he shoved a large bite into his mouth.

"Your father."

"Oh yeah, what did he want?" Not knowing for sure whether his father opened up the can of worms about Andrew requesting he call her on his behalf.

"Well it seems that he is worried about his son, and something about telling the truth."

Trying to be coy, "You gotta love my dad."

"Andrew, why would your father call me and talk to me about determination, obsessions, and what was the other thing, oh yeah, unconditional love?"

Looking sheepishly up at her, "Okay, I asked my dad to call you on my behalf because I thought for sure that I was not in good graces with you given the most recent debacle, and that there would be no way for me to just explain everything to you so that you would understand."

"After all these years do we still need to talk of trust?"

"I just didn't want you to get hurt or worry too much."

"How was I going to get hurt? I'm married to one of the bravest men I know and my faith is strong. However, trust is something a woman clings to, and that is something you have not been honest with lately."

"I know, I know, I should have been more forthcoming and I am so sorry about all of this."

"It's not about apologies anymore Andrew it's about solutions. I know your father went to bat for you down there. Thank God he knows who he knows."

"My father's a good man."

"I know he is, but you could have just sat down with me and we could have worked this all out."

"I know mea culpa Steph, mea culpa."

She rolled her eyes at his religious gesture of forgiveness and sin. "This is certainly no time for making fun of a very serious situation."

The Reunion Reaper

He shrugged his shoulders and lifted his hands toward the sky, "What, I was absolutely sincere there."

There was a brief silence as Andrew stabbed at his pancakes.

"So where do we go from here?" she inquired with genuine eyes.

He drew in a deep breath and slowly exhaled, "I know who it is, or at least I feel ninety percent sure."

Completely exasperated by his response, "Oh Andrew, it's over, we can't...you can't do this anymore." Haltingly, "I patiently and quietly listened to your father explain the Keane sense of determination and obsessing with doing the right thing, but I am not a Keane, I only married one."

"Look, all I need is...twenty four hours and if it is who I think it is and he is where I think he is."

"You see, you still have doubts, how can you go on jeopardizing us, your job, your future..."

"I get it Stephanie we've been down this road before—"

"Too many times it seems."

With a sigh, "Anyhow, I swear to you, if he ain't the guy it's definitely over for me."

With humph like gesture, "Where have I heard that before?"

"I mean it this time, no skirting the edges, this is it. If he's not the one, then I'm done."

"And just how do you plan on getting your man?"

"Well, the sleep definitely helped clear a few things, not to mention a very bizarre dream I had. Anyhow, after I get read the riot act by Hardy, I am going to request a few days off for psychological rest, or something like that. I've got a lot of comp time, so he'll do it. Anyhow, I nail this guy, and once I'm off this case I am completely re-dedicated to the job and of course all of you." Andrew's voice was going a hundred miles an hour.

"I never doubt your commitment to us Andrew, I only doubt whether you can turn away from challenges like these even if they compromise what you have as good in your life."

His head dropped, "I know I can't explain it, but you know how personal this one is to me and with Amy's death it really brings things to a head for me."

"I'm sure it does."

He understood her disappointment in his statement, "Stephanie look at me, Amy meant something to me a long time ago, and sure sometimes feelings you've had for someone remain, but it wasn't about my feelings for Amy, it was about trying to save another classmate and I failed. Now it's about catching that classmate for whom all this misery has been cast."

She dipped her head and seemed to stare into her now empty coffee cup. "I just fear losing you that's all."

"And I have the same fear of losing you, it would crush me." He grabbed her hand, "and that's why I need you to hold on for just a couple more days. This'll all be over one way or another I promise."

She looked him in the eyes, "I believe you and I pray you got the right guy."

He gripped her hand tighter, "I feel it. I've got a really good feeling about this. In fact, I am so jacked I can't wait to get to it." He got up from the table and carried over his dishes and coffee cup to the sink. "I better get to the station I've got a long day ahead of me."

"Well, who do you think it is?"

"I'll call you from the office once I check out one more thing."

The Reunion Reaper

Chapter 97

On the way to the station Andrew flipped open his cell phone to call Sonny. He wanted to know if they could meet. Sonny indicated that he was already on his way to the office. He was anxious to hear Andrew's story of the nightmare that was Florida, but more importantly Andrew revealed that he had a strong sense of who the killer was. Despite the tragic and devastating loss of Amy, Andrew tried to stay positive and driven for her sake.

As they walked inside the station, the two of them were greeted by Tony Moreno.

"Yo guys what's up?"

Sonny stopped Andrew from his walk as they approached Tony, "Oh by the way, here's your snitch."

Andrew stopped while Tony had a look of surprise on his face. "What are you tawkin' about?" Tony asked.

"Tony, why?" inquired Andrew as he faked a look of sullenness.

With a shrugged sense of uncaring, "I don't know what the hell you're tawkin' bout what snitch?"

Sonny quickly cleared the air, "Apparently Tony here was upset he didn't get the LT position and you did, and when he heard us in the locker area talking about this case he ran to Captain Hardy to inform him of your extracurricular duties so to speak."

"That's bullshit Sonny and you know it." Tony bowed his chest.

Sonny's five foot seven frame that was packed full of dynamite stepped up to the five foot eleven Italian from Yonkers.

"Go ahead, why don't you try saying that again, but in front of the Captain, or should I just lay you out right here for being the low life you are?"

Andrew tried to calm the situation, "Guys, guys at least take it outside. I'm just kidding, everyone settle down."

A few passersby began to slow their walk to listen and watch. Andrew stepped up to Tony, "Tony as much as I don't like you I forgive you. I can't believe it, a fellow Paisano too."

Tony stepped back from the two of them, "Hey screw you Irish boy, and you too…" pointing at Sonny, "whatever the hell you are. I didn't snitch on nobody and that's that." He walked away from them abruptly.

Sonny and Andrew just looked at one another as Tony stormed off. Although Sonny didn't have any real hard evidence, he did see Tony perform one of those quick turn and act innocent moments when Sonny emerged from the locker room after he and Andrew discussed a little of the case. Andrew shrugged off the encounter because he was past the point of covering up anyway.

After Sonny and Andrew's encounter with Tony it was judgment time. Would the captain be somewhat understanding of Andrew's request? The meeting lasted less than an hour and Andrew was relieved to know the captain, although not very happy with him, would give him a week to get his act together so to speak, but all this *bullshit* as he referred to it needed to be cleared up before he reported back to work. It was the most animated Andrew had seen from his captain.

Upon walking out of the captain's office Andrew felt a huge weight suddenly being lifted, but he wasn't out of the woods yet. He needed to be right on this his last attempt at apprehending a mad man.

After his talk with the captain, then to Sonny, where they discussed scenarios, he left the building. As He walked out he could hear Sonny shout out to him ooh rah. *Ever the soldier, ever the marine, I love that guy.*

The Reunion Reaper

Chapter 98

Jeffrey celebrated his masterful weave of deception and entrapment by flying to Vegas and blowing green backs on the craps table. He also blew more money by ordering a high priced escort. It had been a while for him, but he had been rather busy he thought, even for that which he sorely needed. It helped him to relieve stress, but then again, so was framing Andrew Keane. His escort that night was a skinny five foot five brunette who could have used a few more pounds. She wasn't quite emaciated, but looked quite withdrawn. He wanted someone to remind him of Amy, in memory of her he thought. She wasn't as tall or as pretty as Amy but for a thousand bucks she would have to do.

He ordered up champagne to the expensive room that went for three hundred fifty a night, but to him it was worth it; the lap of luxury for a man so deserving of such. He only had two pieces of business left, Andrew then perhaps his mother. *All in good time.* Now was the time to sit back and enjoy the fruits of his labor, not to mention the company of a twenty something high priced hooker. He treated her to food, drink, and of course himself, and when the time allotment was up he told her that she should pay him because he knew he was satisfaction guaranteed.

When the celebrating was over it was time to head back home to the comfy confines and consider his plans for Andy's demise. One final act he thought. In some macabre fantasy of delusory thought he pictured her dead body smoldering like a long forgotten cigarette that burned neglected in an ashtray. He didn't know whether to relish her eventual death or vomit from the mere thought of the woman that bore him dying by his hands. Regardless of these feelings he moved forward with her extermination. *All the lies,* he thought, *and all the lost years due to s strung out mother.* He would need little planning, he just needed to have the right opportunity to suffocate her. Aunt Delores was a heavy sleeper he recalled. As for Andrew Keane it would take something clever. He would need to wait on how things played out for ole Andy boy then work from there. When he returned from his three day binge in Vegas he would check the internet to see how ole Andy Boy was holding up in the pen somewhere down in hot, smoldering Ocala, Florida.

****

After blowing bucks, as well as getting blown in Vegas, he was back at home. He brought up the website for Ocala again and began scouring for articles related to the death of Amy McMahon. Suddenly he came across a byline that read *Virginia Officer released in murder case: Police continue search for suspect.* He couldn't believe what he was reading although deep down inside he figured that somehow Andrew would be able to wriggle out of this. He was upset with himself for not being clever enough about framing Andy, but deep down knew that if he wanted him out of the way he would have to do it himself. *Well, at least the framing put him through hell for at least few days. He's got to be hating life right now.*

It really didn't matter if he was or wasn't going to be incarcerated he was going to die anyway one way or another for making him kill Amy McMahon. With disgust, he read how the Ocala Police were unable to hold Officer Keane for the murder of Amy McMahon because his alibi regarding the time of his flight arrival and the time of death were incongruent, not to mention the fact the bullet found

The Reunion Reaper

in Amy's body did not match the ballistics of Officer Keane's weapon. Then he snapped for reason's unknown.

He slid his arm across the desk in anger clearing anything in its path onto the floor. He grabbed the screen of his laptop and slammed it shut. He didn't want to see anymore. Although it was insignificant that Andrew was now a free man, he was pissed. Pissed that Andy wasn't implicated in a crime he surely had a hand in. After all it was that tin badge from Virginia who forced him to kill her. He was the one responsible for driving him to this point, and now it was time for reparations. He had blamed Andy for other offenses in the past, and this was no different. Don't most killers look for some scapegoat rather than accept responsibility for their own actions? Andy Keane had become an obstacle that needed to be moved out of the way. It was time to relieve his anxiety.

Jeffrey paced about the house for a good while contemplating what he should do and how he should do it. The bastard's got to go by hook or crook. He got a brilliant idea and went back to his computer. He placed the CD of Electric Light Orchestra into the stereo and he pushed play. *Hold on Tight* slid easily out of the speakers. It was an absolute inspiration to him. A song about holding on tight to your dreams, and his was about destroying people's lives. It was time to lay the plans for the finale.

Now rubbing the top of his laptop, he apologized to his friend for slamming the screen shut and he gently reopened it and focused on one of the travel websites. He booked a flight two days out from this one, wanting to make sure he had his alibi set up before he set off for work in Roanoke, Virginia. It was all settled Andy Keane had to go, and anybody standing in his way was fair game as well.

Scott A. Reighard

Chapter 99

Andrew returned home that afternoon and began poring over notes in addition to his 1982-1983 yearbook. There was one particular person he was interested in. He turned to page thirty three and looked at the picture of the witty and charming egomaniac Jeffrey Lewis. He stared at his picture, gazing into the blue gray eyes of this young eighteen year old dressed in a Brooks Brothers blazer that blanketed a yellow pin point oxford and solid blue tie, his long flowing black hair that draped his shoulders while his white chops exuded a million dollar smile.

Beside the picture was another, but this one was from his younger years, probably when he was six or seven years old, and in it he was dressed only in shorts flexing his arms like some body builder. *Pure vanity*, Andrew suggested. He flipped through to the back of the book where classmates had signed their well wishes. He was looking for one particular signing.

On the back cover in big lettering he read *Andy boy, what is it that men wish to avoid but hate to lose?* A lawsuit he whispered as he read the remaining words, *Good luck with your law career and Amy McMahon.* It was signed *The Master of Disaster, Jeffrey Lewis.* A riddle he thought, just like some of those sent through the anonymous emails not to mention that Jeffrey always seemed to have these pet names for people. "You were a clever, sneaky little bastard, but why your classmates? Why Amy you sick shit?" He closed the book, sat back in his office chair and closed his eyes. He began reflecting on all those killed. Everyone on the list in some way came to be an enemy to Jeffrey. He went back to the yearbook and looked carefully at every picture of Jeffrey or those who were dead. There were some anomalies within the pictures because Brandon

The Reunion Reaper

Henniker was the primary photographer for the yearbook. He noticed there were no pictures of Jeffrey from spring activities, not even lacrosse. Although Andrew wasn't there, he recalled hearing about an event at a party that took place at Jeffrey's and the embarrassing situation that took place that night. He had forgotten so much over the years. "Surely that wouldn't drive a man to kill twenty five years later would it?" He thought about all the deception, and how Jeffrey was certainly bright enough to pull this off. He felt Jeffrey had a moody side to him, but thought that was the drugs he was on at the time. *He's got to be the guy, a schemer, a player, and a prick all rolled into one. He's got the trifecta and it's my time to collect.*

Andrew felt this was strong enough to pursue since several leads did not pan out. He felt strongly that Jeffrey Lewis was the man responsible for the senseless deaths of seven classmates. It wasn't exactly hard core evidence, but he did have some tell tale signs and a gut feeling. Looking over the list of remaining classmates he couldn't logically discern how any other could pull this off. It's not that Andrew had some sort of epiphany, but after examining those dead, especially Amy, the picture was clearer. He knew that he and Jeffrey weren't the best of friends, but this was difficult for him to fathom. He also remembered that Jeffrey liked Amy. *Why, would he kill her then?* Either way, he felt he finally had the right guy and there was only one way to find out. Deciding to play out the hunch, he pulled out Jeffrey's file then picked up the phone.

Scott A. Reighard

Chapter 100

Looking at the caller ID, Jeffrey thought whether he should pick up the phone.

"Hello."

"Hey Jeffrey this is Andrew Keane."

"Yo, what's shaking Andy?"

"Not too much, actually, things are really bad."

"What's up? Is the family okay?"

"Yeah, the family is fine, but this case…"

"Oh yeah, how's that going?"

Andrew was going to attempt to lull Jeffrey into saying something that would link him to the case.

"Not so good. I got some bad news, Amy McMahon is dead."

"No frigging way, are you serious?"

"Would I kid about Amy?"

"No you wouldn't. How did it happen?"

Come on Jeffrey; say something, anything that will lead me to you.

"Apparently someone got there before I did and killed her."

"Before you did, what do you mean?"

"Well, I figured she would be next."

"Oh you mean the emails?"

Bingo!

"Yeah, he tipped me off by threatening me with Amy or my wife, can you believe that? I mean to involve my family, what a coward and a weasel."

"I hear ya. So what now?"

"Well, I am off the case. I had a little trouble in Florida and my captain took me to the woodshed then threatened to suspend or even fire me."

"So what happens to the case?"

The Reunion Reaper

"I handed everything over to Joe Marketti at the F.B.I."

"Well, that's good news, Joe is a good guy."

Jeffrey flipped the phone from his right to his left hand and took out a notepad. He scribbled down Joe's name, and then wrote, *research Joe Marketti, his family, etc.*

"It's too bad you're off the case though, I think you would have solved it."

"Appreciate that, but it was time, I couldn't dedicate all I needed to it, so this is for the best."

"Well, they say there's a reason for everything."

"Okay, well I guess I'll…oh by the way, how was your trip?"

"My trip? Oh, it was good."

"You went to Greece right?"

"Italy."

Nice try Tweedledee.

"Oh yeah, so how was it?"

"You ask me how Italy was, captivating my friend, captivating."

"All right, well I won't keep you any longer; I just wanted to call you to let you know how things were going."

"Well, I appreciate it; sorry things didn't work out for you. Maybe someday this guy will be caught."

"Hopefully… Okay, you take care."

"You too, Andy boy."

After he hung up the phone Andrew sat down at his desk and solicited several travel websites. He was looking for the earliest and cheapest flight to Albuquerque, New Mexico, the last known address for Jeffrey. *I do believe I have my guy.*

Scott A. Reighard

Chapter 101

For the first time in a long time Andrew actually had something to smile about. Now it was time to talk to Stephanie about his final stab at an inclination that had up to this point been disappointing.

Andrew had to wait until she came home from work. It was early afternoon, the boys were still at day camp and Mary, who was a lifeguard at the YMCA, was working, so Andrew had some time to himself before everyone would get home. Feeling antsy about the next day's flight and possible confrontation, he decided to go for a quick run to clear his thoughts, and then he would pick up the boys and take them to the park, possibly to the Roanoke River for a little splash around and skipping of stones. Sure, it seemed odd that a man who had so much to think about would go splashing around with his kids. But this was a way for him to release nervous tension.

After his run and subsequent taking of the boys to the river, he was remarkably calmer than the angst he felt while on the phone with Jeffrey. He left Stephanie a message at work, so when he and the boys got home she was working on dinner. Mary was chatting with her mother in the kitchen. Everything seemed normal, to everyone but Andrew. He kissed his wife and snuggled her from behind. He was feeling a bit frisky.

"Dad, hello, I'm right here."

Andrew ignored his daughter's observation, "There's something I need to talk with you about." He offered to his wife as he pulled out a chair at the kitchen table. He then looked over at Mary. "Honey, would you excuse us please."

"What, you can talk in front of me."

The Reunion Reaper

Dad gave her that look and she knew it, skedaddle. "Okay, whatever, you say I never want to spend time with you guys and here you all ask me to leave. I don't get it."

"We love you honey, thank you." Andrew used sarcasm, but he meant it.

The conversation returned to its intended subject.

"So, what did you do now?" She responded with sarcasm.

"Well, it's more about what I plan on doing."

There was a brief silence when she broke it with, "Go ahead I'm listening."

"I booked a flight to Albuquerque for tomorrow morning."

"Oh, is the annual Star Trek convention there this year?"

He smiled at her attempt to make humor out of what she knew was a serious situation.

"I think you know why."

"Are you sure he is the one?"

She continued to peel potatoes over the sink not needing to turn to her husband.

"I'd bet the house on it."

"Please don't, you've already drained our savings."

Good point, God I love this woman!

"What do you say if I'm wrong I don't come back?" He leaned back and crossed his legs resting one arm on the table.

"That's not funny Andrew, not funny at all."

"I'm sorry. I was just figuring the dog house can't get any deeper and—"

"Oh, but it can."

Again there was some silence. She continued with her cooking moving around the kitchen like one of those contestants on a cooking show. He marveled at how she glided around the kitchen. He wondered if he looked like that to her when he was cooking for them. He paused before offering up his final question on her, "So, what do you think?"

"That's a pretty loaded question don't you think?"

"What do you think about all of this, me going to Albuquerque, locating Jeffrey Lewis and finding out if I'm right?"

"Jeffrey huh, he kind of gave me the creeps. Anyhow, I never doubted that you want to do what's right it's been the method's you've used that's all. We are now broke from all of your travel adventures and now you want to make another. Supposing your instincts pay off then money well spent, but if you're wrong then—"

"I'm not wrong Steph, I know it. You have to believe me. The only possible obstacle would be for him not to be there, but I plan on taking care of that this evening."

"And just how are you going to do that?"

"I'm going to call him."

"Now I know you're crazy. Why don't you just tell him that you're on the, whatever, flight tomorrow for Albuquerque and ask him if he'll meet you at the airport?"

"Funny. No, my plan is to let on that I am still nowhere with this case and if there was any information he had I would greatly appreciate it."

She finally turned, hands on hips, "You seriously believe he'll buy that? He knows you're on the case and most likely on to him. You call him I say he's gone by tomorrow morning and you don't see or hear from him in a long, long time, maybe never."

He stared at his wife in amazement. What a response he thought, strong and assertive, and very sensible. She continued, "I just say you show up on his doorstep and that's that."

It took Andrew a few minutes to realize but he actually maneuvered his wife into supporting his argument, besides, the phone call had already taken place. *What's another lie in a laundry list of them?*

"So just go to the door and that's that?" reassuring his argument and manipulation.

The Reunion Reaper

"Exactly, anything more may be construed as suspicious."

"You're right. By God you're right, I'm just going to go right up to his house and knock on the door, imagine his surprise when he sees me, ole Deputy Dog, Barney Fife, Jethro."

"You left out Jessica Fletcher, or is it Fletch?" She asked as she returned to cutting up the potatoes for boiling.

"Funny! So, when's dinner ready? Do you need any help?"

"The potatoes have to boil and then you can make the mashed potatoes, thirty…forty minutes maybe."

"Call me when you need the potatoes done."

He took the boys outside for a little go around with the soccer ball. When called he went in and finished the mashed potatoes. The family sat around the table eating yet another of mom's great meals. Andrew gazed at each one of them sitting there, Stephanie, Mary, Michael and Ryan. He loved them so much and wanted this all to be over now. Ryan told a lame joke he made up and everyone just laughed at his laughing at his own joke. Andrew smiled as he thought about how much he had been away too much.

Later that night in bed each of them exchanged I love you, and he whispered to her, "This is almost over… It's time to close the chapter on this crazy ride."

"My prayers tonight will have a special addition."

He rolled over to his spot, and the last thoughts before he drifted off to sleep were hopeful.

Scott A. Reighard

Chapter 102

Andrew's flight arrived at Albuquerque International Airport. He rented a car and drove to the home of Jeffrey Lewis. From his back pack that was lying on the passenger seat, Andrew retrieved the directions he researched via the internet the night before. The air was dry but it was hotter than habanera peppers on the lips.

The drive from the airport to Jeffrey's house would take about forty five minutes, and as Andrew drove to what he hoped was his final destination he examined how the situation took a complete turnaround. If Andrew was correct, the killer of seven innocent classmates was about to go down. If he was wrong, surely it would mean complete and total embarrassment as well as having to give up any chance of further pursuit. The rubber was about to meet the road in the name of Jeffrey Lewis.

Andrew found the location of the home. He drove past it to the end of the street where at a stop sign he attempted a U-turn. He debated whether he wanted to park directly in front of the house. As he passed by the house again he noticed in the driveway a late model BMW Z3. He thought Jeffrey always had a taste for the good life, but then again, inheriting millions will do that for a person. He decided to park a few houses down.

The street was conspicuously quiet. It was a cloudy start to the day, but did little to deter the heat. Andrew was still on East Coast time, his watch indicating that it was afternoon. As he stepped from the rental car dressed in khaki slacks sneakers and a burgundy polo shirt he looked around at the homes that dotted the thick landscape of developments these days in the booming state of New Mexico. As he stepped out of the vehicle he clipped his holstered weapon onto to his belt.

The Reunion Reaper

The neighborhood reflected a working class kind of people. He looked down at his watch again contemplating whether to change the time. *I'll be heading home tomorrow, no need to do something twice.*

Andrew's plan was simple, lay the bait, stroke Jeffrey's ego, and have Jeffrey scoop it up like a vacuum. He continued his walk past a few houses when he came to the front of Jeffrey's modest looking Southwestern designed stucco style home with its terra cotta roof and cinnamon colored exterior. His heart began to pound so hard he actually thought he could see his shirt bulge and then recess, bulge and recess. He slowly made his way up to the walkway and up to the front door. The yard was well maintained and the house looked to be well cared for. Andrew stood for a moment trying to calm his nerves. He had been on several investigations, stood on many doorsteps to deliver bad news or conduct a bust, but never had he stood at the door of a school chum where, especially if his instinct was correct, the school chum was a murderer.

He reached out his hand to depress the doorbell. A sudden chill consumed his body. As he reached the doorbell with his left hand, his right hand instinctively gripped the .40 caliber in his holster. He rang the bell and waited to see if someone would answer the call. For a brief moment he hoped that no one would answer. In the balance hung the entire contents of his investigation, it was the one moment he yearned for yet at the same time dreaded. If he was correct he would have to arrest someone he's known for a very long time. His intent was to arrest not kill a killer, and despite all that Jeffrey had done it was imperative he keep a cool head. There was a final deep breath as he pressed the doorbell again.

He waited for what seemed an eternity, but within a few seconds he heard the lock and then the door opened. There, standing in front of him was a man he had seen just a few months ago joking and laughing with at the reunion. A person that classmates would have a difficult time believing was a murderer, yet here Andrew stood. Either way there he was dressed casually in a pair of cargo shorts, a purple t-shirt and flip flops. His face emitted a look of genuine surprise.

"Andy boy, what brings you all the way out to New Mexico? We just talked yesterday, what's up?"

"How's it going Jeffrey, I was hoping we could talk."

"Well, I hate to break it to you, but the phone is cheaper."

Andrew's demeanor said it all, business.

"Can I come in?"

"Sure, absolutely, mi casa, est su casa."

Jeffrey could sense bad vibes, but he did his best to remain calm. *He's got nothing, only suspicion, if that.*

Andrew softly entered the house looking around for anything suspicious. He had removed his hand from his side arm not wishing to arouse or accelerate the nerves that were already outpacing calmness.

"Are you looking for anyone else?" inquired Jeffrey.

"…No."

"Well, come on in then."

Jeffrey remained remarkably calm given the fact that the person he enjoyed tormenting so often now stood on his doorstep. What he would give to read Andrew's thoughts. Andrew peered around the small living room as he completely entered the house. Jeffrey walked away and toward a rust color padded rattan chair. Jeffrey motioned to Andrew to take a seat on the other chair that sat cantered and adjacent to a rattan couch whose cushions displayed large bamboo shoots of brown and green. The house was sparsely decorated but clean. There were generic Southwestern style pictures of Native Americans that adorned the white walls. The floor was deer skin colored ceramic, and the only rug was a Navajo designed five by eight footer that lay between two chairs and a couch. Andrew obliged and took a seat.

The Reunion Reaper

"So, how's it going?" Jeffrey asked.

"Fine!"

Andrew gazed to his right and down a hallway. He saw at the end two doorways opposite one another. To his left a door that most likely led to the garage based on his orientation of the house upon his approach to entering. In front of him he could see the kitchen and a nook area that served as the dining room. It seemed cozy yet cold. Jeffrey watched as Andrew checked out his home.

"Would you like something to drink? I got some beer in the fridge."

"No, I'm fine," Andrew's voice sounding a bit out of character.

"You look troubled Andrew. So, what brings you all the way out here?"

"Well, in my haste I forgot to mention in our conversation that there is a convention here that starts tomorrow."

What are you up to dog breath? Jeffrey took a seat and motioned for Andrew to so the same.

"Wow, how ironic."

"Yeah, go figure." *Well, you better get to it he's just not going to throw up his hands in defeat because of my presence.*

Andrew was hoping to lure Jeffrey into saying something, anything that would indicate a slip up. Andrew then decided to tell him almost everything, stroke the ego, then strangle the very same ego.

For the next twenty minutes, Andrew opened up. He went for broke then, he did what so many do, go for the manhood angle.

"Here's what I don't get though. The first murders are all accidents, then all of a sudden they become murders and I am the one who is framed. Do you seriously think the killer thought that I would take the fall for those? I mean, I had solid alibi's…" Jeffrey continued to look at him, interested in what Andrew had to say. "I'll tell you what I think; I think the killer is just a stupid jealous coward."

"You think so." Jeffrey leaned in.

"Sure, he's got no balls. Oh he thinks he's got'em, but to pull these surprises on people and then to try to frame someone for his own lack of security or love?" Andrew shook his head as he continued, "He makes himself out to be this genius, but he's definitely no genius. I mean, how hard is it to take people by surprise? People who are helpless and then just taken advantage of. He's no genius like he thinks; in fact he appears to be a piece of shit really."

Andrew gazed at a stoic figure then poured it on. If he was looking for a break, this should do it he thought. "Especially Amy you know. What a totally senseless murder. She didn't deserve to die. None of them did, but seriously, Amy? I mean, it has to be a dick-less prick, who would do this don't you think?"

"Well you did say the guy made the first three look like accidents that sounds pretty genius."

With a stern voice he quickly shot back. "Shit, anyone could do that… You think he is a genius for what he's done? Come on he's remained hidden the whole time." Andrew calmed himself knowing he was getting too excited with his rhetoric. "Someone this vain would absolutely crave attention from law enforcement, yet he stays hidden like the coward that he is." Andrew was sure to emphasize the word coward.

Jeffrey began to move uncomfortably in his chair. Andrew continued to pile it on.

"Oh, and let me add this—"

"Hey would you like something to drink?"

"Uh, no thanks… anyhow—"

"Something to eat?"

"Uh, no I'm great I got something on the way from the airport, so as I was saying—"

The Reunion Reaper

Jeffrey quickly glanced at his watch, "Hey listen you know, I just remembered I got someplace to go, I'm really sorry man."

"Oh, well I'm sorry I bothered you."

"No problem, um listen, are you going to be in town for a while?"

"The convention is two days, then I'm headed back home," Andrew looked him dead in the eyes.

"Oh, well, maybe we can hook up, have some dinner tonight. Where are you staying?"

"The AmeriSuites near the airport," another lie, Andrew had no interest telling him where he was staying.

"Well, anyhow, I hate to run you off but I really gotta go…dentist appointment." Jeffrey stood pointing to his mouth.

"Oh, okay, well I'm sorry I bothered you." Andrew stood.

"So I'll call on you at the hotel."

I'm sure you will. Andrew smiled, "Sounds great, we'll talk more tonight I guess. Again, sorry to drop in on you like this."

"Hey, no problem, friends are always welcome."

The two of them shook hands. Jeffrey's hands seemed noticeably clammy. Andrew walked out of the house and to the rental car. He did not know what to make of the encounter, but he didn't want to be too open or begin pointing fingers. He felt there was something that would emerge from this, and most likely would occur before he left town. It was Andrew's turn to set the bait. He knew Jeffrey was up to something. He finally felt he had the right guy. Sitting there talking and gauging his host answered all his suspicions. As he sat in the car there was a chill that consumed his body. It sounds weird, but when Andrew was hot onto something he always got a certain chill when his instincts felt right. He felt strongly the killer was just a few feet away trying to look and act as cool as ever.

Chapter 103

Andrew continued to sit in the car contemplating whether he should just go back to the house and start slinging accusations. *Surely there's evidence there in the house, there has to be. Maybe I could get a warrant.* He laughed at the absurdity. *Yeah right, explain a Roanoke police officer wanting a warrant in New Mexico. No, I've got to do something. I have to give him credit he held his ground then cleverly ushered me out of the house. I need something, a confession, but how? Plan A failed now for plan B.* He started the car and drove off. He figured Jeffrey was watching him drive away, so he made a point to not look at the house.

As he reached the end of the block he turned left, and then at the next street he turned left again. From the road he could see the back of Jeffrey's house through the yard of the house directly in front of him. He stopped the car, put it in park and sat there contemplating. *Is this a golden opportunity, or a huge mistake?* Everything thus far had been initiated by the killer, was it his turn to initiate? What if he was wrong? Even though the car was running and he had the A/C on he was roasting. His brain was on fire, he had to decide.

He got out of the car and walked across the lawn of the house in front of him and into the back yard of Jeffrey's place. There were no fences to block his path, and few trees to hide his prattling about. He could see, from a short distance, through the kitchen window of Jeffrey's house but saw no movement. He quickly darted to the house and leaned up on one of the walls. He looked around at some of the other houses hoping there wasn't some nosy neighbor gawking out a window. He certainly didn't need any more

The Reunion Reaper

trouble with the law than he had seen in the last month or so.

He slid down the wall to a door near the kitchen area. He attempted to turn the handle and to his surprise it was unlocked. *Maybe it's a trap.* He cautiously opened the door. It was nice and quiet. He took a quick peek in hoping there wasn't a twelve gauge shotgun greeting him with a click/boom. He could see the kitchen was empty and from what he could see into the living room it was empty as well. Then he heard some banging going on. It sounded like dresser drawers closing. He quickly glided into the house and closed the door behind him. He sought refuge behind a counter that looked out into the living room. He pulled his gun from its holster. *Shit, does it have to come down to this?*

He peeked out of the side of the counter looking for another refuge spot. *The large rattan couch.* He tiptoed across the floor, but since he had on sneakers he was more worried about that streak noise they could make on a wooden or ceramic floor. He made it over to the couch and crouched down behind it. Peeking over the top he spotted Jeffrey move from one door way to the other down the hall. He waited, not knowing for sure whether both were bedrooms. He paused. Then he heard some clicking noises.

"Police convention my ass, there's nothing in town amigo."

He continued to click away and talk.

"You thought you could come in here and rattle me? You loser, you just wasted perfectly good airline tickets."

Tap, tap, tap went the keyboard. Andrew inched closer down the hall.

"There you go you friggin' genius, Travelocity is king."

He could hear Jeffrey muttering some words, but was unable to hear his exact words.

"Yes, I would like to book these tickets today." Jeffrey was talking to the computer.

As Andrew heard the clicking he continued to slide silently down the hall. He figured it had to be a bedroom or a study of sorts. His only worry was whether Jeffrey had protection sitting next to him. He wanted this to be quick.

"A coward, you're so full of shit Andy Shit Face Keane. I'm a genius for keeping law enforcement in the dark you ungrateful prick. Well, too late, you missed your chance. I'm outta here and the only way you'll see me is if you come to Jamaica or if I decide to come back and kill your sorry ass."

Andrew hunched in the hallway hearing the comments from the room to his left.
With weapon drawn, he quickly wheeled into the doorway and pointed his gun at Jeffrey.

"You were saying something about missing your chance?"

Jeffrey sat in shock. He was always the one who was able to sneak up on unsuspecting people.

"What are you talking about?"

"I heard everything... Even the part where you threatened to kill my sorry ass."

Jeffrey shifted in his chair, but Andrew gripped his gun even tighter and waved it as if to suggest, don't move you smug little shit. Jeffrey clearly had a look of surprise on his face. He saw a man with a determined look. A look often associated with Dirty Harry just before he pulled the trigger. Andrew's brow was concentrated on Jeffrey as he fought hard to keep from squeezing a round into the bastard's head. Knowing there was nothing he could do Jeffrey just smiled at him, then mockingly put his hands up in the air.

"You got me there Hoss... but you got admit though I had you good for a while."

Andrew shook his head at the smug vanity, "Why Jeffrey?"

The Reunion Reaper

He exhaled, "Well that's an original question." He put his arms back down folding them under one another. "Are you gonna ask me where I was on the night in question?"

Jeffrey looked down as he stretched out his arms in front of him, "So, do you think I should pack some extra tanning lotion?"

"Where you're going you won't need tanning lotion you'll need lubricant."

Jeffrey harrumphed, "Come on, they all deserved to die you know that."

Andrew's brow furrowed and the grip on his weapon grew tighter.

"Who gave you the right to be judge and jury on these people?" Andrew continued to stand in the doorway just in case Jeffrey pulled some weapon from a drawer he would be able to cover behind the wall.

"I did what I thought needed to be done." Jeffrey stated with certitude.

"What you thought needed to be done."

"Is there an echo in here?"

"I just don't get it, what happened to you man?"

"What happened to me? I got wise that's what happened to me." He leaned back in his chair and threw his feet up on the desk as Andrew shook his head in shear disbelief. "You just don't get it do you?"

Andrew looked confused with Jeffrey's question. "Get what?"

"Come on dip shit I did this all for you."

Andrew cocked his head to the side not really knowing what he just heard, "For me?"

"Yeah," Jeffrey laughed. "Come on, you hated these people just as much as I did."

"Now I know you've jumped off the deep end. You're saying I hated Paul and Amy?"

"No, not them, the others," Jeffrey couldn't understand why Andrew hadn't gotten it yet. "Oh, forgot that you told me back in the day how these people and their silver spooned lives irritated the hell out of you?"

Back in high school Andrew wasn't shy about expressing his dislike for certain individuals, but that seemed to be a natural propensity for most people; not everybody is going to like everybody. Jeffrey brought up the time that Judith Barnett spurned Andrew's approach when they were freshman, and that Andrew and Tucker came to blows one day at lacrosse practice and the relationship was never the same after that, or the time when Sharon Bloom called him little dick in front of a group of people. Jeffrey finished his memory playback for Andrew.

"So, I needed to get your attention."

"Attention for what?" Andrew looked lost with Jeffrey's diatribe.

Jeffrey threw up his hands in frustration, "Oye, are you listening? You didn't think I knew that you were a cop? Come on, I knew I could get your attention by knocking off a few classmates. Then all I had to hope for was that you'd bite." He chuckled, "oh boy, you bit hard."

"So if you hated me so much, why not just come after me, why our friends."

Jeffrey shook his head, "they weren't my friends."

He plopped his feet on the floor and Andrew quickly refocused his weapon. "Whoa, take it easy there Barney you're the one with the gun. Oh sure, I could've killed you anytime, but then how would we play the game?"

"You think this is a game?"

Jeffrey smiled but with an angry tone. "It is whatever you want it to be."

Andrew was absolutely stunned, "So you killed these people because of me?"

Jeffrey looked indifferent. "For us my man, these were bad people anyway."

"Oh and you're a candidate for the sainthood." He questioned.

The Reunion Reaper

"I'm a Jew, we don't have saints."

"Well I've heard enough of your crap. This is where you stand and I handcuff you."

Again, Andrew would have preferred squeezing the trigger and then checking Jeffrey's forehead for accuracy after the fact, but he resisted.

"But don't you want to hear the rest of the story?"

"What listen to your bullshit about trying to place the guilt on me? Sorry, come on let's do this the easy way. I nailed you, it's over."

"You got to admit though I kicked your ass pretty good."

"Whatever, I said stand up and turn around."

"What you gonna shoot me in the back?"

"Trust me; if I was gonna shoot you I'd look you in the eye. Now, why don't you act like a man, admit it's over, stand up and turn around."

"You're right; I was just tryin' to bait you. You know, make you look like an idiot again."

"That's okay, enjoy your cracks. The bottom line is you're going down and that's it. Speaking of which, do you like needles? Cause you're going to get them that's for sure."

Andrew cautiously approached him. He grabbed his handcuffs from out of his back pocket. Jeffrey kept jabbering on, but seemed to comply with Andrew's request by placing his arms straight out to each side palms up.

Andrew continued, "Yeah, well game's over, you can tell of your exploits to the Albuquerque police. I'm sure you've seen your share of the COPS program."

"I don't watch television there's too much violence."

"Yeah right."

Andrew grabbed Jeffrey's left hand and placed a cuff on it. He holstered his weapon so he could manipulate the other hand into the cuff. Apparently Jeffrey had seen his share of COPS shows, because he quickly turned and with his left hand that was cuffed struck Andrew in the mouth causing him to stumble backwards. Andrew's vision quickly blurred from the rock solid blow and his mouth filled with blood. He managed to gather himself and pull his weapon, but Jeffrey also managed to retrieve a nickel plated Smith and Wesson .38 caliber from his desk drawer.

The two men were pointing their weapons at one another.

"How ya feeling Andy Boy?"

"Good enough to shoot you between the eyes now put down the weapon."

"Sorry, no can do. Hey, you're dripping blood on my floor."

Andrew then spit a mouthful of blood onto the carpeted floor.

"I'm gonna have to bill you for the cleaning job."

"You shouldn't have blindsided me like that."

Jeffrey pouted his lips, "Sorry old friend, man's gotta do what a man's gotta do."

Each of them stood fixed on one another. There were slight beads of sweat beginning to form on Jeffrey's forehead. The blood from Andrew's mouth continued to drip and the pooling of blood caused the taupe colored carpet to turn burgundy.

"Who's gonna blink Andy boy? I guess we got us a good ole fashioned standoff."

Andrew did not respond, he just continued to look Jeffrey in the eye.

To the two of them it must have seemed like an eternity, but it was only a minute when Andrew noticed something.

"You're arm is shaking, a sign of weakness."

"Hardly, you're the weak ass here." Jeffrey took his left arm and swiped his forehead trying to wipe away the sweat.

What seemed to be another minute or so passed.

Jeffrey wanted to make a deal. "All right, what do you say we declare you the victor and I go on my merry way to Jamaica with a promise to never return?"

The Reunion Reaper

Again, Andrew spit blood on the floor and just shook his head no.

"Damn it, would you stop spitting on my floor?"

"I'll stop spitting when you toss me your weapon."

Jeffrey smiled, although there wasn't the happy go lucky grin that had previously adorned his youthful face. It was now a nervous and agitated smile. He contemplated his next move. What was only a few seconds of silence seemed an eternity to Jeffrey. His arm was getting tired and showed signs of stress as the gun began to slightly shake. Conversely, Andrew's endurance for holding his weapon appeared unbending. Jeffrey finally offered.

"Come on you win, you got me, hooray for Andy."

Andrew remained stoic.

"Come on, I said you got me."

"Then toss the weapon over here."

"You know what, fuck you!" Jeffrey blurted out.

At that moment a shot rang out immediately followed by another.

Chapter 104

Stephanie was just heading home from work when she felt an awful sensation shoot through her body. She was on her way to pick up the boys, but she suddenly became nervous for her husband. *Something's happened.*

She pulled into the parking lot of the day care and got out her phone and dialed Andrew's cell. It rang several times until finally his voice mail asked the caller to leave a message.

"Hey, it's me. I just wanted to know if everything was okay. Call me okay?" She closed the phone. Her hands were wet with sweat. The boys were standing at the door of the day care center wondering why their mother had not gotten out of the car yet.

She was shaking as she opened the car door to let the boys climb in. Michael asked her what was wrong. She did her best to deflect his question, but confessed she was worried for someone. As the boys clicked their seat belts, Stephanie was experiencing a feeling that all wives who love their husband dearly experience when they sense danger; a sudden surge of adrenaline that rushed the heart and the head. She sat in the driver's seat trying to get composed then said a quick prayer. She prayed that her husband was safe and would be home soon.

As she pulled into the driveway her cell phone jingled out its ring tone. She nearly jumped out of her seat. It was Andrew.

The Reunion Reaper

Chapter 105

Andrew was sitting in a window seat on a flight headed toward Roanoke. He stared, gazing out over the tarmac and terminal area of Albuquerque International Sunport Airport. It was a gaze that disguised inner thoughts. It was over. The shot to Jeffrey's heart was instantly fatal. He didn't want to kill him, but he had no choice. One thing was certain there was a lot of anger in that slug. Jeffrey's shot had missed entirely. His misfire slammed into a painting he had on the wall behind Andrew's head. Ironically, it was a painting of a tropical beach scene that looked out over the ocean. There was a catamaran wedged on the beach and the sun was tangerine orange as it was setting just off to the right of where the catamaran sat. Oh how Jeffrey would have longed for that scene instead of the one that befell him.

For Andrew the shot was deadly accurate. Jeffrey stumbled back a step before falling into his executive leather chair. The hand holding his gun went limp and the gun innocently dropped to the floor. The blood oozing from the shot to the heart began to turn the purple t-shirt black. Jeffrey's head tilted to the right and his chin gently rested on his chest. A killer was dead, but at what cost?

Before the authorities arrived Andrew grabbed the pin drive that was sticking out of Jeffrey's laptop. He remained on the scene for a while and was up half the night explaining to the Albuquerque police this bizarre case.

He heaved a heavy sigh as he felt an incredible sense of pressure and stress leave his body. He found himself feeling completely spent, but at the same time energized. This paradox added to emotions that were all over the map and the slouch in his shoulders and sodden demeanor said it all. He felt like he hadn't breathed normal for months. He was upset that it took him so long to get his guy, but he got him. He lost seven, no, make that eight, people he had known very well. People from the graduating class of 1983 will be remembered forever as the class that suffered great losses at the hands of one of their own. It was a sad commentary on what should have been a class that could compare its relative success to others before and after it.

He tried to shrug off Jeffrey's assertion that he killed these classmates because of and for Andrew. It was a preposterous notion, and he didn't want to give Jeffrey the luxury of one last mental victory. He looked toward the heavens as the plane flew over this great country and he prayed for the souls of all those lost, even Jeffrey's. Although he couldn't resist thinking that Jeffrey would be feeling the heat so to speak.

When Andrew's plane landed in a place he was very grateful to see, he greeted his wife at the terminal, gave her an embrace that said, "I've missed you, but I am back to stay." They kissed and both seemed to laugh at the relief at this carousel that finally came to an end. He could see the sheer joy of her eyes as she knew her husband was home and safe. And he knew that he had a great woman who for a while doubted him, but ultimately stood by his side. He understood.

Arriving home he gave each of the boy's a hug that seemed to say it's been a long time even though it was only two days ago that he left for New Mexico. Each of them felt a father's undying passionate embrace. Mary asked him if there was anything wrong and he simply smiled and said, "Not anymore." It was his hope that all would turn back to the way they were before all this started.

Over the course of the next few days he would set things right at the department, especially with Captain Hardy. He talked with Sonny, who was happy to see that the agony consuming his friend was finally gone. He also talked with his father who was probably more relieved than his son.

The Reunion Reaper

His mother mentioned several times to him that her prayers were answered; that her son would be protected because he was just trying to do the right thing. Andrew had ridden a tragic train of events that consumed several months of his life. He was happy about the outcome, but sad about the process to that outcome.

Epilogue

Andrew's life over the course of a few months had changed in a way he never imagined. For the better he wasn't sure, only time would know that answer. He returned to work after the much needed week off and a mini vacation with the family to Virginia Beach and Williamsburg.

Andrew returned to work and on to a new case. It wasn't a serial murder case and that came as a great relief to him. He was more than happy to investigate a string of car thefts in the area. He and Sonny started their weekly running although Andrew was considerably out of shape from where he was five months ago. Those five months spent on the case were ripped away from him no matter how he looked at it. Was it to be a learning experience, or was it just senseless deaths at the hands of a maniac simply trying to get back at a person for whatever selfish motivation he had? Or was it just another example that showed the dark side of man's existence? It was definitely an experience he hoped would never repeat.

On a more solid note, Ryan's cough began to subsist with new treatments and Michael was starting football again. He most likely was going to be the teams lead running back. Mary was excited about entering her sophomore year with the hopes of getting her driver's license before the school year was out. As for Stephanie, well, she kept plugging away at her job, being a mother and a wife. Throughout this whole ordeal she saw parts of her husband that she didn't like, but by the same token fell deeper in love with a man so committed to truth… to justice… to love.

Made in the USA
Charleston, SC
11 November 2013